WE
ALL
FALL
DOWN

Enjoy!

DANIEL KALLA

PUBLISHED BY SIMON & SCHUSTER

New York London Toronto Sydney New Delhi

SIMON &
SCHUSTER
CANADA

Simon & Schuster Canada
A Division of Simon & Schuster, Inc.
166 King Street East, Suite 300
Toronto, Ontario M5A 1J3

This Simon & Schuster Canada edition March 2019

SIMON & SCHUSTER CANADA and colophon
are registered trademarks of Simon & Schuster, Inc.

For information about special discounts for bulk purchases, please contact Simon & Schuster Special Sales at 1-800-268-3216 or CustomerService@simonandschuster.ca.

Manufactured in the United States of America

10   9   8   7   6   5   4   3   2   1

Library and Archives Canada Cataloguing in Publication

Kalla, Daniel, author
        We all fall down / Daniel Kalla.

Issued in print and electronic formats.
ISBN 978-1-5011-9693-5 (softcover).—ISBN 978-1-5011-9697-3 (ebook)

        I. Title.

PS8621.A47W43 2019   C813'.6   C2018-901552-7
                                                   C2018-901553-5

ISBN 978-1-5011-9693-5
ISBN 978-1-5011-9697-3 (ebook)

For my daughters,

Chelsea and Ashley

Praise for Daniel Kalla

OF FLESH AND BLOOD

"[Kalla] plunges us straight into the frenzied pace of the OR and [into] a medical drama that spans a hundred years. He's a strong storyteller who keeps his characters moving and struggling, and we're right there, struggling with them, rooting for them."

Vancouver Sun

"A rich medical narrative that combines the past with the present and throws into the mix visionary doctors, supportive nurses, hospital politics, children with cancer, celebrity patients, a lethal infection, adultery, and unrequited love."

Library Journal

COLD PLAGUE

"Similar in many ways to Michael Crichton and even Dan Brown's bestsellers, *Cold Plague* is testament to just how good commercial fiction can be: entertaining, informative, and downright fun."

Winnipeg Free Press

"Plenty of suspense and layering on the kind of scientific detail that fans of medical thrillers crave. Recommend this one to fans of Robin Cook and other such A-listers."

Booklist

BLOOD LIES

"Kalla strikes again with another perfect page-turner."

LEE CHILD, *New York Times* bestselling author

"Fast-paced and smartly written. . . . Kalla has quickly matured into a force to be reckoned with."

Booklist

"Fans of *Presumed Innocent* will find welcome echoes of that modern classic in *Blood Lies*."

Publishers Weekly (Starred Review)

"Kalla's well-paced medical thriller has twists that surprise us, but always make sense."

Entertainment Weekly

Chapter

One

There he is again. Watching, always watching. *Doesn't the old bastard have anything better to do?* Vittoria Fornero wonders as she rolls up the blueprint and tucks it under her arm.

The little monk has shown up at the site every day since the first crew arrived to tear down the old monastery. As always, he's wearing a traditional black Benedictine habit with the hood down, exposing a wispy ring of white hair around his otherwise bald scalp. Every morning at about nine o'clock or so, he appears with a rusty fold-up chair held under one arm and a black satchel worn over the other. Sometimes he sips from a thermos or reads from a well-thumbed leather prayer book. But usually, like now, he just sits near the edge of the excavation pit and watches like a pigeon perched on a building's eave.

Most of the time the monk blends into the scenery along with the site's other fixtures such as the giant yellow diggers, piles of lumber, and mounds of rubble and rock. But this morning Vittoria has no tolerance for the uninvited spectator.

"*Se n'è andata!*" Vittoria calls out to him, as she bundles her flimsy windbreaker tighter to fight off another vicious chill. "Your relic, she is gone, old man, gone. And the funeral is over!"

In truth, Vittoria can still see the ancient brick and stone monastery in her mind's eye: a simple Romanesque structure that was already crumbling on the south side of the cloister where part of the attached arcade's roof had collapsed years before. Dilapidated as the monastery was, Vittoria had appreciated its decrepit charm. And even though she is an unrepentant atheist, she carries enough childhood memories of intimidating nuns to feel a bit uneasy over her role in having leveled the ancient house of worship.

The old monk responds to Vittoria's calculated belligerence with a friendly wave, making her question his hearing as much as she already does his sanity. Regardless, Vittoria isn't about to be appeased; not this morning, not after he has already compounded her workload and aggravated her piercing headache.

Vittoria wasted fifteen minutes in the cramped overheated trailer that passed for her office trying to calm one of the workers, a pimply-faced apprentice named Emilio.

"Listen to me, Emilio!" Vittoria cut him off in midsentence, unable to listen to another moment of his alarmism. "That freeloading monk is bitter about losing the roof over his head! Nothing more."

"But, Vittoria," Emilio muttered. "Brother Silvio . . . he says it's not just the monastery."

"What, then?"

"Brother Silvio, he says that the monastery . . . it is built on hallowed ground."

"To a monk, maybe. But to us it's just a construction site. No different from any other." Although, she silently conceded, the crypt below the monastery had come as a surprise. The excavators had not expected to unearth such a complex cellar, with its convoluted network of passages. And all those tiny bones. When Vittoria had first glimpsed them, she instinctively thought of her own two children. But she was in no mood to discuss medieval architecture.

"What about Yas?" Emilio asked.

"What about him?" Vittoria demanded, sounding more defensive than she intended.

"The day before last, Yas wasn't feeling so good," he said. "And then yesterday he didn't show up. I haven't seen him since."

"So what? He's probably just hungover."

"Yas doesn't drink. And he's not answering my texts or calls. Brother Silvio says—"

"Enough, Emilio! For the love of God!" Vittoria held up her hands. "Not another word! Or you'll end up on the docks looking for work scrubbing the fishing boats. Just like where Yas will soon find himself!"

Vittoria digs her thumbs into her temples, trying to squeeze away the throb along with the memory of her conversation with the panicky boy. She wishes Emilio hadn't mentioned Yas.

Her legs tremble and another chill overcomes her. The ecstatic TV weatherwoman promised record temperatures for Genoa this morning. The bright April sun has already risen high over the rolling hills above the city, where the site is nestled, but Vittoria doesn't seem to benefit from its warmth.

Maria warned her that she was too sick to work. Of course, Maria was like that, keeping their twins home at the first sniffle. Vittoria can't help but smile to herself. Life hasn't always been easy for two of them, living together in a city as traditional as Genoa, but Maria is still the best thing to have ever happened to her. And, as usual, Maria was right. Vittoria can't remember ever feeling worse. Her breathing is inexplicably heavy. Each step is an effort. Her head is on fire. But it's her armpit that bothers her most. The bluish lump under it has swollen to the size of a robin's egg and throbs like a toothache. Even the light contact against her overalls is agonizing.

But Vittoria hasn't missed a day's work in twenty years. She's certainly not about to take time off now, not when the crew is behind schedule and the boss is so worried over the financing. Her first order of business today is to permanently rid the site of this interloping monk before he scares other workers and puts them further behind. She should have had the security guards deal with him weeks ago, but now she will just have to do it herself. She squares her shoulders and marches toward Brother Silvio.

As she reaches close enough to inhale a whiff of his coffee, Vittoria has to pause to catch her breath. An invisible flame ignites her innards from toes to scalp. Her knees tremble so violently she half expects them to clatter.

The old monk tightens the cap on his thermos and leans forward in his chair. His eyes twinkle. "What is wrong, my dear?" he asks. "Can I be of assistance?"

"Yes! You can get the hell off my—" A sudden coughing fit silences her.

Vittoria feels phlegm climbing up her windpipe and shoots a hand to her mouth. For a moment or two, she can't breathe at all. When the hacking finally subsides, she senses sticky warmth in her grip. Panic seizes her, even before she opens her palm and sees the wad of congealed blood.

Chapter

Two

The poor woman looks like death warmed over, Sonia Poletti thinks as she runs a gloved hand along the patient's forearm in search of a vein. The skin is unnaturally cool to the touch, and the patient's breathing is ragged despite the bulky mask that mists concentrated oxygen over her mouth and nose. Experience tells Sonia that the woman will soon wind up in the intensive care unit on a ventilator, but it's not her place to comment.

Sonia assembles a rainbow array of color-topped test tubes on the stretcher beside the patient's elbow. Once filled, each of them will be destined for a different analyzer, ranging from a highly sophisticated protein spectrometer to a plated slide under a pathologist's microscope.

The woman raises her head off the pillow but can only hold it up for a few seconds before it flops back down. "Are you a doctor?" she asks in a raspy, air-hungry voice.

"I am from the laboratory. I'm here to collect more blood samples."

"More blood? Will you leave me any?"

"Yes." Sonia smiles behind her surgical mask. "More than enough."

The patient coughs so violently that the test tubes on the mattress rattle. "They still don't know what I have?"

The nurses outside the room mentioned possible tuberculosis, but Sonia didn't delve. She's too preoccupied with making sure she gets out of work on time today, of all days. She touches the woman's arm. "We have the best doctors here. If they don't already know, they will soon." She pauses. "You are Vittoria Fornero?"

The patient nods.

Sonia kneels beside the bed. Out of habit, she spins the hospital bracelet over the woman's wrist, double-checking the identity. She applies a tourniquet above Vittoria's elbow, tightly enough for the vein below it to pop to attention. She effortlessly slides a butterfly needle through the skin and into the vein. Blood snakes up the connected tubing. Sonia attaches the other end of it to the first of the test tubes.

"You have children?" Vittoria croaks.

"One." Sonia suppresses a smile. "Florianna—Flori—she is five."

"I have two, myself. Twins. Eight years old. One of each."

"Good for you, the complete set," Sonia says, but there is little chance she will ever have a boy or another girl. Flori's father had left her before the end of her first trimester. Sonia is only thirty-one years old and, as her mother keeps telling her, could still have several more children. But she won't. Flori is joy enough for her.

Vittoria hacks another wet cough. "I wish I could hold mine again."

"Soon," Sonia mutters, but her mind has already drifted back to Flori's dance recital, which will be held later tonight. She must get home in time to finish sewing the tail onto her daughter's tutu.

Vittoria's body jerks with another coughing fit. The noise is awful, like an old truck engine struggling to turn over. Sonia notices Vittoria wiping at her eyes. Blood-splattered phlegm has sprayed out from under the oxygen mask and onto her own forehead.

Sonia grabs a tissue from the box on her basket. She leans forward and wipes the mucus away. Vittoria offers her a small smile. Their eyes lock, and Sonia spots fear in the other woman's eyes.

Suddenly Vittoria convulses with another cough. Sonia feels something wet graze the exposed cheek above her mask, and she jerks her head back.

Dammit! She stumbles back a step, grabs an alcohol wipe—the ones meant for cleaning the equipment—and scrubs roughly at her skin.

Vittoria can't stop coughing now. The stretcher shakes with each fit.

Sonia reassures herself that her own skin test has long been positive for tuberculosis, meaning she had already been exposed to it and cannot acquire it again. She knows she should still report the incident to her manager and to Employee Health and Safety. But there's no time. She promised to send her mother a video clip of Flori's dance, and she still has to charge the camera. So, instead, she scrubs her cheek with another wipe and then sweeps up the tubes and hurries from the room.

Three

Eight years. Alana Vaughn hasn't seen him in over eight years. He has changed so little. True, the cheeks are a bit fuller, ruddier, too. But his smile—"all melty blue eyes and endless dimples," as a smitten English nurse once described it—is the same.

"Ah, Alana. *Ciao bella* . . . Even more beautiful than memory serves!" Dr. Nico Oliva says.

His familiar voice, deep and rich with that perpetually amused timbre, ignites long-forgotten butterflies. "And you, Nico, are even more Italian than I remember."

Nico shrugs in a can't-be-helped way, and she's reminded again why she fell for him in the first place.

His office is predictably minimalist in terms of furnishings and with just a few framed medical degrees and three black-and-white photos of African landscapes, one of which she recognizes from their mission together in Angola. He steps out from behind his desk and kisses her on each cheek, leaving behind a trace of citrus. "You didn't have to come in person."

"Yes. Yes, I did." His text was so unexpected, and so welcome.

"Did you have trouble finding my office?"

"Not really." But she actually did.

Alana has wandered the halls of some of the most formidable hospitals, from Johns Hopkins to the Mayo Clinic, but the Ospedale San Martino is among the most sprawling, seemingly constructed in fits and starts over decades. The signage didn't help. Alana speaks passable German, having lived in Heidelberg as a teen when her parents were stationed there for a year, but her Italian is almost nonexistent. Navigating the curved hallways and hidden staircases of the labyrinthine hospital to reach Nico's office in the Department of Infectious Diseases was no easy feat.

Nico studies her unabashedly. "So much catching up to do. Dinner, soon. I insist." He smiles again. "But you must be anxious to see the patient, no?"

"Yes. Very."

"Come. I will take you." He reaches for her arm and interlocks his elbow with hers, the contact familiar, comfortable. Maybe too much so.

The hallway is lit by fluorescent tubes and smells of bleach. It's crowded with staff and patients, who are lost in conversations, hands as busy as their mouths. No one seems to pay any attention to the sight of two people, one of whom wears a lab coat, walking arm in arm. Alana smiles to herself. *Only in Italy.*

"Where are you staying?" Nico asks.

"The Grand Hotel Savoia."

"Ah, by the station." Nico glances away. "I would've loved to have you stay with us, but Isabella . . . and the children . . . there would be no rest for you."

Of course there's an Isabella. Alana expected nothing less, but she still slips her arm free of his. "Kids, Nico? As in plural? I had no idea."

"Yes. Enzo is three now, and Simona just four months. Can you imagine? Me?" He laughs and looks away momentarily. "A boring family man."

"No. I really can't."

Nico finds her gaze again. "And you? Have you . . ."

"I don't stay in one place long enough to have a hamster, let alone a family."

She can tell that he sees through her levity. "I miss the action, Alana. What we used to do. What you still do."

She thinks of her previous outbreak-containment missions, such as yellow fever in Guyana, drug-resistant tuberculosis in Central Asia, and, of course, Ebola in West Africa. The faces of the dead and dying, particularly the children, who are always most susceptible. "Some things are better left unseen, Nico."

He doesn't comment, but she realizes he's not convinced. As they round another corner, he says, "Tell me, I originally tried you at your WHO email address. The email, it bounced back to me. Of course, I would never misplace your mobile number, but . . ."

Alana remembers his unexpected text, and how excited she was to hear from him, their painful parting forgotten. She might have found an excuse to visit him in person regardless of the circumstance, but two words in his note—*the plague*—had started her packing for Genoa without a second thought. "I'm not with the World Health Organization anymore, Nico."

"Oh? I thought you were what we used to call a 'lifer.'"

I once did, too. For a moment she considers telling him about her disastrous final mission in Liberia during the height of the Ebola crisis. Nico worked for the WHO; he, of all people, would understand. But all she says is, "I needed a change."

"You were in Geneva, no?" he asks, confused.

"Not far away," she says vaguely.

"Alana." He arches an eyebrow. "You are not back with the military, are you?"

"There'll be time later to catch up. Over wine," she says, regretting the words the minute they pass her lips. "Nico, please, tell me about the patient."

"Vittoria Fornero, a forty-two-year-old previously healthy construction worker," he says. "She arrived here at the hospital two days ago. Fever and coughing up blood. Within twenty-four hours, she was placed on life support."

Alana feels the tension building in her shoulder. "You isolated her right away, I hope?"

"Of course," Nico snorts. "Initially, the other doctors thought it might be tuberculosis."

"What made you think otherwise?"

"I found the lump in her right armpit. There was no mistaking it. A classic bubo."

"Did you biopsy it?"

"No need, Alana. The sputum cultures. No question, it is the plague. The *Yersinia pestis* bacteria that causes it grew on the culture plates faster than rats breeding in a slum."

Alana finds the turn of phrase ironic, but she holds her tongue as they join two cleaners inside an elevator who are lost in conversation of their own, speaking what might be Russian or Ukrainian.

She and Nico emerge on the sixth floor. Though they are the only ones in the hallway, Alana still lowers her voice. "Did you start her early on antibiotic coverage?"

Nico grimaces. "The moment I saw her! Even before we had the culture results. Broad-spectrum antibiotics, including both levofloxacin and doxycycline."

"Yet she still wound up on a ventilator?"

"There was a short delay when the working diagnosis was still tuberculosis," he concedes. "She grew so ill, so rapidly. Like almost nothing I've ever seen, Alana."

"When was the last case of the plague in Italy?"

Nico stops, as does Alana. "Six or seven years ago. Two missionaries from Madagascar brought it to Milan."

"So how the hell does a construction worker in Genoa catch the plague?"

"Vittoria was in Africa three weeks ago with her family. In Addis Ababa, where her youngest sister married an Ethiopian. There have been recent cases reported in East Africa."

Alana's thoughts race. "That's too long. The incubation period of the plague bacteria is usually two to six days. She should have gotten sick weeks ago."

"It can take longer. Besides, what other explanation could there be?"

Alana thinks of a few possibilities, but she doesn't share them. "Nico, this isn't just the bubonic plague—"

"Of course not. It's in her lungs. She has the pneumonic plague."

"And when was the last case of *that* in Italy?"

"Three . . . maybe four hundred years? Who knows? Perhaps not since medieval times."

They fall silent for a moment or two until an overhead speaker crackles to life. A voice calls out urgently, repeating the same phrase three times. Alana doesn't need to know the words to understand their intent.

Nico pivots and breaks into a run. Alana rushes after him, ducking through a set of sliding doors just before they close. Inside, the sign above the desk reads CENTRO DI RIANIMAZIONE, and she immediately recognizes the space as an intensive care unit.

Alarms are blaring. Uniformed staff members cluster outside a glassed-in room in the far corner. A woman is howling somewhere, but Alana can't spot her among the throng.

Nico weaves through the crowd, Alana close behind. A plump middle-aged woman grabs him by the arm. "*Dottore Oliva! Mia Vittoria!*" she cries, sputtering rapid-fire words between sobs.

Nico lays an arm consolingly across the woman's shoulders. Her wailing only intensifies.

Alana darts her eyes toward the room's window. The scene inside is reminiscent of the worst days of the Ebola crisis. Four staff members are wearing the maximal personal protective equipment, better known as PPE, from hoods with transparent face masks to waterproof booties. They buzz around a woman on a stretcher, their frantic energy palpable through the glass. Even the patient—who is hooked to a web of tubes and wires—is not still. She thrashes on the bed in an uncontrolled seizure.

Nico glances over his shoulder to Alana, his expression as helpless as that of a lifeguard watching a swimmer drown in waters too rough to permit rescue.

The tube leading from the patient's mouth to the ventilator turns from clear to red, as though it has been suddenly connected to an artery instead of her lungs. "DIC," Alana mutters to no one in particular, recognizing disseminated intravascular coagulation—the patient's blood-clotting factors are failing her as badly as her heart.

"Vittoria! *Vittoria!*" The woman shakes free of Nico's arm and hurls herself at the window. She pounds on the glass until two nurses have to forcibly peel her away.

The patient's back arches, lifting her whole body off the stretcher except her head and her heels, as if she is trying to levitate. She holds the unnatural pose for what seems like ages but then collapses, motionless.

But it's not a good kind of still. Alana knows that even before the blood begins to seep from Vittoria's nose and eyes.

Four

Today marks the twenty-third day of January, in the year of our Lord thirteen hundred and forty-eight.

I, Rafael Pasqua, son of Domenico, was born here in Genova in the year thirteen hundred and eleven. I will most assuredly die here.

Never before have I committed my memories to parchment, but I am compelled to do so now. Forgive me, I am not a man of letters. I am a barber-surgeon, not one of the learned physicians educated at university. However, I was most fortunate to apprentice under the great Antonio Calvi, who practiced our craft in a way few will match and fewer still will ever surpass.

Today, I buried my beloved wife, Camilla. How my hand trembles as I write her name. She was twenty-nine years old, and as beautiful as a spring lilac. I can yet hear her voice. I could fill her grave with my tears.

In this terrible void, I am comforted, however, by one thought. What Camilla and I once viewed a curse, that she could never bear us a child, has amounted to a small blessing. She died, as I will, without ever knowing the pain of having to bury one's own child. Would that I could say the same for so many others in Genova. Oberto, the keeper of the local tavern, has already buried two sons and four daughters. I tended Oberto's wife in her final hours, and I am of the belief that she died not of the pestilence, but of a broken heart.

Such was not the case for Camilla. She went to bed in vigorous health and woke up suffocating in her own phlegm. Another among countless victims of the chest plague.

I dug Camilla's grave today with the aid of my colleague, Jacob ben Moses. Unlike so many other physicians, Jacob has never looked down his nose at my craft. Together we have formed a partnership of sorts. By law, he is only allowed to tend to fellow Jews, but I turn to him for his advice in circumstances when I am most perplexed. In return, I perform surgery on his patients when they require it. Jacob is well past sixty years but he continues to work as hard as any man in Genova. And today I learned that the old Jew has a remarkably strong back for a man of such advanced years.

Why, you may wonder, would two men who have dedicated their lives to the study of medicine be digging a grave with their own hands? Absurd as it may seem, I cannot afford the price of a gravedigger. Besides, blessed is the man who could find a gravedigger still alive and not frightened to take on the work.

I do not presume that I will live long enough to fill many pages of this diary. Perhaps there will be only this single entry. However, as long I draw breath, I carry an obligation, for posterity, as well as all the lost and wasted lives, especially that of my precious Camilla, to record how this pestilence has leveled my once-great city.

Perhaps, as many of the priests and bishops pontificate, the apocalypse has already arrived, summoned by our own sins. But I must record what I see. I have dedicated my working life to science, and what more is science than carefully documented observation?

Like all things to reach Genova, this plague swept in southwest by sea. It was no demon or ghoul who transported the pestilence. It was

Genovese-born merchants and sailors. They carried this curse all the way from the East, from Caffa, beyond Asia Minor.

The first of the plague-infested ships appeared on the horizon in late autumn. We had been forewarned by Neapolitan traders of their approach, and our soldiers were able to turn the vessel back with flaming arrows and other onslaughts. At the end of December, only days after the celebration to mark the birth of our Lord, another infected ship slipped into harbor. The treacherous captain hid the dead and dying belowdecks. He greedily sold his infested wares to unsuspecting traders in the port, poisoning our noble city. Once the damage was done, he sailed his cursed ship away, and is rumored to have spread the pestilence throughout Sicily and Greece.

Within days, the dying began. The rotting carcasses of pigs, goats, rats, cats, and dogs were the harbingers of the pestilence.

Now that the plague has reached us, there is no escaping death in any walk of life. It is not only the gravediggers who put themselves at terrible risk. Doctors who tend the sick, priests who offer last rites, and lawyers who draw the wills, they, too, all perish.

Earlier today, as Jacob and I dug my wife's grave, he muttered away in his unintelligible tongue. I asked him what he was chanting, and he replied that it was a Hebrew prayer for the dead. When I suggested that he would be wise to save his prayers for the living, he laughed and pointed out that the dead were the only ones who still had hope.

I asked him why he would continue to work if he believed this to be so. He replied that he was old and should have died several winters before. Medicine was all he had ever known, and it was too late for him to stop now, despite the futility of the work.

Jacob lowered his shovel. He told me he understood what it meant to bury a wife, as he had lost his Miriam ten winters before. He assured me that the pain lessens, but the loneliness persists. He asked me why I intended to remain in Genova after burying Camilla. Why would I risk certain infection when I could escape north for France or the Holy Roman Empire, where so many of our colleagues already have gone?

Do you not believe that the pestilence would follow after me? I asked.

Undoubtedly, he agreed. But pockets of refuge will be spared.

And what of the sick here in Genova? I demanded. Did we not owe them a debt of obligation?

Jacob indicated the graves all around us and asked, what do we possibly have left to offer the infirm?

I persisted, perhaps only out of the same stubborn pride that vexed Camilla so thoroughly it drove her to once liken me to a blind jackass. I told Jacob that we do make a difference by draining patients' boils, bleeding them when the humors are unbalanced, and applying other time-honored remedies.

Jacob stared at me in disbelief. Then he spoke the words that sank my heart even lower: Rafael, we doctors have failed our patients so utterly that it astounds me they have not yet turned on us.

Even though we have failed them thus far, it does not mean that we always will, I replied.

The old Jew's only response was to strike his shovel into the unforgiving soil. Nothing more was said between us as we gave my Camilla back to the earth.

Do I not fear the pestilence? you might ask. I fear it more with every agonizing death I witness. With each victim who is covered in weeping sores. Every man, woman, or child whose lungs are so filled with bloody phlegm that there is no space for other vital humors. Yet the thought of being one of the few spared, alone and destitute, frightens me so much more.

Chapter

Five

Nico is waiting outside the hotel for Alana with a cup of espresso in each hand and greets her with a quick peck to both cheeks. There's an unexpected chill in the spring air, and she appreciates the coffee as much for its warmth as its refreshing bite.

Nico's hair is slicked back, each strand in place, and his pressed shirt and matching navy jacket are contoured to his chest. But his face reveals a different story. Alana remembers the look too well. Eight years later, it's even more pronounced. The eyes more bloodshot, the bags beneath them deeper. She also notices the tiny clusters of veins snaking along his cheeks that she hadn't observed yesterday. She thinks back to all those nights-before from their time together—Nico insisting on opening a second or third bottle of wine when he should have stopped at least one sooner.

Time hasn't dulled her memories. Alana can still picture the moment she first laid eyes on Nico in the one-room compound that passed for a hospital in rural Angola. She had already heard at length from the chain-smoking English nurse who drove her in from the airport about the "movie-star-gorgeous" Italian doctor, but Alana hadn't expected him to be such a natural leader. He was only thirty-two at the time, a year older than Alana, but he ran the little hospital with veteran authority, seamlessly navigating critical decisions and agonizing dilemmas such as how to ration their limited supply of potentially life-saving intravenous fluids. But Alana, who was fresh out of training and determined to prove herself on her first WHO assignment, refused to be awed or outperformed. She kept her distance at first. It was only after Nico contracted cholera, and Alana had to nurse him to health, that their mutual attraction burst through. Within a week of his recovery, they were sleeping under the same mosquito netting. They got very little rest, though, working eighteen-hour days and spending much of their downtime intertwined in sweaty embraces, their heated sexual chemistry intensified by the life-and-death nature of their mission. After two months in Angola, she was head over heels in love in a way she had never experienced.

Alana doesn't comment on Nico's appearance now, but her expression must give something away. "A long night," he explains with a forced smile. "Not every day do you lose a patient to the plague."

She only nods. There was always an excuse back then, too.

"And Vittoria's wife, Maria . . ." He massages his temples with his free hand. "She is beside herself with concern over their children. The twins."

Alana stiffens. "Are they sick?"

"No. Italian mothers, they do not do so well with bambinos with colds. Imagine the plague . . ."

Six more days until they are clear, Alana thinks, but she doesn't need to remind Nico of the incubation period for *Yersinia pestis*. "Is the family quarantined?"

"Yes. At their house."

"And what about her workplace?"

"Quarantined?" He shakes his head. "She wasn't coughing until the day of her collapse. And it is an outdoor construction site."

"Still, Nico . . ."

The fog of his hangover seems to lift, and his gaze sharpens. "My patient is dead. The only case. It is a matter for Public Health now." He frowns. "And you, Alana? Why are you so invested?"

"The pneumonic plague in Europe! I know it's only a single—probably imported—case. But, Nico . . . in your wildest dreams, did you ever imagine you would see that?"

"Ah. So you will remain here merely out of . . . medical curiosity?"

She shifts from foot to foot but maintains their eye contact. "I'm with NATO now."

He grimaces. "*NATO?*"

"Yes," she says, lowering her voice as if to compensate for his. "Infectious diseases surveillance."

"Ah, of course. Stopping bioterrorism."

"That's a bit dramatic," she says, though she can't help but glance around to ensure no one on the street is listening. "Besides, natural epidemics pose just as much of a potential security threat as biological warfare. Especially the plague."

He chuckles, not buying it. They wordlessly set off for the Ospedale San Martino, walking along the winding Via Cairoli until it expands into the majestic Via Garibaldi. The street is lined with towering palazzos, all baroque arches and pillars splashed with opulent colors. Despite their hurried pace, Nico acts as guide, naming each architectural gem built by a powerful banking family during the Renaissance.

As impressive as the historic street is, Alana is too preoccupied to pay attention. "I won't stay too long," she says. "There are another four or five days where we still could see spread of the plague from Patient Zero."

"Vittoria. Her name was Vittoria Fornero."

"Look, I'm sorry for her family, but my concern lies with the potential spread."

"You are, of course, assuming she *is* Patient Zero."

Alana has wondered that ever since she first heard about the case. "I was hoping to speak to Vittoria's wife."

"Why? What could she add?"

"Details about their African trip. How Vittoria might have been exposed."

"I already discussed this with Maria." He runs a hand through his hair. "Vittoria, too, before she slipped into the coma. She took a day trip without the rest of the family—outside of Addis Ababa—to the Menagesha National Forest. There are many wild animals in that park. All potential carriers for plague-infected fleas."

"But there haven't been any cases reported near Addis," she says. "Or anywhere else in Ethiopia."

"Yes, but next door, in South Sudan. Seven cases in the past year alone."

"From South Sudan to Ethiopia? That's a fair distance for a flea to hop."

"Surely that's up to the WHO to investigate. Not NATO."

"Why don't we at least visit her workplace, Nico? Talk to her colleagues?"

Nico studies Alana skeptically for a long moment and then breaks into the first heartfelt laugh she has heard from him all morning. "Why not? It's been a long while since I chased an outbreak with you. Besides, Alana, those green eyes of yours . . ." She feels her cheeks warming, as he pinches three fingers in front of his face and adds, "A man might crawl over glass for them."

They reach the garage beside the hospital where Nico's silver Audi SUV is parked. Nico drives them through the heart of the city, whizzing past more colorful churches and palazzos—adorned with columns, domes, pilasters, and pediments—than Alana can keep straight. As Nico navigates the winding streets, he offers her a crash course on the city's geography and its past. She has lived and traveled all over Europe, but she can think of few cities that embody as much living history as Genoa does, from the web of narrow medieval streets, known as *caruggi*, in the old city to the Enlightenment-era splendor of the gold-leaf mansions that line Via Garibaldi.

As they head away from the water, the grand walls give way to the rolling hills above the city. Nico explains how Genoa is built like an amphitheater, rising steadily upward from the horseshoe-shaped harbor. Although he grew up in Rome, his pride in his adopted city is obvious. "In spite of our aging population, the economy here is booming again. You might say Genoa is experiencing a second Renaissance."

"Seems like an appropriate locale for one," she says.

"The site where Vittoria was working is particularly high-profile here. Controversial, too."

"How so?"

"To begin with, Marcello Zanetti is behind it." He waits for a glimmer of recognition, but she shows none. "You haven't heard of him?"

"Why would I have?"

"Ah, Marcello is a local celebrity. He was mayor for six years. Many imagined him for higher office."

"So what happened?"

"He retired from politics to return to his construction business. And this San Giovanni redevelopment is his most ambitious project. It will be the tallest apartment tower in Genoa, with spectacular views from the hilltop."

"What's so controversial about it?"

"There was an old monastery there before."

"And the Church was okay with them tearing it down?"

"Marcello says the place was crumbling anyway."

"Hold on. You know him?"

"Of course. Marcello is Isabella's uncle."

"Your wife's uncle? That's kind of coincidental."

Nico shrugs. "Only to our advantage. Otherwise, how else would we access the site?"

He turns onto a dirt road lined with pylons. Dust flies over the windshield and the vehicle shimmies along for half a mile or so until a massive construction site materializes ahead of them. He pulls over into a gravel-lined lot and parks between a pickup truck and a tractor. They climb out into the warmer sunshine under skies marbled with benign clouds, with the smell of diesel floating on the breeze.

As they head toward a cluster of trailers, a diminutive man in a black robe approaches from the opposite direction. He is flanked on either side by two lanky security guards; the contrast in their relative statures is striking. Neither of the guards has a hand on the balding monk, but it's obvious they are escorting him off the site. The monk smiles at Alana and Nico as they pass, and his bright eyes light with amusement, as if the three of them are in on the same inside joke.

Up close, the excavated pit is even more expansive than Alana had anticipated. It cuts deep into the hillside. Slabs of concrete foundation crisscross its base, interspersed with mounds of rubble, piles of lumber, and stacks of rebar. Men in yellow hard hats work in groups while bulldozers rumble back and forth. Saws hum and drills screech. The ground vibrates from the heavy machinery.

The door to one of the nearby trailers flies open and a young man steps out, haphazardly straightening his hard hat. He doesn't make eye contact as he bustles past Alana, but his acne-riddled face is flushed and sweaty.

Two more men emerge from the trailer. One is dressed in construction gear, while the other wears a black suit. Trim, with silver hair, the older man possesses an air of easy authority. As soon he spots Nico, he bounds over with open arms and greets him with a hug and a kiss to both cheeks. Amid much laughter, they chat in rapid-fire Italian while the younger man stands off to the side.

Finally, Nico turns to Alana and extends his hand. "Marcello, please, Dr. Alana Vaughn."

Zanetti clasps her hand in both of his. "It is a pleasure, Dr. Vaughn." His accent is thicker than Nico's. "Nico tells me good things. Such good things."

Although she's pleased to hear Nico has been discussing her with his wife's uncle, she also feels irrationally annoyed, as if he'd disclosed an actual secret between them. "Thank you, Mr. Zanetti."

He squeezes her hand once more before letting go. "Marcello. I insist. Only Marcello for someone of your reputation and your presence, my dear."

"Alana." She smiles, appreciating his Old World charm but wondering how many times the same line has passed his lips.

"Marcello, we were hoping you might tell us about Vittoria Fornero," Nico prompts.

Zanetti's face saddens. "I knew Vittoria for years. Her father, Bruno, was one of my original foremen. He used to bring her to the sites when she was just a girl. She apprenticed under him. As good as Bruno was, Vittoria was even better. The best. And it was never easy for her. Here in Italy, construction is still a man's world."

Alana nods sympathetically. "No one on the site had any inkling she was sick?"

Zanetti waves the suggestion away. "She never said a word. Not one. And she didn't miss a moment of work until her . . . collapse."

Alana still fails to understand how someone with active plague could slog through a day of construction work. "When was the last time you saw her?"

"Perhaps three days ago." Zanetti nods to the trailer. "Yes. She sat down with me and the architects. To review the plans."

"Inside?" Alana frowns.

"Of course." Zanetti glances over to Nico. "Where else?"

"How did she look?" Nico asks.

"The same as always. So serious, Vittoria. So focused."

"You didn't hear her cough?" Alana asks.

"No. Not at all." Zanetti's voice is calm, but his eyes are calculating. "You think she might have already been contagious?"

"No, Marcello," Nico reassures. "Not if she wasn't coughing."

"We have asked everyone here. No coughing," Zanetti says. "Vittoria was well one moment, and . . ." He snaps his fingers.

It seems appropriate to pause, so Alana waits a little while before she asks, "Marcello, have you heard of anyone else at the site falling ill? With a fever? A cough? Even just a rash?"

"Nothing." Zanetti turns to the man in the overalls and converses with him for a few moments before reverting back to English. "No. Not so much as a sneeze. Paolo says he has checked with all of the crews."

"Still, why not just stop work here for a few days?" Alana suggests. "A week at the most. Until we know the risk is completely gone."

Zanetti squints at her. "The other doctors, from the government—"

"Public Health," Nico offers.

"*Sì!* Public Health. They assured us there was no more risk. Besides, my dear, a week . . ." Zanetti flutters a hand up and over his head. "You have no idea what that might cost."

Less than what an outbreak of the plague would. Alana keeps the thought to herself. "Marcello, on our way in, we passed a monk. He was being escorted away—"

"Brother Silvio! Such a character! Funny little man. He comes every day."

"Why?"

Zanetti taps his temple and laughs. "He is losing his mind. Senile, yes? Sometimes he gets in the way. It's not his fault."

"Is that so?" Alana says.

"Do not worry about our little monk, my dear. He will be back tomorrow! That is one thing he never forgets!" He exhales again. "It's such a shame, you know."

She assumes he is still talking about Brother Silvio, but instead he motions toward the construction site. "We tried to save her. The old monastery. We were going to turn her into a beautiful museum. As part of the complex."

"What happened?" she asks.

"The engineers. They took their magical measurements. They tell us she was—" He turns to Nico and switches to Italian again.

"Structurally unsound," Nico translates.

"Unsafe. Yes. We had to take her apart. But we will build a memorial to the monastery right here on the ground floor. Something special. It will make even Brother Silvio proud." He kicks at the loose soil by his foot. "Trust me, the spirit of San Giovanni will soon rise again."

Six

Today is the twenty-seventh day of January, in the year of our Lord thirteen hundred and forty-eight.

Had you asked me a week prior whether the suffering could worsen or the sorrow deepen, I would have told you it was not humanly or divinely imaginable. How wrong I would have been. No person is left unscathed, no family untouched. Death grows insatiable.

I barely have strength left to apply quill to parchment. The muscles in my arms throb. The stench of pus is embedded in my nostrils. I lanced buboes and applied fresh salves long after sundown.

The tempers run short in our once-great city. Earlier, the townspeople jostled violently for position in the queue to consult with me. More than once, the shouting led to fisticuffs. I had to banish one man, the local tanner, after he barged into my room demanding immediate attention even as my fingers were buried deep in the armpit of another.

People are not the only victims of this sickness. So, too, are common values such as decency, compassion, and even order. The spectacles I have witnessed in recent days would embarrass even the most seasoned of men. This pestilence has driven people to the extremes of deportment. I have seen panic on the faces of hardened soldiers and stoic acceptance in the eyes of young naïfs. Some say it has turned men either toward heaven or hell.

Many cling with blind zeal to prayers and rituals. They spend most of their time at church, and to demonstrate their sacrifice to God, some even shun the most basic comforts, including food or drink in the daylight hours and a bed after nightfall.

Others feel abandoned by God, and therefore freed of the obligation to live by His laws. They carry themselves with wanton disregard and, at times, shameless gall. They gamble on the street, drink themselves to stupor in the daylight, carouse openly with those who are not their wives or husbands. I have heard that several among them support their hedonism by looting the property of the newly dead or, even worse, that of those too infirm to resist.

Who am I to judge? We each carry our burden in our own way. Still, I must confess to being saddened to have learned that my former protégé has joined the ranks of the hedonists.

Lorenzo Mirandolo apprenticed under me for two years. The boy showed true promise. I once observed him reset a shattered ankle on a peddler whose weighty cart had rolled over his foot. Lorenzo aligned the deformed foot and ankle with such precision that, within three months, the peddler was walking again with only the slightest of limps.

Sadly, Lorenzo's family served as the earliest of kindling for this newly lit bonfire of death. His mother died before the New Year arrived, and his father, two sisters, and youngest brother all succumbed in the following week. Lorenzo went nearly mad with sorrow.

One morning, early in January, he did not arrive at the appointed hour to help clean the surgical utensils. Punctuality was among his most consistent virtues, so I was concerned that he, too, must have fallen ill. When I told Camilla that I was going to seek him, she warned me to curtail my expectations. Her intuition proved correct. Camilla was prescient that way. I shall never forget the tears of sorrow she cried, two summers before, upon telling me that she was with child. She foresaw then that she would never carry the baby to life.

I found Lorenzo in the lowliest of the local taverns by the harbor. As I entered, a scrawny three-legged dog chased a piglet across the straw floor, stopping only to urinate against the leg of a table. Though it was not yet noon, revelers filled the tavern, which reeked of spilt ale and burnt meat. It took me a moment to sight Lorenzo on the far side of the room, where he tottered on his chair with a whore straddling his lap.

Rafael, he called to me, instead of his usual honorific of Signore Pasqua. Come drink with us, my good master!

You are already drunk, Lorenzo, I observed upon reaching his table.

And so should you be, he announced, causing the wench on his lap to cackle and raise her mug in agreement.

There is work to be done, I said. More work than ever.

Lorenzo laughed bitterly, and his voice grew louder still. The only work left for us is to bide our time until death gets around to claiming each of us, too.

Not all of the afflicted die, I said. There is hope for some. And it is our duty as surgeons to offer them the best opportunity for survival or, at the very least, a modicum of comfort in their dying.

Tell that to my mother, my father, my sisters, and especially my brother!

There are no words to soothe such losses, I said. However, no loss, no matter how great, permits us the luxury of abdicating our duty.

Lorenzo slammed his mug onto the table, spilling ale over it, and labored to his feet, toppling the harlot to the floor. You are a decent man and a good teacher, Rafael, he cried. But you are a cruel fool to confuse high-mindedness for hope!

Seven

The long silences are the worst, Alana thinks, as she listens to her boss, Monique Olin, breathe on the other end of the secure voice-over-Internet line. She remembers the parting words of Gavin Fielding, her Scottish predecessor at NATO: "Don't believe the fuckin' Mother Teresa act! Monique can be one terrifying old cow when she doesn't get her way."

In the eighteen months since Alana assumed her role as director of biological surveillance for NATO, she has come to realize that Fielding was only half joking about their mutual boss. Alana respects and even admires the fiftyish Frenchwoman, who has risen to the level of assistant secretary general, one promotion away from the very top of the old boys' club that NATO continues to be. Among other responsibilities, Olin oversees Chemical, Biological, Radiological, Nuclear Defense, or CBRN as it's always referred to at headquarters. She can be collaborative in her approach, but once her mind is made up she demands absolute compliance. And God help anyone who thinks otherwise.

Olin finally breaks the silence on the line. "So you went to Genoa despite my explicit instructions?"

"Monique, it's the first case of pneumonic plague Western Europe has seen in several hundred years!"

"And what does that have to do with you?" Olin asks quietly. "Or NATO?"

"How can the recurrence of the plague in Europe *not* represent a potential security threat?"

"This is an issue for Italian Public Health," Olin mutters, her exasperation revealing traces of her usually nonexistent French accent. "If NATO were to get involved every time a European tourist brought something back from the developing world—"

"This isn't some sex tourist lugging antibiotic-resistant gonorrhea back from Cambodia. It's the fucking plague, Monique!"

"We only go in when we are invited," Olin says, unmoved. "Not before."

"You could get us that invitation," Alana persists, realizing she would be wise to back off but was unable to stop herself.

"Maybe, maybe not," Olin says. "But I won't try. And you will return to Brussels. Immediately."

"I need another day or so, Monique. Just to establish whether this case is—"

"I said no, Alana! Besides, the WHO is already on the way to Genoa."

The words bristle more than Olin's sharp tone. If Alana had stuck with the World Health Organization, she might have been put in charge of the mission herself. "Who is leading their team?"

"Byron Menke."

Alana shakes her head but holds her tongue. She had never personally worked with the Canadian epidemiologist at the WHO, but she remembers his reputation for being heavy-handed and, at times, tactless—an ends-justify-the-means kind of investigator.

"Come back to Brussels, Alana," Olin says coolly.

"First thing tomorrow morning."

"Any longer and you might not have an office to return to." With that, the line goes dead.

Alana remembers something her mother—an orthopedic surgeon who retired from the army with the rank of colonel—once told her: "The very first words out of your mouth were back talk, darling. How did you ever end up in the military?" It was true. Army brat or not, Alana wonders what self-destructive instinct would lead someone as headstrong as herself to join the most hierarchical institutions in the world, including the U.S. military, the WHO, and, perhaps worst of all, NATO.

Her shoulder aches again, and she rubs it to no real effect. How different life would have been if not for that friendly fire incident, eleven years ago, that leveled the field hospital in the Afghani province of Logar. Four surgeries later, Alana still suffers from chronic shoulder pain and permanent numbness in her ring and little fingers. Sometimes her shoulder spontaneously dislocates if she raises her arm too quickly. Were it not for the injury, she would have been an established trauma surgeon by now, instead of chasing microscopic phantoms across the globe. In her heart, Alana knows she was always destined for this work, but for reasons she doesn't even understand, she still views the injury as a failure, and hides it from most people. Nico used to tell her that the scars made her look sexier. It was a testament to how deeply she trusted him that she ever allowed him to touch them.

The phone vibrates on the bed. Alana wonders if it might be Olin calling back to light into her a second time, but instead, Nico's name pops up on the screen. His three-word text—"Hospital. Come now!"—sets her heart thumping.

Alana bursts through the doors of the Ospedale San Martino. Staff and visitors flow through the lobby as usual. A medical supplier has set up an exhibition in the middle, and several people linger to inspect the wares. But she isn't fooled by the apparent calm.

Remembering her earlier long wait at the hospital's elevator, she rushes up the stairs to Nico's fourth-floor office. Inside, she finds only his receptionist, who speaks no English. The matronly woman tells Alana, through a series of hand gestures, that Nico has been called away. "Where? *Dove?*"

"*Il obitorio!*"

Alana doesn't require a translation. She whirls around and races down the stairs to the basement. She spots the sign for the morgue, but below it two security guards in masks and gloves block the door. Undeterred, she heads for them. The nearer guard shoos her away with a backward wave.

"I'm Dr. Alana Vaughn. I need to see Dr. Oliva right away."

The guard steps forward with palms held up. "*No! No! Solo personale autorizzato.*"

"Nico! It's me!" Alana shouts over his shoulder. "Are you in there?"

The other guard moves closer. "Signora. It is not safe!"

The door behind them flies open and a man in biohazard gear steps out. She recognizes Nico by his gait. Experience alone stops her from following the instinct to dart around the guards to get to him.

Nico addresses the guards briefly and then switches back to English. "These men will get you a PPE kit, Alana," he says before disappearing behind the same door.

The first guard watches with suspicion as Alana suits up, a few feet back from the door. The otherwise tedious drill is second nature to her: wash hands with the sanitizer from the wall-mounted pump, gown, apply mask, goggles, hood, wash again, and then slip on two pairs of gloves. Donning and doffing the personal protective gear in the correct order has been programmed into her brain stem, reinforced by the memory of the Liberian doctor she watched die of Ebola after he deviated from only one of those steps.

As she slips the gown over her shirt, her damaged shoulder shifts and, for a moment, she fears it might pop out of joint, but it doesn't.

When she's done, the English-speaking guard opens the door to the morgue and points her wordlessly down a corridor toward a room at the far end. Her goggles mist under the hood and the cotton booties shuffle over the tiled floor. Her sense of foreboding grows with each slippery step.

The room is refrigerated, but Alana feels a different sort of chill as she glimpses the body on the table. It's not Vittoria Fornero. The woman lying on the slab looks to be in her early thirties. Her hair is shorn on one side of her head and streaked blue in a tint that almost matches her skin's lividity. Her sunken eyes stare lifelessly up at the ceiling.

Nico stands across the table beside a shorter woman. Alana presumes she is the pathologist, but he doesn't introduce her. He motions to the dead woman. "Sonia Poletti."

"The plague?" Alana asks.

Nico nods. "Pneumonic plague. Same as Vittoria."

"Don't tell me that she worked at the same construction site."

"Worse."

"How can it be any worse?"

"Sonia worked here. At the hospital."

"Oh, Jesus! In what capacity? Doctor? Nurse?"

Nico shakes his head. "Sonia was a phlebotomist."

"A lab tech? How much contact could she possibly have had with Vittoria?"

"Not much, apparently. She drew blood on her the day Vittoria first arrived. No contact after."

"Was there a body-fluid exposure? An inadvertent needle poke with contaminated blood?"

"Sonia would have had to report an incident like that. There is no such record."

Alana holds Nico's stare. She knows what he must be thinking: if such casual contact was enough to infect the lab tech, then anyone who crossed paths with Vittoria, or Sonia after she fell ill, might also be at risk, including him.

"Had she been a patient for long?" Alana asks.

"Sonia never made it beyond the emergency room."

Alana hesitates, almost afraid to ask the next question. "How long had she been sick?"

"Hours. Apparently she was well yesterday. But she awoke with a high fever and shortness of breath. She didn't have the strength to climb out of bed."

It feels as if the room's temperature plummets several more degrees. "Was she coughing?"

"*Sì, c'era sangue ovunque*," he says, lapsing into Italian perhaps without even realizing it.

"Nico?"

"My colleagues in the emergency room . . . they say she was spraying blood everywhere."

Chapter

Eight

It is the twenty-ninth day of January. Shortly after dawn, as I was preparing for surgery, I received the most unexpected summons. Two priests arrived, both strangers to me. Without so much as an introduction, the taller of the two announced that the Archbishop requested my presence.

How can I be of assistance to His Grace? I inquired of them. Is he unwell?

It is not for you to ask, the second priest said. You are simply to comply.

I accompanied the priests in silence. I was on foot while they each rode a sturdy horse, up the narrow road to the palace of the Archbishop. Like the nearby basilica of Santa Maria, it is perched on the hilltop in the neighborhood known as Castello and commands a fine view of Genova and the harbor beyond. I was breathing heavily from the climb and, I must confess, was pleased to finally reach its massive doors.

The grand palace boasted the highest ceilings I had ever encountered outside of a cathedral. The walls were adorned with masterful paintings and rich tapestries. The air was dense with the scent of burning incense and candle wax.

I was made to wait in the antechamber. I felt ill at ease to have been summoned by a man as eminent as the Archbishop. The only time I had ever laid eyes on him before was from a distance, as he led the annual Corpus Christi procession through the streets of Genova. I assumed that he, or someone dear to him, must have contracted the plague.

As I waited, an older monk in the black habit of the Benedictine order joined me. He greeted me with a cheerful talkativeness that stood in stark contrast to the cold silence of my escorts. He introduced himself as Don Marco, abbot of the San Giovanni Monastery. He told me he had come to pay his respects to the Archbishop and to ask for his blessing at the monastery, where many of the brothers had fallen ill. When he learned of my profession, his eyes lit like candles and his smile grew wider.

He took my hand in both of his. His palms, rough with calluses, felt more like those of a laborer than a cleric. Good doctor, do you not see how God works in the most magnificent and amusing ways? Don Marco said. Perhaps you would deign to visit our humble monastery in San Giovanni. You see, our local physician has chosen a most inopportune time to seek sabbatical.

I was ashamed to hear that another of my colleagues must have abandoned his duty and fled for his own safety. I felt obligated to accept the abbot's invitation to visit his monastery, and I assured him I would do so before the Sabbath.

He shook my hand gleefully and told me that God loves nothing more than to surprise His supplicants with such unexpected blessings.

Soon after Don Marco departed, another priest, a tidy young man with an officious manner, entered the antechamber to inform me the Archbishop would see me.

I was relieved to discover that Archbishop Valente was not prostrate, as I had feared, but rather seated in a raised chair that resembled a throne in its ornateness. A fire raged in the fireplace at his back. Despite his slender build, thinning blond hair, and fair skin, which stood out against his crimson robe, the Archbishop appeared to be in fine health.

As I stood in front of him, he read from a parchment, tapping the page with a forefinger that bore the most striking jewel-encrusted silver ring I had ever seen. In time, he lowered the document to his lap and assessed me with his intelligent gray eyes.

Doctor Pasqua, my parishioners have told me of the fine work you are doing for the people of Genova in these trying times, the Archbishop said. On behalf of the Church, please accept my gratitude.

You are most welcome, Your Grace, I said. I am simply practicing my craft as best as I am able.

Indeed, the Archbishop said gravely. The Holy Father and we, his servants, are doing all we can to comfort the faithful and to seek their salvation. Until we achieve this inevitable grace, our flock will need the assistance of able earthly practitioners such as yourself.

I bowed my head, but I resisted the urge to add that in my observation the Church is doing little more than adding fuel to the bonfire of panic with apocalyptic sermons.

This scourge, the Archbishop said. You have witnessed it firsthand for several weeks now?

I informed him I had treated my initial case on the first day of the New Year.

Quite the omen, he said. And how is your technique different from that of the other physicians and surgeons?

I do not believe it is, Your Grace, I said. My approach is the same as it has always been. We healers understand that the key to health lies in the balance of the humors. This plague disrupts that balance in the worst of manners. I strive to restore it where I can.

You bleed the sufferers, then? the Archbishop asked.

That is only one technique. There are several vital ways to restore the humors. Cool the overheated with wet compresses. Warm the chilled with fires. Force water and wine into those who have sweated or vomited away too much of their essential fluids. And so on.

The Archbishop tilted his head. And you have seen this approach succeed?

Only in a precious few, I conceded. You see, Your Grace, this plague comes in two forms that are so distinct from one another it is as though they are entirely different illnesses.

Do tell, the Archbishop commanded with a roll of his hand.

The first form is a skin ailment with the agonizing sores and discolored sacs we refer to as buboes. In my experience, two out of three of those inflicted in such a way will eventually die, usually in three or four days to a week at most. With these patients, I have found that an aggressive attack on the buboes by lancing them early and filling them with hostile salves can prove beneficial.

And the other form?

The chest plague, I said, and the words alone tasted bitter on my tongue. This form strikes the lungs with lightning speed. The afflicted rapidly proceeds from a state of good health to complete infirmity. Inevitably, the sufferer is coughing up his final blood-soaked breaths within a day or two, sometimes hours, of the initial symptom. No one escapes the grip of the chest plague with his life.

As I described the pestilence, I could not help but remember my own Camilla. How desperately I had cradled her in those final hours. Her chest rattled with such a cough that it reminded me of a windstorm tearing through an unshuttered house. As I watched the life drain from her soulful eyes, I could not imagine feeling more helpless or useless.

And yet you are still well, the Archbishop said.

So far, yes.

The Archbishop motioned with his hands as if to free a small bird. I can hardly dispatch a priest to offer last rites without learning later that he, too, has contracted the plague, he said. Yet you work day and night with the afflicted and have managed to completely avoid either form of the illness.

His tone was pleasant enough, but discomfort welled within me.

He leaned forward in his chair. What is your secret, Doctor?

I have no explanation for my good fortune, Your Grace. I can only thank God for every single day of good health he grants me.

The Archbishop leaned back. I will pray for your continued good health, he said with a thin smile. And that you will soon share with me more learned insights into this cruel affliction.

Chapter

Nine

Marcello Zanetti studies Don Arturo, the retired abbot of the former San Giovanni Monastery, from the threshold of the seminary's library. Zanetti suspects he, himself, must be even older than the abbot, but there is no question which one of them is more vital or relevant. Don Arturo sits alone in the library, dressed in a black tunic while reading the morning newspaper, even though it's almost dinnertime. *So this is what utter defeat looks like?* Zanetti thinks without feeling an ounce of pity for the man.

Don Arturo greets him with a beatific smile, but Zanetti isn't fooled. When he was mayor, he found it easier to deal with the local crime families than with representatives of the Church. The gangsters were more trustworthy than all those priests, despite their benevolent smiles.

"Ah, Signore Zanetti, to what do I owe this unexpected honor?" Don Arturo asks as Zanetti sits down across from him.

"The honor is mine, Don Arturo. Besides, I feel duty-bound to keep you informed of developments at the San Giovanni site."

"How very thoughtful."

"Also, I wanted to share this with you." Zanetti extracts from his brief-case the glossy brochure that his marketing team had drawn up. He flips it open to show Don Arturo the renderings of the lobby.

Zanetti taps the richly colored drawing with a forefinger. "Here. The memorial to the old monastery. We will plaster the whole wall with photographs and old paintings. Glass cases for a few of the relics—alarmed, of course." He moves his finger to the center of the page. "And right here, a most detailed replica of San Giovanni that will stand three feet high."

"It will be as if the monastery were never demolished."

Zanetti hides his irritation behind a somber smile. "We would have saved her if we could have. The engineers, they would not allow it. They say it would never have been safe."

"We were lucky it hadn't collapsed on our heads anytime in the past eight hundred years. Still, sometimes even those of us in my line of work must defer to science."

Zanetti slides the brochure toward the abbot. "Please, for you."

"Thank you." Don Arturo pushes it back. "It is wasted on me. I am not in the real estate market. The Church provides for all my worldly needs here at the seminary."

Unperturbed, Zanetti gathers the document and slides it back into his briefcase. "One of your monks continues to spend much of his time at our construction site."

"My monks? Even when I was still the abbot, they were never my monks." He glances skyward. "Only His. And now that I have been retired . . ."

I can play this game all day, you cagey son of a bitch. Zanetti nods solemnly and says, "Yes, of course. A Brother Silvio."

Arturo only rolls his eyes in response.

Zanetti taps his temple. "Is he all right?"

"That is a difficult question to assess. Brother Silvio is definitely single-minded."

"He is a jovial man. He enjoys engaging my workers in conversation. Too much so. They really have no time for such chats. And . . . he can be an alarmist."

"An alarmist?"

"Yes. He shares stories of the old monastery with anyone who will listen. Legends about curses and so on." Zanetti clucks his tongue. "Such superstitious nonsense is not always good for morale, you understand?"

"And how do you know it all to be nonsense?"

"I am a man of faith, too. Mass every Sunday. Well, most of them, anyway." Arturo makes no comment, as Zanetti searches for the right words. "No disrespect, Don Arturo, but I thought you were more . . . worldly . . . than to believe in this kind of folklore."

The abbot studies him for an icy moment, before the smile finds his lips again. "Regardless, I cannot be of much assistance with Brother Silvio."

"Oh? Why not?"

"I do not even know where he is residing."

"My associates can easily find out for you," Zanetti says. "Besides, he is very easy to find. He's at the construction site almost every day."

Arturo nods. "Perhaps so. However, I never held much sway over Silvio even when I was his superior. Now that you and your associates have seen to my retirement, I am certain it would be a waste of time for me to speak to him."

Zanetti doesn't bother to argue. As he rises to leave, Arturo says, "Can I offer you a small piece of advice, Signore Zanetti?"

"Yes. Please."

"Every once in a while, science—and, yes, even real estate developers—ought to defer to God."

Ten

The English and Italian meld into an incoherent jumble. Alana has already forgotten many of the names and titles of those crowded around the conference table, but most of them are senior government officials at the civic, regional, and even federal level. Everyone is speaking over each other again.

Dr. Byron Menke, the Canadian epidemiologist leading the World Health Organization's response team, stands motionlessly at the head of the long table. He's handsome—with gray-blue eyes and prominent cheekbones—but he's more noticeable for his ruffled appearance; his brown hair is tousled, and his dress shirt half untucked. His lips are parted in a half smile, as though amused by the kerfuffle around him. After watching a few moments more, he casually raises the thick file in his hand and releases it. It slaps the table with a thud that quiets the room.

This guy is exactly as billed, Alana thinks.

"Let's begin with what we know, rather than what we assume. Agreed?" Byron glances around the room, seeming to puff his chest slightly.

Heads nod around the conference table. Alana senses that the Italian authorities have already ceded the leadership of the outbreak containment to Byron and his WHO team. She has been around long enough to know that it's politically expedient for local governments to do so, providing them with a convenient scapegoat when things get worse or go wrong, as they so often do.

The top floor room in the Municipo, or City Hall, is brightly lit by the midday sunshine streaming through the windows that frame the famed Via Garibaldi below. Alana paused on her way in to admire the iconic building with its vaulted ceiling and tiered balconies. It reminded her of how little she had seen of Genoa in her two and a half days here. Normally, visiting a city so rich in history for the first time, she would've found time to soak in the local ambience and culture through morning jogs and evening strolls. But there's nothing normal about this visit. Not only is her mission unsanctioned, but she feels an urgency she hasn't experienced since she joined NATO.

Aside from Byron, four other members of the WHO task force are squeezed around the table among the Italian officials. The highest-ranking is the country's deputy minister of health, a doughy-faced man who has thus far remained silent.

The table is so crowded that Alana's knee keeps brushing against Nico's. His cologne is a constant distraction. She hasn't shared this kind of proximity with him since that last morning in Palermo when they lay naked and winded in the four-poster bed, plotting out future reunions that were never to materialize.

It's been over eight years, Alana reminds herself. There have been other relationships since, two of which lasted longer. She came close to marrying the last man, a gentle but, as it turned out, insufferably idealistic water engineer whom she had met in Geneva. But Nico was different. He was her first love after her shoulder injury, and their romance hadn't sputtered out like most of the others had. They had chosen their careers, which kept them constantly separated in different hot spots across the globe, over their relationship.

Byron's voice pulls her back to the meeting. "Just to review: the plague is spread by the rat flea, or *Xenopsylla cheopis*, which transmits bacterium through its bite." He clicks the remote in his hand and the screen above him fills with the image of a golden translucent creature that resembles a lobster without claws. "These fleas require an animal vector, or carrier, to 'host' them. That can be almost any mammal, especially rodents like rats, mice, squirrels, or even prairie dogs. But in most cities the plague is usually spread by the black rat." The slide above him dissolves and re-forms as a photo of a mischief of rats, clumped together and crawling over one another. The image, although static, gives Alana a queasy sense of movement.

"As most of you know, there are three clinical variants of the plague," Byron continues. He speaks in English, not allowing time for translation, even though this meeting is in Genoa to discuss an Italian outbreak. "All are caused by the same bacterium: *Yersinia pestis*. The most common form is the bubonic plague, which presents with classic skin buboes, or swollen lymph nodes, that are discolored from internal bleeding." The next slide is that of a wide-eyed young boy whose neck is distended on both sides by darkish lumps. "But there are two other, even deadlier forms. The rarest is a type of blood poisoning known as the septic plague." The body of a pale, thin woman, with a bar drawn across her eyes to hide her identity, fills the screen. Her skin is riddled with small purplish red spots, known as pur-pura. Both her legs are blackened from the knees down with the patches of dead skin or necrosis, and it's obvious to Alana the photo was taken postmortem. "And, of course, the other form is known as the pneumonic plague, which attacks the victims' lungs . . ." The screen comes to life with a grainy video clip. A middle-aged man writhes on a hospital bed. His cough is so harsh it almost made Alana hack. Even though he covers his mouth with a hand, bloody sputum sprays between his fingers with each violent hack. "Both the septic and pneumonic plagues are uniformly fatal without early and aggressive antibiotic treatment."

Byron lets the uncomfortable clip run on a bit longer than necessary, Alana thinks, before the screen finally goes blank. "The bubonic plague *only* spreads through infected fleabites, not via person to person," he says. "The pneumonic plague can begin as a skin infection, with the usual buboes, that travels to the lungs. However, more commonly it spreads from one person to the next through coughing, and it's as contagious as the flu. So far, we have two confirmed cases of pneumonic plague in Genoa. Patient Zero is a forty-two-year-old construction worker who presented four days ago. She developed her first skin symptoms, buboes in her armpits, two days prior to hospitalization. Once there, she had direct contact with the second case, a thirty-one-year-old lab tech. The second victim had no skin involvement of any kind, only chest symptoms. She, like Patient Zero, died from respiratory complications."

"So we can presume respiratory spread from the first victim to the second," Nico says.

"We can, I suppose," Byron says with a cursory glance at him. "It doesn't mean we would be correct to do so."

"We would be foolish not to," Nico fires back.

"Foolish . . ." Byron grins. "Say, like not immediately placing a feverish woman who presents to hospital coughing up blood on full isolation precautions?"

"Easy to say in hindsight," Nico snaps. He turns to the person on the other side of him and mutters something in Italian, loud enough to be heard by everyone. The room erupts into a medley of unintelligible voices.

Byron holds up his hands. "Point taken," he says, in the tone of someone appeasing an irrational toddler. "You were astute to diagnose the plague. Besides, what's done is done. Why don't we finish taking stock before we move on to the next steps?"

There are a few reluctant nods and the din settles.

"We do not as of yet have a confirmed source for the *Yersinia pestis* bacteria," Byron continues. "We do know that Patient Zero traveled to Menagesha National Forest in Ethiopia twenty days prior to showing her first symptom."

"And that park is chockablock full of high-risk critters," Dr. Justine Williams pipes up. The petite woman of Asian descent with the dark eyes and long lustrous black hair has made an impression with her job description alone—Alana had never before met a rodentologist, let alone "one of the world's leading zoologists in the study of rat behavior," as Byron had introduced her.

"All kinds of potential endemic plague vectors could be hiding among those lovely juniper bushes," Justine continues. "From *Desmomys harringtoni*—better known as Harrington's rat—to *Praomys albipes*, aka the white-footed rat. Though their feet aren't any whiter than mine." Her giggle is almost contagious. "And don't forget, our dear old friend *Rattus rattus*—the common black rat—is also found in the same park. Word on the street is that black rats have had a brush or two with the plague in the past."

Byron eyes Justine with a mixture of amusement and annoyance. "The usual incubation period for the plague is two to seven days, not twenty," he says.

Justine shrugs. "Bugs mutate. Shit happens."

"There hasn't been a case of bubonic plague reported in Ethiopia—in man or animal—in over twenty years. Besides, the two cases in Genoa have behaved far more aggressively than any of the ones seen in Africa recently."

"See my earlier point about mutation . . . and also . . . shit happening."

The deputy minister raises his hand. "Dr. Menke, a question, if you will allow me?"

"Of course."

"Are you saying that this outbreak did not originate in Africa?"

"No. Not yet, at least. As Dr. Williams points out, there are all kinds of mammals living in that ecosystem, including black rats. We also know that the rat flea is endemic to the same park. We've got a WHO team on the ground in Ethiopia collecting samples at the national park, and we should know better in the coming days. Meantime, all I'm saying is that we have no confirmed source and we shouldn't presume anything."

"But if the so-called Patient Zero was not infected on her trip to Africa, then she could only have acquired it here in Genoa."

"It is too early to know."

"Where else could it possibly come from?" the deputy minister persists. "There have been no such infected animals in Italy for hundreds of years!"

"Underestimate the ingenuity of rats at your own peril," Justine says. "To them, intercontinental travel is little more than a jaunt in the park."

Alana can't hold her tongue any longer. "How do we know the first victim became infected through a rat or any other animal vector?"

All eyes turn to her. "Would our NATO colleague care to elaborate?" Byron asks.

Alana introduced herself only as an infectious diseases colleague of Nico's, but she realizes it's not the time or place to confront Byron for calling her out. "As you said yourself, Dr. Menke, we can't presume anything about the source," she says calmly. "Including that there ever was a zoological source. Or, for that matter, that the person whom you're calling 'Patient Zero' is in fact the index case."

Byron holds her gaze for a moment, and then looks around the table. "I think we can all agree that, whatever the source, containment is now the top priority." Heads nod and there are murmurs of concurrence. "To that end, we need to start every casual contact of both known victims on antibiotics."

"We have already done so at the hospital," says Dr. Sansa, a distinguished-looking older man who was introduced as the city's chief Public Health officer. "Everyone who had direct contact with the victims has been started on doxycycline and ciprofloxacin, or some alternative if allergic."

"What about immunization?" Nico asks.

Byron motions across the table to a man with reddish blond hair and a boyish face, whose bushy beard makes him somehow look even younger. "For that I will defer to our immunization expert, Dr. Larsen."

Larsen removes his glasses. "The World Health Organization does not, as of yet, have ready access to mass quantities of *Yersinia* vaccine."

"But the U.S. military does," Alana says.

"Even their capacity is limited. Besides, the plague vaccine is notoriously unreliable, with post-exposure immunity rates of only seventy-four percent. It would leave roughly three out of ten people unprotected."

"Better than ten out of ten," Alana points out.

"Also, the vaccine doesn't offer any proven protection against exposure to the pneumonic plague. Only post-exposure antibiotics are effective. And they must be given within twenty-four hours."

"Nonetheless," Byron says. "We will expedite access to the vaccine, prioritizing the health care workers on the front line and in the lab. Meantime, we need to focus on aggressive contact-chasing. Find anyone and everyone who might've been within a stone's throw of a plague victim."

Dr. Sansa nods gravely. "We have been doing little else. Around-the-clock."

"Good," Byron says. "There is one other vital aspect we need to agree upon. Communications. It's a miracle this story hasn't hit the mainstream media. But it will. And soon."

Sansa exhales. "Our office received several calls this morning."

"It's essential we get ahead of the media and control the message, rather than vice versa. To that end, I'll turn to our communications specialist, Yvette Allaire, to review the fundamentals."

"Thank you, Byron," says a painfully thin Frenchwoman at the far end of the table. Alana has the mental image of her holding a martini glass in one hand and a cigarette in the other. "As we all know, the biggest immediate risk facing Genoa is not so much the outbreak as the overreaction that will inevitably follow . . ."

While Alana agrees that mass panic will only compound the problems, she doubts it's the plague's most imminent threat. She feels the vibration of Nico's cell phone against her leg.

"Excuse me," he says, rising from the table.

Instinctively, she follows him.

Nico speaks into the phone at first in a whisper, but his voice rises sharply even before he clears the door. By the time Alana catches up with him in the hallway, his pupils are wide and he is barking into the receiver in a machine-gun staccato.

"What is it?" she asks, grabbing his arm.

Nico pulls the phone away from his ear. "Two new patients. One of them is a doctor. He's one of my best friends."

Chapter

Eleven

Today is the first day of February.

It is not for me to interpret the vagaries of fate, but I cannot help but wonder the same as the Archbishop did. Why have I been spared? To be left behind is more a burden than a mercy.

I write by candlelight now. I have only just now returned home from an arduous trek up to the San Giovanni Monastery. I had not anticipated the extent of the suffering I would encounter there.

The plain stone and brick buildings of the monastery stand humbly in relation to the palace of the Archbishop. But what the monastery lacks in color or charm is compensated for by the abbot himself. Don Marco greeted me at the doors with the affection of a man chancing upon a friend at a tavern, rather than welcoming a near-stranger to the plague-stricken commune.

I never doubted God would deliver you to us, Doctor Pasqua! he cried, as he patted me on the back.

He led me by the elbow through a doorway into the central room, the

Warming House, where a fire was blazing even though it was still morning. The dreary chamber was nearly empty, the floors cold stone, the walls unadorned. A single long wooden table was the only furnishing. Our voices echoed as we spoke.

Where are the other monks? I asked.

Don Marco held up a helpless hand. We have delivered last rites to forty-one brothers already this month, he said. Almost half of our order. The others are either ill or caring for the ill or burying them. Even the scriptorium lies empty. We house one of the most enviable libraries in all of Genova, but there are no calligraphers free to continue the Lord's work.

I had run out of words to comfort for such losses, so I held my tongue.

God has a plan for us all, though, does He not? Don Marco said as he summoned another smile. Where did you leave your horse?

When I told him that I had arrived on foot, he rushed over to a shelf on the wall. He pulled down a wineskin and removed a partial loaf of bread from a clay pot. You must be parched from the climb, he said. I am sure the Archbishop would not dare serve such slop to his lowest serf, let alone an honored guest, but I am afraid we have no better to offer.

Though I suspected the food was carefully rationed, I knew better than to insult my host by refusing. The wine was sour but drinkable and the bread nourishing, despite its saltiness. When I had finished the last bite, I asked him where they kept the infirm.

I wish we had time for a little spiritual and scientific discourse, Doctor. How I miss those days. But these times do not allow for such luxuries, do they?

I followed him outside and into a low-ceilinged building with a thatched roof. It was only then that I heard throaty moans and inhaled the stench of decay that so often heralded the afflicted.

We have converted the sleeping quarters of the novices into an infirmary, Don Marco said. After all, why not? All twelve of our novices have already departed this earthly world.

More than twenty wooden beds were occupied. Wet coughs and

agonized groans filled the room. Three or four monks hurried from one bed to another, stopping to ladle water or kneeling to offer prayers.

The first man we came across was already dead. At initial glance, I thought the second, with his ghostly face, was as well. But despite his blackened fingers, which in my experience always portend an imminent demise, he was awake enough to look up at Don Marco with a weak smile. The abbot knelt at his bedside and prayed for him, bravely dabbing water on the monk's forehead while whispering words of encouragement between his prayers.

It was not until we reached the fourth bed that I recognized a condition I could actually address. This monk's armpits were painfully swollen with massive buboes. He lay before us silently, but the dried tears on his cheeks evidenced his agony. I hurriedly pulled my surgical instruments from my satchel. I stood as far back from the bed as I could as I lanced his swellings. Even still, I had to back away from the eruption of pus that greeted my knife.

And so it went all morning and into the afternoon. Two more brothers, including the one with the blackened fingers, died. I cannot claim to have made much, if any, difference for the fate of those cursed monks. But as we returned to the cloister, the abbot praised me as if I were a returning hero of war. He insisted on serving me more wine and bread. And I have to admit, it was hunger more than politeness that compelled me to accept this time.

As I was finishing my wine, I heard scratching somewhere below me. Two black rats emerged from under the table and scurried toward the wall, their long tails disappearing through a hole between the bricks.

It took a moment before I realized why the commonplace sight seemed so striking. I had seen more rats over the past month than I had in my entire life, but none of them had been alive. After all, this sickness was indiscriminate in its choice of victims. Livestock and animals were equally susceptible as people. Dead dogs, cats, and goats rotted on the streets of Genova until the stench became so unbearable that someone was forced to clear the carcasses. But dead rats outnumbered every other dead animal by at least ten to one.

What is it? Don Marco asked me.

Those rats, I said. They appear to be in good health.

It is true, good doctor, Don Marco said. In the initial weeks of this pestilence, we would find dead rats littered all over. However, in the past week I have seen robust rats scurrying about the premises. We have even caught the miserable vermin trying to feed off the remains of our brothers, he said with a shudder.

You no longer see rat carcasses? Only healthy rats?

He considered this for a moment. Yes. I suppose so. And it can only mean one thing, good doctor.

What is that?

For whatever reason, God has blessed these rats.

My chest pounded as if I were climbing the hill to the monastery again. It indeed meant something. However, I did not believe it had much to do with divine providence.

Twelve

Alana grips the armrest of Nico's SUV, as the vehicle races around another corner. The Ospedale San Martino appears ahead. The media vans are her first tip-off to the mayhem awaiting them.

Nico abandons the car on the opposite side of the street and rushes for the entrance. They elbow their way through reporters and camera crews crowding the main door. A security guard at the door checks Nico's ID, before letting them enter.

Inside, voices are unusually low, faces grim. Another checkpoint has been established in front of the emergency room with a changing area and a makeshift decontamination zone walled off by freestanding dividers and sheets of plastic. Alana and Nico have to step into full PPE outfits before the security guard will allow them inside. Slipping the hood over her head, Alana experiences an uneasy flash of déjà vu.

The dread inside the ER is tangible. Bedside monitors blare their alarms, while voices yell over the cacophony. Masked staff bustle everywhere. No one is still.

Nico rushes toward a room in the far corner. Alana begins to follow, but she pauses when she glimpses a commotion out of the corner of her eye. She turns to peer through the window beside her. Inside, someone is straddling a patient on a stretcher and performing vigorous chest compressions. With every thrust, dark blood sprays out around the man's breathing tube to form a red mist in front of his lips.

Disheartened, Alana turns away and heads into the room Nico entered. A patient lies on the bed, propped up by the head of the stretcher. An oxygen reservoir covers the lower half of his face, but he's not connected to a ventilator. Nico rests a gloved hand on the man's shoulder. At first glance, Alana assumes the patient is gasping for air, but then realizes he's actually laughing. So is Nico.

"How is any of this funny?" Alana says.

Nico looks over. "Claudio told me that his ex-wife still blames him for every cold or flu he ever brought home from work. He just asked me to send for her now."

Alana steps closer. "Does Claudio understand English?"

"Barely. If you speak slowly and use tiny words—"

"I speak better English than this clown!" Claudio rasps. "Better Italian, too. Also, French, German, Spanish, and Portuguese. Even Latin, if we are counting."

"Good to meet you, Claudio. I'm Alana Vaughn."

Claudio turns to his friend. "*Nico, questa è lei? La Alana?*"

Nico dismisses the question with a self-conscious wave, but Alana feels a tinge of excitement at the idea of him still referring to her as "the Alana."

"Dr. Claudio Dora here is my colleague," Nico says. "Well, not so much. He's only an emergency room doctor. He didn't do so well in medical school."

"Then why you did copy off me on all our exams?"

"Copy from you? Of all the stupid ideas—"

Claudio silences Nico with a sudden coughing spasm. He jerks both his hands to his face, covering the oxygen reservoir, pointlessly. When he pulls his hands away, the clear plastic is speckled with blood.

Nico squeezes his arm. "Are you all right, Claudio?"

"No." Claudio clears his throat noisily. "I feel worse than the last time I drove with you." He looks at Alana. "My life flashes before my eyes every time I get into his car."

"Seriously, Claudio!" Nico snaps. "No more joking. How do you feel?"

"I ache all over. The chills and shakes come and go. I feel very short of breath without oxygen. The cough is worse than anything I've ever felt. But I am relieved I can still talk . . . even if only to you."

Alana's throat tightens. "There's no doubt it's the pneumonic plague?"

"None. The pathologist studied my sputum under the microscope. She's certain it is *Yersinia*."

"From which patient?" Nico asks.

"Sonia Poletti."

"Not the construction worker?" Alana presses.

"I never came across her. But I was Sonia's physician in the *pronto soccorso*—the emergency room." Claudio's voice cracks. "I also worked with her for the past seven years. Every week, a new photo of her *bambina*. Florianna. She loved that little girl so. The father wasn't involved. Only Sonia."

"The poor kid," Alana says, though at the moment she's thinking more about the child's risk of acquiring the plague than about her future life as an orphan. "Claudio, were you masked when you attended Sonia?"

"Of course. We were aware of the risk the moment she came in to emergency. I was as protected then as you are now."

"Then how . . ."

Claudio's cheeks color. "The day before she came in as a patient . . . we finished our shifts at the same time. We left together. She coughed, maybe twice. She told me she was coming down with a chest cold. It was late. I was tired. It never even occurred to me . . ."

Nico pats his shoulder. "How could you know?"

"When did you feel your first symptom?" Alana asks.

"This morning. I woke up in a sweat," Claudio says. "As soon the cough came . . . I realized."

"So less than forty-eight hours from when you walked out with Sonia?" Alana asks, troubled by the numbers.

"More like thirty-six. It was an evening shift."

"Did you not take antibiotics yesterday?" Nico asks. "I thought they started everyone who was in contact with Sonia."

"You know how sensitive I am to antibiotics, Nico. Multiple allergies. Besides, I took full precautions yesterday in the emergency. I never thought I would be at risk."

"*Idiota*," Nico mutters, his sympathy gone. "You know better!"

"I'm taking them now. Besides, if this plague was going to kill me, it already would have." But Claudio's worried eyes belie his casual tone.

"What about your family?" Alana asks.

"I am divorced. No children. It's just me and the plague now." Claudio forces a laugh. "Frankly, it's no worse company than the ex-wife."

Someone steps into the room. It takes Alana a moment to recognize Byron Menke behind his hood and mask. "Dr. Oliva, Dr. Vaughn, can I have a word in private?"

Nico doesn't budge. "We can speak here. Claudio is a colleague."

"I realize." Byron nods to Claudio and then turns to Nico. "But this concerns only the task force members."

"Speak to Alana. I will catch up later. I am staying here with this fool."

Alana follows Byron out of the ER. They slip off their gear inside the decontamination zone. As they wash their hands for a third time, Alana asks, "Have you ever seen an outbreak of the plague comparable to this one?"

"Bigger," Byron says. "In Madagascar, three years ago. There were ten times as many patients—"

"That's not what I meant. I'm talking about casual spread from one person to the next with minimal contact. Patients dying despite antibiotics. All of them from overwhelming pneumonic plague."

"You're thinking it might be something else?"

"Possibly."

"Bioterrorism?"

"I don't know what this is, Byron. And neither do you."

"I suppose if all you have is a hammer, then all you see are nails."

"Bullshit! I'm saying we should consider everything. Including that this could be man-made. After all, the Soviets weaponized the plague in the seventies and eighties. So did the U.S. government. Maybe one of those strains of *Yersinia* got loose somehow?"

"How would that happen?"

"I'm not sure yet," she admits.

Byron eyes her skeptically. "We'll keep the possibility in mind. Meantime, I need to see the construction site where Vittoria Fornero worked."

"Then go see it."

"I would, but I also want to speak to Marcello Zanetti, and he hasn't returned my calls." He hesitates. "I hear Nico is friends with Zanetti."

"Okay. I'll ask Nico if he can put in a word."

He looks as if he has something else to say, but instead he just nods. "Thank you."

"Byron, the other patient in the ER just now. The one they were performing CPR on . . ."

"He died."

She nods, unsurprised. "Where did he work?"

"We're not sure yet. He was unconscious when he arrived."

"He's not medical?" She tenses.

"No. He was Sonia Poletti's neighbor."

The words are as jarring as a slap. "Oh, Christ, it's already spreading in the community."

Chapter

Thirteen

Today, on this fourth day of February, I, Rafael Pasqua, trudged through hell. What I saw there bore no resemblance to the paintings of inferno by the master artists that adorn the walls of the grand cathedral. No, as God is my witness, it was far worse.

I had not visited the market in the main square for ten days. I ventured there this morning in need of food and supplies. Even from a distance of a hundred paces, the air was thick with the stench of decay more foul than any slaughterhouse. There were men and women lying in the streets, some already dead while others lay suffocating on blood and unholy secretions. Not even the children were spared. Many of them died alone, abandoned by parents, through cowardice or death, and seemingly by God Himself. All the while, starving wild dogs struggled to drag corpses from open pits and mass graves that were too shallow.

Far worse than these spectacles was something which could not be seen at all. It came to me at first as a howling, as though baying wolves had gathered in the heart of Genova. But then I recognized the noise for what it was: voices, young and old, man, woman, and child, melded into a horrible cacophony. The cries came from a row of houses that lined the northern edge of the marketplace.

The market itself was immune to the horrors enveloping it. Merchants hawked their wares of meats, skins, wine, and spices as usual, while visitors haggled over the cost as if it were a day like any other.

I stopped a man whose highborn status was apparent from his fine purple tunic. He introduced himself as one of the town councilmen.

Good sir, I said. What is the source of this terrible commotion?

Have you not heard? The councilman gawked at me as though I must be simple. He flung his arm in the direction of the frailly constructed row houses. Those dwellings are all plague-infested!

What part of Genova is not? I asked.

Maybe so, but it has been found that the sickness is spreading from those houses to the rest of our community.

Found by whom?

Why, the Archbishop himself!

There was a sinking at the pit of my stomach. I did not ask the gentleman why or how the Archbishop had determined that a single row of houses could account for a pestilence that was known to spread anywhere and everywhere. Instead, I asked what could cause the people inside such agitation.

Is it not obvious? The doors and windows, man!

When I looked closer, I could see that wooden slabs covered every opening. The doors and windows had all been boarded shut, the fates of the houses' inhabitants sealed as tightly as the openings.

The council has confined them inside there to die? Whether or not they are even infected?

What choice do we have? the councilman said. This is the will of God.

Are you so foolish as to believe that mere wood and nails can somehow contain a pestilence that is immune to air, fire, or water?

I believe the word of God, sir.

You mean the Archbishop, do you not?

Here in Genova, he speaks for God.

With that pronouncement, the councilman marched off.

I hurried to purchase the few essential supplies I had come for. However, I did not return directly home. Instead, I followed the narrow path up to the palace of the Archbishop. Without escort or invitation, I rapped on the imposing doors. When there was no response, I banged harder.

The door creaked open. A soldier filled the threshold, his sword drawn. He stepped forward and swung it toward my head, close enough that I could feel the air across my cheek. I stumbled back.

What business have you here? the soldier shouted, twisting his blade back and forth at the level of my heart.

I need to address the Archbishop.

His Grace sees no man without an appointment! he barked in his rough street dialect. Who knows who carries the pestilence in their chest or on their shoes?

I carry no plague. I am Rafael Pasqua, the barber-surgeon. His Grace has summoned me before.

The large door slammed shut so hard it shook on its hinges. I stood there in the street like a fool, uncertain whether to stay or retreat. Moments later the door rumbled open again and the same soldier stepped out. He looked as unwelcoming as before, but his blade was now sheathed. Come! he barked.

I silently followed the soldier through the palace and into the Archbishop's chamber. The fire was again raging, making the room uncomfortably warm. The Archbishop was perched on his elevated seat, and he again read from parchments.

Why are you intruding upon my time of reflection? he asked.

His tone was quiet and yet I still felt as if he were yelling. Your Grace, I have come to see you about the houses.

Which houses?

The ones near the marketplace that have been boarded shut.

What of them?

I was led to believe, Your Grace, that you had instructed that the boards be erected.

That is a civic concern.

I was told by a councilman that you might have offered the council guidance on this particular matter.

Of course I did, he said without a note of contrition.

I opened my mouth to reply but he silenced me with an extended finger while the reflection of the flames danced off his bejeweled ring. My supplicants have informed me of how rapidly the death spreads in the vicinity of those houses, he said. So much so that there is no time or space to bury or consecrate the corpses.

But Your Grace, surely not everyone inside is afflicted.

These are cataclysmic times. Perhaps even End of Days. You of all people should know this.

Why board one building shut, Your Grace, when we know this sickness to be borne by man and animal alike? It spreads in the air and poisons our wells. No doubt it also seeps up from the ground and falls from the heavens with the rains.

To contain one significant source is to prevent the suffering of many. My personal physician, Doctor Volaro, believes this step to be prudent. Perhaps we should invite him to contribute to this discourse?

The Archbishop lifted a small bell and rang it. A servant rushed to his side. The Archbishop muttered instructions. Within minutes a stooped old man hobbled into the room, his neck crooked and one shoulder tilted higher than the other. I might have mistaken Doctor Volaro for a peasant were it not for his maroon cape, gilded with golden thread.

The Archbishop recounted our discussion to the aged physician.

Mister Pasqua, Volaro said. I do not pretend to know all the primitive ways of you barbers. But there is very little of the methods of the physician that I have not studied in my many years.

I am deeply honored to be in your presence, Doctor, I said with a small bow.

Surely even you, a common barber, must have noticed how quickly the pestilence spreads from one person to the next? Volaro asked, his voice rattling as only the elderly's will.

Indeed, sir, I see it every day.

Then you must understand how vital it is to prevent the contact between the sick and well.

I could not agree more, I said. However, Doctor Volaro, even if those houses were the origin of the city's plague, it has long ago spread beyond them. And the people trapped inside represent little more than a drop in a bucket.

Buckets are filled one drop at a time, Volaro said.

I could see I would need a more compelling argument if I were to find any hope of freeing the entrapped denizens. What about the mice, rats, and other vermin? I asked.

What about them? the Archbishop asked.

No boards will be tight enough to prevent them from entering or leaving those premises at their will, I said.

I did not need to explain to these learned men how the rotting corpses would soon become a food source which would infect the rodents and lead to further spread. I stood as still as I could while they silently considered my words.

Even before Volaro spoke, I could see from his countenance that the cause was lost. If they die on the street, the vermin will have even easier access to them, he declared.

This is indisputable, the Archbishop agreed. He stared at me for a long spell, and his eyes darkened with suspicion. Only you, Doctor Pasqua, appear to be immune to infection despite your constant contact with the sufferers.

I had the sudden premonition that I would now be required to argue for my own freedom. But Your Grace, I said, I am not the only one who has avoided this plague.

Who else has?

The rats of the San Giovanni Monastery.

Rats? What on earth do you speak of?

I told him of the rats and how Don Marco had attested to their new-found health. I suggested that the vermin might have developed some form of natural protection, which perhaps could be shared with human sufferers.

There are only two possible protections from this scourge, the Archbishop said. The first is the blessing of God. And the second is witchcraft. Are you suggesting that God has chosen to bless these vermin over all the inflicted men, women, and children?

I would never presume to know His will, Your Grace.

And, for that matter, why has God chosen to protect you above others? the Archbishop asked with menace.

Chapter

Fourteen

Alana steps out of the hospital to find even more reporters and cameras clustered at the entrance than when she arrived. Ravenous for updates, they shout questions at anyone in the vicinity. Alana can picture the explosive fallout that is bound to follow once the news breaks of this morning's victims. Undoubtedly the Italian logos on the sides of the media vans will soon be replaced by those of huge international outlets such as CNN and the BBC.

Shouldering her way between the reporters, she keeps her head down and ignores their questions. She keeps walking until, two blocks farther, she ducks into a narrow side street, where she finally finds a moment to call Monique Olin in Brussels.

"I dropped by your office earlier this morning," her boss says icily. "You must have been in a meeting."

"I couldn't leave, Monique," Alana says flatly.

"I was not aware that staying was an option."

"Things have gotten worse." Alana hurriedly summarizes the recent developments.

"All right," Olin finally says. "Stay. Be our official lead there. But, Alana, we cannot afford to upset the apple cart."

"In what sense?"

"The WHO. We need to work with them. Tread lightly. You, of all people, know how they can be."

"I do."

"That is history, Alana," Olin says. "Learn from it, yes, but do not dwell. It's not constructive."

Easy for you to say, you weren't there in West Africa. "I won't get in the way."

"And you won't antagonize them, either?"

"No. Promise. But, Monique, we need to find out exactly what we are dealing with here."

There's a slight pause, and Alana pictures her boss peering warily over her reading glasses. "What are you asking for, Alana?"

"We have to share our samples with the WHO's Level Five laboratory in Geneva."

Olin inhales sharply. "Are you suggesting we simply hand over samples of the plague bacteria that the Soviets weaponized?"

"Yes."

"We are talking about one of the world's most dangerous pathogens, are we not? On a level with smallpox and anthrax, or worse . . ."

"We don't have to share live samples. Just give the WHO a map of the bacteria's genome—its genetic fingerprint—for comparison. And not only the Soviet bioweapons. The American one, too."

"Is this wise, Alana?"

"Monique, what we are dealing with here is not like any other form of plague we've seen in the last fifty years or more."

"It does not mean it's a weapon, either."

"Maybe. But how can we know we're *not* dealing with bioterrorism until we compare its genetic fingerprints to those bioweapons? We have to, Monique. You know we do."

"All right. I will speak to the secretary general about releasing the samples. Of course, I need to consult the Americans, too."

Alana thanks Olin and promises her another update soon. Moments after she hangs up, a dark blue sedan pulls up beside her. Byron is at the wheel and Justine Williams is in the passenger seat. Alana climbs into the back.

"So, why NATO?" Justine asks, apropos of nothing, as the car pulls away from the curb.

"What about NATO?" Alana says.

"You used to be on our team, right? The WHO. You know. The winning team?"

"Not so sure the WHO is always the winning team."

"And you think NATO is?" Justine laughs. "Come on, you got to admit, it's a pretty weird transition from public health to this quasi-military stuff."

Alana isn't about to discuss the debacle of her final WHO mission in West Africa. "I come from a military family," she says instead. "I was in the army before I joined the WHO."

Justine aims an imaginary rifle at her. "As in combat army?"

"Yes, Afghanistan. I was training to be a trauma surgeon."

"So what got you booted out?"

Alana eyes Justine for a silent moment, deciding whether to rise to the bait. "I was injured," she finally says.

"Oh! Like an ambush? A roadside IED? Or friendly fire?"

"Ease up, Justine," Byron interjects.

She looks at him in feigned shock. "This, from you? The king of tact?"

"What about you, Justine? Why rodents?" Alana asks.

She shrugs. "They're generally more trustworthy than people."

"Bet you've used that line a few times before," Alana pushes back. "But it's not an answer."

"I grew up on a farm in Kansas. My parents are real hicks," Justine says with a note of affection. "Come to think of it, that's probably true of my biological family back in China, too. Who knows? Never met them." She shrugs. "I was always around animals. Fascinated by them. Way more so than humans. Zoology was the natural choice for me when I went away to college in the big city of Manhattan—the one in Kansas, not New York—and one of my profs got me into rodents. The rest is history."

"There's no one in the world better at chasing down zoological vectors and their spread," Byron says.

"Love all the smoke up my ass, boss," Justine says. "But all in all, I'd prefer a raise."

The laughter is contagious, and they make small talk for the rest of the ride.

Byron turns off onto the dirt road and parks his car between the construction vehicles in the same gravel lot as Nico did. Alana notices that the stench of diesel is even thicker today. New frameworks of wood and rebar have already popped up in the base of the gaping excavation pit since yesterday. Numerous workers scurry around the site, but Alana doesn't see any sign of the old monk whom Zanetti had described as a fixture on the site.

Zanetti greets them alone in front of the trailer-office. He wears another dark suit, and his silver-framed sunglasses match the color of his carefully swept-back hair. He shakes hands with Byron and Justine, and leans in to kiss Alana on both cheeks. "Such a pleasure to see this gorgeous face again so soon."

Alana suppresses the urge to roll her eyes. "Hello, Marcello."

"So now the World Health Organization is interested in my condominiums?" he asks.

"Mr. Zanetti, the WHO is interested in the woman we believe is the index case behind the spread of the plague," Byron says.

"Ah, Vittoria. Such a terrible loss." Zanetti sighs heavily. "I was told she acquired this . . . thing in Ethiopia."

"We haven't confirmed that," Byron says.

"You will, no doubt," Zanetti says.

Justine pipes up. "What about rats?"

"I do not understand your question, signora."

"Rodents." Justine makes a scurrying motion with two fingers. "Have there been reports of rats, mice, squirrels, et cetera, around here?"

"Not to my knowledge. No."

"What about carcasses or small skeletons? Have you seen any of those?"

"This was once an old monastery. There could have been rats underground, I suppose. There usually are."

"Not usually. Always."

"Mr. Zanetti," Byron says. "We understand that you saw Vittoria Fornero at a time when she might have been most contagious."

"I am taking the medicines the Public Health people provided to all of us here." Zanetti turns to Alana with palms extended. "Alana, we discussed this," he says, sounding like an exasperated father. "Did you not tell your friends?"

"The infection has spread from Vittoria to others, Marcello. Two more have already died. We want to make sure it doesn't spread here, too."

Zanetti motions to the nearby workers. "Do any of these men look as if they have the plague?"

Byron smiles. "Did Vittoria before she collapsed?"

Zanetti eyes Byron coolly, but says nothing.

Realizing they will need Zanetti's cooperation, Alana opts for a more conciliatory tone. "Marcello, I'm sure we're driving you crazy with the same questions. But can you tell us, has everyone reported in to work today?"

"I do not check every day. I will have to ask Paolo."

"Please." Alana wraps her fingers around Zanetti's elbow and squeezes. "Meantime, will you tour us around the site?"

Zanetti bows his head slightly. "*Prego*. A pleasure."

He calls out to some nearby workers. A few moments later, Paolo, the brawny contractor whom Alana had met the previous day, hurries toward them carrying three hard hats. Paolo and Zanetti exchange a few clipped words, before the developer turns to the others and says, "No one has called in sick. Everyone is accounted for."

"Thank you, Marcello," Alana says.

"Come." Zanetti extends a hand proudly toward the pit. "Come see *il futuro di Genova costruita sul suo passato!*"

"Which means?" Byron asks.

"Our marketing slogan. How would you say in English? 'The future of Genoa built on her past.'"

Zanetti leads them down a wooden staircase and into the excavation pit. They wander among the diggers and bulldozers, between the wooden frames where the cement has yet to harden. At one point, Justine wanders off. Zanetti doesn't seem to notice. He's an enthusiastic guide and treats them more like potential condo buyers than doctors tracking a plague outbreak, painting an optimistic picture of the luxurious residences that will soon tower overhead.

Minutes later, Justine rejoins them at the base of the staircase. She pulls a clear plastic container out of her bag and shows them the dark rice-shaped flecks inside. "Droppings," she announces.

"From?" Byron asks.

"Can't be positive. But from the size, I'm guessing *Rattus*. Our old buddy, the black rat."

Byron nods. "Where did you find them?"

Justine points to a mound of dirt and rubble about a hundred feet away.

"That would make a good rat's den," Byron says.

"Ideal. Very cozy."

Zanetti crosses his arms. "Show me a construction site that does not have a few rats."

"Perhaps, Mr. Zanetti," Byron says. "But we're going to have to scour that pile. This whole site, if need be. Until we find those rats."

"So go ahead and look."

"I mean with an entire team. A proper forensic search."

"And what do you expect us to do in the meantime?" Zanetti asks, his tone now as cold as his glare. "Stop construction?"

"As a matter of fact, yes. This is a public health emergency."

"And this"—Zanetti taps the ground with a foot—"is the biggest construction site in all of Genoa. Every delay costs a fortune."

"Your government has given us the authority to investigate wherever and however we deem necessary." Byron motions to the rat droppings. "This is as necessary as it comes."

"Tell that to my lawyer!" Zanetti pivots, and marches up the stairs.

They return to Byron's car in silence. As Alana opens the passenger door, she senses a presence behind her. She looks over her shoulder to see a young man in a hard hat. As he shifts from foot to foot, Alana recognizes him as the anxious-looking teenager whom she saw leaving the trailer yesterday. He's not sweating today, but he doesn't seem much calmer.

He glances around and then asks in barely above a whisper, "*Sei un dottore?*"

"I don't speak Italian."

"A doctor?"

"Yes. How can I help you?"

He looks nervously over either shoulder again and then slips her a damp piece of paper.

"What's this?" Alana asks as she unfolds the crumpled note, but the young man is already rushing away. She resists the urge to call out after him as she watches him disappear behind a cement truck.

She looks down at the note and sees the name "Emilio" with a phone number scrawled beside it.

Fifteen

How much did I drink? Marianna Barsotti wonders as she rolls over in bed. She only remembers a Chianti. It's possible there were a few bottles. Nothing too out of the ordinary for a Thursday night. But her head pounds so hard it feels as if someone is using her skull for a drum.

Marianna pats the spot beside her. It's still warm and indented from where he was lying, but he is nowhere to be seen. What was his name again? Alberto . . . Adamo . . . no, Adriano! He was funny, that one. And good-looking in a Sicilian way. But the cologne! She can still inhale the vanilla and spice. They always overdo it with the scents.

She bundles the blanket tighter around her. The chill in her apartment is unusual for April. Maybe she will have to turn on the heat today.

She wonders if her guest is in the kitchen or if he's already gone. It doesn't really matter. Marianna won't see him again. She never does. Since her divorce, she prefers it that way—brief intense encounters. The initial eye contact and slow mating dance that, if all goes well, reaches a frenzied conclusion in her bedroom. At thirty-five, Marianna has no problem attracting new men, but a couple of flings a month is plenty.

Adriano was good in bed. She came twice with him, almost effortlessly. Sometimes, it takes all her energy to climax even once with the awkward or selfish ones. She didn't mind that Adriano smoked, but his cough was off-putting. It almost prevented her from taking him home. But he assured her it was only a smoker's cough. Now she wonders. And with her trip to Paris less than a month away, she cannot afford to take any more sick time from work.

Marianna's head throbs as if the imaginary drummer dropped his sticks and started to just whack her scalp instead. *Oh, Mother of God, don't tell me Adriano gave me the goddamn flu!*

Sixteen

Alana can see that Nico hasn't slept. It's more than just his bloodshot eyes or the dark pouches beneath them. The shadow on his cheeks and, more strikingly, the unruly spikes of hair tell the story. The messiness is so unlike him. She wonders if he remembers texting her at 1:37 a.m. and then again at 2:04 a.m. The two rambling messages—both filled with misspelled words and Italian phrases—expressed his drunken fear that it might already be too late to contain the outbreak. But it was the last two lines in his second text that stuck in her mind and kept her up an extra hour or two. "I cannot resent this plague too much," he wrote. "After all, it brought you back into my life."

Alana gets angry again thinking about it. Nico is the one with the family. The adorable kids. The loving spouse. They both had made their choices. And, while she had never felt the urge when she was younger, now, in her late thirties, she wonders more and more what life might have been like had she settled down and had kids of her own. It's unfair of Nico to drunkenly toss around verbal grenades such as "back into my life." He has things she might never have.

She knows it's not the time or the place to confront him over the texts. The little café behind the hospital is teeming this morning. People chat in English around them. She assumes some, if not most, are with the international media, who seemed to have jumped en masse on the outbreak overnight.

They have to lean across the table and speak in low voices to avoid being overheard. "So this Emilio . . . he has not answered your calls?" Nico asks.

"Or my texts," Alana says.

The creases in his brow deepen. "It probably has nothing to do with the plague."

"Maybe," she says, but her gut tells her otherwise. "How is Claudio today?"

"No worse. Perhaps a little better. The plague certainly has not claimed his sense of humor . . . unfortunately." He squeezes his forehead between his thumb and forefinger. "Alana, did you hear about the latest death?"

"Yes." Byron woke her at five-thirty with a text detailing the fourth known victim. The young woman had apparently been one of Sonia Poletti's closest friends. "The infection is grabbing a foothold in the community."

"At least three more new cases overnight," he says. "One of them is admitted across town to a different hospital, Ospedale Centralino. And, Alana . . ." He pauses. "This patient only has buboes in his armpits and groin. It's not in his lungs."

"How does that happen, Nico?"

"*Mannaggia*, Alana!" he groans. "How does any of this happen?"

"You know what I mean! The only way to transmit the plague from person to person is through the lungs, not the skin."

"It's true."

"Maybe he picked it up from the same place Vittoria did?"

"The construction site?"

"Where else?"

Nico drains the last sip of his espresso. "Speaking of the site, Marcello came over last night."

"To see you?"

"I wasn't home, but Isabella says he was beside himself. He begged her to talk to me. To put a good word in for him with the WHO."

She grimaces. "Marcello really thinks your wife would try to intervene?"

"He is her favorite uncle."

Alana senses how conflicted Nico must feel. Perhaps a fight with his wife over her uncle's request had launched him on the previous night's bender. Empathy edges out her frustration with him. She rests a hand on his wrist. He looks surprised, but makes no move to pull away. "Why is Marcello so opposed to a search for a few rats?" she asks.

"He thinks the search could bankrupt him. The delays and so on."

"Or is it possible he's just worried what they will find?"

"Perhaps. Marcello says that if the press learns that the WHO is searching his site, it will ruin the development. Even if they find nothing, the new condos will still be worthless."

"He might be right. But his financial viability is the least of our problems."

He slips his arm free. "Just another victim of the plague, no?"

She looks at him. "Not sure it will help, Nico, but I can ask Byron to conduct the search as discreetly as possible."

"Discreetly? Byron? Have you met the man?"

She chuckles. "Good point."

"So what are the next steps?"

"I heard from my boss this morning. NATO is willing to share the genetic architecture of all known plague bioweapons with the WHO lab. The entire genomes."

"You don't really believe it will be the source, do you? Bioterrorism?"

"It's my job to consider the possibility."

His tired eyes show a glimmer of pity. "Sounds like a morbid job, Alana. Do you not miss the clinical work?"

"Sometimes," she admits.

He grins, and years dissolve from his face. "Remember Angola? During the cholera outbreak? We made a difference there, you and I."

How could I forget? she thinks. But she refuses to let herself reminisce. "During the Cold War, the Soviets developed the most elaborate bioweapons program ever seen."

"Using the plague?"

"There were other diseases, too, like anthrax and smallpox. But the Soviets recognized *Yersinia* for the ideal weapon it could be. Their scientists developed a highly contagious flea-borne form of the plague as well as an aerosolized version. We estimated that a single airborne release over a densely populated urban center would kill upward of a hundred thousand people."

"A hundred thousand?" He cringes.

"And that was a conservative estimate. They never did use it, of course, but it didn't stop them from mass-producing the stuff."

"But this all would have been decades ago, no?"

"Maybe so, but after the Soviet Union fell apart, the Russians lost track of some of their supply of bioweapons. Particularly in their labs in former satellite states such as Uzbekistan, Kazakhstan, and Ukraine."

"How could they let that happen? Like losing track of a nuclear bomb. Alana, if this outbreak is related to that . . ."

He doesn't need to finish the sentence. She has harbored the fear since the moment she first laid eyes on the dying Vittoria. "Did you ever hear how the plague reached Europe during the Middle Ages?"

"What do the Middle Ages have to do with biological warfare?"

"Caffa."

"What is Caffa?"

"A port in the Ukraine. On the Black Sea. Now known as Feodosiya. But in the fourteenth century, Caffa was the key trading port between

East and West. And you'll never guess which great merchant seafaring state colonized Caffa at the time."

"Genoa?"

She nods. "In 1347, the Mongols laid siege to the walls of Caffa. They probably would have made short work of it, too, if the plague hadn't swept in from Asia around the same time. The Mongols died off in droves. They assumed the Genoese inside the fort were somehow responsible. So— in maybe the first-ever documented example of biological warfare—the Mongols began to catapult rotting corpses of their own soldiers over the walls of Caffa. Soon the Genoese became sick, too. It caused mass panic, and many of them fled for home."

"Bringing the plague back to Europe with them?"

"Exactly. Via the so-called plague ships," she says. "To Sicily, to Venice, and eventually, of course, right here to Genoa."

They lapse into a despondent silence. Alana feels her phone vibrate. Relieved for the distraction, she reaches for it. Her pulse picks up as soon as she recognizes the cell number for Emilio's. The text reads: *Via Capodistria e Via Vincenzo Bellini. Un'ora.*

Alana turns the screen out to show Nico. "Emilio wants to meet!"

He nods. "In one hour. I know that neighborhood. Cornigliano. I will take you."

"Should we let Byron know?"

"Byron has more than enough on his hands."

Alana vacillates a moment. If they arrive with too many people, Emilio may not show or might be too spooked to talk. She replies to Emilio's text with one word: "*Sì.*"

Nico drives, but with less urgency than on their last frantic ride. Alana's phone rings, and when she sees Byron's name on the call display, she answers on speakerphone.

"Where are you?" Byron demands.

She glances at Nico, who shakes his head. "Tied up. NATO business."

"Nice to know NATO has more pressing priorities when all hell is breaking loose around here."

"What happened?"

"Multiple new patients. Worse, there are two cases on the other side of the city that are definitely the bubonic plague. Neither have any connection to Vittoria Fornero or Sonia Poletti. We can't even say for certain that Vittoria is Patient Zero anymore."

"For this to be spreading through the skin, not the lungs . . ."

"There has to be some kind of animal reservoir. It must be incubating among rats or other rodents before being transmitted by fleas."

"Unless we're talking bioterrorism."

"Of course. It always has to come back to that with you."

She takes a long breath. "Byron, Brussels is willing to release the DNA blueprints on the Cold War–era bioweapons."

After a slight pause, he says, "Okay, let's compare them. At this point, I'm willing to try anything."

"What about the vaccine?" Alana asks.

"We don't have any here yet. And unless you can convince your government—"

"I work for NATO, not the Americans."

"Well, unless someone can convince the U.S. military to release their supply—as in yesterday—the vaccine will do us no good. Besides, even if they had enough to share—and that's a *huge* if—we have no idea how effective it would be."

Nico nods in silent agreement.

"What about mass prophylaxis?" Alana suggests. "Starting everyone in the affected neighborhoods and hospitals on preventative antibiotics?"

"We've already begun," Byron says. "But you know what's bound to happen if we put everyone on antibiotics willy-nilly?"

"Resistance," she concedes.

"Exactly. We'll inadvertently breed out the most antibiotic-resistant strains of *Yersinia*. And then we'll have no treatment options left for the sickest patients."

"So it's a catch-22."

"A razor-thin balance, at least. If we cover everyone with antibiotics, we risk creating an even worse outbreak. But we have to cover the most vulnerable."

Alana locks eyes with Nico. He looks as despondent as she feels. "What about the airport and train stations?" she asks.

"We've started to screen all departing travelers, just like we did for Ebola," Byron says. "But there must be a thousand ways to get out of Genoa. Land, sea, or air. Besides, someone could hop on a plane while incubating the plague without ever knowing it."

"What's your next step?"

"Epidemiology 101. Contact-chasing. We keep tracking anyone who might have crossed paths with infected patients. At least that's one thing this media circus can help with." He pauses to mutters something indistinct to someone else, then says, "Oh, hopefully we'll secure our court order to search the construction site by this afternoon. It would be a help if your friend Nico could convince his uncle to just let us start now."

"I'll run it by him," Alana says.

Nico shakes his head vehemently.

"One last thing," Byron says. "The lab in Geneva confirmed that this strain of the bacteria is not the same subtype as the one currently active in Ethiopia. So Vittoria definitely didn't pick it up there. In fact, so far, this bug doesn't match any known isolate of *Yersinia*."

None of this fits! Alana wants to scream. "Byron, it's more important than ever to consider the possibility of a genetically engineered strain—" But the line goes dead before she can even finish the thought.

"I thought Canadians were famous for their politeness," Nico says.

"I think he's trying to single-handedly torpedo that reputation." She runs a hand through her hair. "No known matches, Nico."

His silent acknowledgment is troubling. She soon lapses into her own thoughts.

As they drive eastward, the city transforms in front of Alana's eyes. Genoa's high curved walls and grand buildings, with their bright colors and intricate embossments, give way to more working-class neighborhoods. One street begins to resemble the next, all of them lined by drab low-rise apartment blocks of indeterminate age with laundry drying from lines strung between windows.

Eventually Nico pulls the car over to the curb near an intersection. Alana checks her watch and realizes they're a few minutes early. She scans the narrow street. An elderly woman sweeps the sidewalk in front of a café. Four screaming boys chase a soccer ball down the street. Two young black women in headscarves push strollers past. But she sees no sign of anyone who could be Emilio.

"Over there," Nico says. Alana follows his gaze, but she has to squint to see the figure.

Someone is standing back in the shadow between two buildings, beckoning them with a hand held close to his chest. As they approach, he retreats from view.

They find Emilio wedged in the doorway of a building with his back against the entry. Dishes clatter somewhere behind him. The faint stench of garbage wafts over them. Emilio shuffles from foot to foot, his eyes constantly scouring the street. Alana wonders if he might be high.

Emilio motions at Nico with his chin but keeps his eyes on Alana. "Who is the man?" he asks in a thick Italian accent.

"Dr. Oliva. A doctor, like me. He is a specialist at Ospedale San Martino. Vittoria was one of his patients."

Nico speaks to Emilio in a rapid-fire exchange that leaves Alana in the dark. "Please," she finally interrupts. "English."

"Sorry," Nico says. "Emilio says there was something strange about the construction site. Like it was . . ." He turns to Emilio and says, "*Maledetto*," and the boy nods vigorously. "Cursed. Apparently the old monk—the one we saw being escorted away from the site—he warned Emilio. Something about tampering with sacred grounds."

"*Sì, sì!*" Emilio wipes his sweaty forehead. "Bad, very bad. As soon as he got sick! Brother Silvio speak true. *Terribili segreti.*"

"Terrible secrets," Nico translates.

"And then he disappear!" Emilio cries. "*Andato!*"

"*He?*" Alana says. "Vittoria didn't disappear, Emilio. *She* is dead."

"Vittoria?" Emilio grimaces. "No, no. No. Not Vittoria. Yas!"

Alana glances at Nico who shakes his head, as bewildered as she is. "Who is Yas?" she asks.

"My friend, Yas," Emilio says as if she should already know. "Yasin Ahmed. He works like me. At San Giovanni. Yas got sick before Vittoria!"

Chapter

Seventeen

Today is the seventh day of February. Three days have passed since my audience with the Archbishop, and his soldiers have yet to return for me. I expect them still. The Archbishop all but accused me of sorcery. In these turbulent times, there is hardly a more serious charge.

I returned to the market this morning in search of food and supplies. A quiet had fallen over it that was somehow more discomforting than the raucous hubbub of my previous visit. There were few vendors or shoppers and besides, little was available to purchase. The stalls were as barren as they had been after the last great drought.

On my way home, I passed the row houses that had been the target of such scrutiny. The doors and windows were still boarded shut. Not a single sound emanated from inside. But the terrible fetor seeping through the cracks told me all I needed to know about the fate of the residents.

I am relieved that my dear Camilla has been spared from having to witness all of this suffering. For her, the loss of decency and humanity would have been even more troubling than the ubiquitous death.

At times, in moments of weakness to be sure, I think I would welcome a quick end to this life for the chance to be reunited with Camilla, if only in the ground. However, I know it to be the coward's path. I am beholden to duty and obligation. My services are more sought-after than ever before.

Among the many people who came seeking my care today, the most unexpected was my old colleague Jacob ben Moses. His youngest daughter, Gabriella, brought him to my surgery. Jacob could not have made the trip on his own. He could barely stand. At first glance, I thought he had contracted the plague. However, I soon saw that both of his eyes were blackened. The right one was swollen shut. I noticed that he was cradling his left arm against his chest. I looked closer and saw the deformity at his elbow, where the forearm was bent at an unnatural angle. The bones were clearly out of the joint. With his daughter's assistance, I positioned him on a stool and supported his arm with mine. He did not utter so much as a moan as I applied force until a loud clunk indicated that the bones had slid back into place.

Jacob laughed in relief. He bent and extended his arm to prove to himself that he once again could. As often as I have seen my own patients suffer, he said, one can never appreciate another's pain until one has endured it himself.

Who did this to you? I asked.

What is done is done, he said. And you have reversed the damage. Thank you, Rafael.

I turned to his daughter and repeated the question. I had only met Gabriella once before, prior to her husband's death the previous winter. I knew her to be the youngest, by several years, of Jacob's three living offspring. His unexpected blessing, as he had once described her. She possessed a kind face that was striking in its contrast with hair as dark as nightfall but eyes as pale as the summer sky. There was sadness in those eyes, but also resolve.

Our neighbors beat my father, Gabriella said. The very same Christians who rush to see him in the middle of the night if their wives or children take ill, even though their own Church forbids them to.

Enough, daughter, Jacob said.

It is true, Father. They will borrow our money, bargain for our wares, and take whatever else they need from us. But as soon as ill fortune befalls them, they always blame us.

We are fortunate, daughter. Other kingdoms have forced Jews to live in ghettos. Or banished them altogether. The gentiles treat us well here in Genova.

Your face would suggest otherwise, I said.

They blame us when the crops fail or if their livestock are not thriving or if the weather is too hot or too cold, Gabriella said. The worst is when they return home drunk from the tavern with heavy gambling losses. That is somehow always the fault of the Jew.

Forgive my daughter's outspokenness, Jacob said.

Gabriella was too impassioned to desist. You Christians will forever hold the Jews responsible for the death of your Messiah. I wish only that you would acknowledge Gesù Cristo was one of us himself.

That is enough, daughter.

Fear clouded Gabriella's pale eyes. Doctor Pasqua, the neighbors, they were accusing Father of somehow being responsible for the spread of this pestilence, she said. One of them even suggested that he might have poisoned the well.

They are terrified, Jacob said. They are desperate for an explanation for something that is beyond explanation.

They look for a scapegoat, Father.

Maybe it is best if you depart Genova for a while? I suggested.

Jacob shook his head. They may accost us, yes. They may even strike us in frustration. However, I know these neighbors to be decent people. They will not do worse. And it shall pass. It always does.

I could see that Jacob had made up his mind, so I said nothing more.

However, as I record this now, I think again of those doomed residents who were effectively buried alive by order of the council at the mere suggestion of the pestilence spreading from within their homes. No, my learned colleague is wrong in his belief. Dangerously so. They will do worse. And this shall not pass.

Chapter

Eighteen

Alana braces herself as she steps into Byron's temporary office inside City Hall. It's as messy as she expected, with boxes piled haphazardly, paper strewn across his desk, and a jacket crumpled on the floor behind his chair.

"Let me understand this, Alana," Byron says pleasantly, as he leans back in his chair. "NATO is now running an investigation parallel to ours?"

"No. Emilio—the young construction worker I texted you about—contacted me. I had no idea what it was about until I met him."

His grin only widens. "Of course. Could have been about anything, right? Traffic congestion in Genoa, global warming, the isolating effect of social media on millennials . . ."

She feels her cheeks heating. "He wanted to meet urgently."

"And you decided you didn't need to include me?"

"I'm qualified to handle it. And, besides, I don't work for the WHO anymore. My capacity in this investigation is now official. And separate from yours."

"Alana, I have been up-front with you from the outset. I've included you—when I didn't have to—in every development. I haven't hidden a thing."

Byron's unrelenting smile tells Alana just how pissed off he is. She squirms inside. It reminds her how her dad, who was an amazingly soft-spoken man for an army surgeon, used to react when he was most disappointed in her. Once, after she had caved in the side of his car on an unlicensed joyride, he didn't say a word to her for a week, offering her only grim smiles instead. It was worse than the grounding and all her mother's yelling.

"You're right." She clears her throat. "I should've called you, Byron. I'm sorry."

He acknowledges her apology with a half shrug. "Our lab in Geneva received the genomic data NATO sent us on those plague bioweapons," he says as he sits up straighter. "We'll hear if there's a match within forty-eight hours or less."

"Good." But two days strikes her as far too long.

"All right, say we assume for a reckless moment that terrorists have gotten into the bioweapons business. How would they possibly get their hands on the plague?"

"Central Asia would be their best bet," Alana says. "We've been keeping our eye on the region for years because it was once home to the major Soviet biological warfare program."

"That would've been thirty years ago or more."

"Maybe, but when the Soviet Union collapsed, the Russians were negligent in cleaning up the mess. There's this place in the Aral Sea called Vozrozhdeniya Island. It straddles the border of Uzbekistan and Kazakhstan. You should see it."

"Have you?"

"Yes. Last year. We were invited by the Kazakh government, but they had to sneak us in, since the Uzbeks didn't want us there. The island was the nerve center of the old Soviet bioweaponry program for developing anthrax and the plague. The Russians abandoned it in the early nineties with minimal containment effort. There's still equipment and discarded canisters—I even saw one marked with a biohazard symbol—scattered around the site. They buried some of the most sensitive material less than six feet underground. And what concrete they did pour is less than six inches thick."

"Guess they figured it wasn't going to be their problem anymore."

"The worst part? It's not even an island anymore."

"Did the Russians take the water with them?"

"The Soviets originally chose Vozrozhdeniya Island because it was so close to land. Around the same time, they started damming the rivers that fed the Aral Sea, which is really just a big lake. Predictably, water levels dropped. Eventually a natural land bridge formed to the island."

"You can't dream this stuff up."

"Maybe the Russians assumed the water would act as a permanent natural barrier. Who knows? But ten years after they left, poof." She snaps her fingers. "The lake dries up. And lab animals are free to roam right off the island. Rumor has it that strange illnesses began to pop up soon after. I spoke to one local doctor who swears that it caused an outbreak of an unusual respiratory infection that's resistant to any and all treatment."

"Are there any Islamic extremists active near this . . . this non-island?"

"Not officially. At least, not according to the Uzbek and Kazakh governments."

"But?"

"We know there are factions active in the region. My local sources confirmed it. In fact, that's why I was sent there in the first place. To assess the risk of any bioweapons being found and stolen."

"This Yasin Ahmed who's gone missing. I assume you've already checked into his background?"

"Brussels doesn't have anything on him. Neither does Interpol. In fact, as far as we can tell he's not known to any national security service."

"Does he happen to be from Central Asia?"

"No, he was born here in Genoa. His parents are Tunisian immigrants. He's nineteen years old. No criminal record. No known suspicious activity."

"Religious?"

"Emilio told us Yasin is an observant Sunni Muslim."

"And he's just . . . what . . . vanished?"

"He hasn't shown up to work in over six days," Alana says. "According to Emilio, he hasn't answered any texts or calls since then."

"Have you gone to the police?"

"No, not yet."

"It's time we did, don't you think?"

"Might not be necessary," Alana says, determined to dissuade him. The dictum in NATO is that involving local law enforcement always introduces uncontrollable variables. If and when a manhunt for Yasin were required, she would far prefer to let the intelligence agencies run it. "I have the address for Yasin's family home. We should talk to them first."

"Let's go." Byron rises from his chair. "We're going to need to a security escort, though. I'll speak to the mayor."

"Let me take care of that, Byron. I can go through Brussels. Faster and more secure."

He eyes her doubtfully but says nothing.

"We don't know that Yasin is even connected to the outbreak, let alone that he's a terrorist. Besides, if we go in there with a fleet of police, lights and sirens, we're only going to spook everyone. And it will be splashed all over the news." He still doesn't comment, so she adds, "Let me handle this, Byron. It's what I do now."

He hesitates a moment. "All right."

"I'll call Nico. He should come, too."

Byron shakes his head. "Nico might be your friend, but he's not a part of this investigation."

"He knows this city. He understands the people. And the only reason we're here at all is because Nico sounded the alarm."

Byron stares back, unswayed.

"We owe it to him," she says. "Besides, how's your Tunisian? Because I'm pretty sure you don't speak Italian, and Yasin's family probably doesn't speak English."

Alana contacts Monique Olin, who says she'll secure their escort through the Agenzia Informazioni e Sicurezza Interna, better known as AISI, the Italian equivalent of the FBI.

Two hours later, an intelligence officer arrives at Byron's office. He introduces himself as Sergio Fassino, the head of tactical operations for AISI, and explains that he has flown in directly from Rome. His rank alone confirms just how seriously the Italian government is taking the threat of possible bioterrorism.

With his good looks and impassive manner, Sergio reminds Alana of the lead actor from a detective series whose name she can't place. His English is impeccable, but he's a stickler for detail. She has to negotiate with Sergio for over thirty minutes before they finally compromise on the size and role of the AISI detail: six plainclothes operatives in total, but only two will accompany them inside the building while the other four will secure the perimeter.

Alana and Byron head out in Byron's rental sedan, while the AISI team follows at a safe distance in a pair of unmarked SUVs. At Nico's request, Byron picks him up a half a mile away from the hospital.

"It's a disaster" are Nico's first words as he climbs into the backseat.

Byron glances over his shoulder. "Have there been new cases in the past two hours?"

"At least three others, two of them critically ill. The hospital is under siege by the media. And the emergency room is overrun with the worried and the neurotic. To them, every cold and sniffle must mean the plague."

"Always happens," Byron says. "Next, some of the staff will get too scared to report to work."

"Yes, it's already happening. The hospital has had to close two wards because of staffing shortages."

"Wait until people hear that the spread might be deliberate," Alana says. "Then you'll see real panic."

They fall into somber silence. Alana suspects that Byron and Nico must harbor the same dark fear that she does: while the body count might still be relatively low for this epidemic, it's rapidly approaching the level of critical mass—the dreaded point in any new outbreak when there are enough cases to simultaneously propagate the spread in multiple places. If that were to happen, the death toll would skyrocket. It could reach into the tens of thousands or more.

The car's GPS leads them deeper and deeper into Cornigliano, the same working-class neighborhood where they met Emilio. Once the GPS announces that they have arrived, Byron rolls the car to a stop with two wheels perched on the sidewalk. One of the two black SUVs pulls up behind them, while the other drives past, carrying the four agents who will guard the perimeter.

As Alana walks between Byron and Nico, she feels on edge. Sergio and his younger partner, both in dark suits and ties, seamlessly fall in line a few yards behind them. As silent as they are, she's aware of their presence as acutely as footsteps behind her in a dark alley.

Halfway down the block, they reach the nondescript apartment building with the address that matches the one Brussels forwarded to her. The lobby door is ajar. Alana inhales the scent of cooked meat and spices. Two men in traditional North African tunics walk past, one of whom glances warily at Alana, and she wonders if it's because her head is not covered.

Sergio opens the door to the stairwell. Alana starts to follow when she feels Nico's hand on her elbow. She turns to him. His encouraging nod doesn't conceal the concern in his eyes. She flashes him a reassuring smile. There's something so painfully intimate in the brief interaction that she has to break off eye contact.

As they step out of the stairwell onto the third floor, Alana hears a man and woman shouting angrily from behind one of the nearby doors. She notices Sergio and his partner unbutton their jackets to allow easier access to their holstered weapons.

They continue down the hallway and stop at the second-to-last apartment. Sergio and the other agent stand in front of the door, while the rest of them line up behind. Sergio raps firmly. Tense moments pass before the door finally opens a crack. Alana can see the junior AISI agent instinctively slip a hand inside his jacket. Her shoulder aches in anticipation.

Sergio speaks through the gap. A timid voice responds on the other side. The other agent relaxes his hand. After a lengthy Italian exchange, the door opens wider.

A thin black woman with a white veil wrapped around her head and neck stands at the threshold. She rocks on her feet and keeps her chin down. She speaks in a soft but urgent staccato.

"What is she saying?" Byron demands.

Sergio holds up a hand to interrupt the woman.

"This is Yasin's mother, Thewhida Ahmed," Sergio says, which surprises Alana because the woman looks no older than she is. "A widow. She admits that Yasin lives here but she swears she hasn't seen or heard from him in almost a week. She says she's extremely worried about him."

"Yasin didn't tell her where he was going?" Byron asks.

Sergio shakes his head.

Nico elbows his way between the two agents and speaks to Thewhida. After a few moments, he turns to Alana. "She says the last time she saw her son—six days ago—he was complaining of a fever. He left for work and never came home."

"Was he coughing?" Byron asks.

Nico shakes his head.

"What about rashes or buboes?" Alana asks.

Before Nico can ask, Sergio speaks up in Italian. The woman raises her hands and stumbles back as if he pulled a gun on her.

"What did he say to her?" Byron asks.

"He asked whether her son associates with radicals or Islamists," Nico explains.

Sergio's tone turns soothing, but it only seems to agitate Thewhida more. She speaks even faster.

Nico translates for Alana and Byron in snippets. "Yasin is a good boy . . . Religious, yes . . . Not political . . . Doesn't associate with radicals . . . She forbids it."

Sergio asks something else. Thewhida begins to answer, but her voice cracks and her words dissolve into incoherent sobs. Nico reaches out to console her, but she recoils from his touch and covers her face. She mutters something in a whisper.

"The Al Halique Mosque," Nico translates.

Sergio looks over his shoulder at the others. "I know the Al Halique Mosque."

"How?" Alana asks.

"Last year I interrogated the imam after three teenagers from the mosque were caught trying to get to Syria." He pauses. "To join ISIS."

Nineteen

Today is the eighth day of February. It is also the day I have been stricken with the plague.

In truth, the first chill came over me yesterday while Jacob ben Moses and his daughter were still present. When it passed without another soon following, I tricked myself into believing that the cool evening combined with my light dress were to blame. The chills returned once I retired to bed. Not even the extra blanket provided me warmth. As soon as the fevers and violent shakes, known to us practitioners as rigors, possessed me, I was certain it was plague.

I awoke this morning in nightclothes so drenched it was as though I had slept in a pond. Every inch of me ached as if I had been clubbed by the same mob that had beaten Jacob. The worst of all was the pain in my right groin. I recognized it for a bubo by the outline of the firm swelling alone.

In spite of the discomfort, the sweats, and a fatigue like none I had ever known, my initial response was not one of fear. On the contrary, I felt relief. My toil would come to an end and my loneliness would soon be dispatched. I would be reunited with Camilla. The thought brought me peace. And I allowed myself an indulgence I had not in years. I continued to lie in bed as daylight saturated my room.

After several minutes, the ache in my bones lessened or, perhaps, I was just dulled to it. However, it was the sense of obligation, not survival, that eventually forced me up from bed.

Even through the haze of fevers and sweats, I recognize I was being given an extraordinary opportunity to document the suffering of the plague firsthand through the senses of a learned practitioner. The same duty to posterity that compelled me to begin my diary weighs even heavier upon me now. However, strong as my conviction remains, determination alone might not be enough for me to see this endeavor through. A pronounced quiver has crept into my script. This pestilence saps my strength further by the minute. God alone knows how many entries I have left in me to compose.

After rising from bed, I forced myself to drink a few sips of water and swallow a few pieces of bread. I had to rest after such minimal effort. The bulge in my groin was even more incapacitating than the fatigue. Each step was agony. When I donned my trousers, the pressure of the wool against the swollen bubo was too much to bear.

I had only one option for addressing the bubo, to lance it myself, but I broke out in a sweat at the prospect. The logistics of the procedure also presented a unique challenge. In the end, I had to tie a mirror to the post above the bed in order that I could lie down and still observe my hands during surgery.

My fingers were trembling as I dug the sharpened blade into the center of the bubo. So intense was the pain that I had to bite down on a leather strap to endure the procedure without crying out. Thick yellowish discharge burst forth like a miniature fountain. The stench was more awful than even the sight of it. But the relief was deeply gratifying. It was as if a heavy boot had been lifted off my thigh.

As I lay there, pressing a rag to my groin to stop the bleeding, my thoughts turned again to the rats of the San Giovanni Monastery. Could it be true? Could those godless vermin really have become immune to this plague?

My old mentor, Antonio Calvi, had taught me well that no tool in medicine is more powerful than observation. God created man, Antonio would say, but He left it up to us to heal each other, without revealing the secrets of His creation. We do most of our mending in the dark, stumbling for our way like the blind. If one happens across a treatment that helps one patient, it will likely help others.

Unlike Don Marco, I refused to believe that God would choose to spare rats from this pestilence above all other creatures. There had to be an earthly secret to their salvation. Something that must dwell within the humors of the rodent. Perhaps that protection could be shared, I reasoned. I felt compelled to find out.

I waited several hours while I forced more water and even a little wine into my objecting stomach, as I hoped to rally a modicum of strength. But it was to no avail. I realized that I would only grow weaker. There would be no better time to visit San Giovanni.

The journey on foot up the hill to the monastery was the most taxing of my life. Every ten paces or less, my legs and lungs demanded rest. At some point, I collapsed on the path just as a farmer's family approached from the opposite direction. The father steered his cart off the path to avoid me while the mother wrapped her children's faces in cloaks as they passed. Eventually I summoned the energy to rise and finish the trip. I collapsed again in the wet dirt outside the gates of the monastery. Don Marco himself found me there.

Even though he must have seen in a glance that I was afflicted, Don Marco sat down at my side and revived me with sips of warm cider from his wineskin. Unconcerned about my contagiousness, he lifted me to my feet and supported me with his body. Leaning heavily on him, I shuffled inside the monastery and slumped into the first chair I reached.

Though it was still daytime, the room was warmed by a roaring fire.

And for the first time, I witnessed black-cloaked brothers performing functions other than tending the sick or dying themselves.

Don Marco appeared as hale as ever. His mood was, if possible, even more ebullient than before.

Our humble home has been blessed! he said. We have not lost a brother in almost two days. And no one else has fallen ill in almost twice that time. It appears that the accursed infliction has tired of our monastery and moved elsewhere.

That is remarkable, I said.

And you, good doctor! Your visits have been almost as restorative as our Savior's intervention. But clearly you are afflicted now, too.

Yes, as of this morning.

Then the least we can do is tend to you as you have for us.

No, Don Marco, I am not staying.

Then why have you journeyed this far, as ill as you are?

The rats.

Of course! he cried. Those blessed creatures.

Do they still appear as robust as on my last visit?

We see more of them than ever. Not one of them is stricken. They truly have been the harbingers of our salvation.

I did not want to offend him with my skepticism. And in truth, I had no energy to argue. With your blessing, Don Marco, I would like to bring some of these rats home with me.

You mean to bask in their restorative powers?

I mean to examine them.

Examine them, Doctor Pasqua? How will you accomplish this?

Through dissection, of course.

Don Marco recoiled as though I had blasphemed. You mean to kill these holy creatures?

I would have to, yes.

But, Doctor, they have been chosen by God. To sacrifice these anointed animals as though they were some pagan offering is not right.

No, not sacrifice! Somehow their humors protect them from this pestilence. If I can unravel the magic of that feat, not only will I be able to cure myself, but I might be able to help many others.

But to kill those which God has spared?

I do not require all of them. Only a handful. These are rats. No animal alive replicates as rapidly. No one will notice their absence. Not even God Himself.

Don Marco weighed the request for several moments. Finally, he smiled and said, I would never relinquish them to anyone else. But we brothers could not be more indebted to you, good doctor. And I would do anything in my power to see you well.

Thank you, I said. Could I impose upon you for one further favor?

Anything, my son.

I do not believe I have strength left to capture the creatures. Will some of the brothers help trap them for me?

That will not be necessary.

How so?

We are housing them in special cages. We have even selected a brother to tend to them.

You found a brother willing to play the role of rat keeper? I asked in disbelief.

Agreeable to be the keeper of God's rats? It was all I could do to choose between the many brothers who vied for the honor.

Twenty

After a few fitful hours of sleep, the buzz of her phone against the nightstand wakes Alana. The top of the screen reads 5:23 a.m., and the text from Byron below contains only three words: "Sixteen more cases." It's enough to launch Alana out of bed, as if doused by ice water. The spread is far worse than feared. No epidemiological simulation or model would have ever predicted the number of plague cases to have more than doubled in a single day. Not naturally, anyway.

She brushes her teeth, ducks in and out of the shower barely long enough to lather and rinse, and then throws on the same outfit she wore two days earlier. She had come to Genoa with only clothes enough for three days. She hadn't expected to stay. Then again, she never expected any of this.

Outside, a taxi is idling near the entry. Alana climbs inside and the young driver greets her with an over-the-shoulder grin. But his expression turns from welcoming to wary when she informs him that she's heading to the Ospedale San Martino. Only after she manages to convey that she is a *dottore*, not a potential patient, does he agree to drive her there at all.

As soon as the cab pulls away, Alana phones Sergio Fassino. She spent much of the previous day with the intelligence officer after the search for the missing Yasin Ahmed intensified. By day's end, they still hadn't found him, but AISI agents had rounded up the imam at the Al Halique Mosque along with two other men from the mosque who were on the Italian equivalent of a no-fly list.

Despite the early hour, Sergio answers on the second ring, sounding as if he has been up for hours. Alana has little doubt that his blazer is buttoned and his tie already knotted. "The imam and the two others from the mosque claim they know nothing of Yasin Ahmed's whereabouts or any of his recent activity," Sergio offers, before she can even inquire. "The imam was the only one to admit being even familiar with Yasin."

"Do you believe them?"

"Not necessarily," Sergio says. "We searched their homes overnight. We discovered militant propaganda on one of the computers. But we have not found anything to connect any of them to Yasin or this outbreak. Still, we will keep an eye on them."

"No other leads on Yasin's whereabouts?"

"We're interviewing more friends and family, but nothing so far," Sergio says. "His cell phone has not been active in over a week. The last traceable signal came from the construction site where he was last seen."

"His mother and Emilio both say Yasin was already sick that day," Alana thinks aloud. "Yet he still worked at the site?"

"Apparently."

"Why would you do a day of hard labor if you were trying to spread an infection as a weapon of mass destruction?"

"To expose as many people as possible?" Sergio suggests.

"All right, then why not go somewhere crowded? A concert? A soccer game? Or just board an airplane?"

"Perhaps he didn't want to draw attention."

"Isn't that the whole point of terrorism?" It was one of the inconsistencies that had been gnawing at her overnight. "If Yasin is our Patient Zero—our bacterial 'suicide bomber,' as it were—he couldn't have done any of this without support. A lot of it. And if other terrorists are involved, why has no group stepped forward to claim credit?"

"Maybe they are waiting for the damage to increase? Until the body count is high enough to draw even more attention."

"I suppose," she says, but something doesn't sit right.

Alana hangs up just as the driver pulls up to a curb. He points to the front window and indicates the hospital, which is at least two blocks away. She accepts the premature stop with a simple "*Grazie*" and pays in cash.

Alana can't blame the driver for his reticence. Fear of the unknown is instinctual for humans and, probably, healthy in this instance. She has been following the incessant coverage on TV and online when she can. Dread of the plague has already crawled into public consciousness. Cafés are less crowed. The usually tactile locals are less willing to kiss, hug, or even shake hands. And, in the most telltale sign of all, a number of people wear surgical masks in public—a common sight on the streets of Shanghai but extremely unusual in Italy. Once word of the new surge in cases leaks out, she imagines it will be difficult to find a cabbie who will be willing to venture within a couple miles of the hospital.

The usual media mob gathers out front of the hospital, their nervous energy manifesting itself in their loud chatter and the faint stench of cigarette smoke and body odor. Alana squeezes her way through the throng without responding to their questions.

Security has been heightened. At the entrance, the guard scrutinizes the photo on her ID badge and then runs the card through a scanner. Two young cops with rifles slung over their shoulders and glares fixed to their faces oversee the checkpoint. One of them keeps a hand on the barrel of his weapon as he vigilantly monitors his surroundings. Alana suspects that the local authorities must have already been alerted to the potential of a terrorist threat.

Inside the hospital, the process is equally rigorous. Alana slips into her gown, gloves, and hood in the makeshift change room in the lobby while a plump nurse stands, with arms folded, and watches every step of the process to ensure that there are no breaches in protocol.

As Alana trudges down the corridor toward the ICU, her PPE suit feels more constrictive than ever. Inside the unit, it's the quiet that disturbs her most. Staff move about purposefully, but no one is talking. It reminds her of Liberia at the height of the Ebola crisis. The hopeless silence in those hospitals was almost tangible, as well.

Byron meets her at the nursing station, holding a sample bag in his gloved hand. Alana gestures to the rooms. "How many of these are plague victims?"

"Six." He nods to the right. "They've separated the unit, as best they could, for infection control. All the patients on this side have the plague, and all the rooms have negative pressure ventilation." She knows that means that air is being sucked into the potentially contaminated room and blown safely out of the hospital through filtered pipes.

Alana glances through the window into the room beside her. A woman lies motionless on the bed with a ventilator tube fed through her lips. Her face is ashen, and her exposed legs are mottled in a lacy deep purple indicative of severe shock. Two tubes that are each the size of a garden hose and engorged with blood run from her groin to an elaborate machine at the head of the bed. Alana recognizes the device for an ECMO—extracorporeal mechanical oxygenation—apparatus, meaning that the patient's heart is failing so badly the doctors have had to place her on a heart-lung bypass circuit. Even still, the blood pressure on the monitor above her reads so low it's barely compatible with life.

"Six of sixteen new cases have already ended up in the ICU?" Alana asks.

"Five others have already died overnight," Byron says.

"Five more? Already?"

"Probably even more since I last checked an hour ago," he says. "It's chaos in the ER. Not just here. The other hospitals in the city, too. So many real cases, but we're also being flooded with mimics in terms of colds and flus."

"We have to assume it's the plague until we know otherwise."

"We're advising doctors to treat all patients with any fever as potential plague, regardless of how unlikely."

"How is the supply of antibiotics holding up?"

"So far, we have enough. What we don't have enough of is time. This strain kills people faster than anything I've ever seen. Faster than the antibiotics can work, in some cases."

"Even faster than necrotizing fasciitis?" she asks, referring to the feared flesh-eating bacterial infection. "I once saw a woman lose her whole arm within twelve hours of getting a paper cut on her finger."

"Even faster."

"Can we connect the dots in the new cases back to Vittoria?"

"No. We've done extensive contact-tracing. The two cases yesterday from the east side of the city have no connection to Vittoria or any of her collateral spread."

She breathes out heavily enough that her face mask fogs momentarily. "So Vittoria isn't our Patient Zero, then."

"Probably not, no." Byron eyes her intently. "Can we say the same of Yasin Ahmed?"

"How can we know? He's disappeared."

"We have to release his name and photo to the media."

"It's too early, Byron. Even Sergio agrees. And he's the lead Italian agent on this."

"What's the point of waiting?"

"One, we still don't know if Yasin is involved. And two, if he's the source, publicizing his name might only spook him and make him and his network that much harder to trace."

"We don't have to announce he's a terrorist. Only that he might be infected."

"People will put it together. Imagine the fallout."

"I don't give a flying fuck about fallout!" The sudden outburst is a departure from his usual more composed defiance. "More people are going to die. Plenty more. You know this as well as I do, Alana. If anyone out there can help us find Yasin . . ."

She sees his point. It's also a rare glimpse into the passion that lurks behind his cool, at times arrogant, exterior. "Okay. Give me a few hours to discuss it with Brussels and Rome. Please, Byron."

"All right," he says, making a visible effort to calm himself. "I see your point."

"Thank you."

His shoulders slump. "I have worse news, Alana."

She braces herself. "Which is?"

He points to the patient on ECMO behind the glass. "Marianna Barsotti."

"Who is she?"

"She's not just any other plague victim." He reaches into the bag and extracts a disc-shaped container. It's an agar and petri plate, which labs use to grow bacterial samples to test for antibiotic resistance. The plate is gray with bacterial growth. There are small white dots demarking where the antibiotic samples were placed around the outside, resembling numerals on a clock face. Alana knows that on a normal culture plate there would be dark halos surrounding the antibiotics where the bacteria had been killed off. But on this plate there are no such "kill zones."

Alana feels the dread crawling up her spine. "Is that her *Yersinia* culture plate?"

Byron nods. "Ms. Barsotti might be the first-ever case of multi-antibiotic-resistant plague."

"Jesus."

"Not even sure He could help us."

"But it does make some sense, Byron."

"How so?"

"If we are dealing with a genetically engineered bioweapon, it would have been programmed to accumulate resistance."

"Regardless of where it comes, if the antibiotic-resistant strain of the plague continues to spread beyond the walls of this hospital . . ."

He doesn't need to finish the thought. Alana knows all too well that, if that were to happen, containment might be impossible.

Twenty-One

Today is the ninth day of February. It will also likely be my last one on this earth.

In whatever time I have left, I will attempt to record my final struggles in the clutches of this pestilence. However, I do fear that my penmanship has grown so tremulous that these last pages might not be legible to anyone who were to chance upon them.

The fevers pounce upon me like nothing I have ever imagined. First comes the deep chill, a cold that is colder than snow. My teeth clatter and my bones shake similarly to the convulsions we see when the regulars from the tavern go too long without ale or wine, except, unlike them, I am awake throughout my fits. I yearn for warmth that is not attainable even through layers of blankets. Invariably, the fever follows. It is so intense that I can only compare it to the hottest of kilns. My elixirs and my salves offer no relief, and no wet compresses or exposed skin suppress the fire that rages to my very core.

What demonic force must this pestilence possess, to take a man from the coldest of cold to the hottest of hot in a matter of moments? It defies any science I understand.

New buboes have also developed in my armpits. They make it impossible for me to extend my arms above the level of my waist. There is no possibility that I can drain them myself, were I to possess the strength or resolve to do so.

A day has passed since the brothers of the San Giovanni Monastery collected six live rats for me in a satchel and then carried me home on the back of a mule. Upon returning to my room, once I had mustered strength enough, I grabbed the biggest of the rats. I suffered his scratches and bites, for I needed his heart to be still beating as I turned him toward me and slit his throat. The warm foul blood spurted into my mouth in pulses. I drank it like the lowest of savages might. It took every modicum of the strength I had left in me to keep the contents of my stomach down. However, hard as I tried, I could not swallow down his raw flesh. After two bites, I vomited repeatedly, uncertain after a time whether it was his blood or mine that was spewing forth.

I washed my mouth with wine and waited several minutes before I repeated the barbaric procedure with a second rat. This time I consumed only the blood. With great effort, I warded off the vomiting.

Several minutes passed before I had strength to sit down at the table and dissect the second rat. My study confirmed what Don Marco had told me to be true. The creature's organs, from his heart to his intestines, had been spared from the ravages of the plague. But the secrets of his imperviousness remained invisible to me. I could only hope, now that I had consumed his blood, those protective humors would invisibly transfer to me.

However, I awoke this morning to the realization that it was not to be. I was more afflicted than ever and barely strong enough to get out of bed. In the name of experimentation, I killed a third rat and drank its blood. Aside from that and two or three sips of water, nothing has passed my lips since.

Death hovers near. The fever and chills take turns assailing me, with no reprieve in between. My body aches to the bone, whether I boil or freeze. My breathing has become ragged. Before, I only struggled for breath when I moved, but now even lying still winds me.

My last wish and prayer is for this diary to survive and provide some utility to those who follow, be there any, in understanding how this miasma toppled our great city and, perhaps, all of civilization.

Most Sacred Heart of Jesus, I accept from Your hands whatever kind of death it may please You to send me this day with all its pains, penalties, and sorrows, in reparation for all of my sins, for the souls in Purgatory, for all those who will die today and for Your greater glory. Amen.

Your humble servant, Rafael Pasqua

Chapter

Twenty-Two

The moment Alana steps into Claudio Dora's hospital room, she notices the improvement in Nico's friend. A pair of nasal prongs under his nostrils has replaced the bulky oxygen mask that he wore the last time she saw him. His hair is combed back and he wears a navy silk robe over his gown. But his cheeks are still gaunt, and his eyes sunken. And he has to struggle just to sit up at the side of the bed to greet her.

"So now we have antibiotic-resistant plague on our hands?" Claudio says.

"Nico told you, huh?" Alana stands at his bedside in the full PPE gear. "This plague kills fast enough as is. But if it's resistant to antibiotics . . ."

"*Mio dio!* Perhaps it's an ideal time for a career change. For us both, Alana."

"In a way, resistance was inevitable," she says, battling the urge to tell him about the possible human genetic manipulation of the bug. "With all the different bacteria in the hospital trading their DNA among themselves."

"Ah, yes, hospitals. The world's breeding grounds for antibiotic resistance. Grouping all those sick patients together. It's not so different from filling a children's pool with piranhas." He shifts in his bed. "But to happen *so* quickly?"

"This strain of plague does everything quickly."

"Reminds me of another strain." Claudio reaches for the bedside stand and lifts up a book. The cover is filled with a medieval depiction of a hooded grim reaper, scythe held menacingly overhead. In blood-red dripping letters the title reads: *La Grande Mortalità d'Italia*.

Alana takes a stab at translation. "*The Great Death of Italy?*"

"Close, yes. It tells how the Black Death leveled Italy, including Genoa. For some twisted reason, your friend Nico thought it would make for light reading during my recuperation."

Alana laughs. "Most thoughtful of him."

"Actually, it's fascinating. Terrifying, too. The descriptions of the spread . . . how quickly the plague jumped from town to town and country to country. In a time with so little travel." He lowers the book.

"What about you, Claudio? You are getting better?"

"Almost fully recovered," he says, but his pallor belies the remark. "The antibiotics have worked on me, thank God. I would have been released home already if they did not still consider me to be a modern-day Typhoid Mary."

"You've been lucky."

"This kind of luck I can do without."

"Nine people have already died. Six more are on life support and may not make it."

"And that was before the antibiotic resistance emerged."

"You don't have to remind me."

"Alana, if this reaches critical mass. A tipping point . . ." He raises the book again. "Like what happened during the Middle Ages."

"That was a primitive time. Long before modern medicine."

"Maybe so, but . . . one-third to a half of all of Europe was wiped out in only three years. The worst natural disaster in all of recorded history. It took five hundred years just to repopulate the Continent back to the same level as before the plague. Can you imagine?"

"We won't let that happen," she says, though she realizes how hollow the words sound.

Claudio nods noncommittally. "Nico says there have been other cases across Genoa that have no possible connection to our original case here."

"It's true. Vittoria wasn't the index case."

"Then who?"

"We don't know for sure."

"You have someone in mind, though?"

She innately trusts Claudio. Moreover, she knows Yasin Ahmed's name will soon become public, but until then the information is still classified. She backs a step away from the bed. "I should let you rest."

"Ah, sometimes I forget that you are a regular Jane Bond."

"Not quite."

"Tell me, how does an infectious disease specialist end up running NATO?"

"Running? Hardly. I'm just a peon." She snorts. "I ended up working at NATO by chance. Like most of my other life decisions."

Claudio stares at her expectantly. Behind his levity, there's an intensity that Alana finds compelling. "I was on my way to becoming a trauma surgeon with the army, like my mom and dad, but my shoulder was torn apart in Afghanistan. My surgical career was over before it even started. Not to mention my tennis game." She's surprised to find herself opening up to him in a way that she rarely does, even to close friends.

"Tennis, my favorite. You play?"

"I did. Varsity-level at college. Loved it. It was my favorite release. But I can't serve a ball now without dislocating my shoulder."

"A shame. We could've played. My game is only so-so, but I'm a world-class cheater." His grin dissipates. "So once you couldn't operate anymore . . ."

"Didn't know what I was going to do with myself. One day, I ran into my favorite prof from med school. A microbiologist. Dr. Crawford. He was ancient and eccentric as hell, but he always made the field of infectious diseases feel so vital. He used to portray it as a microscopic battleground as important as any war. Dr. Crawford convinced me to give it a whirl. After finishing my residency, I ended up at the WHO because, in my mind, it embodied the battle." She laughs self-consciously. "Or maybe the truth is that I just love to travel. My whole life, I've never really settled in one place. Even as a kid, I was always on the move with my parents from base to base and country to country."

"So why NATO?"

"My last mission with the WHO in Liberia, it . . . disillusioned me. And I'm nothing if not pigheaded—just ask my dad. I quit on principle. Or maybe impulse? On my way out of Geneva, at the airport, I had another chance encounter, with an old family friend who works for NATO. He encouraged me to speak to his colleague Monique Olin, who happens to be the assistant secretary general. My medical and military background fit what Monique was looking for. One thing led to another, and here I am . . ." She runs a hand over her gown. "In this fumigator getup."

"It suits you. You look like a sexy beekeeper. Now I understand why you have Nico so flustered."

"He's married, Claudio."

"Technically, yes."

Alana squints in suspicion. "What does that mean?"

"He never told you about Isabella?"

"Very little. What about her?"

"There was another man." Claudio shrugs. "Nico and Isabella were already separated when he found out she was pregnant with Simona. He thought it would be a good idea if he stayed and gave it another try. I didn't think so. I still don't. Things are not good between them."

Alana says nothing. She can't even discern her own response to the news. She wonders why Nico wouldn't have told her any of this. While she's still digesting it, her phone vibrates in her pocket under her gown. The rapid triple buzz identifies Byron as the sender.

She bids a quick goodbye to Claudio and heads out. As soon as she strips out of her protective gear and clears the final security hurdle, she calls Byron and arranges to meet him across the street from the hospital.

Outside, Alana weaves through the hive of media at the main door. She crosses the intersection to where Byron and Justine wait on the sidewalk.

As Alana approaches, Justine shakes a finger at her. "Your friend went and did it!"

"Which friend?"

"That developer. Zanetti!"

"He's not my friend."

"You two seemed pretty cozy."

Alana crosses her arms. "What the hell are you talking about, Justine? What has he done?"

"He cleared the construction site. Every last trace."

"What? You couldn't find any rats?"

"Find any? It's like rats never existed in Genoa. Our first visit there, I found two piles of droppings within five minutes. This time I couldn't find so much as a single hair after hours combing the site."

Byron shakes his head. "Zanetti stalled us with a court injunction long enough for his team to sanitize the site."

"Why would he do that?" Alana wonders aloud.

"Because he's corrupt as sin!" Justine cries.

"Even so," Alana says. "If Yasin Ahmed really was spreading the plague at the construction site and other places across the city, why would Zanetti need to cover it up?"

"He obviously ordered the cleanup before he heard about the other cases," Byron says.

"Besides, crime scenes aren't usually helpful for condo sales," Justine says. "Try selling your house after someone's been iced in the bedroom."

Alana ignores the morbid joke. "So you don't expect to find any live rats at the site?"

"I'm more likely to find a brontosaurus stomping around," Justine says. "They did a very thorough job."

"Can you prove Zanetti did it?" Alana asks.

"How do you prove something that no longer exists? Someone covered up the evidence. No question."

Alana remembers her first visit to the construction site. "There was this monk from the old monastery. I saw him there my first day. Zanetti told us he loitered at the site. Emilio mentioned him, too. What was his name? Brother . . ." She snaps her fingers. "Brother Silvio. Yes, that's it . . . Silvio."

"How can he help us?" Justine asks.

"Not sure," Alana admits. "I assume he lived there a long time. He might know things about the site. Also, it sounds as though he was chatty with Emilio. Maybe he talked to Yasin, as well?"

Justine rolls her eyes. "Oh, this sounds like a sure bet."

"Do you have a better idea?" Alana asks.

Before Justine can respond, Alana feels her phone vibrate again. This time the slow staccato tells her that it's from her boss. She pulls out her phone and looks at the screen. The message from Olin only contains a single hyperlink and no other text. Alana clicks on it and her screen fills with an online article. The headline screams: "Plague outbreak linked to terrorism!" On the next line down, the subhead reads: "Authorities searching for fugitive Yasin Ahmed."

Alana turns the screen around and holds it out to the other two. "What the fuck, Byron?"

Twenty-Three

Mamma tells Rosa that Papà has gone to live with the angels. Rosa doesn't understand what she means. Why would Papà live with the angels when they moved into such a nice house with Nonna? And besides, Papà promised to take her to the park on Saturday. The big swings. Papà always keeps his word.

"Everything is going to be fine, precious one," Mamma says as she sits behind Rosa and weaves her hair into braids.

But if that is true, Rosa wonders, why is Mamma crying so hard? "Papà won't stay with the angels too long, Mamma," Rosa says. "He will miss us too much."

The laughter only makes Mamma sob louder. Rosa doesn't know how else to comfort her. And she feels guilty for lying. She told her mother that she had drunk all the yucky medicine that the doctor promised would keep her safe after what happened to Papà. But Rosa couldn't swallow it. It tasted worse than that oily fish her auntie cooks. So Rosa only pretended to swallow the medicine and went and spat it out in a tissue after each spoonful.

Rosa feels chilled. For a moment she wonders if Nonna or Papà opened a window. But Nonna is not home and Papà is with the angels. "Mamma, you won't go live with the angels, will you?" she asks.

Her mother kisses the top of her head and wraps her arm tightly around Rosa's chest. "No, no, darling. I will never leave you."

Rosa squeezes the back of her mother's hand. "Promise, Mamma?"

"I promise, precious!" Mamma grabs Rosa's hand and clutches it in hers. "I will never let you go."

Rosa doesn't understand why the room is getting so cold. She snuggles in closer to Mamma, but it doesn't really help. "Mamma, can I have ribbons on my braids?" Rosa asks.

"Of course, darling. What color?"

Rosa hesitates. "I like pink and blue."

Mamma laughs through her tears again. "Why not both, then?"

"Why not, Mamma?" Rosa echoes as her legs and arms begin to tremble from the cold.

Twenty-Four

Nico hasn't said more than three words since he got behind the wheel. Alana can't remember seeing him this angry. She tried to talk him out of confronting Zanetti, but recognizing how futile it was, she insisted on accompanying him instead.

They are heading south of the city along the Ligurian coastline. The two-lane highway is congested with late afternoon traffic. Nico drives aggressively, quick on his horn and veering out often into the opposite lane to look for any opportunity to overtake the cars ahead.

Alana finally breaks the silence. "I saw Claudio this afternoon. He's doing better."

Nico only nods.

"He also told me some things." She clears her throat. "About you and Isabella."

Nico glances over at her. "Like?"

"He said you two went through a . . . rough patch around the time Simona was born."

"A rough patch?" Nico snorts. "I suppose you could call it that."

"How would you describe it?"

"Isabella thought I had become distant. And that I was working too much." He shrugs. "Who knows? Maybe she was right."

"These things usually take two."

"Then again, I thought she was fucking one too many men."

Alana's gaze drops to her lap. "I'm sorry, Nico."

"Her boss. At the bank. Can you believe it? Such a cliché." He scoffs. "And I was the one who had 'the wandering eye.' Isabella, she would get so jealous." Alana doesn't say anything, so he continues. "Never once, Alana. Not with Isabella or you or anyone else have I ever crossed that line."

"I believe you, Nico."

"We had troubles. What marriage doesn't? But to climb into bed with Roberto? What kind of answer is that?"

"Was that what she was looking for? An answer?"

"She tells me she was lonely. Feeling neglected." He exhales heavily. "I work too much. I know. And yes, I probably drink too much wine, too. But we all need to unwind somehow, no?"

Alana doubts Nico believes the rationalization any more than she does, but it's not the moment to argue.

"Sometimes, when I look at little Simona, *mia bambina preziosa*," he shakes his head, "I wonder if she's even mine."

"Of course she is! Regardless of the circumstances."

"What Isabella has done . . . I am not sure I can get over this."

"You say that now, but your feelings might change over time."

Nico's only answer is to veer left and accelerate into the oncoming lane to overtake the car ahead of him. A motorcycle flies toward them directly ahead. Alana grips the armrest. "Nico . . ."

He swerves back into the right lane, missing the motorcycle by what seems like only yards. The biker rides his horns and flips his arm furiously as they pass.

"Nico! Is it worth getting someone killed?"

"This is how we drive here."

"How *you* drive!"

His shoulders bob up and down.

"Besides," she says. "Even if you don't kill me on the road, Byron probably will."

"For what?"

"Going to see Marcello without him."

"Marcello is not Byron's uncle."

"Maybe so. But after the Emilio incident, I promised to cooperate fully with him."

Ignoring the comment, Nico motions ahead out the window to the striking cluster of colorful villas that are perched along the coastal waterfront at the foot of rolling hills. "They call this area Golfo Paradiso. These beautiful old seaside towns. Suburbs of Genoa." He barely slows as he turns off at an exit. "Marcello lives here, in Bogliasco."

The road quickly tapers into a narrow stone street. They follow it for a few blocks farther before Nico turns into the driveway of a red stucco villa. Though it has a lovely view of the ocean, the house is no bigger than the neighboring villas and far more modest than what Alana had expected from the developer.

Just as Nico parks the car, Alana's phone vibrates. She glances at the display and, recognizing Sergio's number, answers the call on speakerphone.

"Where are you?" the AISI agent demands.

"Just outside the city. Why?"

"We need you here."

Alana glances at Nico, who holds up a finger and mouths the words, *One hour.*

"We can be back in town in an hour or so," Alana says.

"No longer," Sergio says. "We're assembling the team now. We'll be ready in an hour. And, Alana, no one else. Only you."

"The team?" She peers at the phone. "What's going on, Sergio?"

"Ibrahim Hussein."

"Who is he?"

"One of the men we interviewed from the Al Halique Mosque."

"What about him?"

"We kept all three men from the mosque under surveillance after releasing them. The imam and the second man, they returned home. Not Ibrahim Hussein. He made his way to an apartment in the Cornigliano neighborhood."

"What's so suspicious about that?"

"Hussein didn't go there directly, Alana. He took three buses and a taxi."

"As if trying to lose a tail?"

"And he almost did," Sergio says. "This apartment, it's less than a mile from where Yasin's family lives."

"Is he still there?"

"As of now, yes."

"What else do you know about him, Sergio?"

"The windows are shuttered but we were able to lower a listening device from the rooftop. There are at least two others inside with Hussein."

Her pulse pounds in her temples. "What have you heard so far?"

"Hussein told the other two that the authorities were onto them," Sergio says ominously. "He keeps telling them that they need to act now or go into hiding."

Chapter

Twenty-Five

Marcello Zanetti adjusts the tight knot on his navy tie as he steps onto the driveway to greet his nephew-in-law and the woman from NATO who was meddling at his site.

Zanetti hugs Nico, who is uncharacteristically stiff in his arms, and then kisses Alana on both cheeks. He steps back to appraise her again for a moment. She's undeniably attractive, with long auburn hair, angular cheeks, and full lips. Her dark green eyes are striking, a color that reminds him of the ocean churning in a storm. But she's too slender for him. And, besides, he doesn't trust her; especially not now, when she seems as on edge as Nico is.

Zanetti buries his suspicions behind a welcoming smile. "Nico, what would my niece think?" He winks conspiratorially. "You alone with this vision? Out on a romantic seaside drive."

Nico ignores the comment. "Is Anna home?"

Zanetti isn't about to let them know that his wife has left him. Instead, he says, "She is never home. This board and that board." He laughs.

"Apparently Genoa would have no art, opera, or culture of any kind without my wife's constant presence."

Nico heads through the open doorway without invitation. Zanetti follows him in, as does Alana. They step down into the sunken den that, Zanetti proudly knows, reveals the villa's hidden grandeur to first-time guests. The bright open floor plan is all-white and is furnished with sofas and chairs of the finest Italian leather. Marble countertops complement the kitchen's sleek cabinetry and appliances. And a retractable glass wall leads to the wraparound mahogany deck that is perched over the sea. The wall is open now, and the warm breeze drifts through the room.

Zanetti motions to the leather couch facing the water. Alana sits beside Nico. Still standing, Zanetti motions to the décor. "So, Alana, you like?"

"It's quite spectacular," she says.

"We renovated last year. It was all Anna. Every single detail down to the lining of the drawers." Zanetti smiles again as he wonders if his wife is even still in the city. Could she be ill? He hasn't heard from her in days. "What would you like to drink? Grappa? Wine? I have a Barolo from just north of here that is quite tasty."

"Not for me, thanks," Alana says. "We're in a bit of hurry, Marcello."

"Nico?" Zanetti asks.

He shakes his head.

"Nico, since when do you say no to a glass of Barolo—"

"This is not a social call."

Unfazed, Zanetti sits down in the chair across from them. "They seldom are with you, these days."

Nico eyes him with a sternness he hardly recognizes in his nephew-in-law. "What have you done, Marcello?"

"Done?" The hair on Zanetti's neck bristles. "With what?"

"The construction site."

"Not as much as I would like. This wild goose chase—searching the site and questioning my employees—has already cost me two days in delays. That is a fortune in my business." Zanetti breathes slowly, swallowing his annoyance. "And for what?"

"You destroyed evidence, didn't you?" Nico snaps.

Zanetti squints, as if genuinely confused by the accusation. "What are you saying, Nico?"

"The rats! You got rid of every last trace of them."

"*Chi vi ha detto*—"

"English, Marcello, please!"

"Who told you this? The Chinese lady?"

"Justine is a world expert," Alana says. "She claims the site has been tampered with to eliminate all trace of rodents."

"Why would I do that?"

"To cover up the source of the plague," Nico says.

Zanetti hops to his feet. "It was that worker Yasin Ahmed! It's all over the news. He brought the plague to my site. Gave it to poor Vittoria. They say it's terrorism!"

"Maybe, maybe not." Nico rises to his feet, too. "Either way, someone cleared the site."

"Not me!"

Nico raises his finger. "First you tell us no one else was sick at the site besides Vittoria, when clearly this missing worker already was—"

"I didn't know about Yasin until later!"

"And then you refuse to cooperate with the WHO's search of the site," Nico continues. "By the time they get a court order—presto!—the rats are gone."

Zanetti glares at Nico while his mind races as he considers his options.

Alana rests a hand on Nico's arm and then turns to Zanetti. "Marcello, is it possible someone else could have done this without you knowing?"

Zanetti weighs his words carefully before speaking. "I do not believe my team would act without my permission."

"Someone did, Marcello," Nico says. "And I doubt it was without your permission."

"*E tu devi sempre saperne più degli altri* . . ." Zanetti mutters.

"I wish I always knew better, Marcello," Nico says icily. "Especially when it came to you and your family."

"Nico, we better go," Alana says. "Sergio's waiting."

Nico and Alana turn for the door without another word. Zanetti stands motionless as he watches them leave.

What exactly do you know? he thinks with growing alarm.

Twenty-Six

Today is the seventeenth day of February. And I, Rafael Pasqua, have lived eight days longer than I expected to.

It is also the first day I have vigor enough to contribute again to my diary. My grip on the quill is still weak, and each word is an effort to construct. However, I feel compelled to document my experience while it is still fresh in mind. I have no memory of the first three of those eight days, as I was unconscious with delirium. To account for them, I will have to rely on the recollections of others.

A week ago, after my previous diary entry, I crawled into my bed, closed my eyes, and waited for Death to claim me. The last recollection I have from that day is the ethereal sound of Camilla's voice raised in song. I cannot articulate the intensity of my elation upon mistaking this slumberous fantasy for my earthly departure, or the extent of my disappointment to awaken later to a face that was not my wife's.

In my feverish haze, it took me some time to recognize the woman hovering over me as Jacob's daughter Gabriella. She was dabbing at my brow with a damp cloth. And the rivulets of water that dripped onto my lips tasted better than the best of ales.

I am alive? I asked her in disbelief.

I believe so, she said with a kind smile. She ladled a small spoonful of water into my mouth. I gulped it thirstily.

How is this possible? I asked. Despite the welcome liquid, my voice was still no more than a croak.

Gabriella explained the she and her father had come to my home the same day I had lost consciousness, bearing the gift of meat to express their gratitude for my efforts in repairing his arm. They found my door ajar. I lay stuporous in my bed, burning up with fever and muttering unintelligibly.

It sounded as though you believed you were conversing with your wife, Gabriella said.

I attempted to lift my head off the mattress but lacked the strength. You have attended me for these last three days?

Not only I. She explained how her father and her older sister had taken turns in nursing me.

But the risk to you all, I protested.

Gabriella eyed me as though I were still delirious. The pestilence is everywhere, Doctor Pasqua. So is the risk.

Maybe so, I argued. But for you to be in such close proximity to my festering wounds, it surely places you in danger.

My father has observed that the people who care for the afflicted with the chest plague are at far higher risk of falling ill than those who attend ones with only buboes. And you have not coughed once in my presence.

I realized she was correct. I did only have the skin affliction, not the chest plague. Surely it was the only reason that I had been spared.

Gabriella fed me two more welcome spoonfuls of water. She looked down at her hands. Doctor Pasqua, may I ask you something?

Yes, of course.

When we first arrived at your home, we found several rats, she said.

Some were still alive and others were in various stages of dissection. Were they a part of some form of remedy?

Yes, a failed one, I said. I described the rats of the San Giovanni Monastery and how I had hoped to transfer their protective humors to myself.

But why do you assume this remedy to have been a failure when you are still alive?

I would surely have died if the two of you had not intervened.

I am not so convinced. Yes, we have tried to diminish your fevers and feed you sips of water and soup. But we have offered similar treatment to many of Father's patients. Very few of them have survived.

I had observed the same in my practice. Is it possible that the blood of those impervious rats might offer some form of protection to the stricken?

Our brief conversation exhausted me, and resist as I tried, I soon lapsed back into slumber.

I have seen much of Gabriella over the past five days. She tells me that since her husband's death she has no one to care for but her father, whereas her sister and brother have families of their own.

Gabriella is unlike any woman I have encountered. Behind the shy and kind demeanor, there is intelligence and a resoluteness of principle that would well suit a priest or lawyer. But science is her passion. She has confessed to me that, with her father's blessing, she has studied his medical texts. Her knowledge of medicine is more extensive than that which some of my colleagues might possess. I have no doubt that, were she a man, she would be a fellow doctor.

She also possesses the ability to loosen my tongue like no one other than Camilla. We even share memories of our lost spouses. I have come to admire her Isaac for his stoic devotion to her, and Gabriella seems to enjoy my recollections of Camilla. She laughs heartily at the stories of Camilla chastising me for the sin of pride of which I was so often guilty. Gabriella tells me that she is convinced that she would have been friends with Camilla in life.

I do not remember ever spending an idler few days than these last ones.

And yet, I have enjoyed the time spent in the company of this family, despite their foreign religion and my illness. I have also regained my appetite. However, my recuperation has not been without setback. Three days ago, Jacob had to lance the growing buboes in both of my armpits. I endured the procedure with the aid of the leather strap to bite upon, but I worried I was going to break a tooth against it. After the second lancing, the wound under right arm began to spurt blood in the arc of a fountain, the way only a severed vessel will. I grew faint from the loss of blood. Jacob had to compress the wound so tightly with a cloth that I could see his hand turn blue from constriction.

After the bleeding finally abated, Jacob was deeply apologetic and appeared ashamed. I am not the doctor I once was, Rafael, he said. These old eyes and knobby fingers do not cooperate as well as I wish and need them to.

You and your daughter have saved my life, I said. How many doctors can claim the same in this dark age, my old friend?

My reassurance and gratitude fell on deaf ears. It was then that I realized something else was troubling Jacob. What is it? I asked.

This affliction shows no sign of reprieve. I have heard that for every three residents of Genova, one has already perished. They bury the dead by the cartload or, as often as not, dump the bodies straight into the Ligurian Sea.

Did you expect any different?

The sadness and grief are to be expected. The fear and the helplessness, as well. What I did not anticipate was the rage. I see it in the faces of the men in the street. They need someone to blame for all the loss and suffering. My daughter was right, Rafael. Their God and their church will not be scapegoat enough.

You are worried they might turn on the Jews?

I am not worried they will. I know they will.

Twenty-Seven

The black SUV is waiting for Alana out front of the hotel with its engine running. The back door opens and a man in a black commando-style uniform, whom she doesn't recognize, beckons her inside. The two men in the front seats are dressed the same. The car takes off as soon as the door closes.

"No news on Hussein? Or Yasin?" Alana demands.

The agent beside her only shakes his head, leaving her uncertain whether he even understands English. No one else speaks and, aside from the hum of the engine, a palpable silence engulfs the car.

Minutes later, the vehicle turns off into the entrance of a garage in the heart of the Cornigliano neighborhood. The driver steers down a ramp, and circles two floors lower until they reach a level filled with vehicles and commandos. They pull up beside another SUV. As soon as Alana spots Sergio, clad in the same black uniform as the others, she hops out and hurries over to join him.

The garage smells vaguely of urine and cigarettes. Fifteen or more uniformed AISI agents gather beside four unmarked black vans with dark tinted windows. Standing beside Sergio, Alana makes eye contact with the only other woman in the group, an agent with her hair tied back behind her cap and an assault rifle slung over her shoulder. The woman offers Alana a stone-faced nod before turning away.

"Hussein and the others have been in there for hours," Sergio says. "They could move anytime. You understand?"

Alana nods.

"Once the grounds are secured, we will need you to tell us what we might be dealing with. How to handle any material that could be contagious."

"Yes, of course." She has begun to knead her shoulder without even thinking about it.

He shepherds her over to the side of an open van. Inside, it is piled with equipment. He reaches for a self-contained breathing apparatus that she recognizes by the hood and tank. Another agent steps out from behind the van already fully garbed in the same outfit, down to his gloves and booties.

Sergio points to the equipment. "Will these protect my agents if there are active germs inside?"

"They should. So long as they decontaminate properly afterward. I'll show them."

Sergio steps into his outfit as if sliding on a wet suit.

"Where's mine?" Alana asks.

Sergio nods to the van. "You don't need to put it on yet. Not until we have secured the grounds."

Alana steps up to the van and grabs one of the suits. "I'm coming with you."

He shakes his head adamantly. "We cannot risk lives. Yours or ours."

"I'm ex-military, Sergio."

"No!"

"What if something is released during the raid? You can't afford to wait. You need someone on scene who understands bioweaponry. In real time. Not afterward, when it's already too late."

Sergio hesitates. Finally, he says, "You will stay behind us."

"Of course."

They suit up in silence. Sergio reaches inside the van for something else. He holds a gun out to Alana, handle toward her. She takes the weapon from him and weighs it in her hand. It's lighter than she expected.

"Beretta," he says. "Nine-millimeter. You are familiar with it?"

Alana nods. She hasn't been to a firing range since her discharge from the army, but she had always been proficient with handguns, scoring high marks throughout marksmanship training.

Only four others in the garage are wearing breathing apparatuses, but all of the agents are armed. Most of them, including Sergio, carry automatic weapons. They gather in front of the vehicles, where one agent, a balding man with a thick neck and baritone voice, leads them through a short briefing in Italian that Sergio doesn't translate. After he finishes, Sergio directs Alana and the rest of the respirator-clad team into the back of one of the vans.

The vehicles head out of the garage in a convoy. No one speaks. The taut atmosphere reminds Alana of her experience in an Afghani field hospital, moments before casualties were expected. Her pulse pounds in her ears, just as it used to back then.

Sergio adjusts his earpiece and slips his hood on. Alana does the same as the van hops the curb and slams to a stop in front of a nondescript apartment block. Sergio mutters a few clipped words to his team as the doors slide open and they spill out of the vehicle. Alana rushes along with the others and through the propped-open door into the building. They climb one flight of stairs and step out onto a landing. Sergio brings a finger to his lips and points down the narrow corridor.

They stop in front of the second-to-last apartment. Sergio glances over to her and raises his rifle. Alana nods once and slips off her gun's safety. Her hands are still and her breathing steady, but the jitters intensify.

Sergio jabs toward the door with two extended fingers. An agent steps forward and raises a compact battering ram in both his hands. Two other men flank him, their automatic weapons leveled at the door. Alana doesn't breathe as Sergio counts to three with his fingers. The agent thrusts the ram into the door, and it explodes off its hinges with a metallic shriek.

Heart in her throat, Alana storms into the apartment with the others. There is shouting and the sound of glass shattering. Feet stomp. Chaos. Two bearded men kneel on the floor with their hands clamped to top of their heads. Between them, a dining table is piled high with coils, pipes, and wires.

Suddenly the bedroom door bursts open. Alana sees the flash of a muzzle even before the sounds of the gunshots erupt in her ears. A bullet whizzes past her head. The agent in front of her cries out and drops to the floor. Alana swings her gun toward the source of the gunfire. Before she can squeeze the trigger, the shooter topples backward, still firing shots into the ceiling. More gunshots. One of the two suspects kneeling by the table falls over as if tipped, while the other screams in protest and waves his hands above his head.

The next minute passes in what seems like an hour. Dropping her gun, Alana sinks to her knees and applies pressure to the right side of the fallen agent's chest. She can feel blood and air leaking out between her fingers, as his chest moves weakly up and down.

Sergio hovers over her shoulder, speaking urgently to the injured agent, who doesn't answer. "Is he alive?" he asks Alana.

"Yeah, but his right lung is collapsed," she says. "His chest is filled with blood and air. It needs to be drained. *Now!* Where are the paramedics?"

Sergio barks into his headset and then says to Alana, "Coming!"

The fallen agent breathes choppily, his chest hissing with each aspiration. Alana holds her hand as tightly as she can against his chest, trying to form a seal. He looks up at her with the glassy eyes of someone in hemorrhagic shock.

She's catapulted back in time to her trauma residency. If she had a chest tube and a scalpel, she could insert it in two minutes or less. But the only tool available is her own palm, so she keeps it clamped to his chest.

"Slow deep breaths," Alana says in the most soothing voice she can muster. "You'll be all right. The paramedics will be here soon."

He only mutters unintelligibly.

Alana can't tell whether he understands English, let alone is conscious enough to hear her. But she keeps repeating her reassurances anyway.

Sergio taps her on the shoulder and then motions to the table piled with equipment. Beside it, the other agents are pinning the third suspect face-first to the floor. "There is no lab here," he says. "Not for germs, anyway. Those are all bomb-making supplies."

Twenty-Eight

The bathroom is no cleaner than the rest of the grimy motel room. He is repulsed by filth, but it's just one more hardship, along with the loneliness and isolation, with which he has to cope. None of them are real sacrifices; not compared with the honor of doing the Lord's work.

He sorts the pill bottles alphabetically along the edge of the sink. He has been told it makes no difference which he swallows first, but the order appeals to him. He reads each label, including the directions, even though he could recite the words in his sleep. He extracts a pill from each of the bottles labeled DOXYCYCLINE and the CIPROFLOXACIN—the two medications that are supposed to protect him—and swallows them with a sip of bitter water from the tap. He leaves the other containers untouched.

A squeaking noise comes from the other room. They always seem to know when it's dinnertime. Best not to leave them too long without food. As intelligent and social as they are, eventually, if hungry enough, they will devour the youngest and the weakest of the mischief.

He heads back into the bedroom and reaches for the large carrying case under the bed. The bag stirs in his hand. The squeaking intensifies. He feels a pang of guilt as he unzips the bag, but he forces himself to banish the doubt.

He has never had a pet of his own, but the case reminds him of the rat cage he used to see in the window of a local pet store. He sprinkles pellets of food among the seething gray forms. He watches them eat for a while, and then smooths the bedcovers before sitting down to watch the local news.

"Authorities are not saying whether the raid on the terrorists' lair is connected to the outbreak of the plague. However, the World Health Organization is looking for one Yasin Ahmed." Despite the anchorwoman's somber tone and expression, she wears an immodestly low-cut sleeveless blouse and bright red lipstick that only flaunt her sexuality. "The authorities are saying only that Ahmed is a potential victim of the plague. He was born in Genoa but is of Tunisian descent." Her words drip with implication. "Officials will not confirm or deny any possible links to terrorism."

"Where do they get such information?" he asks the rats. But the creatures are too busy feeding to pay any attention.

The anchorwoman moves on to other plague-related news, describing new cases and recent deaths. It pains him to consider all the suffering. The doubt creeps over him again like a chill.

If there were any other way . . .

But there is none, he reminds himself. He has been chosen. To doubt is to blaspheme.

Despite the regret, he also feels satisfaction. After all, a foothold has been established. The first step of the mission is complete.

He glances down at his rats. Cacio squeezes past Grappino and sidles predatorily up to Fresca, the plumpest female. Cacio pauses to look up at him, poking his long snout upward. His whiskers twitch as he sniffs the air. He is not the biggest of the nine remaining rats, but he is clearly the alpha male.

"You never doubt, do you, my friend?" he asks the black rat.

Cacio only stares back with those dark fearless eyes.

At the sound of a man's voice, he turns his attention back to the TV. A male reporter appears in front of a hospital entrance. Police, paramedics, and reporters crowd the screen. A wailing ambulance races past with lights flashing. Pandemonium.

Unable to watch or listen any longer, he presses the power button on the remote. "There is too much attention for us here," he announces to the indifferent animals.

Twenty-Nine

"Where in your job description does it mention 'leading armed assaults'?" Monique Olin speaks over the secure line in an ominous hush.

"I wasn't leading it." Alana sits on side of her bed, her wet hair wrapped in a towel. "They needed me there to identify and secure potential bio-weapon threats."

"Perhaps you were able to convince the AISI team of this, Alana, but I know better."

Alana rubs her neck and shoulder. The hot bath did little to loosen the knots that were aggravated by clamping her hand over the oozing gun-shot wound for fifteen minutes. "I stayed well behind the advance team. I was never in any danger."

"So you were in no danger whatsoever, and yet the agent standing right beside you was critically wounded?"

"He was in front of me," Alana argues, realizing it's pointless but persisting anyway. "He's in stable condition now, after his surgery."

"Use your head! You represent NATO. You're not there for gunfights. Your pigheadedness could have gotten you killed or, worse, embroiled in an international incident."

An incident would be worse than my death? But Alana adopts a conciliatory tone. "I will be more careful from now on. I promise."

"What's the English expression? Hope springs eternal." Olin sighs. "What else have they learned about those radicals?"

"I just got back from the debriefing with the AISI team." Alana can feel the adrenaline washing out of her system, and she struggles to keep her eyes open. "Forensics confirmed what we already knew: there's nothing to connect the bomb-making lair with the plague. Or, for that matter, with Yasin Ahmed."

"They still haven't found any sign of him?"

"He's vanished. His cell phone and credit cards have been dormant for over a week. All they found on his home computer was some hidden porn. Not a shred to connect him to the radicals, let alone this outbreak."

"His disappearance alone is suspicious enough, is it not?"

"Maybe, but by all accounts, he's just a regular teenager."

"He wouldn't be the first one of those to be radicalized. What about Ibrahim Hussein?"

"Hussein is a die-hard fanatic. All three of them in that apartment. They were planning an attack with homemade explosives. Looks like the target was the Church of St. Peter in Banchi. But Hussein is the only one who survived the raid, and he's not talking."

"He seems to be the only one who isn't. We've been fielding calls non-stop from the national security services, including your National Security Agency. The Americans want to send their own team to Genoa."

"That will only confuse things," Alana says, trying not to sound defensive.

"Perhaps it's time for me to come there myself?"

"We need you in Brussels to support us, Monique. On the political and diplomatic level."

"You mean out of your way, do you not? I will expect another update in the morning." With that, she disconnects.

Alana checks her voice mail. There's another message from Nico, the third one tonight. He sounds rattled. She's touched by his genuine concern over her well-being, but she picks up on the slight slur in his voice. And after he mentions their long-ago romantic escape to Palermo, she decides not to return the calls.

Her eyes close as soon as her head touches the pillow.

The alarm jolts her out of a deep dreamless sleep just before six o'clock. As she groggily pats the nightstand, she hears the loud clunk even before she feels the stabbing pain in her shoulder. Suppressing a scream, she grabs her wrist with her other hand and forcibly rotates the arm away from her body until the bone pops back into the socket. The immediate relief is welcome, but she wishes the agony of each dislocation would lessen after so many episodes.

Still breathing heavily, Alana climbs out of bed. She turns on the TV and half listens to it while she dresses. The international coverage of the raid on the terrorists' lair competes for airtime with the update on the spread of the plague in Genoa. None of it is news to Alana, until a reporter appears on-screen standing in front of a mosque. One of its walls has been spray-painted with dripping red letters, and several of the arched windows above are shattered. Disheartened, she switches off the TV and heads downstairs.

Byron is seated at a high-top table in the lobby café. Alana braces herself for another rebuke, but if he's upset about being excluded from the confrontation with Zanetti or the AISI raid, he doesn't show it. He even offers her a small grin as she joins him. "I'm guessing your night might have been more eventful than mine," he says.

"Possibly." She swallows. "Byron, it all unfolded so quickly, and Sergio insisted that no one else—"

He stops her with a raised hand. "Just tell me what happened."

She takes a quick glance around her. Aside from an inattentive waiter, they're alone, so she feels comfortable speaking freely. After she finishes updating him about the raid, she says, "Did you hear about the local mosque?"

"Yes. I was told they even tried to light it on fire while worshippers were still inside."

"It's our fault, Byron. If I hadn't pressed so hard on Yasin . . . and if his name hadn't been released to the media . . ."

He shakes his head, unrepentant. "Would have happened anyway. As soon as the news got out about the shoot-out with those terrorists. Anyone could've put it together. People are on edge. Looking to blame something or someone."

"It's only going to get worse."

"Maybe, maybe not," he says distractedly. "Alana, listen, I heard back from Geneva this morning. This *Yersinia* outbreak here isn't a genetic match for any known plague bioweapon."

Relieved as she is to hear it, she also feels strangely deflated, as though they've lost further momentum. "If it's not a match for a bioweapon or any documented naturally occurring plague, then maybe we're facing a new spontaneous mutation?"

"Maybe. But it's still got to come from somewhere."

"Exactly. And we better figure where. Soon."

"Right now we need to deal with the spread," he says. "There have been nineteen more cases since yesterday. Four of them children. One was a friend of Sonia Poletti's daughter."

"Was?"

"The little girl—six years old—died. Five others have died, too, including the woman with the antibiotic-resistant strain, Marianna Barsotti." He rubs his eyes. "And another child."

"Oh, fuck," Alana groans. Over the years, she has learned, out of necessity, to emotionally detach herself from the plight of victims. But it becomes almost impossible when children are involved. The prospect of having to watch helplessly as kids die here in Italy, like she did in Liberia, is beyond discouraging. "The death toll of this thing, Byron . . . we're nearing critical mass."

"There are going to be more deaths. A lot more. Our job now is to minimize them as best we can."

"How do we do that?"

"Most of the other patients—even the ones in the ICU—improve on antibiotics. The biggest issue is how quickly people die from this plague. If we can keep them alive for twenty-four to forty-eight hours, the medicine seems to do the trick."

"Not for Marianna Barsotti. And if her antibiotic-resistant version of the bug gets loose in the community . . ."

"We haven't seen any other cases."

"We will. There have got to be other options. Any progress on the vaccine?"

"Not really. Even if we can get enough of it here in time, there's no evidence it will be effective for preventing the pneumonic plague."

"What about using antiserum?" Alana asks, thinking of the technique of passively immunizing newly infected patients by infusing antibodies derived from the blood of recent plague survivors. "It's pretty old school, but we tried it with Ebola to some success."

"We're working on that, too. We've harvested antibodies from Claudio Dora and a few other survivors. But it could take weeks, maybe months, to engineer enough antibodies to treat more than a handful of patients."

"So we're back to Epidemiology 101?"

"When all else fails . . ." he says quietly.

So far it all has. But she keeps the thought to herself.

"I want to show you something, Alana." He pulls his chair around to her side of the table and extracts a thin laptop from his bag, opening it on the table in front of them. The screen fills with a detailed map of Genoa. "This is a time-synced map that charts the spread of the infection." A red spot glows faintly in the northwest corner of the city. Byron taps it. "This is Zanetti's construction site on what we're calling 'Day One'—the day Vittoria Fornero collapsed at the construction site. It's possible—likely, even—Yasin Ahmed was sick before her, but since we don't know for sure . . ." A central spot in the southeastern core of the city turns red. "This is the Ospedale San Martino. Day Three, when the second confirmed victim, Sonia Poletti, came down with the plague." He taps a button and more red spots glow on the map, clustered mainly around the hospital. "This is the spread on Day Five. All of these cases, so far, can be traced back directly or indirectly to Vittoria."

"Okay . . ."

"But this is Day Six," Byron says, and a green dot appears in the far eastern corner of the city. "A new case of the plague is seen way over here. At least six miles away from the other two clusters. This one cannot be linked to Vittoria. Moreover, it's a skin-related infection with buboes."

"So it's not from human-to-human spread."

"Exactly. Had to have come from an infected fleabite."

Alana touches the green dot on the screen. "So, either Vittoria and Yasin contracted their original cases of plague over here in the eastern end"—she moves her finger to the red spot by the construction site and draws an imaginary line back to the green one—"*or*, an animal loaded with infected fleas traveled six miles here from the construction site without infecting anyone in between." She pauses. "Of course, there's one other possibility."

"Which is?"

"There were infected animal vectors in both places."

"Simultaneously?" He shakes her head. "Not possible. At least not naturally."

"Not without human intervention, no."

Byron eyes her for a long moment. "We can assume that one, if not both, of the clusters of infection began somewhere around here in the east." He taps his finger right next to hers, and they both pull away from the touch. He clears his throat. "There's a big park around there called Parco Serra Gropallo. Justine is scouring it for rodents. She's hoping to trap some and test them for *Yersinia*."

Her gaze drifts back to the largest of the red glowing points, near where the San Giovanni monastery once stood. "But if the infection really came from the east end of Genoa, then why did someone go to the trouble of sanitizing the construction site of all rats?"

He only shrugs.

Her phone vibrates with a familiar buzz. It's a text from Sergio, listing a name and an address that Alana asked him to research. She rises from the table. "Let's go find our monk."

Byron drives them to the Seminario Arcivescovile di Genova in the heart of the city. She is expecting another Renaissance or Baroque treasure, but the rental car's GPS leads them to a relatively modern building perched partway up the hill and offering a panoramic view of the old city and the harbor below.

They are met at the entrance of the seminary by a young Hispanic priest whose intentions, Alana quickly realizes, are better than his English. "Arturo Corcione," she repeats slowly, and, at a loss for an appropriate hand signal, crosses herself. "The abbot of San Giovanni Monastery. Don Arturo."

A middle-aged cleric, with sunken eyes and a widow's peak, appears behind the other priest. "I will take you to him."

"Thank you," Alana says.

"I am Brother Samuel," he says as he leads them down a long hallway. "Is the Father Abbot expecting you?"

"No," Byron says. "We are with the World Health Organization."

"Ah," Samuel says, blank-faced.

At the end of the corridor, he ushers them inside a wood-paneled library. The only person in the room is a gray-haired man in a simple black tunic, who looks up from his open newspaper. Samuel speaks to him in a low voice. The older man nods, lowers his paper, and then rises to his feet. "You are looking for me?" He frowns as though puzzled.

"Are you Don Arturo?" Alana asks. "Of the San Giovanni Monastery?"

He smiles wryly. "There is no San Giovanni Monastery anymore," he says in his flawless English.

"But you were the abbot there? Before?"

"For twelve years. Yes. Come, please, sit." He extends a hand to invite them to join him, and she senses quiet authority behind his humble brown eyes.

Once seated, Alana explains with deliberate vagueness that she and Byron are part of the international response team dealing with the plague outbreak.

"Doctors." Don Arturo nods, seemingly impressed. "How can I possibly help?"

"Have you been back to the site since the monastery was demolished?" Byron asks.

"No." A pained expression crosses Don Arturo's face. "It is so difficult. Like seeing the remains of your home after it has been destroyed by fire. It was only a matter of time, though. The old building, she was not safe. One small earthquake . . . Or so they said."

"You didn't believe them?" Alana asks.

"The developer—our former mayor, Signore Zanetti—he had detailed engineering reports."

"But you don't trust him?"

Don Arturo hesitates. "Signore Zanetti, he has . . . grand ambitions. However, the Church tells me the report was accurate. Although I never felt unsafe." His shoulders bob. "Of course, one never does until the moment the roof falls in."

"So you never met Vittoria Fornero?" Byron asks, trying to refocus the discussion. "The construction worker who collapsed at the site from the plague?"

"No, never."

"How about a young carpenter named Yasin Ahmed?"

"Ah, the young man the newspapers say the police are searching for? No, I never met any of the workers. I have not been to San Giovanni since the day they moved us out. It is not . . . my place."

"What about Brother Silvio?" Alana asks.

"Brother Silvio?" Don Arturo laughs in surprise. "Has he joined the construction business?"

"He has spent a lot of time at the site," Alana says. "I saw him there once myself."

"Brother Silvio is nothing if not determined," Don Arturo says good-naturedly. "He is even older than I am. And he is a little—how do you say . . ."

"Demented?" Byron suggests.

"I would not say for sure," Arturo says. "He is eccentric, to say the least. Sometimes I wonder if he has lost a little touch with reality. You understand?"

"Yes," Alana says. "Does Silvio live here now, too?"

"At the seminary? No, no. The Church has put him up in an apartment while he waits for his next placement."

"Is he here in Genoa?" she asks.

"I believe so, yes."

"Can you get us his new address?"

"Brother Silvio, he is a character, that one. How he ever found the monastic life is a mystery to me. He loves to talk and talk."

"Do you know where he lives?" Byron persists.

"I imagine I can find this out. I honestly do not see how Brother Silvio will be of much, if any, assistance to your cause, though."

"We would like to interview him," Byron says flatly.

"*Prego.* I only hope you do not end up wasting precious time while more people suffer."

Chapter

Thirty

He had expected to stay awake all night, but the hypnotic motion of the overnight train had put him to sleep within minutes of departing, and he didn't wake up again until they were nearly pulling into the station in Naples.

The morning rush hour at Stazione di Napoli Centrale is bustling with commuters and travelers. Businessmen and -women in suits hurry past in every direction. Several speak on phones. Others keeps their heads down, walking almost blindly as they tap away on their mobile devices. Everyone seems to be in such constant contact these days. No one is disconnected, except for him. There was solitude in his previous life, certainly, but never the kind of loneliness he has experienced since launching on his mission.

Aside from the business types, backpackers and other tourists fill the terminal. He has to avert his eyes from some of the women with their revealing tops, exposed midriffs and buttocks poking out of their miniature shorts. *O Lord, surely You never meant for this!*

Realizing it is time to take his morning pills, he heads for the nearby washroom and locks himself in a stall. It's even filthier that the rest of the terminal.

His backpack vibrates slightly as he lowers it to the floor and digs the bottles out from the side pocket. He swallows down one tablet of each antibiotic with only saliva. He pulls out the other full bottles, wondering why he even brought them along. He reads the labels again: lithium, olanzapine, and sertraline.

"Mood-congruent psychosis secondary to schizoaffective disorder," Dr. Lonzo had pronounced.

He never questioned Dr. Lonzo's mouthful of a diagnosis. He has nothing but respect for the medical profession and, particularly, Dr. Lonzo. But why would he take the medications? His mood is stable and his thoughts have never been clearer. Besides, when he was taking the drugs, he found it so difficult to commune with the Almighty. The voice went almost silent, leaving him without guidance. And never more had he needed divine counsel.

The voice returns now. "Lust. Gluttony. Greed. Sloth. Wrath. Envy. Pride." Each of the seven deadly sins is articulated softly inside his head, in little more than a whisper, but the force behind them could move mountains. "Man has turned against man. Man has turned to Satan. Man has turned from Me."

I understand, O Lord, but what you ask . . .

"To me belongeth vengeance and recompense," the voice commands. "Their foot shall slide in due time. For the day of their calamity is at hand, and the things that shall come upon them make haste."

He recognizes the verse from Deuteronomy. He doesn't dare argue.

As he puts the bottles back in the bag, a muffled squeak emerges from deep inside. The rats will need to feed soon. At least, the ones who will be continuing on with him. He hasn't decided whether he will leave Cacio or Grappino behind. Both are born survivors. Either would fare well among all the garbage and discarded food at the train station.

"*Here* is the chosen site," the voice commands.

As he steps out of the bathroom back into the maelstrom of travelers, he wonders why he hadn't thought of it sooner. *Why spread the scourge myself when these godless sinners can do the work for me?*

He strolls the terminal, pretending to wait for a train, while he surreptitiously scans for the best place to release one of the males. He is leaning toward Cacio.

He wanders over to a platform where a train is loading. At the far end, tucked behind a pillar, he spots an overflowing yellow garbage bag beside a metal trash can.

He reaches for his bag and then takes another quick glance around. He notices a group of young girls in matching school tunics waiting to board a train. They look to be perhaps seven or eight years old. They line up in pairs, each holding the hand of a partner. One of the little girls has reddish hair tied in a ponytail. She looks over in his direction and grins. He can't tell if she is smiling at him or not, but it hardly matters. Her expression is the epitome of innocence.

No, not here. He involuntarily backs away from the trash can.

"This is the chosen site!" the voice rails inside his head.

The girl turns her head away, lost in laughter with her partner.

Anywhere but here, O Lord. Just not here.

Thirty-One

Alana has never before visited the Istituto Giannina Gaslini, Genoa's renowned children's hospital, but she wishes she didn't have to come today, especially not to the pediatric ICU. She stands with Nico and their host, Dr. Lina Montaldo, beside a wall painted in an ironically cheerful pastel color near the nursing station. With her freckled unlined face, Montaldo doesn't look much older than a child herself, but according to Nico she is already one of the most well-respected pediatric infectious diseases specialists in the city.

The hood of Alana's PPE suit feels particularly constrictive today, and sweat beads along her upper lip. The warmer temperature alone doesn't account for her overwhelming urge to bolt, nor do the children inside the unit, who are barely clinging to life with the aid of ventilators. No, it's the parents who trouble her so much. She can't begin to imagine their degree of anguish and helplessness as they hover at the bedsides, separated from direct contact with their critically ill children by layers of rubber and latex.

Montaldo leads them to the first of the rooms, where they gather outside the glass door. "Rosa is only three and a half," Montaldo announces.

Inside, two nurses busily attend to lines and tubes attached to a little girl on a stretcher. Her skin is pale to the point of gray. Her long dark hair is pulled back in braids and tied at the ends with blue and pink bows. Her mother sits on a stool at the bedside, hunched over and motionless. Her gloved hand clutches her daughter's as if hanging on to it for life.

"Rosa acquired her chest infection from her father," Montaldo explains. "We have added gentamicin, a third antibiotic, to her treatment regimen. She only began to cough yesterday. Just hours after her father died. But now Rosa is the most critically ill of all the patients."

Alana looks back over to the mother. There's such defeat in her slouched shoulders that she has trouble taking her eyes off the woman, even as Montaldo moves on to the next room.

Inside, a boy lies on his back with arms outstretched in an almost biblical pose. He is also connected to a ventilator, and even more lines and tubes crisscross his body than Rosa's. A nurse adjusts the intravenous infusion pump on one side of him. On the other side, the boy's mother strokes his hair while his father paces up and down in the narrow gap beside the bed.

"This is Angelo. Eight years old." Montaldo turns to Nico. "He is the reason I consulted you, Dr. Oliva."

"The sputum cultures?" Nico asks.

"Yes. The preliminary bacterial culture results are concerning, most concerning. It's *Yersinia*, of course, but so far it is resistant to all the antibiotics we have tested."

"Not another one," Alana murmurs.

Montaldo's jaw drops. "There are other cases of antibiotic resistance?"

"At least one other, at the Ospedale San Martino," Nico says. "A patient of mine."

"How does a new strain of bacteria develop antibiotic resistance so rapidly?"

"We aren't certain," Alana admits. "It must have a particular affinity for developing resistance through genetic mutation or by 'borrowing' DNA from other resistant bacteria inside the hospital."

"Perhaps," Montaldo says, unsatisfied, before turning to Nico. "How did you treat your patient with antibiotic resistance, Dr. Oliva?"

"We could not, Lina. She died."

Montaldo turns from the window without comment. She starts toward the next room but is stopped by the screech of an alarm. Her head jerks toward the nursing station, and she calls out, "*Quale stanza?*"

"*Il primo!*" someone shouts back to her.

Montaldo rushes back to the first room and bursts through the door. Alana and Nico follow. The nurse is already leaning over Rosa's stretcher, her two palms interlocked as she rapidly pumps the girl's chest up and down in piston-like compressions. The overhead monitor wails its alarm, while its warning lights flash like a strobe.

Other suited staff members storm into the room. Alana recedes back against the glass wall, aware she has nothing to contribute to the little girl's resuscitation. She glances over at the mother, who sits bolt-upright, still clutching her daughter's hand. One of the staff speaks soothingly to the woman as she tries to free her grip to gain access to the girl's arm. But the mother refuses to relinquish hold of her daughter. She just keeps muttering, "Rosa, Rosa, Rosa . . ."

Nico says a few words to the nurse, who moves away. He kneels down beside the mother's stool and, without saying a word, lowers an arm gently over her shoulder. Still clinging to her daughter's hand, the woman turns and buries her hooded face into Nico's neck, breaking into a heavy sob.

The silence in Nico's car is broken only by the gravelly Italian voice on the radio. Alana tries to focus on the broader picture—an overall impression of where this outbreak stands and where it might head—but she cannot shake the mental image of little Rosa. She can still hear the soft crunch of each chest compression accompanied by the desperate sobs of her mother, as the ICU team worked frantically but futilely to restart the girl's heart.

"*Tale stronzate!*" Nico grunts, pulling Alana from her despondent thoughts. "Such bullshit!"

"What is?"

Nico shakes a finger at the radio panel. "Such an idiot. This Tommaso Crispi!"

"Who is he?"

"A local politician with the Leagua Nord—the Northern League— the anti-immigration party here in Liguria. Crispi is the worst of the lot. He's defending the vandalism of that mosque. He calls it self-defense."

"You can't be serious."

"Crispi doesn't just blame Yasin Ahmed for the spread of the plague. No. He's says *all* Muslims are to blame. And they should all be deported. The Northern League is holding a rally later today. They are expecting thousands."

"Thousands? The threat of the plague turns this city into a ghost town, yet thousands of people are willing to turn out to protest its imaginary source?"

"Ignorance."

Alana experiences a pang of guilt over not having done more to the delay the publication of Yasin's name, which after all has whipped up this racist rancor, but she keeps it to herself.

They drive a few miles farther, until Nico slows the car to a stop in front of a tree-lined park. "Parco Serra Gropallo," he announces. "I was here only last week with little Enzo. He loves the big slide in the playground."

Alana can picture Nico horsing around with his son on a playground. She has little doubt he would thrive as a dad, he's so loving and playful. It raises the specter of what might have been.

As soon as they step onto the grass, Alana spots the commotion in the clearing between the trees. People stand inside a ring of yellow barrier tape secured around trees. Armed police guard the perimeter. As Alana nears, she can see that it's not a typical crime scene. Byron and Justine are wearing masks, gowns, and gloves. Justine holds a branch in her hand. At her feet lies a grayish black blob the size of a large bread roll. It's not until they reach the barrier that Alana recognizes it for a partially decomposed rat covered by a clear plastic bag.

"Another senseless victim of gang violence," Justine jokes as they reach the barrier.

Alana leans over the tape but knows better than to cross it. "What have you got?" she asks, dreading the answer.

Justine points with the branch to the rat's mouth, which is encrusted with dark blood. "Hemorrhagic shock." She runs the stick along the animal's hind limbs. "Buboes. This little fella died of the plague."

"Who found him?" Nico asks.

"Who do you think? This is what I do, McDreamy."

Nico motions to her mask and gown. "Is that the only protection you have been wearing?"

"Yeah."

"You'll need to start on prophylactic antibiotics. Immediately." Nico turns to Byron. "And anyone else who was exposed to that rat before he was covered."

"This is not our first time in the field, Nico. All of us took doxycycline and cipro before even coming out here."

"Is this the only rat you found?" Alana asks.

"The only dead one," Justine says.

"You've trapped live ones, too?"

"Two of them."

"Healthy?"

"I mean, I didn't check their cholesterol or blood pressure or anything . . ." Justine pokes the carcass with a stick. "But unlike this poor little fella, they don't look like they've come down with the plague."

"You will test them, of course?" Nico asks.

"More helpful advice," Byron says.

Nico shoots Byron a withering stare but holds his tongue.

"I'm far more interested in testing the fleas we found on them," Justine says.

"You sure they were carrying fleas?" Alana asks.

"Hundred percent. The male rat we trapped—aggressive little guy, total alpha male—he was scratching up a storm."

"Justine knows her stuff," Byron says with a touch of pride. He turns to Alana. "I heard from Don Arturo. He sent me the address of that monk you wanted to speak to."

"Let's go see him," she says.

"Soon as I decontaminate."

Nico glances from Byron to Alana. "I better get back to the hospital," he says as he turns away.

Minutes later, Byron meets Alana on the other side of the tape and they cross the street to his rental car, a nondescript dark sedan. He plugs the address into the car's GPS, which guides them deep into the distinctly working-class district of Sestri Ponente. He parks in front of a drab yellow and gray four-story building. They climb a flight of stairs to a second-floor apartment.

The same tiny monk from the construction site opens the door to them dressed in a traditional black habit. His eyes are hooded and the skin over his bald scalp is blotchy from sun damage. He could be anywhere from seventy to ninety years old.

Alana makes introductions. Brother Silvio ushers them inside his small apartment, speaking English in an almost musical cadence. The vanilla-and-must scent of old books permeates the room, reminding Alana of the old college library where she loved to study during med school. There's hardly any furniture, aside from a few chairs stacked with papers and a small wooden desk that supports a laptop computer. Leather-bound books cram the bookshelves and spill out onto piles on the floor.

"Too early for a grappa?" Silvio asks merrily.

"For me, I'm afraid," Alana says with a smile, and Byron shakes his head.

Silvio clears a stack of papers off two chairs and insists they sit down. Once seated, Alana motions around her. "Quite the collection, Brother."

"*Sì, sì.* My little passion. I was the librarian at our monastery. We monks love to collect writing! Hoarders, you might call us." He chortles. "The diocese, they took away the most precious volumes. But the bishop, he trusts me to sort and catalog the rest."

"How long did you live at the monastery?" Alana asks.

"For more years than either of you have walked on this earth. I had a good run—is that not how you say it in America? So did San Giovanni. Six more years, and she would have seen her eight hundredth birthday."

"It's amazing the Church let them tear it down," Alana says.

"Yes, but like me, San Giovanni was not in very good shape." Silvio smiles. "During the war, she was hit by a stray bomb. Part of the arcade collapsed. Besides, she was always a basic working monastery with none of the architectural charm of, say, the Cervara Abbey up north. Or the old San Fruttuoso Abbey in Camogli." His eyes light. "Have you ever been? Now, there is a structure that pays proper tribute to God in her—"

"Brother Silvio," Byron interrupts. "Do you remember a young carpenter at the construction site? His name is Emilio."

"With the angry skin, yes? A nervous boy, but very respectful."

"Exactly," Alana says. "He told us that you had warned him about the site."

"Perhaps"—Silvio smiles, amused—"Emilio is being a little dramatic, no? I told him the grounds were hallowed. I still believe this to be so."

"As in cursed?"

"I am a simple man of the church," Silvio replies vaguely. "As such, I am quite superstitious."

"How so?"

"I do not believe it can be such a good thing to tear down a house of worship to build a skyscraper." His smile falters for a moment. "Can it really be what God intended?"

Alana has no interest in a theological debate. "How about rodents? Were they ever an issue at San Giovanni?"

"An issue? How do you mean?"

"Any infestations of mice or rats? Do you remember seeing many of them inside the monastery or on the grounds?"

"I would hear the patter of the odd mouse sometimes. But I do not remember encountering any rats."

"What about another construction worker, Yasin Ahmed?" Byron asks. "Do you remember him?"

"I do not believe so," Silvio says.

"A boy of about Emilio's age," Alana prompts. "North African. His family is from Tunisia."

"*Sì!* I do remember him. He was with Emilio. The boy, he said nothing. But his color was not good. Sweating. He did not look so well. Not well at all. I even offered him aspirin, but he would not take it."

"When was this?" Byron asks.

"Last week." Silvio stops to think. "I cannot remember precisely, but it was two or three days before the woman in charge collapsed. This boy, Yasin? He looked just the same as her. It was the plague for both of them, no?"

Byron shoots Alana a warning glance. "The woman, yes," she says. "We still don't know about Yasin."

Silvio shakes his head gravely. "The plague, she has visited Genoa before. And she left a mark on San Giovanni then, too."

"You mean the Black Death?" Alana asks.

Silvio nods vigorously. "In 1348. The plague nearly wiped out the monastery."

Alana stiffens. "As in San Giovanni? Your same monastery?"

"*Sì.* Long before the bulldozers and cranes visited." Silvio waves to the volumes squeezed into the bookshelf. "It is all documented there. In the history books and journals. Some of them are even written by eyewitnesses."

Alana is still digesting the news after they part ways with Silvio. Outside, in the stairwell, she grabs Byron by the arm. "It's a big coincidence, don't you think?" she says.

"You mean that the plague was in Genoa before?"

"Not just Genoa, Byron, but at the San Giovanni Monastery."

"The Black Death was everywhere back then, Alana."

"Maybe so."

"You're not thinking . . ."

"There's no living sample anywhere in the world of the strain of Yersinia that caused the Black Death. Not even in a Level Five lab. I checked."

"But . . ."

"Scientists in England have reconstructed its ancient genome from bone marrow found in a burial site in Hereford. They've cracked its full genetic code, Byron."

"And you want us to compare the DNA of our current outbreak to the strain that caused the Black Death? Like we just did for the bioweapons?"

The implications of what she is suggesting suddenly sink in, and she almost shudders. "I think we have to."

He studies her for a moment as if he might argue, but then he nods. "I think so, too."

Chapter

Thirty-Two

Today is the twentieth day of February. Eleven days have passed since I contracted this pestilence. My fever has broken, the wounds are healing, and I grow a stronger by the day. However, I have shrunk to the point that my skin puckers between my ribs, and the mere effort of rising from bed to table tires me.

One of the cruel oddities of this infliction is that those who survive often go on to perish from weakness and neglect, because other members of their family are either dead or too terrified to tend them. I have no doubt I would be among those victims were it not for the attention I have received from the family of Jacob ben Moses.

Gabriella comes every morning. She carries with her fresh water from the well and more than enough food for a day. I am so hungry that perhaps I would find any victuals to be delicious, but I have developed a taste for the Hebrew food that they call kosher. My mouth waters at the scent of it.

Gabriella has also become my eyes and ears to the world outside of my room. The news she brings is not what I would want to hear but is no less than what I expect. The affliction continues to sack our once-proud Genova in a way that no invading army ever has. Gabriella tells me that the market is barren and public order has decayed in the heart of the town, forcing her to alter her route to and from my home to avoid the danger. Ne'er-do-wells maraud freely, stealing from the homes of the dead and the dying. They imbibe and gamble wantonly out on the streets in a manner that the city council and the church never before would have tolerated. The few remaining gravediggers charge such a king's ransom that only the wealthiest can afford Christian burials for their loved ones. More and more victims of this plague are dumped into the sea or, sadder still, left to rot where they fall.

The horror of these revelations is only diminished by the grace and kindness of the messenger herself. Listening to Gabriella, I am reminded of the dark fairy tales my mother would recite to me when I was a child, and how they never really frightened me because her voice was the most soothing sound in the world.

Had someone suggested earlier that I could share so much in common with a widowed Jewess, I never would have believed it. However, I have spent more time with Gabriella than anyone since Camilla's passing. We pass hours in easy conversation. Her passion for the art of healing surpasses even mine. Her knowledge of the writings of Galen, the Roman father of all medicine, is exceptional.

We are bound by more than just a shared interest in medicine. I had always assumed Gabriella and her husband to have been as childless as Camilla and I were. Yesterday, I told her of our despair over the many miscarriages and the one stillbirth Camilla experienced. Then I admitted what I had not shared with anyone before, not even to a priest in confessional: my wife blamed herself for our fate. Camilla believed that she must have been a sinner to have remained so barren. As I hurried to explain that I was not suggesting Gabriella was also somehow responsible for her own childlessness, she interrupted me.

I was not childless, Doctor Pasqua. I had Ester.

You had a daughter?

Ester was four years old when Jehovah took her.

I am so sorry. How did it happen?

She was bitten by a dog.

A stray attacked her?

No, the neighbor's mutt. Ester loved the old dog, even though he was near death and crippled by rheumatism. She would rub his belly and scratch behind his ears. One day, the cur's ear was swollen, so when Ester went to touch it, he bit her on the finger. It was little more than a nip. I thought nothing of it until a week later when Ester developed a high fever. And then her limbs began to stiffen.

With the lockjaw?

Yes. Ester did not survive another day after the first spasm.

I was at a loss for words. Even before this pestilence struck, I had seen too many children die from all manner of illness or accident. However, I was particularly saddened to learn that Gabriella lost her only child to such a cruel and casual whim of fate. I almost reached out to take her hand in mine, but I stopped myself before committing an act of such impropriety.

Her eyes welled with tears, but I was surprised to see her lips form a melancholic, yet almost joyful smile. Every day I had with Ester was a blessing, she said. I am grateful for each one. God did not take her from me to punish my sins, any more than Camilla's barrenness was a penalty for hers.

I agree, I said. I only wish Camilla had believed it.

I am sorry for you both that she blamed herself, Gabriella said. In truth, I feel more fortunate than the mothers from whom the plague has stolen children. At least Isaac and I had the opportunity to bury our Ester and mourn for her in the proper Jewish tradition. I cannot imagine having to dispatch the most precious being in my life to the sea or worse.

Perhaps we both revealed more than we had intended, but we fell into a shy silence after this conversation and Gabriella departed earlier than on previous days.

Gabriella returned again this morning, but soon after she arrived, I received two other visitors. I could tell by the heavy knock on my door they were of the less welcome variety. The same two priests who had come for me before stood warily outside the open door, covering their mouths with their sleeves, as they announced that His Grace requested my presence.

Gabriella protested that I was far too weak to travel.

The taller priest looked at her as if he had just inhaled a foul odor. Is this woman a Jew? he asked me.

I told them that Gabriella was the daughter of a colleague who brought me daily supplies. I tried to silence her with my stare, but she would not abide.

He is in no condition to leave his home, she insisted.

The second priest turned to her with a fiery glare. We do not answer to any woman, he said, let alone a Jew.

I pretended to be overcome with a fit of hacking. The priests jumped back as if they had been startled by thunder. I panted as though struggling to catch my breath. This plague, I said. I do not have the lungs or strength to walk to the Archbishop's palace. Perhaps in another week or so.

We have a horse for you, the taller priest said.

I argued that I was not fit for an audience with the Archbishop, as I had not shaved or changed in almost two weeks. But they were deaf to all my excuses.

The priests rode together on the lead horse while I trotted ten paces back, as per their instructions, on the second animal. At the palace, I was led to the Archbishop's chamber and made to wait outside the door while the priests entered. After a delay, they emerged from the chamber and the taller one commanded me to go inside.

The Archbishop was seated in the same raised chair as before while a fire raged even more intensely at his back. He clutched a handkerchief across his mouth and nose. No farther! he cried the moment I crossed the threshold.

I stopped and bowed to him from across the room.

So you have been afflicted after all, Doctor Pasqua, he said through the cloth.

Yes, Your Grace.

And yet here you are. It seems my prayers for you have been answered, unlike those for so many other of my parishioners.

Thank you, Your Grace. I have been more fortunate than most.

So it would seem. Would you care to elaborate on the secrets of your recovery?

There is no secret, Your Grace, I said, and explained how I had contracted the skin form of the pestilence, which had spared my lungs. I described how I had applied the time-honored traditions such as balancing humors and applying salves, but I made no mention of Jacob or his family.

The Archbishop grew impatient. Tell me, then, who was this Jewess who was at your bedside when my priests came for you?

She is no one. An errand girl. Her father is a colleague.

A doctor? A Jewish doctor?

A physician, yes. Doctor ben Moses. But he is merely an old acquaintance.

Surely you must realize it is against the law for a Jewish doctor to treat a Christian? the Archbishop said.

I do. He did not treat me.

It is not only illegal. It is blasphemous.

Your Grace, I also treated myself with a remedy that is most extraordinary, I said, as I was most anxious to direct his attention away from the involvement of Jacob or his family.

What is it?

The blood of the rats. From the San Giovanni Monastery.

You drank rat's blood? he asked as he stood in outrage. What kind of pagan ritual is that? It reeks of Satanic worship.

These are no ordinary rats. These are the creatures I described to you and Doctor Volaro. The ones blessed with the ability to ward off the pestilence.

No animal is blessed, let alone a lowly vermin!

Not blessed by God, of course. But somehow they possess the ability to resist this illness like no other creature alive. Ask Don Marco. He will tell you the same.

The Archbishop sat down and brought the handkerchief back to his mouth as he considered my argument. Are there more of these vermin at the monastery? he asked.

I believe so, I said, sheepish for having betrayed the confidence of a friend.

This is most unusual. I will speak with Don Marco.

My legs were growing weak from standing, but the Archbishop seemed in no hurry to dismiss me.

What of the Jews, Doctor Pasqua? he asked.

What of them, Your Grace?

You said the rats of San Giovanni were the only creatures who escaped the plague, and yet clearly so, too, did this Jewish physician and his spawn. What about other Jews?

They are as susceptible as anyone else. I hear the losses in their community are as great as ours.

Their losses? The Archbishop grunted. These infidels live off of our good grace. By our protection. And what do they provide us in return? Do they contribute to our harvest? Do they build our houses? Do they worship our God? No! At most, they lend us their money and charge us usury in exchange for our Christian charity.

I had to bite my tongue so as not to point out that the Jews were banned from participating in guilds or most other forms of commerce.

The Archbishop motioned around him. Even now, I still repay David ben Solomon for the exorbitant loan he bestowed upon me to complete this house. This humble shrine to the Lord, built with money from an Israelite. A debt my parishioners might never be able to repay.

It is unfortunate, Your Grace, I said.

There are those who believe the Jews have been spreading this pestilence all along. I have heard whispers that the rabbis, those pagan priests of the Jews, are poisoning the wells.

But Your Grace, how is that possible when this miasma spreads through the air like a vapor?

The Archbishop did not appear to hear me. When he spoke again his eyes seemed to look right through me. Doctor Pasqua, is it not my duty as a spiritual leader to take any and all steps to protect the faithful?

I thought again of those doomed residents who were barricaded into their own homes and left to die. For the first time in days, I experienced another chill.

Thirty-Three

Even though Alana sat at the same long conference table only three and a half days earlier, it feels more like a month. Her good shoulder aches for a change, after being vaccinated a few minutes before. The limited supply of American military plague vaccine arrived that same day, and the meeting's attendees were among the first to receive doses.

Sunlight streams through the thin shade covering the window of the Municipo's top-floor conference room, bathing the room in a bright glare. The table is as crowded as before, but many of the faces have changed. The Italian minister of health, Laura Pivetti, has joined her doughy-faced deputy at the table. Pivetti is a good-looking, olive-skinned woman of about Alana's age who has an air of someone accustomed to getting her way. Several other officials are also present, including Sergio Fassino, Genoa's mayor, and the entire WHO team.

Byron spends the first ten minutes updating the attendees on the outbreak. He projects on the screen above him the same image of its spread that he shared with Alana. Charts, maps, and tables demonstrate the geographical and chronological extent of the disease.

"We have fifty-six infected. Twenty-two dead so far." Byron pauses and the room goes dead silent. "Inevitably, this will only be the tip of the iceberg."

"So just to review, Dr. Menke," Pivetti says in a tone that only heightens the already taut atmosphere. "This epidemic has increased from two cases to almost sixty in the time since the WHO has been managing it?"

"That is correct, Minister." Byron breaks into a smile of pure defiance. "Of course, almost half of those cases were incubating before we arrived. And in that same time frame, we have seen the fatality rate drop from one hundred percent to roughly forty percent. There has been no further in-hospital transmission. And so far, no spread beyond Genoa."

Pivetti views him icily. "Yet I would not describe the situation as controlled. Would you?"

"Not in the least, Minister. As I said, it's only going to get worse. We have a reservoir of infected animals and fleas in a park in the heart of the city. This infection kills faster than almost any other one we know of. The spread is accelerating. And, most worrisome of all, we have already seen two cases of multi-resistance. This bacteria has the potential to become an international epidemic or, worse, a pandemic."

"Resistance? What does this mean?" the mayor asks in a pained tone.

"This bacteria has an uncanny ability to rapidly acquire resistance to antibiotics."

The color drains from the mayor's cheeks. "Are you saying we might soon not have any treatment available?"

"It's possible, yes."

"Then how will we control it?" the mayor asks, gripping his upper arm. "With this vaccine?"

Byron turns to the bearded Swedish vaccine expert. "Dr. Larsen, care to comment?"

Larsen pulls his glasses off and taps them against the table. "At best, the American military vaccine will provide seventy percent immunity. Besides, there is only enough to immunize a few thousand people, not the whole city."

"That is all we have?" The mayor looks as if he might jump out of his seat.

Larsen taps his glasses even faster. "Our Geneva lab is already working on developing a vaccine for this specific strain of *Yersinia*, but it will take a minimum of four months before it's available."

Byron glances at Alana. "We are also developing an antiserum using antibodies from the blood of survivors. But its availability will be measured in weeks, if not also months."

"And in the meantime?" Pivetti demands.

"We continue to do what we are already doing, Minister," Byron says. "We treat anyone with suspicion of the plague with antibiotics. We quarantine known victims and do aggressive contact tracing. We screen all air, sea, and rail travel points for symptomatic people. We apply aggressive pest control measures to the local rat population, especially in the parks."

"Good luck with that!" Justine pipes up. "Unless the plague does the pest control for us."

"And finally, we are about to embark on a strategy of ring prophylaxis."

"What does that involve?" Pivetti asks.

"In the sixties, the WHO effectively eradicated smallpox using the same approach," Byron says. "They would locate any villages or towns with smallpox victims and then immunize everyone living in the ring— the immediate vicinity—surrounding that hot spot." He levels an infrared pointer at the map on the screen and encircles the areas around the construction site, the hospital, and the Parco Serra Gropallo. "We're going to do the same with these foci of outbreaks here in Genoa. We intend to treat everyone living in a one-mile radius of these hot spots with antibiotics, even if they've had no known contact with any victims."

"How do you expect to stop this . . . this organism, when you do not even know where it originates?" Pivetti challenges.

"I didn't say we expect to stop it," Byron says with an affable smile that contradicts his tone. "At least not yet. At this point, we're focusing on containing or, to be more accurate, slowing its progress."

The minister turns to Alana, her stare penetrating. "Dr. Vaughn, what does NATO have to say? Have you determined whether or not this is an act of terrorism?"

"No, not for certain. This microbe isn't a match for any known form of bioweapon. But we still cannot rule out deliberate spread."

"How do you explain Yasin Ahmed?" Pivetti asks. "And his disappearance?"

"I can't," Alana admits. "Not yet."

"There has been no trace of him in over a week, Minister." Sergio speaks up for the first time. "However, we have found no evidence to link him to Islamic extremism. The terrorists we arrested yesterday were working on an attack unrelated to the plague."

The minister folds hers arms across her chest. "So, to summarize: we do not know where the germ comes from, how it spreads, who is spreading it, or how to stop it." She glances around the table. "Does *anyone* have anything helpful to add?"

The simmering room explodes in multiple voices. Byron eventually quells the racket with a whistle. The heated discussion devolves into a rehash of conflicting ideas. Pivetti soon loses patience. She cuts the discussion off and sets another meeting for the same time the following afternoon. As she rises from the table, she stares at Byron. "By then, hopefully, we might have a few actual answers."

"Minister, in all deference to your expertise in managing emerging epidemics"—Byron's smile is pure frost—"in my experience, this outbreak is unique. We may not have a specific answer for weeks or more."

Alana and Byron leave City Hall together and step out into the bright sunshine. Once out of earshot of the others, she asks him, "Why do you do that?"

"Do what?"

"Antagonize people that way. Especially the minister."

His nose crinkles. "You didn't think she was challenging me?"

"Okay, maybe not the best example. But you have a way of goading people with that smile of yours. The way you do with Nico."

"Ah." The same grin reemerges. "That's what this is about."

"It's only an example," she says, maybe a little too quickly.

He views her with curiosity. "You're very protective of him. You two have a . . . relationship that goes beyond the professional."

It's Alana's turn to fold her arms. "That's none of your business."

"No offense intended." He looks away. "Aside from your . . . um . . . credentials, I don't know a lot about you."

Byron seems awkward all of a sudden. Alana realizes she doesn't know much about him, either, beyond his professional status. She's not even sure whether he has a partner or children.

Before she can reply, Sergio Fassino strides up to them. "You need to come with me," he announces. "Both of you."

"Where?" Alana asks.

"The hospital."

Byron lifts his chin. "What's going on, Sergio?"

"Yasin Ahmed."

Alana's throat thickens. "He's in hospital?"

Sergio walks on without answering.

Less than thirty minutes later, Alana, Byron, Nico, and Sergio—who appears fidgety and uncomfortable in his protective gear—gather around a bedside on the sixth floor of Ospedale San Martino. The man on the stretcher looks up at them from behind his hospital mask with wide fearful eyes.

It takes Alana a few moments to recognize the patient as Paolo, the contractor from the San Giovanni construction site. "Paolo has the plague?" she asks.

Sergio shakes his head. "He showed up at the emergency room an hour ago thinking he did."

"He was terrified," Nico cuts in. "But the blood tests and X-rays confirm that he only has a chest cold."

"In his panic, though, Paolo has solved a mystery for us," Sergio says.

"Which is?" Alana asks.

"Yasin Ahmed."

Aside from the occasional cough, Paolo is breathing easily, but he seems to grow more anxious by the second as Sergio questions him, with Nico translating for the others.

"Paolo swears that on the morning they found Yasin collapsed at the site, the boy was already dead," Nico says.

"Who is 'they'?" Byron asks.

"Paolo and Vittoria." Nico listens to the interrogation. "Vittoria was first to arrive . . . She found Yasin at the bottom of the pit. The boy had fallen in it during the night . . . He was sick the day before, yes, but they didn't know he had remained on-site overnight." He waits again. "Paolo says they panicked . . . They were behind schedule . . . under such tight time and money constraints . . . Vittoria reminded him of the time INAIL had shut down a site for a week after a worker died in a crane accident."

"INAIL?" Alana asks.

"The Institute for Insurance Against Accidents at Work," Nico explains. "Paolo says Vittoria convinced him they couldn't take the chance . . . It would draw unnecessary attention to the site."

Sergio's tone grows pointed, and Paolo shakes his head frantically.

Nico grimaces behind his clear mask. "Paolo says they lowered Yasin's body into one of the forms and poured him in concrete."

"That would make him a bit tougher to find," Byron grumbles.

Nico intervenes to ask Paolo a question. The contractor frantically waves his hands in front of his chest as he spouts his reply.

"Paolo swears Marcello didn't know about Yasin," Nico says. "That he and Vittoria decided to hide the body on their own."

"Do you believe him?" Alana asks.

Nico shrugs. "Who knows with this bunch?"

They don't learn much more. According to Paolo, no one had asked Yasin about his illness. Apparently Vittoria had assumed that the youth was just hungover and had refused to let him go home early. The next time they saw Yasin, he was dead in the pit, and they impulsively hatched the plan to hide the body before the authorities started sniffing around. Paolo even offers to lead Sergio to the precise slab where they encased Yasin but concedes it would be of little help, as they had already built on top of it.

They leave the unit together. Nico and Alana emerge out of the decontamination station at nearly the same time, but they have to wait a few minutes in the lobby for Byron to appear. When he finally joins them, his expression is grim.

"What is it?" Alana asks.

"I just got a call from Geneva," Byron says. "They finally have a match for this strain of the plague."

"Which is?"

"*Yersiniai pestis orientalis.*"

Nico shakes his head. "I've never heard of this subtype."

"Because it hasn't been seen in hundreds of years," Byron says. "Not since the Middle Ages."

"No . . ." Alana murmurs.

Byron locks eyes with her. "It's one of the only two known variants of the medieval plague."

She goes cold. "The return of the Black Death."

Chapter

Thirty-Four

*A*rmageddon. Perhaps it has descended already without any form of divine intervention.

He feels dirty just being here. He read up beforehand on Scampìa, the crime-ridden neighborhood in northern Naples, but only in person does he appreciate the ungodliness of the place. A modern-day Sodom or Gomorrah. The dilapidated buildings are protected by chain-link fences and locked gates. The street is littered with garbage, much of it in the form of humans. Drunks and addicts totter down the streets, a few push their possessions in shopping carts. The neighborhood stinks of sin— body odor, tobacco, and rotting garbage.

He crosses at an intersection and passes two young women who stand on stiletto heels under the bluish haze of a streetlight. Both smoke cigarettes. Each of them is squeezed into a tube top and tiny skirt. One of them is taller than him, with shoulders as broad. And the other one with the purple-dyed hair, who looks to be no more than fifteen or sixteen years old, can't stop giggling. It's obvious they are intoxicated. He wonders if cocaine or even amphetamine—the crystal meth he read was so rampant in this neighborhood—is to blame.

"Hey, lover boy," the taller one calls to him in a deep voice. "Want to play?"

He is shocked to realize that she must have once been, or possibly still is, a man. He shakes his head and continues walking, but the girls follow, falling into stride on either side of him.

"For seventy-five euros, I'll blow you good," the purple-haired one offers.

"And for a hundred fifty, you can do us both," the masculine one coos. "Bet you've never had a threesome, lover boy. Not as special as one with the two of us, anyway."

O Lord, what has this world come to?

"Don't be shy, lover boy."

"Tend Your sick ones, O Lord Christ," he mumbles to himself. "Rest Your weary ones. Bless Your dying ones. Soothe Your suffering ones. Pity Your afflicted ones."

"Ooh, we got a religious one here." The taller one claps her hands gleefully. "My absolute favorite kind to corrupt!"

"Looks like your pants are saying yes," the purple-haired one cries out as she points at his crotch.

To his horror, he realizes that his member has stirred to life. The shame and guilt overwhelm him. He has worked so hard to banish those urges. He wants to vomit. He wants to run. Instead, he just mutters, "I have no money."

The jezebels seem to lose interest and fall away. He scampers on for three or four more blocks, until he's convinced they are no longer following. Then he doubles back to the streetlight where he met them, but the two whores are nowhere to be seen.

He surveys the landscape around him. Ten or twenty feet to his right, a man lies slumped at the foot of a chain-link fence, either unconscious or dead. The woman sitting beside him ignores the fallen man altogether. Instead, she jabs a needle into the crook of her elbow.

O Lord, this is so much better than the railway platform, he thinks. *Please forgive me for defying Your earlier command.*

But his prayer, like all the others he has uttered since leaving the train station, goes unanswered.

Undeterred, he backs into an alcove, a shadow away from the streetlight. He extracts a glove from his pocket, removes his backpack, and lowers it to the ground. He reaches his gloved hand inside until his fingers find the cordlike tail. As soon as he pulls on it, the rat squeaks in protest. He can feel the pressure of the bite around his finger, but the teeth don't penetrate the glove. He pulls Cacio out by the tail.

The rat stills with fear as it dangles in front of his face.

His sympathy stirs for the petrified animal. "Not to worry, Cacio. You will love it here. So much to eat. So many places to hide."

The rat stares back with dark blank eyes.

Then he parrots the same phrase his mentor sometimes says to him: "You should feel honored. After all, you will be doing the Lord's work."

Thirty-Five

The second vodka neat tastes better than the first. Alana finds the slight buzz welcome after this deflating day. Byron is still nursing his first beer while she's already considering a third drink, as she toys with the straw in her glass.

She can't even remember which one of them suggested drinks. Byron gave her a ride back to her hotel and their conversation regarding potential containment strategies continued into the lobby and up to the bar. Now, after midnight, they're sitting at a table with the whole bar to themselves. *No wonder*, Alana thinks again. *Who would visit this doomed city?*

"Back in the Middle Ages, it wasn't called the Black Death," she says apropos of nothing. "That term wasn't coined for centuries."

"What did they call it?" Byron asks.

"The Great Mortality."

Byron studies the rim of his beer bottle. "It does kind of fit."

"You figure?" Alana is aware that alcohol sometimes brings out an edge in her, but she makes no effort to suppress it. "Truth is, 'The Great Mortality' was a massive understatement."

"It does explain a lot, though. Like why this outbreak is so much deadlier than what we've seen with the modern-day bubonic plague."

"That's about the *only* thing it explains."

"It's as if they're not even the same bug. Like comparing a cold virus to Ebola."

"You're gonna tell me about Ebola?" She taps her chest indignantly. "I was there. In West Africa."

"So I've heard." His eyes glint with sarcasm.

"Then again, the plague does have one major epidemiological advantage over Ebola that will make it far deadlier."

"Which is?"

"Ebola kills most of its sufferers. It's too damned lethal. It usually burns itself out by running out of fresh victims. But if we are looking at a survival rate of one-half or two-thirds for those infected, then the plague can just keep spreading and spreading."

He nods grimly. "And it has a separate animal reservoir—in rats and fleas—whereas Ebola only infects primates."

"Yup. The Black Death could be as big a killer now as it was in medieval times. Half of Europe gone in three years. We're talking tens of millions of people in today's terms. Maybe more." She hums the tune to a familiar nursery rhyme and then, as she lets the straw topple to the table, mutters, "Ashes, ashes. We all fall down."

"Come on, Alana. You're getting a little carried away."

"Am I?" She raises her empty glass and shakes it in the direction of the waiter. "We might be truly fucked this time around, Byron."

"So this is you after two drinks, huh?"

Alana laughs. "Yeah, but they're doubles."

"Can't wait to see what a third does for you."

"Puts me to sleep, I hope."

His smile fades. "Tell me about West Africa, Alana. Seriously."

"What's to know?"

"I heard it's why you left the WHO."

"You heard right."

He leans closer. "What went so wrong?"

"I've seen a lot of pointless death in my day. I've been to some of the most hopeless places the world has to offer. And before the WHO, I was stationed for four months in Afghanistan. Christ, I almost died there. But Liberia . . ." She closes her eyes. "That was worse. Way worse."

"Worse how?"

"The WHO sent us in unarmed and unprepared. We were as useless as a rescue boat without life preservers . . . or rope . . . or a fucking rudder or compass, for that matter." She looks up at him. "There were only three of us on my team. It was so bad, so much worse than what we expected. I warned Geneva every single day. And they just sat on my reports. All we wanted to do was to protect local doctors and nurses who were caring for the sick and dying. They were begging us for simple stuff like sterile gloves and masks, body bags for the dead. The most basic infection-control gear. And all I got from Geneva was the runaround."

"That surprises you? You know how the bureaucracy creaks along at the WHO. Takes a special task force just to get the printer paper refilled."

"Tell that to Moses Conteh."

"Who?"

"A local doctor who ran a clinic in Ganta, in the north. Maybe the bravest guy I've ever met. Moses worked day and night with Ebola victims. He used to plead with me for supplies to protect his staff. Right up until the day the virus killed him." She shakes her head. "Moses was thirty-four years old."

The waiter drops off a fresh vodka for her and sweeps the last glass away with a quick "*Prego.*"

"Okay, time for me to drink and for you to talk," Alana announces. "Tell me your story."

"I've never been to West Africa."

She rolls her eyes. "Why the WHO?"

"You ever been to Montreal in February?"

She swallows such a big sip of vodka that her throat burns. "Bullshit."

"You'd be surprised what a Quebec winter can drive you to."

"For real, Byron."

He studies the label on his beer bottle. "I was at McGill University for seven years—on a full professor tenure track—but I got tired of academic life. Too competitive and cutthroat, even for me. Besides, I always preferred fieldwork. One day, three years ago, a colleague at the WHO made me an offer I could have easily refused—for even less money than my academic salary—but I took it." He hesitates. "I needed a change."

"What about the wife and kids?"

"No kids. Dana and I tried for a while, but . . . just wasn't to be. Maybe for the best, because we didn't last." He looks down again. "Apparently I'm not the easiest guy to get along with."

"You?" Alana feigns shock. "Hard to even fathom."

Byron grins self-consciously. "Dana and I were still colleagues at the university. It was hard after we split. That, more than anything, sent me to Geneva. I needed a fresh start or change of scenery or whatever you want to call it."

"Aha! You're still in love with her!" Alana wags a finger at him. Tomorrow she knows she's going to be embarrassed by her behavior, but right now she doesn't care. "Admit it!"

He rolls his shoulders. "Change isn't easy for me. Plus, you might not have noticed, but I'm kind of stubborn."

"No! The shocking revelations are coming fast and furious."

"Okay, okay." He laughs. "This soul-baring is exhausting. Your turn. Tell me about you and Nico."

"There's not much to say."

His grin widens. "That's kind of cute."

"What is?"

"The way your eye twitches when you lie."

She doesn't even bother denying it. "I met Nico when I started at the WHO. We dated on and off for a year or so, but it ended about eight years ago."

"It's not really over, though, is it?"

"Yes, it is. He's married with kids."

"That doesn't always make a difference."

"Well, it sure as fuck does for me!" She slams her glass down, spilling some vodka.

He reaches out and touches her wrist, so fleetingly that she wonders if she imagined it. "I know how it feels, Alana."

Her face heats up, and she suddenly feels almost sober.

She's thankful when he changes subjects. "It's pretty obvious that Yasin Ahmed was no terrorist," he says.

"Yeah, it looks more and more like the poor kid was our actual Patient Zero."

"So where did he get his infection from?" he asks. "The Black Death hasn't existed in hundreds of years. Not even in a lab."

"Got to be the construction site. It's an eight-hundred-year-old monastery they ripped apart. One that, according to Brother Silvio, barely survived the Black Death. God knows what the excavators dug into over there."

"Say that were true. How would the bacteria survive for more than six hundred years underground?"

"Who knows? Maybe it survived in some kind of spore form? Other bacteria do. For example, *C. difficile* can live dormant as spores for years. A kind of suspended animation."

"Six hundred years? Seems like a stretch." He frowns. "Even if we assume the microbe did originate somewhere in the monastery, how did it travel all the way across the city to Parco Serra Gropallo to become endemic in the rat population there?"

Alana just stares at him, lost for a plausible explanation.

The silence is broken by a loud voice. "There you are!"

Alana looks over to see Justine Williams striding toward them.

"Finally. It's like finding two annoying needles in a haystack. Hey, boss," Justine says to Byron. "I'm not asking for one of your kidneys or anything, but how about checking your phone every once in a while?"

"What is it, Justine?" he asks evenly.

She motions from the glass to the bottle. "Since I didn't get the memo about the pub crawl, I decided to get a little work done on preventing the next apocalypse."

"Are you going to get the point?" Alana asks.

"Eventually. I'm not quite done guilt-tripping you two for drinking on the job. And worst of all, without me!" Justine grabs a nearby chair and pulls it up to the table. "Okay, we just got the results on the rats we found in the park."

"And?" Alana prompts.

"We found *Xenopsylla cheopis*. Classic rat fleas. Lots of them. And according to the rapid PCR screen on their saliva, the little buggers are carrying *Yersinia*."

"But that's not a big surprise," Byron says. "We knew the rat died of the plague."

Justine shrugs. "Who said anything about the dead rat?"

"Hold on," Alana says, thinking she must have misunderstood. "You're saying you found infected fleas on the live rats?"

"All the rats! Including the live ones. The big aggressive male. His fleas were loaded with the plague."

"The healthy one?" Alana asks, pushing herself up from the table.

"Healthy as a horse. Well . . . not so much after we euthanized him. We're going to do a necropsy, of course, but there's no sign he ever had the plague."

"Then he must have recovered from it," Byron suggests.

"Nope." Justine shakes her head so hard her hair shakes. "There's zero evidence he was ever sick with the plague."

Alana feels on edge and, suddenly, fully sober.

"Justine, are you saying this rat was an asymptomatic carrier of plague-infected fleas?" Byron asks.

"You catch on quick for a Canadian."

Alana squeezes her temples between her palms. "So now we have rats that are immune to plague but can still spread the goddamn Black Death."

Thirty-Six

Kemal Attila doesn't smoke, but he's happy to keep his younger brother, Basim, company, if only to escape the stagnant heat inside their father's convenience store. There are no customers anyway. Business is bad this week. Ever since the news of the plague broke. Kemal doesn't understand the big deal, but since he's facing a mountain of schoolwork at the university, he's happy for the quiet.

"Hey, Basim, CFC is going to crush Fiorentina tomorrow night," Kemal says, referring to their favorite football club, Genoa CFC.

"At home, for sure." Basim takes a long drag of his cigarette from where he sits beside Kemal on the stone steps. "But on the road? I wouldn't bet on them."

"Don't be such a downer. They'll pull it off. You'll see. Tomorrow at Padano's."

"We might be the only ones at the bar, brother." Basim laughs. "This is a ghost town."

"People are too easily scared."

Basim winks. "Hope the plague doesn't scare away all the ladies."

"Brother, you only think with your—"

A stranger's voice interrupts them. "What are you two doing here?"

Kemal looks over to see four young men approaching. One of them has a mustache and another's head is shaved, but they all wear white T-shirts, jeans, and boots. A hand-painted sign dangles from the hand of the mustached one. It takes Kemal a moment to read the upside-down scrawl that reads: ITALY FOR ITALIANS! He realizes they must be returning from the anti-Islam rally the Northern League organized, which, according to his Twitter feed, some of his friends were planning to counter-protest.

Basim is already on his feet. "We are Italians," he says. "What's your excuse?"

"Come on." The bald one scoffs. "What are you ragheads, really? Syrians? Iraqis? Pakis?"

Kemal knows his younger brother too well. They are only a year apart in age, but their temperaments are night and day. If Basim loses his temper, it won't end well. Kemal grabs his brother by the elbow and begins to pull. "Let's go back in."

"Yeah, and take your filthy plague virus with you!" One of the others calls.

Basim shakes free of Kemal's grip. "You morons better get the fuck out of here."

The bald one steps closer to him. "Or what, raghead? You'll infect us?"

"Something like that." Basim's fist comes out of nowhere and slams into the bald guy's jaw. He stumbles back and grabs his bleeding lip with both hands. Before Basim can swing again, the other three pounce. One tackles Basim to the ground. Another kicks him repeatedly in the belly. The bald guy rushes back over and begins stomping wildly on his chest as if he's trying to crush glass.

Kemal hurls himself at the bald one, wrapping him in a bear hug.

"I'm going to kill you, you camel-fucker!" the man screams in Kemal's face, spraying spittle and blood along with the stench of stale beer.

A searing pain shoots across Kemal's scalp and then everything goes dark. He feels himself falling but he's helpless to stop it. Only when he opens his eyes does he realize that he's lying on his back on the ground. He looks up into the hateful eyes of the one with the mustache, who is now holding a brick. "You should've never ever come here!" he cries as he swings his arm down.

Kemal hears the thud before the pain explodes inside his skull. Then darkness falls again.

Thirty-Seven

Today is the twenty-first day of February. While my vigor grows by the day, the same cannot be said of my spirit.

I did not sleep last night. It was no fever or bubo that kept me awake, but rather the threatening words of the Archbishop that were only compounded by the frightening spectacle I witnessed upon my return home from his palace.

The same two priests led me back on horseback, but they did not take me all the way. They left me instead, without explanation, at the door to their church, a half a league or so from my home. The streets were not as empty as they had been on my departure. On the contrary, they were more crowded than a typical day even before the time of the plague. I assumed by the way the townsfolk were lining the streets that a religious procession of some form must be winding its way past.

There was indeed a procession, but none like I have ever observed before or hope to ever again. The men participating could be heard even before they could be seen, though their words were unintelligible. Not only was their tongue foreign to my ears, but they cried out over each other and many just howled or moaned.

The sight of them was more shocking still. There had to be twenty men or more. They staggered along the street in a loose collection like a group of revelers stumbling out of a tavern after dark. They wore cloaks and togas, but most of the garments were torn enough to expose their chests and backs. They had once been white but were now thoroughly stained with blood, dirt, and sweat. A few wore crowns of thorns fixed so tightly on their heads that blood trickled from their foreheads. The man at the front of the procession lugged a wooden cross over his shoulder that was so large its base dragged along the street behind him.

They trudged along the street stopping often to flog themselves with lashes that were adorned with sharp objects. Many of the vicious strokes drew blood. All the while, they chanted, shrieked, and moaned as if in a state of ecstasy. At random intervals, each man would drop to his knees and mutter some form of garbled prayer. Some foamed at the mouth, while others smeared their faces with their own blood like barbarians applying paint before a battle.

The sight of them was enough to make a man question his sanity. But when I looked upon other spectators, few appeared as revulsed as I felt. Some looked amused. Others watched in rapt attention as though witnessing an epiphany. Many even spurred the eccentrics on with shouts of encouragement.

I recognized a neighbor of mine standing among the crowd, Giacomo the cobbler. I asked Giacomo if he knew who these strangers were. He said they were Germans who had come from north of the mountains.

What form of madness is this? I asked him.

They claim that man's sins have brought the pestilence upon us, he said. Gesù Cristo died for those sins. And only by them paying the ultimate penance, scourging themselves as they do now, will God vanquish this plague.

You cannot believe this to be so.

I do not know what to believe anymore, Rafael. This pestilence has claimed my wife and two of my children. The priests and you doctors have been powerless to stop it. Perhaps these flagellants are right in thinking that only such extreme measures might spare the rest of us from the same plight.

I was too distraught to argue. There was something so ungodly in the barbaric ritual that I could not watch a moment longer. Besides, I was tiring rapidly, as I had not stood on my feet so long in over two weeks.

I returned home with a heavy heart. Even in the darkness of my room, I could not escape the visions of the flagellants in my head. I have seen many abominations and cruelties since the dawn of the plague. However, nothing rocked my faith in humankind as much as the sight of those eccentrics mutilating themselves while the townspeople cheered. It suggested to me that there would be no limits to the savagery or depravity to which our once-noble society might sink.

All night long I dwelled on this revelation. By the next morning, when Gabriella arrived bearing a basket of heavenly smelling delicacies, I had no appetite for them. I sat her down at my table. I did not mince my words as I recounted my audience with the Archbishop.

Gabriella displayed neither shock nor alarm.

Surely you must see how dangerous it would be if the Archbishop himself were to level the accusation that Jews were poisoning wells? I asked.

Your people have been doing this forever, she said.

What do you mean?

You ban us Jews from joining guilds or owning lands or working in most trades. You only borrow from us, because according to your Bible, it is a sin for Christians to charge interest on a loan to another of the same faith. You have no one else to call upon when you are in need of money. However, no sooner has the loan been granted than you resent the loaner even more for practicing the only trade available to him.

This all may be so, but the risk to you Jews is even greater now.

It is true, she said. The Archbishop would not be the first man to try to erase his debt by eliminating his creditors.

I was so consumed in my thoughts that without a preconceived notion I reached out and took her hand in mine. Her fingers went stiff and her eyes lowered to the floor, but she made no effort to withdraw her hand.

I must confess there was unexpected exhilaration in the contact. But it came with guilt. Camilla has been in the ground for less than a season, and here I was hand in hand with a widowed Jewess. However, I also knew that Gabriella's presence in my home would not and could not last much longer.

You and your family must leave Genova straightaway, I said.

Where would we go? she asked without looking at me.

South toward Naples or even east toward Venice. Anywhere out of reach of the Archbishop.

Father is too old to travel those distances.

It is far more dangerous for him to remain here! You must believe me.

Gabriella squeezed my hand a little tighter. I do believe you, she said. But I do not wish to leave the only home I have ever known. And, Rafael, I do not wish to leave you.

Thirty-Eight

Alana's head seems to ring louder than her cell phone. *What the hell was I thinking?* The three vodkas seem far more like triples than doubles in retrospect. She might as well not have even bothered to sleep. The phone's screen reads 4:47 a.m. and announces that, not unexpectedly, Monique Olin is the caller.

"There has been another new case," Olin says by way of greeting.

"Must've been several more overnight," Alana mumbles groggily. "That's the pattern so far."

"Except this one is in Rome."

Alana sits up involuntarily. "What?"

"A thirty-six-year-old man showed up at the hospital coughing up blood. He is on life support now, I am told."

"Does he have a connection to Genoa?"

"He is from Genoa. Works in textiles. He came to Rome the day before for a trade show but ended up in the intensive care unit instead."

"Thank God for that," Alana mutters, falling back on her pillow.

"You and I must differ on what constitutes good fortune."

"Monique, it means his infection must have been imported from Genoa and therefore not a case of local spread in Rome."

"Perhaps, Alana, but how many others might he have exposed on the flight there alone?"

"That depends. He only would have been contagious if he were sick and coughing on the flight."

"We had better find out. Perhaps you should go to Rome?"

"Maybe." But Alana isn't ready to leave Genoa. Not when the plague is still raging out of control and they have yet to crack the puzzle of its nongeographical spread. There's at least one major missing piece, and obstinate or not, she's determined to uncover it.

"I didn't quite understand your last email," Olin says. "What is the significance of this rat that they found in the park? The one that appears to be immune to the plague?"

"It's a problem. A big one. It tells us that some rats can be asymptomatic carriers of this medieval strain of the plague. In other words, they won't get sick themselves from the bacteria, so they can house infected fleas on their bodies indefinitely."

"And therefore continue to spread the plague indefinitely?"

"Exactly. It's well documented that a small percentage of rats are immune to modern-day bubonic plague. There's evidence that some people in the Middle Ages were protected by a similar genetic mutation to their immune system. But to have a modern-day carrier of the Black Death? That will make it so much harder to eradicate."

Olin is silent for a few moments. "I have come to agree with you."

"About?"

"What you said earlier regarding the security threat," Olin says. "No question. The recurrence of the medieval plague in Europe poses a potential threat to the NATO alliance."

"Even if no terrorists are involved?"

"Regardless."

"I feel badly for sounding the alarm," Alana admits. "If I hadn't pushed so hard on Yasin Ahmed's disappearance . . ."

"Then three terrorists would still be free to bomb Genoa."

The justification isn't enough for Alana. "But Yasin was innocent. And the backlash against the Muslim community is real, Monique. Someone tried to burn down a mosque. And there are people, politicians even, who are calling for their expulsion."

"Fear makes people irrational. Always. The best way to combat it will be to eradicate the plague."

"I suppose." But Alana doesn't feel particularly reassured.

"What else do we know about the construction site?"

"Aside from the fact that a group of Zanetti's workers conspired to hide the probable first victim of this plague?"

"Yes."

"Not much. But, Monique, that old monastery they demolished . . . it somehow ties this whole outbreak together."

"Then you had best figure out how."

"Good advice. Any other helpful ideas?"

"Alana, I chose you for a reason."

After she hangs up, Alana texts Byron to inform him of the developments. Although it's barely five o'clock, he texts back immediately. He is aware of the case in Rome and asks her to meet him at the Ospedale San Martino.

Two hours later, Alana and Byron cluster together with a group of doctors, nurses, and other public health officials in the ICU. Every room in the unit is occupied by at least one ventilated patient, and some house two. It speaks to the impact of the crisis on the local health-care system that the ICU has had to admit multiple patients to the same room, an extremely unusual occurrence for a First World hospital.

Despite the relative silence, the atmosphere is charged. Alana senses that the staff are nearing the breaking point. No matter how many patients recover or die, more arrive by the hour to overwhelm them. It must feel as unrelenting and unforgiving to the medical staff as it did for the doctors and nurses in West Africa at the peak of the Ebola crisis.

An alarm wails from the room across from Alana. She watches through the window as someone applies electric paddles to the chest of the patient inside. The man's body jerks off the stretcher from the defibrillator's shock. But it doesn't work, and someone else begins to perform CPR. One of the doctors in their group peels away to help, but the others ignore the alarm. Even Alana is numb to the sight of another plague-induced cardiac arrest. *Is this what it has come to?* she thinks.

Byron grabs Alana's elbow and gently pulls her back from the others until they're out of earshot. In the room beside them, she notices another patient connected to a ventilator, but his head is bandaged and his arm is wrapped in a fiberglass cast from his fingers to well above the elbow.

"There are twenty-one new cases of plague in Genoa since yesterday, and it's barely breakfast time. And eight more deaths, bringing the total to thirty." Byron clears his throat. "Including Angelo, the eight-year-old with the antibiotic-resistant infection."

The unwanted image of the critically ill boy—his mother stroking his hair while the father paced frantically at the bedside—pops to mind. She also thinks of Rosa, the little girl with the colorful ribbons in her hair. But there's no time for pity or grief. She shakes off the memories and instead asks, "Still just the one case in Rome, right?"

"So far. I connected with the head of Public Health there. They're tracing all passengers who were on his flight and placing them on home quarantine and antibiotic prophylaxis."

"Good. And what's the status of the ring prophylaxis campaign here in Genoa?"

"On schedule. Over a hundred local public health workers are fanning out this morning across the neighborhoods identified as hot spots. We have enough antibiotics to start ten thousand people on prophylaxis, if necessary."

"It's going to be necessary, Byron."

Their eyes meet. "We could end up breeding a lot more antibiotic resistance," he warns. "Especially if people don't bother to finish their whole course of antibiotics."

"You're preaching to the choir." Alana knows that doctors bear much of the blame for causing worldwide antibiotic resistance through overprescribing, but in mass prophylaxis campaigns like this one, it's inevitable that some patients will fail to complete courses of prescription and thereby spare enough bacteria that could "learn" to acquire resistance.

Her eyes are drawn again to the patient whose arm is casted. "This guy doesn't look like he's suffering from the plague."

"Apparently he was one of the kids who was beaten so badly yesterday."

"Which kids?"

"You didn't hear? Two Turkish teens were attacked outside their dad's convenience store. This one got clubbed in the head with a brick."

"Are they saying the attack was racially motivated?"

"A bunch of local thugs got all fired up after some anti-Muslim rally. He and his brother were just in the wrong place at the wrong time."

"Jesus," Alana mutters, but she stops herself before adding, *it's my fault*.

Thirty-Nine

Letizia Profumo sits beside her husband, Francesco, at the very same table where he proposed to her almost three years earlier. On that memorable day, the quaint family-run restaurant was packed, whereas tonight only one other table is occupied. Though it's the night of their second anniversary, Letizia would still rather be at home. She's exhausted. And her nausea is intractable.

Letizia pushes the *cima ripiena*, the restaurant's signature dish, around on her plate. She has no appetite for the veal specialty that's normally her favorite. The thought of another bite turns her stomach. She never expected to feel this sick or overheated so early in her pregnancy.

Francesco is too busy sopping up the white sauce from his penne dish to notice right away. But as soon as he does, he grips her wrist in his meaty hand. "What is it, Leti?"

"My stomach is not right."

"Are you sick?"

"In a way, I suppose."

His face crumples with concern.

Letizia smiles and then reaches for her handbag. She extracts the used home pregnancy test that reveals the pink plus sign, and flips it over to show him.

"*Amore!*" His eyes light with joy. "You really are?"

"Yes, I really am. Happy anniversary!" She throws her arms around his thick shoulders and hugs him tightly.

Letizia isn't sure if it's the hormones or just happiness, but a thick ball forms in her throat and tears spill down her cheeks. It takes her a few moments to realize that the constriction in her throat is not going away.

Choking, Letizia wriggles free of her husband's grasp. She coughs hard, trying to clear the obstruction. She feels something give, but her hand doesn't reach her mouth in time. The blood and phlegm spray across her husband's plate, as if intending to turn his white sauce into a pink.

Chapter

Forty

Desperate for fresh air, Alana slips out of the hospital without telling Byron or Nico that she's leaving.

The sun is high and a light breeze carries the scent of fresh blooms, but the perfect spring weather does little to quell her dark thoughts. As she walks along the relatively deserted sidewalk, Alana reminds herself that she has no connection to the assault on the Turkish teens. But that doesn't prevent the guilt from gnawing. She forces the thought to the back of her mind and focuses instead on the recent developments in the outbreak: the accelerating death toll, the growing antibiotic resistance, and the discovery of healthy rat carriers. It feels as if events are conspiring to create the perfect epidemiological storm. She wonders if, hundreds of years before, similar bleak factors propelled the original Black Death to the point of critical mass.

She thinks again of Zanetti's construction site, where Yasin died. She is more convinced than ever that the old monastery has to link the current outbreak to the medieval one. *But if so, where could the plague have hidden all those years?*

On a whim, she hails a cab. Ten minutes later, she is dropped off in front of Brother Silvio's dreary apartment building. It takes the diminutive monk a minute or two to answer his door, but he does so with a big smile as he welcomes her inside his cramped apartment. The smell of old books seems even stronger today.

"I hope I'm not disturbing," Alana says.

"Not at all. I am happy for the company. Many believe a monk's life to be one of solitude. But for me, it was the opposite, living as I did among my brothers. I miss the humanity."

She can't help but return the cheerful monk's grin. "Brother Silvio, I was hoping to learn a little more about the monastery."

"*Prego.* What can I tell you?"

"Were there ever any unexplained illnesses among the brothers who lived there?"

"Unexplained?" He grimaces. "I lived at San Giovanni a long, long time. Over forty years. Long enough to see several of the brothers pass."

"Of course. But were there any sudden illnesses? Fevers? Rashes? Bad chest infections? And so on."

He frowns, deep in concentration. "Brother Simone, he died of pneumonia a few years ago. But he was almost as old as me, and he had the cancer. The doctors, they said it was a blessing."

"No one else you can think of?"

He squints at her. "You believe this plague comes from San Giovanni?"

"You have to wonder," she admits. "The first two known victims worked at the construction site. They died of the very same infection that almost wiped out the monastery during the Middle Ages."

Silvio taps his veiny nose but says nothing.

Alana nods toward the bookshelf. "You told me last time that you had historical records of the Black Death in Genoa."

"I do."

"Could you show me?"

He spreads his palms in front of him. "Do you read Latin?"

"No, but I can get them translated if necessary."

"Of course." Silvio ambles over to the bookshelf and thumbs through the volumes on the shelf. He extracts a leather-bound volume and waves it in the air. "This one. Written by the fifteenth-century Genovese historian Ugo Cavotti. He tells how almost half of Genoa died from the plague."

"Fifteenth century? So he would have been born after the time of the Black Death?"

"Yes."

"You mentioned eyewitness accounts?"

Silvio wavers a moment, then he slips the book back into its slot and reaches above him for another volume. It is slimmer and appears even older than the previous one. "This is the diary of a Genovese doctor. Rafael Pasqua."

She reaches for it. "May I?"

He hands it to her gingerly, as if passing her a robin's egg.

She accepts it with both hands. The plain brown cover is scratched and stiff as she turns to the first page, which is written in Latin script.

"It is special, this one," he says. "The other historians like Cavotti wrote about the big details and the tragedies. But Doctor Pasqua, he writes of his own experience. It is very . . . moving."

"Do you think I could borrow it?"

He seems to hesitate again, but then says, "Yes, of course." He takes the volume back from her and carefully replaces it on the shelf, and then hurries over to the laptop on the desk that is almost hidden by a stack of papers.

When Alana views him in surprise, he laughs. "Even we monks have had to accept the modern age. We do not transcribe with quill and parchment anymore, Dr. Vaughn. I have scanned a copy of the text into a PDF document. This, I will email you."

Alana provides her email address and thanks Silvio, then heads downstairs. She flags a passing cab and takes it back to the hospital. Once there, she gowns up and heads straight for Claudio Dora's private room in the isolation ward.

Claudio sits on the side of the bed. Though his cheeks are still hollow, he is no longer wearing any kind of oxygen tubing. His navy robe makes him look more like a guest at a spa than a plague victim.

"You look much better, Claudio," she says. "Less pale."

He motions to her protective garb. "And you still look like a glamorous beekeeper."

"They say it's all the rage in Milan this season."

"Certainly in Genoa, at any rate. It's all I ever see these days."

"How are you, Claudio?"

"Better. I still tire easily, though. This Black Death can really wear a person out."

She musters a smile. "Nico told you?"

"About the Black Death? Yes." Claudio pauses. "Other things, too."

"Like what?"

He looks skyward. "He struggles, our friend Nico. More so since you have arrived."

"He drinks too much, Claudio." She feels slightly sheepish voicing the concern in light of her previous evening, but it has been weighing on her mind.

"True. Even by Italian standards." Claudio's expression turns serious. "He was doing better. Much better. For years. And then Isabella . . . and the affair . . . It's been hard on him."

"That's just an excuse, Claudio."

"Sometimes we need those, though, Alana." He falls silent for a moment, and then exhales heavily. "It's amazing."

"What is?"

"One unlucky construction worker shovels into the wrong pile of dirt, and presto, he drops dead from the plague. If his coworkers had reported Yasin's death instead of trying to cover it up . . ." He shakes his head.

"Then perhaps he would have been the only case instead of the tip of the iceberg."

"Yeah, maybe," she mutters, but her mind is elsewhere. "Unless . . ."

"Unless what?"

"That explains the second cluster."

"What are you talking about, Alana?"

"The other hot spot, in Parco Serra Gropallo. We couldn't figure out how the plague traveled from the old monastery all the way across the city to infect the rats in that park."

"Do rats not travel?"

"Not that far in such a short period of time. Not even a healthy carrier."

"So how does what I said explain anything?"

"The cover-up at the site. We already know they hid Yasin's body. And then later they cleared away all the rats to make it seem as if the plague had never begun there."

"Yes? So?"

"What if they took it a step further? What if they relocated the rats somewhere else to deflect suspicion away from the site?"

"Would someone do such a thing?"

She thinks of the explosives piled on the table in the extremists' apartment. "You'd be amazed what lengths people will go to."

He reaches for the book at his bedside with the grim reaper on the cover and raises it to show her. "During the time of the Black Death—the last go-around, anyway—they went to extreme measures, too."

"So I've heard."

"It's ironic, isn't it?"

"What is?"

He wiggles the book. "That the Black Death has come back home. To Genoa. After all, it was Genovese sailors who brought it to Europe from Asia in the first place."

Alana takes the book from him and studies the cover. "I have my own text on the Black Death in Genoa. An eyewitness account." She tells him of the medieval doctor's diary Silvio emailed her, and then adds, "It's written in Latin, of course. I will have them translate it into English for me in Brussels, but that could take a while." She bites her lip. "Didn't you once brag to me that you knew Latin?"

"I am far too accomplished to brag about anything," he says with a fleeting grin. "But yes, I can read Latin."

"Would you mind . . ."

"Email it to me."

"Are you certain?"

"I am bored out of my mind, Alana. And I've got at least two more days until I will be released from quarantine. My parole cannot come soon enough."

Somehow, he already seems like an old friend. "I'm really glad you beat this thing, Claudio."

"I am relatively pleased myself." His smile falters. "How many others won't?"

She has no answer for him. Instead, she pats his shoulder and says, "Listen, Claudio, I have to run. I've got another meeting to get to."

"Of course, you do, Miss Bond. Probably in an abandoned gondola on some treacherous mountain peak."

"Something like that." She grins as she turns for the door. "See you soon, Claudio. And thanks."

Alana leaves the hospital and heads straight to the biology building of the University of Genoa, where she has arranged to meet Justine. The rodentologist is already garbed in PPE gear and waiting for her in the basement hallway. She passes Alana a matching set.

"So?" Justine views her expectantly. "Got another Tinder date tonight?"

"Byron and I weren't on a date!" Alana snaps, immediately regretting her defensiveness.

"If you say so."

Biting back her annoyance, Alana shakes open the folded gown, raises it over her head, and jabs her hand into the sleeve. Her shoulder pops, and she gasps in pain.

"What's the matter?"

Alana forces her arm outward and feels the instant relief of her shoulder slipping back into place. "An old injury," she says as she carefully slips the rest of the gown on.

"From Afghanistan, right?"

"Yeah, a wall collapsed on me after our hospital was bombed. My arm was trapped. Ripped all the tendons in the rotator cuff. My shoulder has been unstable ever since."

"Ouch. They couldn't fix it, huh?" Justine asks with what sounds like genuine concern.

"I've had enough surgeries."

"If you say so," Justine says. "He's not so bad, you know?"

"Who?"

"Byron. Nothing wrong with him that a couple martinis and maybe a baseball bat couldn't fix. You could do a helluva lot worse." She laughs. "So could he, come to think of it."

Alana only sighs. "What about you, Justine? Are you married?"

"Unfortunately. I got a husband back in Atlanta. A real lab geek, too. He's a royal pain in my ass."

Alana picks up on the affection behind her flippant words. "Any kids?"

"No. Not yet. I like the fieldwork too much."

"Yeah, well, don't wait too long."

Justine eyes her with a knowing smile but says nothing. Instead, she opens the door beside her with a gloved hand.

Alana follows Justine into the sterile-looking lab. In the center of the room stands a high table surrounded by wooden stools. On top of it, a grayish rat lies belly-up on a green towel, surrounded by an array of surgical instruments.

Justine picks up a scalpel and taps the animal's hind leg with its blunt end. "This is the largest of the rats we found in Parco Serra Gropallo. I call him Vin Diesel."

"Why?"

"I name all my animals, alive or dead. And this one kind of reminds me of the action movie actor. You know? A buff alpha-male type. Bet he was a real lady-killer in his day!"

"Oh, God." Alana can't help but chuckle.

Justine flips the scalpel over and reaches for a pair of forceps. "Okay, Vin, let's see what's under the hood!"

She pinches the skin at the base of the rat's abdomen with the forceps' teeth, lifts it up, and incises it with the scalpel. Once she's created a small cut in the lower center, she runs a pair of pointed scissors upward, opening the flaps of skin and fur on either side like unzipping a jacket, exposing the shiny lining of tissue, known as the peritoneum, beneath. She slices through the peritoneum using a similar technique, and the intestines and liver spill out of the opening. Finally, she uses the scissors to chew through the animal's breastbone, revealing the heart and lungs underneath.

Justine says nothing as she leans forward and examines the organs using two slim metal probes, occasionally exploring with her fingertip. Finally, she drops the probe on top of the stack of used tools. "Nada," she says.

"Meaning?"

"No lung involvement. No lymph nodes. No skin buboes. Nothing. This animal was never sick with the plague."

"But you're certain he was infested with the same fleas that carried the plague."

"Positive."

"Perfect." Even though it only confirms what they already suspected, Alana's heart still sinks. "How do you stop an outbreak when the carriers are the only ones immune to it?"

Justine doesn't reply. Instead, she folds the abdominal skin flaps back into place. She motions to the overlying brindle markings and white patches. "A very unusual pattern."

"How so?"

"I've never seen these kinds of markings on a black rat. And look." She flips the rat over and pries opens his mouth, exposing two long yellowish teeth above and below. "You see the size of his upper two incisors relative to his lower ones?"

"They look about the same to me."

"Exactly! Usually a rat's lower incisors are twice as long as his upper ones."

"Wait, Justine, are you suggesting that this rat isn't native to Parco Serra Gropallo?"

"Forget the park. I'm saying I don't know of another black rat *anywhere* that matches this particular sub-breed."

Chapter

Forty-One

Today is the twenty-fourth day of February. I mustered strength enough to go to market today. I confess I went with trepidation. I was most relieved to not encounter any of the flagellants or their devotees. In truth, I met few people along the way, for the market was a site of great desolation. I spotted only three vendors at the market, whereas in the time before the pestilence there would have been scores present. Even the dead and dying were few to be found. I wonder if it is possible that the plague has run out of fresh victims.

I stopped at the stall of a baker to inspect his sparse offerings. I was vexed when he demanded two silver denari in exchange for two loaves of bread, particularly as they were so misshapen and burnt at the crust.

Before the affliction, two pennies would have bought me ten loaves, I said.

Before the affliction, you would have had ten bakers to choose from instead of only me, he replied without apology.

That does not make it right to hold the rest of us to ransom. It is not Christian of you.

Christian? he said with an angry laugh. Why would anyone adhere to Christian scruples when God has so clearly abandoned us to the devil?

So it is more important now than ever to show charity toward our fellow man.

He raised one of the loaves in his filthy hand. Before the affliction, he said, my wife would have shaped them, my oldest son would have baked them to perfection, and my youngest son would have brought them to market. Now there is only me. And I do none of their jobs as well. You worry about two precious denari? I would trade a wheelbarrow of gold florins to have any one of my family back.

I was ashamed for having bartered so hard with the grief-stricken man. I passed him the two coins and expressed my sorrow for his loss.

You had better get accustomed to rising prices, friend, he said. Mark my words. If any of us survive this pestilence, then surely the world order will change.

How so?

There will not be enough tradesmen or laborers left alive for the well-born to continue to value our worth at nothing, as they have always done before.

As I made my way home, I considered the baker's words. Perhaps he was correct. I have heard that six hundred perished in Genova in a single day alone in January. Before the plague's descent, people would complain that the streets of the town were too crowded and the countryside over-farmed. I suspect we will not hear the same complaints muttered again for generations to come, if ever.

Upon my return, I was surprised to see a welcome guest waiting at my door. Don Marco greeted me with even more exuberance than usual. It is true, good doctor, the effusive abbot cried as he patted my shoulders. God has answered my prayers and here you are in fine health.

I would not describe my health as fine, but I am thankful for your prayers. They could only have helped.

I invited Don Marco inside. I served him wine and bread, which he hungrily devoured.

How do the brothers fare? I asked.

Sadly, three more brothers have passed. However, such tragedies are much less frequent than in the days before God blessed the San Giovanni Monastery with those invincible creatures.

I am pleased to hear it.

Don Marco lowered his cup and viewed me with unusual gravity. Doctor Pasqua, the Archbishop told me you drank the blood of our rats, he said. Could this really be so?

It is so, Don Marco. When I was most ill and convinced there was no other possible hope of cure.

And you believe it was the humors from our rats that has saved you?

I cannot say with certainty. However, I would very much like to experiment with the same remedy on others who are afflicted, if you would be willing to provide me with more rats.

Don Marco shook his head. The Archbishop has requested the same of us, but I cannot condone these requests, he said. Besides, as blessed as these creatures are, they carry a risk all of their own.

How so, Don Marco?

Of the three brothers we have lost in the past two weeks, two of them have been the keepers of the rats.

Are you sure it is not coincidence?

They both fell within days of assuming their post, he said, and he viewed me with great puzzlement. How can it be that the same sacred animal that offers protection from the pestilence can also be the agent of its spread, good doctor?

It is a paradox, I agreed.

There has to be meaning behind it, Don Marco said. I have to believe that the Lord blessed San Giovanni with these creatures for more than simply the salvation of us inconsequential brothers.

What more, then?

Don Marco did not answer me directly. We will move the animals somewhere farther from their keepers, he said. However, Doctor Pasqua, I am most reluctant to share these sacred creatures with you or the Archbishop. It cannot be what God has intended for them.

I understand.

In truth, I have practiced medicine for long enough to realize that fate plays a far greater role in the recovery of a patient than any single remedy. However, I cannot help wonder how much the humors from those rats contributed to my survival. I would have liked to experiment on other sufferers. But Don Marco appeared resolute, so I did not persist. Instead, I turned my inquiries to another issue that was heavy on my mind.

Don Marco, you know the Archbishop well, do you not? I asked.

I would not necessarily say so, he said. However, being as old as I am, I have known Archbishop Valente for a very long time. Since he was just a young priest serving under the Archbishop who reigned even before his predecessor. When that grand palace of his was only a glint is his eyes.

The Archbishop is a stern and pious man, I said, choosing my words carefully.

Yes, he is, Don Marco agreed. He is also cunning and ruthlessly ambitious.

The abbot's candor surprised me. I was emboldened to speak more freely. I told Don Marco about the rumor the Archbishop had conveyed to me regarding Jews and their possible involvement in the deliberate spread of this pestilence.

But our Savior was a Jew Himself, Don Marco said.

Indeed. I am not convinced that the Archbishop believes the rumors of the Jews' involvement to be true.

The abbot smiled knowingly. I see, he said. You are also not convinced that the truth would stop the Archbishop from acting upon such rumors?

I was tempted to tell Don Marco of the Archbishop's disdain for the Jews and his resentment over the debt he still owed to one of their own. Instead, I said, In such desperate times I worry how people might respond to such hearsay, especially if it were to come from the lips of someone of authority.

Doctor Pasqua, we are all God's creatures. I abhor cruelty and maltreatment, particularly toward the helpless. However, with all the suffering that envelops us, why are you concerned over the welfare of a few Jews?

I have a colleague, Jacob ben Moses. He is an honorable man with a good family. He is my friend.

Don Marco considered that for a quiet moment. A soft answer turns away wrath, but a harsh word stirs up anger, he quoted from the Book of Proverbs. Yes, I will speak to the Archbishop. And you should pray that he listens.

Forty-Two

Alana has been going nonstop since leaving the university that morning, and yet she's still troubled by the sense of time slipping away. Outbreak responses are always races against the clock, but she has never felt the pressure more acutely. With the confirmed case of plague in Rome, the threat of the epidemic going global is more real to her than ever.

Nico is fifteen minutes late to pick her up, which only compounds her anxiety. His SUV finally rolls to a stop at the curbside shortly after five p.m. As she climbs inside, one glance at Nico makes her forget about his tardiness. His hair is askew and the veins in the pouches beneath his eyes appear as if they could pulsate. He looks as if he hasn't slept in days. "What is it, Nico?"

"The hospital."

"Is it that bad?"

"Worse." He sweeps a hand through his hair. "So many more have died. I had to break the news to a patient's fiancée just now. She wouldn't believe me. Kept saying I was lying. Screaming at me." He exhales. "The wedding would have been tomorrow."

Alana reaches out and touches his arm.

His shrug doesn't hide his pain. "It's not only the new cases. Or even the deaths."

"What else?"

"The hospital, it is under siege. Outside, reporters and cameramen multiply faster than the victims. And inside, I do not know what is worse: the sense of panic or defeat." He swallows. "For every real case, we have twenty hypochondriacs arriving with nothing. And the staff . . ." He thumps the steering wheel in frustration. "Alana, the staff are losing hope."

None of this is news to her, but it's still deflating. She withdraws her hand from his arm. "It's only been one week, Nico. That's all."

"And every day is worse than the previous."

"It's to be expected, Nico. That's how it is with a new outbreak. Always. Until you contain it."

"You're convinced we will?"

She hesitates, perhaps a moment too long. "I think so, yes."

Nico glances at her, his face creased with skepticism. "And you? How was your day?"

"Feels like I spent much of it chasing my own tail. Speaking of tails, I reviewed the rat necropsy with Justine today."

"The rat that was immune to the plague?"

"Yes. Justine says those rats they found at the park have never been seen in Italy."

"So where do they come from?"

Alana shakes her head. "Justine doesn't know. She's never seen them anywhere before."

The traffic comes to a stop. He turns to her with a despondent look. "This outbreak . . ."

"I know. It's not following the usual rules of epidemiology, is it?"

"Everything is wrong about it, Alana. Everything."

They lapse into silence for a few minutes, before Alana finally says, "I accompanied the WHO team door-to-door on their ring prophylaxis outreach this morning. I wanted to get a sense of the logistics."

"How was it?"

"Similar to your experience in the hospital. Dread and distrust everywhere. Some people were too afraid to answer the door, even though we could see they were home. Others had endless questions for us. And the anger and blame. You wouldn't believe it."

"Blame? Who?"

"The politicians, the government, and the WHO for not doing more. Especially us doctors. And a lot of people still blame Islamic extremists— all Muslims—for the outbreak."

"*Idioti.*"

"One of the nurses with us was born here but she's ethnically Indian. A few people slammed the door in her face. One woman screamed at her to 'stop poisoning real Italians!'" Alana sighs. "At this rate, there are going to be other victims of racial violence. Like the Turkish teen who was almost killed."

"You didn't hear?"

"Hear what?"

"The boy, he died this afternoon from the head injury."

The guilt stabs. She looks away and distracts herself by studying the shoreline. Dark, low-hanging clouds now extend to the horizon and threaten rainfall. Even in the haze, the rolling hills and rocky beaches remind her of somewhere else—a vague childhood recollection of a family vacation somewhere along the Gulf Coast during much happier times.

They reach Bogliasco, and Nico turns into Zanetti's driveway. The developer isn't waiting outside this time. Nico has to ring the doorbell twice before Zanetti finally answers. Instead of a dark suit, he wears a bathrobe and pajamas, despite the hour. He makes no excuse for his wife's absence, saying only that "she is gone."

Inside, in the sunken den, Zanetti refills his stemless wineglass from an open bottle of red and pours two more glasses. Alana's stomach flip-flops at the sight of it. Nico shakes his head, too. Zanetti drops onto the couch facing the ocean, while they remain standing.

"We need to know about the construction site, Marcello," Alana says.

"The truth this time!" Nico adds.

"*È finita!*" Zanetti glances to Alana. "There is no more site. It is totally worthless. Just like me!"

"You're not the only one to suffer, Marcello," Alana says. "And it all traces directly back to your site."

Zanetti juts out his lip. "Why do you assume this?"

"Wake up, Marcello!" Nico snaps. "The Black Death! She is gone for over six hundred years and returns to Genoa only weeks after you excavate a monastery that was once overrun by the plague."

Zanetti only shrugs. He looks so much older than he did only days before. "I know nothing about plagues."

"Your man on the site, Paolo, does," Alana says. "He told us how he and Vittoria hid Yasin Ahmed's body. And how he later cleared the rats from the site."

Zanetti eyes them coolly. "Did Paolo tell you I was involved?"

"No," Alana admits.

"So why are you here?" Zanetti asks, lifting the glass to his lips again.

"People are dying," Alana says. "Lots of them. Young people. Children, too. Yesterday there was a case in Rome. It all started at *your* construction site."

"I . . ." Zanetti starts to say, but instead buries his nose in the glass.

Nico sits down beside Zanetti. He lays an arm over the older man's shoulder. "How could you not have known, Marcello? You were there all the time."

Zanetti drains the last drop of wine from his glass and then slowly lowers it. "*Sì, io sapevo,*" he says, his voice cracking.

"How long have you known?" Nico asks.

"I knew nothing about Yasin," Zanetti says quietly. "That was all

Paolo and Vittoria. I swear to you. I only found out after Vittoria became so ill."

"You've lied to us many times," Nico says in an even tone. "Why should we believe you now?"

Zanetti sighs. "We were behind schedule. Over budget. The economy in Genoa, for new construction, she is not so good. Paolo and Vittoria worried that an investigation of any kind into Yasin's death would cause more delays and, perhaps, bankrupt us. They panicked. They decided to bury the body. Paolo told me only minutes before you came to see me the very first time. I had just found out they involved me in a . . . *una trama criminale*."

"A criminal conspiracy," Nico translates.

"I thought I would go to jail, Nico!"

"So you helped cover up the rest of it?" Alana says.

Zanetti nods. "We trapped the rats and cleaned up their mess. We thought it could only help. What was done, was done. What difference did it make?"

"What difference?" Nico yanks his arm free of Zanetti's shoulders. "I just had to tell a woman that her fiancé is dead!"

Zanetti turns to Nico with pleading eyes. "It's not my fault!"

Nico shakes his head. "We could have responded sooner, and better, if we had only known last week where the plague was coming from. Who knows what we might have found at the site if you had not tampered with it? Or how many would still be alive if you hadn't valued your precious investment over their lives!"

"Jail, Nico! I was not thinking right . . ." Marcello pats his chest frantically. "Look at me. I do not sleep. I used to be mayor. I love this city. The people are my people. Like family. I did not mean for any of this . . ."

Alana stares hard at the shaken man. "We need to know everything, Marcello. Do you understand?"

Zanetti swallows. "*Sì*."

"This cover-up," she says. "How deep does it go?"

"What do you mean?"

"We found an infected rat in Parco Serra Gropallo, on the other side of the city. We believe it came from your site. It couldn't have gotten there on its own."

Zanetti shakes his head frantically. "No! No! We did not move any rats. I swear! *Sulla tomba di mia madre!* On my mother's grave!"

"So what did you do with the rats you trapped?"

"We were so very careful. We burned them right there at the site. Every one of them!"

"How many rats?" Alana demands.

"Not many. Ten or twelve. We hired an exterminator. I saw all the rats. They were dead in the traps."

"Did you find other rats before?" Alana asks. "When you first excavated the site?"

Zanetti shakes his head. "No."

"None?"

"I never saw any animals, not even droppings, until the day the Chinese lady came to the site with you." Zanetti stops to rub his face. "Although . . ."

"What, Marcello?" she asks.

"After we tore down the old monastery, Vittoria showed me the crypt below the main floor. It went so much deeper and farther than expected. It had all these narrow . . . how would you say . . . *scanalature.*"

"Passages," Nico says.

"Yes. Some of them, not even the smallest child could fit. And there were bones. Many, many of them. Vittoria, she thought the monks were breeding small animals of some kind."

"As in rats?" Alana glances at Nico. "Why would anyone breed rats?"

Zanetti holds up his hand again in bewilderment.

Alana and Nico continue to interrogate the developer, but he has little more of use to add. As they are leaving, Zanetti stops them at the door. "You will tell the police?" he asks.

"Yes, of course," Nico says flatly.

Zanetti grabs his shoulder. "Everything I told you today is true. All of it. I would never have done it if I thought others would get sick. You must believe me, Nico. Yes?"

Nico glances down at the hand on his arm. "You remind me of Isabella," he says coolly. "Just like with your niece, it's impossible to know where your lies even end."

On the drive back to town, Nico offers to take Alana for "the best fish in all of Genoa." Despite how little she has eaten in the past few days, she's too tense to sit down for a meal, especially an intimate dinner with Nico. They end up instead at the same high-top table in the lobby bar where she sat with Byron the night before. This time, though, she nurses a chamomile tea while Nico drinks red wine.

"Nico, what you said to Marcello about Isabella earlier . . ."

"He knows what I meant." He drains the last of his glass. "So do you."

"Isn't that over?"

"Maybe it is. Or, at least, we will be soon."

"I meant her affair with her boss."

He raises his empty glass to the waiter and jiggles it. "So Isabella says."

"You don't think you can trust her again?"

"Not sure I want to try."

"Your children, they're so young. Don't you owe it to them?"

"People make mistakes," he mutters. "All the time."

"Exactly."

"For example, you and me."

"It wasn't a mistake, Nico. We were young. Ambitious. We chose our careers over our relationship. Remember?"

"Precisely." He swallows. "Too young to know better."

His pained expression softens her resolve. "How could it have ever worked for us?"

"We were in love, Alana. We could have made it work. We should have."
He reaches out and takes her wrist, gently caressing it between his fingers.
The touch has less impact than she expected. "Perhaps we still can?"

The waiter interrupts to sweep up his glass and replace it with a full
one. As soon as he's gone, Alana asks, "And the drinking?"

"For two or three years, I hardly drank," he says with an indifferent
shrug. "Then I found out about Isabella and Roberto . . . Perhaps I was
just a coward. Hiding in the bottle." He searches her eyes. "Then you
came back."

Alana doesn't know how to respond. She struggles to separate her
sympathy for Nico from other emotions.

"I tried to call you," a voice says behind her. "A bunch of times."

Alana jerks her arm free of Nico's grasp. She glances over her shoulder
to see Byron striding for the table. "My phone is in my bag," she says.
"Didn't hear it ring."

Byron glances from Alana to Nico and back. "I didn't mean to interrupt personal time."

"And yet you did," Nico says.

Alana ignores the remark. "What's going on, Byron?"

"Naples."

"Naples?" She frowns. "What about it?"

"There's a new case of plague there."

Alana goes cold. "In a traveler from Genoa? Like the one in Rome?"

Byron shakes his head. "She's a local drug addict who hasn't left Naples in years."

"How, Byron?" she presses.

"No idea. But she has the bubonic, not pneumonic, plague."

"So she must have got it from a fleabite?" Nico says.

"Brilliant deduction," Byron says.

The implication hits Alana like a punch to her stomach. "How the
fuck does an infected rat get from Genoa to Naples?"

Chapter

Forty-Three

Rome? He wonders if he misheard. He turns up the volume on the TV and focuses on the words spoken by the anchorwoman while trying to avoid looking at her. There is no doubt. She is discussing Rome.

"The man suffering from the plague had flown from Genoa to Rome two days prior to his admission to the hospital," the anchorwoman says. "All fellow travelers on the plane have been placed on home quarantine. So far there have been no other reported cases in Rome, but officials across the city are on the highest alert."

So it has begun to propagate itself, just as it was prophesized. He supposes he should be pleased. His mission will be complete only once he has become redundant in God's plan. But as he looks around the bleak motel room—which smells even mustier than the last one—he feels anything but satisfaction.

God has not spoken to him since the morning he arrived at the train station in Naples. At first he assumed he was being punished for defying His command. But it has been days, and his doubt grows by the hour.

He grabs his head in his hands. He cannot help but remember Dr. Lonzo's words: "The voices you hear, they sound as real to you as mine does. But they are not real. They are nothing more than auditory hallucinations. A symptom of your schizoaffective disorder. No different from a runny nose caused by a cold."

Dr. Lonzo is such a kind man, and so easy to talk to. Were he not a doctor, he would have made a wonderful priest. What if Dr. Lonzo has been right all along? Maybe the voices are all attributable to "persecutory delusions," as the doctor called them.

He rocks on the bed, squeezing his temples as hard as he can. *What if I spread all of this death and suffering for nothing? Have I been acting in the service of Satan instead of God?*

He feels the sweat forming under his arms. His throat tightens. The walls seem to encroach on him. The guilt smothers like a cloth to his mouth.

"Hear me!" the voice booms in his head, louder and angrier than ever before. "To doubt my word is to sin!"

He pulls his hands from his head and sits up. As much as he respects Dr. Lonzo, the voice is purer than any sound he has ever heard.

"Will you defy me again?" the voice challenges.

No, Lord. I have been so very weak.

"Go forth!" the voice commands.

Go where, O Lord?

"You will spread my righteous discontent beyond the shores." The voice grows so loud that his head throbs. "All of mankind will soon know my wrath!"

Forty-Four

The awkward silence continues for most of the short flight from Genoa to Naples. Byron has been working on his laptop since take-off and has hardly acknowledged Alana.

She checks her watch. They won't be touching down in Naples until after ten in the morning, as their departure was delayed for almost an hour. Alana and Byron had been partly responsible. Like all passengers departing Genoa, they each had had to answer at the security gate an extensive questionnaire about potential plague exposure. The screeners had even measured their body temperatures, twice, with digital fore-head thermometers. As soon as the authorities had learned of their involvement in managing the epidemic, they whisked them off to a special holding area. Despite their diplomatic credentials, it had taken a phone call to WHO Headquarters before they were freed to board the flight.

"This isn't right, Byron," Alana says.

Byron looks up distractedly from the computer screen. "Which part?"

"Any of it. Sure, we could concoct some wild hypothesis of how the plague accidentally spread from the construction site to a park on the other side of the city."

"Such as?"

"Who knows? A rat hiding in one of the workers' backpacks?"

Byron snorts his doubt as his eyes drift back to the screen.

"But there's no plausible explanation for how an infected rat traveled four hundred miles from Genoa to Naples on its own."

"So we're back to bioterrorism?"

"It's always been a possibility. But this isn't typical of terrorism. No one's even taken credit for it."

"What else could it be?"

"Not sure," she admits, thinking aloud. "Okay, let's assume the plague did recur by accident at the excavation site when the workers there dug into something they shouldn't have. Maybe it had been hiding dormant all these years—in the form of spores or whatever—somewhere in that network of channels below the monastery that Zanetti described."

"But . . ."

She locks eyes with him. "Since those initial cases related to the construction site, the spread of this plague has been anything but natural."

He doesn't argue. "So if it is intentional, do you think Zanetti is involved?"

"In the cover-up, for sure. But . . . no . . . not the spread to Naples. What would he stand to gain by that?"

"Who the hell would gain from the spread of the plague? Aside from maybe terrorists?"

"Not sure." Her ears pop as the plane descends. "If we don't figure it out soon, we might not be able to stop it."

As soon as they land at Naples International, Alana receives a text from Claudio Dora asking her to call, but she doesn't have time to reply. Sergio Fassino is already waiting for them outside the baggage area in a black suit, with his sculpted hair swept back as always.

Alana greets him with a handshake. "How long have you been in Naples?"

"A few hours," he says, as he leads them out of the terminal to a waiting sedan with tinted windows and no official markings. "I am working with the Naples AISI office. Rome has taken charge of the investigation here."

"Meaning you?"

"Yes."

Once in the car, Byron asks, "Have they trapped any rats in the vicinity of where this local case came from?"

Sergio opens his palm. "The Public Health people are searching the neighborhood."

"We need to speak to the patient," Byron says.

"We're going there now," Sergio says.

In less than fifteen minutes, they pull up in front of a modern-looking hospital with a sign that reads OSPEDALE MONALDI. Unlike in Genoa, there is no media circus gathered outside the hospital. *Not yet, anyway*, Alana thinks. But inside, the hallways ripple with the same undercurrent of fear as elsewhere, as if there might be a bomb hidden in the basement.

The medical director, Dr. Debora Orrifini, greets them at the door and hurries them through the hospital. She is a fidgety middle-aged woman who speaks little English. Sergio translates as Orrifini explains that the patient in question is a sixteen-year-old drug user who lives in the "underprivileged" neighborhood of Scampìa.

Ten minutes later, they are gowned and hooded and standing inside the third Italian ICU Alana has visited in under a week. She stares through the glass at yet another plague victim—this one four hundred miles from the others. And since the skeletal girl with purplish hair already has a breathing tube between her vocal cords, she will not be able to answer any of their questions about her exposure. The sense of futility is crushing.

A nurse at the bedside adjusts the intravenous drip into the patient's left arm, but it's the other exposed arm that Alana can't take her eyes off of. The girl's limb is reddened from the neck all the way down to the fingers, which are swollen to the size of sausages. Pus leaks out from multiple ragged wounds across the arm. It appears to have burst open spontaneously from the pressure. At the elbow, a blackish bubo the size of a golf ball stretches her skin. Even if the girl can survive the plague, Alana has serious doubts that her arm can be salvaged.

Orrifini explains that the patient, Lalia Renzi, showed up in the ER the afternoon before. The medical staff originally assumed her infection was related to injecting with dirty needles. Then one of the doctors noticed the darkish bubo. Before Lalia was connected to a ventilator, she denied encountering rats or noticing any fleabites. But, Orrifini adds, Lalia was high from crystal meth and sick with infection, so perhaps she was not the most reliable witness. When the doctors finally tracked down Lalia's mother, they learned that none of the family had been in contact with the girl for over six months.

On their way out of the hospital, they stop to interview a few other staff members who treated Lalia, but they learn nothing of obvious value.

As they step into the warm Naples sunshine, Alana mutters, "That arm . . ."

Byron shakes his head. "How the hell are we possibly going to provide reliable antibiotic prophylaxis to other addicts and residents in a neighborhood like hers?"

"You had better get a WHO team down here ASAP," Alana suggests.

"Why is Naples so much more of a concern than Rome?" Sergio asks.

"Night and day," Alana says. "The Roman case was in a traveler from Genoa who brought the plague with him. Lalia got hers from a fleabite. In other words, through an animal vector."

"What does this mean?"

"Unlike in Rome, the plague must have already found a home in Naples."

Sergio opens his mouth to ask another question, just as a tall woman in a tight skirt and high heels marches up to them. "*Sei un medico?*" she calls out in a much deeper voice than Alana expected.

Sergio shoos her away with his hand.

"What does she want?" Alana asks.

"You are doctors?" the woman asks in English.

"Yes," Alana says. "Is something wrong?"

"Lalia!" the woman cries. "She is like a little sister. They will not let me in. How can they do this? How is she?"

"She is ill," Alana says. "Very ill. She needs surgery."

"What happened?" the woman demands. "She was well yesterday. Her arm, it swelled so fast!"

"You were with her?" Alana asks. "When she came in?"

"I brought her. Now they stop me at the doors. *Figli di puttana!*"

"And you?" Alana asks. "Are you feeling all right?"

"I am good," she says defensively. "Lalia is the sick one."

"Was anyone else with Lalia?" Alana asks.

The woman shakes her head.

"What is your name?" Byron asks.

She thrusts her hands on her hips. "Who needs to know?"

"We want to help," Byron says kindly.

"Juliet," she says, pursing her lips.

"Has Lalia been to Genoa in the past week or two, Juliet?" Alana asks.

"Genoa? Of course not!" Juliet laughs dismissively. Her eyes narrow. "Why would you ask such a thing?"

"Lalia has the plague."

"*Dio mio!*" Juliet backpedals in shock. "How can she have this?"

"That is what we are trying to figure out," Alana says.

Juliet throws up her hands. "It was him, wasn't it?" she cries.

"Who?"

"*Il lunatico religiosa,*" Juliet says.

"A religious lunatic?"

"Yes! In Scampìa, we met him. Lalia and me. He was very nervous. He looked guilty. He was saying some prayer to us. But it sounds more like a curse!"

"*Uno paziente mentale?*" Sergio suggests to Juliet, and then turns to the others. "Many mental patients live in that particularly neighborhood."

"No, no!" The woman shakes her head wildly. "I know *paziente mentale*. He was not one of them. He dressed clean, with short hair."

Sergio speaks rapidly to her. She appears increasingly irritable, and, eventually, she throws her hands up again and snaps in English, "No, there was no sex! We never saw him again."

Juliet spins and stomps off for the hospital door. Sergio hurries after her.

Alana feels her phone vibrate. When she sees the name on the screen, she answers it. "Yes, Claudio?"

"You need to come see me, Alana."

"I'm in Naples."

Claudio laughs. "I thought I'd heard every excuse a woman can make to avoid me."

Alana's thoughts are still on what Juliet just told them. "I should be back in Genoa this evening."

"Good. I will be finished translating the diary by then." His voice is uncharacteristically somber. "But I can tell you already, we need to discuss it."

Forty-Five

Today is the twenty-seventh day of February. As I write by candlelight my hand trembles, not from illness or fever, but rather from the horrors I have witnessed this day. In an age where shock, suffering, and grief have lost most of their currency, I still quake from an abundance of all three.

My day began hopefully enough with the arrival of Gabriella, even earlier than usual. I should have recognized something was amiss since she carried no food with her. However, it was not until I could see her face up close that I appreciated the extent of her distress. In a heartsick voice, she informed me that her father had developed a fever overnight. I donned my cloak and grabbed my instruments before she said another word.

After a long walk, we reached the Jewish quarter off the Via del Campo. Several wooden houses with thatched roofs stood clustered together. There was little to distinguish the simple homes of the Jews from those of their Christian neighbors.

Gabriella led me to the house at the back that belonged to her father. As soon as we entered, we were enveloped by heat from a roaring fire. Jacob lay on his bed on the far side of the room wrapped in a fur blanket. In spite of the warmth, he shook violently. I was reminded of the chills I had endured at the whim of the pestilence, which even the fires of hell could not have warmed.

Stay back, Gabriella! Jacob said in a voice no louder than a croak and yet still heavy with authority.

Gabriella turned to me with pleading eyes. He will not let me tend him, she said.

With good reason, I said, as Jacob began to cough.

His wet bark sounded like bones rattling. And I knew it to be a death sentence as certain as the noose of the hangman around his neck.

Leave us for a minute, please, Gabriella, I said.

Her eyes held mine for a long doubtful time before she turned and left the house.

Jacob held out a hand in warning, but it did not deter my approach. My phlegm is rife with foul blood, he said. You of all people must understand how contagious it makes me.

Have you ever seen a man contract the pestilence twice? I asked.

So few have survived the initial bout, he said. But no, I have not seen the same person twice afflicted.

As I neared, Jacob still turned his head from me and covered his mouth with the edge of the blanket. The color of his skin, what I could see of it, was pallid. He shook as if taken by a fit. When he spoke, his voice trembled as much as his body. Each word was a labor for him to produce.

I am surprised to have survived the night, he said.

Was it only last night that you fell ill?

With fever, yes. The aches overcame me the day before. I had no doubt the plague was taking grip, but I could not bring myself to tell Gabriella.

I could go to Don Marco, I said. To ask if he will provide more of his special rats.

Even if those humors did help you, and I am not convinced they did, it is too late for me.

Maybe so.

I am ashamed to confess it, Jacob said. Cowardly as I am, I was hoping death would claim me in my sleep.

There is no shame in that. I remember feeling the same when I was most afflicted.

Jacob broke into a weak laugh. Look at us two, he said. We have dedicated our lives to a profession of such futility and folly.

You cannot believe this to be so, my friend.

At least the builder has his buildings and the farmer has his crops. But what do we have? We might as well have practiced as soothsayers, for all our lack of usefulness.

Were it not for you, I would be long dead, I reminded him.

I am not so convinced, he said.

And without me, you would not be able to bend your elbow.

It is true. Perhaps, you are right. My Miriam used to always say that I had a penchant for pessimism.

You are a good doctor, Jacob. I am most proud to call you my colleague and my friend.

And I likewise. Now I have a favor to ask of you.

Anything.

You and Gabriella have become friendly in recent days.

She has cared for me as well as any doctor would have.

I am not blind, Rafael. I see how fond you have grown of one another. I hold no grudge or resentment over it. I understand affection does not follow the dictates of society or religion.

It is true, yes, Jacob.

Gabriella has her sister and brother, Rafael, he said. But they have families of their own and she will be still alone in this world. Promise me you will protect her as if she were your own kin.

I will, I said without hesitation. With my life, you have my word.

If she cannot be with one of our faith, it brings me peace to know that at least she will be with a learned doctor and a kind man, he said as he closed his eyes.

We spoke no words for a few minutes. Only the crackles of the fire and the gasps of his labored breathing filled the void. At one point I wondered if Jacob was slipping into the slumber of the dead, but then he stirred again.

Rafael, my family will never abandon me, he said.

Of course not, I reassured him.

You misunderstand me. Every moment I draw breath, I risk exposing them to this curse through my hostile vapors. Gabriella, in particular, will not be deterred.

Are you telling me that you want to die?

I will die. It is a matter of hours, a day at most. Why my frail body still resists when my mind and soul have already accepted my fate, I do not understand.

I reached out to him, but he recoiled. It will not be long now, my friend, I said.

It should be right now, he said as he directed his gaze toward the animal skin at his feet. It would be so easy.

I suddenly understood what he was asking of me. I backed a step away from the bed. No, Jacob, I said. You cannot ask this of me. My religion would not permit it. Neither would yours. It is a sin of the highest order.

How is it a sin to expedite the inevitable? he asked. Is it not our duty to address the suffering of our patients?

Please, Jacob, I said. Do not ask this of me.

If I had the strength and courage to suffocate myself I would do so, he said. I am ready to die. I should be dead. Only you can help me, Rafael. Only you can help protect Gabriella from my affliction.

Before I could reply, the door flew open. Gabriella stood on the threshold. They are here! she cried. The flagellants!

I rushed over to her and took her by the shoulders. Stay inside, by the door, but do not approach your father, I instructed.

I stepped out into the street. A group of Jewish men identifiable by their long beards and robes stood side by side in front of the row of houses, as though to protect them with their bodies. Across from them, at least ten or more flagellants gathered beside a cart that was loaded with hay. They held clubs, whips, and other weapons. Two of them held lit torches even though the sun was high in the sky. I recognized their leader from the previous sighting, when he had worn a crown of thorns and dragged a heavy cross behind him. Today he was encumbered by neither. He stood at the front of the gang, holding a bulky wooden club in one hand and shaking his fist with the other.

Where is David ben Solomon? he cried in a heavy Germanic accent.

The Jews looked fearfully from one to the next, but no one answered.

Where is David ben Solomon? the leader asked again, and the men holding the torches moved forward with deliberate menace.

We will burn down your houses with your vile women and progeny still inside, the leader said. Is that what you prefer?

A corpulent man took a hesitant step forward. I am David ben Solomon, he said weakly.

The leader marched over to ben Solomon without uttering a word. As soon as he reached within arm's length, he swung his club and smashed it across the man's crown. Ben Solomon crumpled to the ground. A younger man rushed to the aid of the older man but he only made it a few steps before he, too, was felled by the same club. The rest of the flagellants surged forward, while the Jews backed up in response.

How many more of you want the same? the leader shouted.

The younger man with the blood pouring from his forehead struggled to rise to his knees. The leader bashed him on the head again, and kept hitting him even after he fell still to the ground.

Three or four of the flagellants carried armfuls of hay and spread them around and over the two fallen men until it was piled to knee-height.

I stood paralyzed by revulsion, unable to look away from the abomination that I could see was imminent.

The men with the torches sauntered around the pile and lit the hay at multiple spots. Murmurs of protest emerged from the mouths of the other Jews, but none of them moved to stop the flagellants.

The fire soon took hold. The younger Jew might well have already been dead, as he lay still in the flames that consumed him. However, ben Solomon screamed out and managed to rise to his feet. His clothes were aflame as he staggered out of the blaze, only to be set upon by the leader, who bashed him over and over with his club.

After ben Solomon collapsed back to the ground, the leader turned to the other Jews and shook his fist again. Let this be your warning! he cried. You heretics, you murderers of our Savior! You have brought this cursed plague upon us believers. You will all be punished for it yet!

Forty-Six

Byron and Alana spend much of the afternoon with Dr. Pietro Polese, Naples's chief public health officer, a heavyset man with a quick laugh and a good command of English. Polese drives them out to the Scampìa suburb where Lalia Renzi fell ill. As they walk, Alana hugs the bag holding her passport and wallet a little tighter to her chest. Even in broad daylight, the neighborhood feels less safe than some of the worst inner cities she has seen after dark.

"Scampìa was built in the sixties and seventies to house Napoli's rapidly growing workforce," Polese says sadly. "High-rises everywhere. Then the economy—especially in manufacturing—slowed. Many of the working people left. In the last twenty years, Scampìa has been overrun by unemployment, addiction, and crime, especially the gangs. It's so very sad. A black eye for all Neapolitans."

As if to prove the point, they have to slow to step over the legs of an addict who is sprawled across the sidewalk. His beard is crusted with food, or possibly dried saliva, and the stink of his body odor follows them for several feet. Half a block farther, a man with wild spiky hair stops digging through a dumpster to look up at them and scream obscenities. Metal fences and padlocked gates line the building fronts, and Alana notices surveillance cameras mounted at regular intervals high up on the walls. Graffiti and litter are everywhere. The faint stench of garbage wafts through the air. The neighborhood strikes Alana as a dream ecosystem for rats. She realizes that trapping any infected animals among the undoubtedly huge endemic rodent population could prove to be a challenge of needle-in-a-haystack proportions.

As they get back into his car, Polese receives a phone call and speaks urgently for a few minutes. After he hangs up, his tone is grim. "They have found a second victim."

"Where?" Byron asks.

"Here in Scampìa," Polese says. "In an alley. A few blocks from where we were just walking."

"Let's go talk to him," Byron says.

"It won't be much of an interview, I am afraid," Polese says. "He is dead."

"How do they know it was the plague?" Alana asks.

"The police found his body about two hours ago. It was assumed he died of a heroin or fentanyl overdose. So many of them do. However, once he arrived at the morgue, the pathologist found buboes in his groin. He took a biopsy. It is *Yersinia*. No question."

"Perfect," Byron groans. "Public Health is going to have to quarantine this whole damn neighborhood. Lock it down."

"How can we quarantine an entire suburb?" Polese asks in disbelief.

"What choice do you have?" Byron says. "With the self-neglect and lack of hygiene we just saw, it's almost as bad as the Middle Ages. Can you imagine how quickly the plague could spread under those conditions? At the very least, everyone in Scampìa is going to require antibiotic prophylaxis."

"*Prego*," Polese says. "This we can try. I will put my entire staff on it."

"We'll send a WHO team to help," Byron says.

Alana doubts those steps will be enough, but with one glance at her despondent colleagues, she decides to keep the thought to herself.

Polese drops them off at the airport. As soon as their flight is airborne, Byron opens his laptop and furiously types more notes. Alana studies him while he works. "What is it, Byron?"

He barely looks away from the screen. "What is what?"

"What's troubling you so much?"

"Everything. You saw and heard what I just did."

She won't let it go. "C'mon, Byron. There's something else, isn't there?"

He shakes his head and begins to type again. After a short while, he slams the laptop lid shut. "I didn't expect this, all right? Is that what you need to hear?"

"Expect what?" she asks quietly.

"Any of it!" He takes a breath and lowers his voice to avoid being over-heard. "I'm good at what I do, Alana. Very good. When they asked me in Geneva to lead the response team, I believed I was the right choice. The best choice. I never doubted that we would contain this outbreak."

Alana can see that he needs to talk, so she just nods.

"Look where we are a week later," he says. "The plague has gripped Genoa and has now spread to Rome and Naples. And you just saw the disaster that is Scampìa. How the hell will we contain *that*?" He looks away for a few moments. When he speaks again, his voice drops to a near-whisper. "The best choice? I am not even convinced I've been a competent one."

"You've done as well as anybody could." She puts a hand on his leg. "You were the one who told me that our primary job is to minimize further spread and death. And that's exactly what you've been doing."

"But you said it yourself. We can't contain this until we figure out where it comes from and how it's spreading."

"Agreed. We'll figure it out. In the meantime, we can only do what we can. One step at a time." She forces a grin. "Epidemiology 101, remember?"

"Yeah, I do." He lays his hand on top of hers and gives it a squeeze. "Thank you."

The unexpected moment of intimacy confuses her. Up until a few days ago, she hadn't even particularly liked Byron. She's still not sure how she feels about him. Flustered, she pulls her hand free.

Byron smiles shyly, avoiding eye contact. "We make a decent team, huh?"

"Especially with Justine here to keep our feet to the fire."

"True." He turns back to his laptop.

Once they touch down in Genoa, Alana's phone buzzes with several text messages, including two from Olin and another one from Claudio.

Byron checks his phone, too, as they leave the airport. "Four more dead in Genoa and several new cases," he says with a shake of his head. "I have to go meet the health minister and my WHO team at City Hall. Do you want to join us?"

"Can't," she says. "I have to go the hospital."

"To meet Nico?" he asks, almost too casually.

"No. Claudio."

"We can debrief later tonight? Maybe even grab a bite, time permitting?"

"Yeah, maybe, time permitting," she says, surprising herself with the answer.

Forty-Seven

Today is the first day of March. So much has happened in the two days since I last took up my quill that I hardly know where to begin. Perhaps I would best start with a confession.

The miscreants who call themselves flagellants did me an unintentional service with their act of barbarism. They spared me from a dilemma with no acceptable resolution. They also permitted me a coward's escape from the final request of a dying friend. By the time I went back inside Jacob's house, he was no more. Gabriella was weeping a few steps from his bedside. I later learned that she was respecting his last words, which were that even in death she should not approach him.

Ignoring the conventions of decency, I embraced her in my arms. She cried against my shoulder for so long that I lost track of time. Not a word was spoken between us, but her pain was as present as a scream. I thought of Camilla and how, in the hours after her death, it felt as though I had been gutted alive.

Gabriella began to wobble on her feet, so I guided her to the chairs by the table and sat her there. She took a few sips from the wineskin I offered. When she spoke, her voice was steady. Tell me what happened with the flagellants, she said.

It is over now, was all I said.

I heard the shrieks, she said. I smelled the smoke that carried the stench of burning flesh. Tell me, Rafael, please.

I told her of the two men who were put to flame and the ominous warning the leader of the flagellants uttered upon their departure.

Gabriella accepted the news with calm and poise. They sought David ben Solomon by name? she asked.

Yes, they did.

It cannot be a coincidence, then.

What cannot be?

You have told me the Archbishop also complained of his debt to ben Solomon, did he not?

He did.

So the Archbishop stood to benefit from his demise?

True, I said. But the Archbishop could not have been the only man to owe money to ben Solomon. After all, he must have been a successful lender, to have enough money to loan for the building of a structure as grand as the Archbishop's palace. Other debtors would surely gain from ben Solomon's death, too.

Perhaps. But who else would hold such sway over the flagellants?

I am not certain, I confessed.

I hope it was the Archbishop who dispatched them to kill ben Solomon.

How can you say this, Gabriella?

Do you not see, Rafael? If the Archbishop was motivated by his debt, then it is now canceled. And he might forget his grievance against the rest of us.

No, I said, as I clutched her hand in mine. The Archbishop will not forget. Neither will those crazed beasts in their bloodied robes. Their leader blamed this pestilence on the Jews. They will come back, Gabriella.

We were interrupted by the arrival of her older brother and sister along with several of their children. Between the death of their father and the terror of the flagellants, the family was in such a heightened state of agitation that it prevented further rational discussion. I used the distraction as opportunity to go see Don Marco.

I arrived at the gates of the San Giovanni Monastery more breathless than ever. It was the most effort I had expended since I had contracted the pestilence, and the climb up the hill seemed thrice as steep as before.

I was surprised to find such a hubbub of activity outside the monastery. Monks and peasants labored alongside each other, as they sawed and nailed planks. On the eastern side of the main church, mounds of dirt ringed a pit that was so deep I had to stand at its edge to see its base. At the bottom, men with spades hacked at the firm ground. A stocky man who looked to be neither peasant nor monk marched about, shouting directions to the other workers.

Don Marco rushed over to shake my hand with great affection. Your recovery must be complete if you are able to make the journey here, he said.

I am much improved. What is happening here, Don Marco?

We are building a sanctuary.

Underground? I asked in confusion.

Not for the brothers. For the harbingers sent to us by God.

You mean the rats?

At this juncture, the burly man shouting the orders joined us. I once constructed noble edifices, churches, and palaces! he exclaimed. Now I build underground crypts for rats.

Don Marco introduced the man as Giuseppe the builder, a master craftsman originally from Milano. Giuseppe was quick to respond that all great builders come from Milano.

What is the intention of this crypt? I asked.

Other churches house the relics of holy saints and apostles, Don Marco said.

These rats are hardly relics.

No, they are far more important, he said with unusual gravity. For they carry the Lord's forgiveness along with His wrath.

How so?

These divine creatures possess the power to heal as well as to damn. God did not dispatch them to San Giovanni as a mere blessing for us insignificant brothers. No, I believe the Lord has entrusted them to us for safekeeping.

Safekeeping? For what reason?

The next time.

I shook my head in bewilderment.

Doctor Pasqua, this pestilence has been sent to punish man for our sins, Don Marco said. As mortals, we are destined to sin and sin again. The Lord has tasked us with preserving his messengers. For the time when atonement is again required.

I know nothing of this superstitious nonsense, Giuseppe interrupted. However, I will build the rats a crypt so secure and impenetrable that they will still be here when Gesù Cristo returns for the Second Coming.

I was tempted to argue, but my issue was far more pressing than the fate of these vermin, whether blessed or cursed. Instead, I asked Don Marco if there was somewhere we could speak in private.

He led me inside the empty Warming House and sat me down at the long table. Don Marco explained that all of the brothers, except those in prayer or in the scriptorium, were participating in the construction. He told me that there were no newly afflicted monks, and they had not buried another man in seven days.

I expressed my genuine happiness over the order's turn of fortune. Then I raised the subject I had come to discuss and asked whether he had had opportunity to speak to the Archbishop.

I have, yes, he said.

I cannot thank you enough, Don Marco, I said with my head deeply bowed.

Your gratitude is not in order, Doctor Pasqua.

Was he not amenable to your intervention?

The Archbishop possesses an iron will. He is not a man to be easily persuaded. Especially by an old monk.

What did he say about the Jews?

I would not describe his opinion of them as high. However, he did not indicate to me that he wished any particular ill will upon them.

Someone has.

How so?

I recounted the earlier happenings in the Jewish quarter. As I spoke, the good humor drained from Don Marco's countenance.

This not the way of God, Don Marco said with great disappointment.

It does, however, appear to be the way of the flagellants.

Are you certain the Archbishop was even aware of the murderous intentions of those savages?

No. It is no more than speculation on my part.

I had best speak to the Archbishop again.

I would not ask it of you a second time, I said. Besides, I doubt you would have any more success than on the first.

Perhaps not.

However, there is one more favor I hope to impose upon you.

What is it, good doctor?

The Jews of Genova, I said. I worry that the flagellants have not finished their business with them. I fear for the safety of my friend's family.

I did not even need to ask. The smile returned to his lips. Of course, my son, he said. Our humble church is a haven to those in need, as all churches are meant to be. Believer or nonbeliever, they are all welcome here at San Giovanni.

Forty-Eight

Alana finds Claudio in his hospital room, standing at the bedside and packing a knapsack. He still wears the same blue robe, but he's no longer connected to any intravenous lines.

"Are you taking a trip?" Alana asks.

"Yes, thank God." Claudio grins. "I have been 'sprung.' Is that the right term?"

"If you happen to be a character in a fifties gangster film."

"I'd rather be trapped in one of those than stay in this room for another minute." He laughs. "My quarantine period is over as of this evening."

"And you're fully recovered?"

"Like a new man." He flashes a thumbs-up sign. "Like someone who has been given a second chance . . . to ruin his life all over again. What do you think?" He winks. "Want to get married?"

Alana laughs, her mood improved by his presence. "So what's so urgent about the diary?"

"It's incredible. Truly incredible." Claudio pulls his tablet computer out of the bag and motions to the bed. "Come. Sit with me."

They sit side by side as Claudio scrolls down a screen filled with bullet points. "I have read it twice," he says. "I didn't have time to type out a proper translation, but I have made notes. Will they suffice for now?"

"Of course."

"This doctor, Rafael Pasqua, he was such a wise and thoughtful man." Claudio sounds reverential. "And brave! You have no idea the hell he went through."

"Tell me."

He consults his notes. "Pasqua was a local barber-surgeon. He was thirty-six years old when the plague struck Genoa in the winter of 1348. He started his diary on the very day he buried his wife. He never expected to survive the plague. Pasqua recorded his observations only for the sake of science and history."

"That is some dedication."

"You have no idea, truly," Claudio says. "It's bad enough for us now, but we can't imagine what it would have been like in Pasqua's time. So much superstition and ignorance! They didn't have a clue what caused the plague. Some blamed astrology, others the apocalypse. Even Pasqua—who was very enlightened for his day—thought it came from some kind of miasma or evil vapors." Claudio pauses to check his notes again. "Every day, Pasqua would see one victim after another in his surgery. He lanced buboes, treated wounds, and did what little he could for the other symptoms. And the scale of this epidemic! Pasqua writes that on one day alone, more than six hundred people died in Genoa. I looked it up. The population of the whole city was little more than a hundred thousand at the time. They ran out of places to bury the dead. And gravediggers to do the work. Eventually they simply dumped the bodies in the harbor."

"This is fascinating, Claudio, truly," Alana says, beginning to overheat under her hood. "But how does any of it apply to our situation?"

"Indulge me," he says with a mischievous grin. "I've been alone in here with my thoughts for too long."

She nods. "Go on."

"People weren't the only victims of this epidemic. Soon the whole social order began to decay. Without laborers and farmers, the economy fell apart. Crime became rampant. Relatives abandoned loved ones. Eventually people turned on each other, looking for scapegoats."

"They usually do, in bad times." She thinks again of the slain Turkish teen. "Even today."

"Pasqua himself, he was deeply involved."

"In the scapegoating?"

"No, the contrary," Claudio says. "Inevitably, Pasqua contracted the plague. He was nursed to health by another doctor and his family. A Jewish family. In those days, the Church was everything. And not very tolerant of outsiders, especially Jews."

"I can imagine."

"But for Pasqua it was personal. You see, he fell in love with his colleague's daughter." Claudio describes Pasqua's relationship with the Jewish family, and how he struggled to protect them from deadly persecution. He pauses to look over his notes and then nods to himself. "There is one other big coincidence between his experience and ours."

"What's that?"

"Pasqua spent a lot of time at the San Giovanni Monastery."

"The monastery again." Alana shakes her head in surprise. "Why? What was he doing there?"

"At first he went to tend to the ill brothers."

"What do you mean, at first?" she asks, sensing significance. "What changed?"

"This part is . . . what's the expression . . . mind-blowing! When Pasqua fell sick himself, he went to San Giovanni to find antiserum."

"Antiserum? In the 1300s?"

"It seems the clever monks had noticed that some of the rats inside the monastery had stopped dying. As if they were immune to the plague."

"*Immune?*" The word runs through Alana as viscerally as an electric shock.

"Yes," he says. "The monks, they viewed these rats as a sign from God. They worshipped them. Like the relics of some long-dead saint. The abbot, Don Marco, even had them build a pen and assigned a monk to watch over the rats. But the first few rat keepers—or the *Custodi di ratti*, as they referred to them—died from infection. You see, these rats were still contagious. So the monks built a special place to house them safely away from contact with the rest of the brothers."

"The monks deliberately preserved infected rats?"

"Yes."

"Why would they do that?"

"Two reasons. One, despite the deaths, Don Marco believed the presence of the rats offered the brothers a kind of paradoxical protection from the plague itself."

Alana sits up straighter. "And the other reason?"

"To preserve the rats for the next time God needed to punish man for his sins. Or as Don Marco put it . . ." Claudio uses a finger to scroll down his laptop's screen. "'For when atonement is again required.'"

"*Atonement?* Jesus!" The hairs on her neck bristle. "These monks were storing the plague like an incubator in a lab? So it could be released again?"

"Yes, but they also might've been housing the cure," Claudio points out. "When Pasqua became sick, he reasoned that if he drank the blood of these rats, he might get better, too. It apparently worked for him. You see? A primitive form of antiserum, no?"

Alana's heart leaps in her throat. She's not thinking of antiserum or curses. "Where did the monks build this rat sanctuary?"

"Under the monastery."

"Like a crypt?"

"Precisely! It was sealed off. The brothers installed a hole to feed the rats, but the crypt went deep enough to safely isolate them from the rest of the monastery. Thus protecting the animals and the monks."

"And also preserving the plague," she mutters. "Oh, my God!"

"What is it, Alana?"

"Don't you see, Claudio? An enclosed ecosystem for rats who carried the plague but were immune to it themselves."

"You do not think . . ."

"Yes. Yes, I do. The healthy rat Justine found was also carrying plague. She said it was different from any known breed. What if it was a direct descendant of those rats the monks buried under their church over six hundred years ago?" Her voice goes hoarse. "Claudio, what if the time for atonement is now?"

Alana bids a hasty goodbye to Claudio and hurries out of the isolation ward. Their discussion about the medieval monks reminds her of Juliet's comment about the well-groomed "religious lunatic" that she and Lalia had encountered in Scampìa. As soon as she clears the decontamination station, she extracts her cell phone and dials Sergio. "The surveillance cameras, Sergio," she says by way of greeting. "The ones mounted on the walls all over Scampìa."

"What about them?"

"Can you get your hands on the footage?"

"All of it?"

"If need be, yes."

"Even if we could, Alana," he says, exasperation creeping into his tone, "the number of agents and hours it would take to go through all of that video . . ."

"So narrow it down. Can you check the footage on the day Juliet and her friend Lalia ran into that 'religious lunatic' she told us about? Juliet should be able to give you the approximate time and location."

"Perhaps," he says. "But Juliet's story changes by the hour. The drugs . . ."

"I know, Sergio. Maybe it's not related, but it can't hurt to track down an image of this guy's face. Figure out who he is and what he was doing there."

Sergio is silent for a moment. "I will see what I can find out."

After she hangs up, she tries Byron's mobile number but only gets his voice mail again. She assumes he's still tied up at City Hall.

Just as she reaches the automatic sliding door exit, Nico calls to her from behind. He jogs over and greets her with a kiss on both cheeks. His stubbled chin grazes her face. But his proximity and familiar scent have little of the previous impact.

"You disappeared, Alana," he says.

She eases out of his embrace. "I was in Naples most of the day, Nico."

"Yes, the new case. Tell me."

"Cases." She summarizes what she knows of the two new victims in Naples. "But there's a breakthrough here in Genoa. It could be even more relevant."

He frowns. "What is it?"

"The diary Claudio translated."

"How is that related?"

Alana tells him about the medieval rats that were immune to the plague and how the monks sequestered them under the monastery in a subterranean sanctuary.

Nico's eyes go wide. "Could the rats survive down for centuries?"

"That's what I intend to find out. I'm on my way to see Justine now."

"I will come with you."

Outside, they weave through the reporters, ignoring the questions shouted at them. They turn a corner and step inside the little café behind the hospital. Justine is already seated at a table by the window with a teacup in hand. She giggles as they sit down on either side of her. "Damn it, girl! Guessing which date you're going to show up with is harder than predicting the next Super Bowl champ."

Alana ignores the barb. "We need to talk about the rats," she says.

"Yes, we do! We discovered something else really interesting today. You know how I told you that Vin Diesel could never have—"

Nico's face scrunches. "Vin Diesel?"

"The big alpha male rat from the park that I dissected," Justine says as if it should have been self-evident. "Anyway, we know Vin was immune to the plague, right?"

"Yes," Alana says.

"So I thought the only way he could be carrying *Yersinia* would be through the infected fleas on his back."

"It's not?"

"No, ma'am!" Justine taps her hand above her eyebrow in mock salute. "His entire skin was colonized with the bacteria. Millions of them. You know, the way human skin is colonized with all those staph and strep bacteria that live on us but hardly ever cause infection?"

"So you're saying this rat was a true carrier of the plague?" Alana says. "With or without fleas onboard."

"Exactamundo." Justine nods proudly. "So, what did you want to ask me about the rats?"

Alana relays what she just learned from Claudio about the rats and the crypt.

"Holy shit!" Justine cries. "You think Vin Diesel might have been a direct descendant of those medieval plague rats?"

"Is that even possible?" Nico asks. "A colony of rats living under the monastery for all those centuries?"

"It sure would explain a ton!" Justine says. "Like why he had such different markings and teeth from contemporary Genoese rats."

"And also why he was immune to the plague," Alana says.

"But how could rats survive trapped down there for so long?" Nico asks.

"Find me another mammal that comes even close to being as resilient as the rat!" Justine looks from Nico to Alana. "Have either of you ever heard of the *Heterocephalus glaber*? AKA, the naked mole rat."

Alana and Nico share a blank stare.

"Not that easy on the eye, your basic naked mole rat," Justine says. "Not a stitch of hair. Bald as the real Vin Diesel. And with two sausage teeth that would embarrass even a British dentist. *Ugly!* But these suckers live under the ground twenty-four-seven in Africa. Some of them don't surface once in their whole lives. And they don't live in any cushy underground gangsta crib. Nah, they get by in the tight burrows that they dig themselves that are up to ten feet below the ground."

"How do they survive?" Nico asks.

"They've got freakishly good adaptive skills. They don't need light. And they can function at a fraction of the oxygen level other mammals do. They get most of their food from eating the roots of vegetables while still in the dirt. And they have this awesome social structure where each nest has one queen rat who calls all the shots. How great a gig would that be? She doesn't even have to see how ugly all the males are that she mates with. Kind of like Tinder for the blind." Justine laughs. "And while most mice or rats live one to four years, even in captivity, naked mole rats can live up to thirty."

Nico holds up a palm. "But surely, Justine, these creatures evolved over millions of years, not a few hundred?"

"My point is, McDreamy, this is what rats do. Adapt. They have this uncanny ability to maintain a steady-state population, even through cannibalism and infertility when need be. So, if you're asking me whether a colony of rats who were living in a protected underground enclosure could survive hundreds of years down there? Then I'd say: hell, yeah!"

Alana hops up from the table. "Thanks, Justine."

"Where are you off to now?" Justine grins. "Not *another* date?"

"Sort of." Alana grins. "With a monk."

Nico follows her out of the café and hails a cab for them. Alana shows the driver the address in the Sestri Ponente District on her cell phone.

"You are convinced?" Nico asks her.

"Of what?"

"That our outbreak comes from these rats the monks buried back centuries ago?"

"Not convinced, no, but leaning that way."

"It does not explain Naples," he points out.

"True. It doesn't even explain Parco Serra Gropallo or much of the rest of the spread through Genoa. That required human intervention." She bites her lip. "So it seems to me the next step is figuring out who else knew about the crypt and these rats."

"Aside from Brother Silvio?"

"Yes." Although at this point she's not willing to discount anyone or anything.

After a quiet few moments, Nico reaches out and lays a hand on her forearm. "I meant what I said last night, Alana."

"Which part?"

"All of it," he says, his stare painfully intense.

There was a time when those same words might have melted her, but now they only evoke a pang of melancholy—the happy memory of a time that can never be recaptured. "Nico, what we had was incredibly special. But us? Now? That's impossible."

"How can you be sure?"

"Your home is here. If not with your wife, then, of course, still with your kids. Mine?" She shakes her head. "Mine is elsewhere."

Nico releases her arm and flashes her a smile tinged with wounded bravado. "I suppose it's for the best." He lets go of her wrist. "I wouldn't survive a week in Brussels, anyway. It's so boring, it makes Genoa seem like Las Vegas."

The cab drops them off at Brother Silvio's building. They mount the steps to his apartment. The black-robed monk answers the door with as welcoming a smile as ever. Alana introduces Nico, and Silvio ushers them into his apartment. He again clears the papers from the chairs and insists that his guests take a seat, but he remains on his feet. "How can I be of assistance?"

"Rafael Pasqua," Alana says.

Silvio's eyes light with recognition. "*Prego!* The other good doctor. You read the diary, yes?"

"Not in full yet," Alana says. "But a friend of mine did. He described some of the highlights. For example, the crypt under the monastery."

Silvio tilts his head in curiosity. "Yes? What about it?"

"The monks built it to enshrine the rats."

"They did."

"But also to keep them alive for future generations," she says. "In case God wanted them to be released again."

"Well, of course no one could ever reach the crypt once it was built," Silvio explains. "We did not speak of rats anymore. They were only . . . symbolic. But I always believed there to be a kind of divine presence below us."

"Is that why you warned Emilio about tampering with the hallowed ground?" Alana asks.

Silvio nods.

"And what about the rat keeper? Was that a role that had been passed down through the years?"

"No. Not since the Middle Ages," Silvio scoffs. "Most of the brothers did not even know of the rats. Or what the . . . *scivolo* . . . was built for—"

"The *scivolo*?" Nico interjects. "Like a slide?"

"Yes, like when you throw the dirty clothes down the hole?" Silvio fumbles for the English translation. "Except this one is for garbage."

"A chute?" Alana offers.

"*Sì*," Silvio says. "Made of stone. Don Marco had the brothers install it. The only connection to the crypt. But not so long that the rats could ever reach it from below. We would throw food that is rotting down the *scivolo*. It was a tradition."

Alana jerks her head back in surprise. "So, it's true! The brothers have continued to feed those rats for over six hundred years!"

Silvio grimaces. "What rats?"

"The ones who brought the Black Death back to Genoa."

"No! They would have died off long ago."

"They didn't," Alana says. "Our team trapped one of them."

"*Non è possibile.*" Silvio shakes his head adamantly.

"The plague, Brother Silvio. Don't you see? It returned as soon as they tore down your monastery. As soon as those rats were freed."

He goes quiet for a long moment. "Could it be? The plague returned from San Giovanni? From our very monastery?"

"Yes," Alana says. "And we think someone deliberately released those rats."

"Why would anyone do this?"

"We can't answer that, not yet. But who else at the monastery would have known about the rats?"

Silvio only shakes his head.

"Then who else read Pasqua's diary?" Alana asks.

"I . . . I cannot say," he says, avoiding her gaze. "Maybe ask Don Arturo. He knows such things better than I do."

Chapter

Forty-Nine

He feels so exposed sitting at the far terminal in the Internet café. His fingers tremble on the keyboard. To calm his breathing, he has to remind himself that the seats beside him are unoccupied and that no one seems to be paying any attention to him. He is accustomed to going unnoticed. Brother Silvio used to describe it as God's gift to him. "You must view it as more of a blessing than a curse, my boy. Some people thrive in the shadows."

Just like my rats, he thinks. The more time he spends with the creatures, the more he can relate to them. They shun attention, too. And they understand their place in this world.

He glances over either shoulder before he taps in the password to his email server. There is only one new message in his in-box. Anxious as he is to read it, he pauses to take another discreet scan of the room. Satisfied no one is watching, he taps the mouse and the message appears.

"You must always abide His word," the email instructs. "When He tells you to go forth, He means for you to carry His sacred creatures eastward. To Asia. I am convinced of it. You must release them in the Far East, the squalor of civilization, where they do not heed His word." The sender then quotes a familiar verse from the Book of Psalms: "Let death steal over them. Let them go down to Sheol alive, for evil is in their dwelling place and in their heart."

He swallows hard, trying to steel his courage. He has never before left Italy, let alone the Continent. "New ships depart for the Far East every day," the message goes on to say. "If I were the chosen one, I would go to the harbor and find a working ship. Perhaps a freighter? They are always in need of new crew. Is your passport in order?" The email ends, as they all do, with the same phrase, "You will be forever blessed."

He replies with three words—"passport in order"—and then deletes the messages. As soon as the screen confirms that he has been logged out of the email server, he rises to his feet and heads for the door. He keeps his eyes straight ahead but makes no attempt to cover his face. After all, no one remembers seeing the invisible.

As he steps into the warm Neapolitan air, his resolve is stronger than ever. He does not doubt that Dr. Lonzo is a good man and an able psychiatrist. But in this case, he must be wrong. If only he could tell him: *Do you not see, Dr. Lonzo? It is not only God who is instructing me.*

Fifty

The two men in white biohazard suits wheel the sealed black body bag out of the ICU room. The gurney almost grazes Alana's gown as they pass her. The twenty-nine-year-old on it died only minutes earlier, following another failed resuscitation that ended in as much blood spatter as any Alana had witnessed. The woman had apparently been out celebrating her second anniversary with her husband only the day before. Now she represented Genoa's thirty-ninth plague-related victim in the one week since Vittoria's death. Fortieth, if you were to include her fetus, Alana thinks miserably.

She feels an elbow brush up against hers and glances over to see Byron at her side. "I want to show you something," he says, grinning.

"What's there possibly to smile about, Byron?"

"Couple of things," he says, as he guides her toward another room in the ICU. "First of all, there have only been eight plague-related deaths today."

"And that makes you smile?"

"There were eleven yesterday."

Alana sees his point. In epidemiological terms, any decrease in the number of daily deaths or new victims in the acute phase of an outbreak represents a potential indicator of containment. But she's not ready to concede. "The day's not over."

"Will be in fifteen minutes." He nods to the digital clock above them that reads almost midnight.

"And you're not even counting new cases in Naples," she points out. "At least six more, with two deaths already."

"We can only manage this outbreak city by city," he says, undeterred. "If our model works here, then we can replicate it elsewhere."

Alana isn't buying it. "What are you not telling me, Byron?"

He steers her to another one of the rooms and motions to the patient who lies on the stretcher on the other side of the glass. With all the lines running into him, it takes Alana a moment to notice that he isn't connected to a ventilator. Only a simple oxygen mask covers his face.

"This is Pietro Molaro," Byron announces. "Pietro is the fifth patient to contract antibiotic-resistant plague. The other four are dead. Yesterday, it seemed certain Pietro was about to join them."

Alana watches the patient reposition himself on the bed without help. "You mean he's improving?"

Byron's smile brightens.

"How?"

"Thanks to Claudio Dora."

"Claudio? What does he have to do with this? He only left hospital today."

"Yes, but the lab managed to extract the antibodies from the blood of a few survivors, including Claudio. Specifically, the immune globulins active against *Yersinia*. From that, they were able to genetically engineer enough antiserum to treat Pietro."

"And it worked?" She waves the question away. "Well, obviously it did. But I thought it was going to take weeks or months to produce antiserum."

"Originally, so did we. But the lab used an experimental technique. They cloned the DNA for the specific antibodies, then expressed them in a non-secreting myeloma cell line and purified the immune globulin from the supernatant."

To most ears, the explanation would have sounded like gobbledygook, but Alana listens with growing excitement. She understands it means that scientists were able to splice the genetic information from Claudio's antibodies into the genes of cancer cells and then use those rapidly multiplying malignant cells to produce enough of the protective antibodies to treat another patient.

"How much antiserum did they produce?" she asks.

Byron's smile dims. "Enough for just one patient. But they're ramping up to make more. With any luck, they'll be able to produce hundreds of doses in the next couple of weeks."

"Hundreds? That's good. Very good. But it's not a silver bullet. Not yet, at least. We're going to need many more doses, and sooner than a couple weeks. By then the dam might've already burst."

"True."

"Meanwhile the plague continues to spiral out of control in Naples. And we still don't have a goddamn clue as to how it actually got there."

"Agreed."

She throws up her hands. "We haven't even really tied those mutant rats—and the medieval monastery that hid them for all these years—back to this outbreak."

Byron points to the patient, who sits himself up in the bed with ease. "Granted, Pietro over there represents a small victory. But it's a significant one. Maybe our first since this all started. He's worth celebrating, Alana."

An hour later, they end up at an all-night restaurant, an ancient diner in the old town with low ceilings and red-checkered tablecloths. The only other guests are two students who each sit at separate tables with laptops open and earbuds in.

The penne marinara is so delicious that Alana can't help but wolf it down. Byron watches her in amusement. "Are you ending a hunger strike tonight?"

"Practically," she says unapologetically as she swallows the last bite. "I might be the first person ever to spend a week in Italy and actually lose weight."

Byron lifts his beer bottle to his lips without really sipping it. "You look . . . um . . . amazing tonight . . . all things considered."

"All things considered?" She grabs her chest, feigning insult.

"Dana used to tell me I was never much good at that."

"What? Compliments?"

"Small talk. What I'm trying to say is that after a week of nonstop outbreak-chasing and practically no sleep, you look really—"

He stops when she breaks into a laugh.

"Dammit! I'm useless at this."

"Beyond useless," she says. "Do you still think about her much?"

"Dana? Less than I used to, but I still do. After she left, I hung on to the belief that we were going to somehow work it out. We always made so much sense together. To me, anyway."

"How so?"

"Similar interests, same career, matching life goals—at least, I thought so." His gaze falls to the tablecloth. "I guess we were just one of those couples who looked a lot better on paper than in real life."

"It's easy to get fooled, huh?"

He nods. "Is that what happened with Nico?"

"Nico and I never made much sense on paper."

"Really?" His expression is skeptical. "A couple of idealistic infectious diseases doctors who both worked for the WHO . . ."

"One of whom has an alcohol problem and two young children?" she counters. "He has a huge heart, though. And we both shared real passion for the work. That first mission—the cholera outbreak in Angola—was all-consuming. We were young. Naïve, too. You know what it's like in the field."

He studies the label on his bottle. "Yup. I do."

"I guess we confused those emotions for something more."

"Or maybe you were just in love?"

"Yeah, maybe. No, you're right. We were. But if there's one thing this past week has reinforced for me, it's that Nico and I never would have had a future together."

"Can you really know for sure without—"

"What the hell, Byron? You asked me to dinner just to sell me on an ex?"

Byron laughs. "Mea culpa."

Alana bites her lip. "Don't start in on the Latin now, charmer! I will lose it."

The server approaches with a bottle of house wine to top up her glass, but Alana waves him off. She rises from the table, pulling Byron up by the hand with her. "It's crazy late. Pay the bill and take me home."

As soon as they step outside into the cool night air, Alana spins and leans into him without another thought. Her lips find his and she kisses him. She feels his arms wrap tighter around her. Warmth runs from her chest to her thighs. She kisses him more urgently, sliding her tongue between his teeth, expressing a need she didn't even realize she had.

As soon as the cab pulls up to the curb, Byron fumbles for the door without releasing her from his grip. They maneuver themselves into the backseat. As the taxi pull away, she climbs onto his lap and kisses him ferociously. His warm breath excites her. He squeezes her breast. She grinds her hips into his. His hardness presses between her legs, and it arouses her more. She strokes him through his pants.

Just as the cab pulls up to her hotel, her phone dings with multiple new text notifications. She's tempted to ignore them, but she recognizes the unique chime for the one she has assigned to Sergio. Still straddling Byron, she digs the phone of out of her purse.

A grainy photo pops up on the screen. It's a close-up of a clean-shaven, nondescript young man. His face is tilted but his features are clear, particularly the smallish eyes and square jaw. She scrolls down to see a second, wider-angle photo of the same man taken from above, undoubtedly by a surveillance camera. He's standing beside two women. Even though the taller woman is only caught in profile, Alana recognizes her immediately for the transgendered Juliet.

Below the photos, Sergio has written: "The religious lunatic?"

Fifty-One

Today is the third day of March. I write with a heavy heart and a conscience laden with guilt, for yesterday I committed more sins in a single day than a virtuous man might in a lifetime.

I was awoken at dawn by a pounding at my door. I opened it to find two soldiers at the threshold. Before I could say a word, the bearded of the two grabbed hold of my arm. The other, stouter one announced that, by order of the Archbishop, I was to accompany them. I had to plead with them for time enough to gather my cloak and hat.

The soldiers marched me on foot up the hill. Inside the palace, the stout soldier shepherded me roughly down a narrow dark hallway in the opposite direction from the Archbishop's quarters. I assumed he was leading me to the dungeon or the stockade, and my breathing quickened with trepidation. However, the chamber he shoved me inside was no prison. The room bore no windows and was lit only by torchlight, but I recognized it for an infirmary of sorts, with four straw mattresses spread out across the stone floor. Each was occupied.

The stout soldier would not cross the entryway, but he motioned to the man on the farthest of the mattresses near to the wall. Him! he commanded.

The wet rattles emanating from the chests of the men inside confirmed they had been afflicted by plague. I did not recognize the first person I passed, nor the second, although I could tell from his vacant countenance and still chest that he had already died. However, I had met the third man before. He was one of the two priests who had previously escorted me to see the Archbishop. He looked up at me with a face drenched in sweat and eyes large with fear, but he said nothing as I continued past.

When I reached the far mattress, I did not immediately recognize the old man lying at my feet. His complexion was gray and he shook like a leaf in a storm, despite the furs bundled about him. It was not until he opened his eyes that I realized I was gazing down upon the Archbishop's esteemed physician, Doctor Volaro.

I did not call for you, Volaro said in a voice that trembled as violently as the rest of him.

When did you fall ill? I asked as I knelt beside him.

Send for a real physician, he commanded in a weak voice. I want none of the primitive ways of you barbers.

I am doubtful any doctor, physician or surgeon, will be of service to you, I said truthfully.

And yet you can?

No, sir, I said in the kindest voice I could summon. Your condition is too advanced for intervention.

Your opinion is not worthy of my consideration, Volaro said as he struggled to roll over and show his back to me.

The soldier beckoned me over to the doorway. He led me down the corridor to the Archbishop's chamber. We had to wait at the door for several moments before being granted access. I stepped into a room that was as warm as a fever. The fire inside raged like a funeral pyre. The Archbishop sat as before on his raised chair and fidgeted with the ring on his finger as I approached. As I neared, he shook the same finger at me. You have at-tended Doctor Volaro and my priests? he asked.

I have, Your Grace, I said, bowing before him. They appear to all suffer from the chest plague. One of them has already died.

Yes, he said. Despite our best precautions, the plague has still invaded this house of God.

It appears to be inescapable, Your Grace.

And yet you have escaped it, Doctor Pasqua.

I did not escape it, Your Grace. However, I was fortunate to survive it.

By consuming the blood of rats. Is that not so?

I cannot say, Your Grace.

You will share with me the remedy that has offered you such protec-tion! he shouted.

It was not so much the Archbishop's sudden show of temper, but the demand itself, that made my neck hairs bristle. I thought of Don Marco's offer to provide sanctuary for Gabriella and her family. The idea of the Archbishop's men harvesting rats at the monastery troubled me. What if they were to happen upon the Jews?

Your Grace, I said. It is my humble opinion that no remedy will be of assistance to the good doctor or the still-living priest confined with him.

It is far too late for them, he said with a dismissive wave. They are merely biding time until their imminent heavenly summons.

For whom do you need the remedy?

Me!

Are you unwell, Your Grace?

No, not yet. However, now that the pestilence has crept into my home, no one is safe. I wish to be prepared.

I was overcome with the urge to protect Gabriella's only possible route of escape. Therefore, I did what I never would have imagined possible. I lied to the highest representative of God in all of Genova. Your Grace, I said. The blood of rats has no curative power whatsoever.

The Archbishop leaned forward and narrowed his gaze. You told me the contrary in this very room.

I did, Your Grace, I said. At the time, I believed it to be so. But, alas, every patient I have since treated with the humors of those rats has died an agonizing death.

Except for you, he said with an accusatory glare.

No. I was not spared by the rat humors. There is an alternate remedy.

And why have you not disclosed this to me sooner?

I was not convinced of its benefit until recently, I said, inventing the words as I spoke them. To be frank, you were most clear about your skepticism and your suspicion of sorcery. I feared that you might view this remedy as such.

What remedy?

I will tell you, Your Grace. However, it is an unseemly concoction, I am afraid.

These times do not allow for sensitive ears.

The paste is made from ground daffodils, crocus, and peonies, I said the names of the first flowers that came to mind. I mix in several spices along with the blood of a healthy sheep and the urine of a cow. And forgive me, Your Grace, but there is one more ingredient that is most indelicate.

Tell me!

To this mixture, I add the semen of a male goat. It is an essential element.

Disgusting. And yet, you are convinced of the effectiveness?

The medicine can work miracles, I said. The proof is standing here before you.

The Archbishop viewed me silently for so long that it felt as though he were peering directly into my dishonest soul. It took all my strength to hold his gaze. Finally, he said, You will prepare me this medicine.

It will be my honor, I said with another deep bow.

Go now!

Your Grace, may I impose a small request of my own?

I am God's holy servant. You do not expect payment for this concoction?

Not at all, Your Grace. I merely wanted to ask your assistance in another matter regarding the family of my friend Jacob ben Moses.

A Jew, he said as if referring to an odious highwayman. What sort of assistance?

I described to the Archbishop, in vague terms, the assault upon the Jews by the flagellants. As I spoke, I sensed he was already aware of the happenings inside the Jewish quarter.

The flagellants are foreigners, he said. These Germans are not part of my flock and do not follow my guidance.

These flagellants have dispatched one of the few elders left among the Jews, David ben Solomon, I said in order to emphasize that the Archbishop's creditor was already dead. I made a promise to Jacob on his deathbed to protect his family. If anything were to happen to them, I fear that I would feel so guilty my gift of apothecary might desert me.

The Archbishop stared at me for another long period. Then his lips curved into a callous smile. You may have overestimated my influence, Doctor Pasqua.

I think not, Your Grace, I said as I steeled my nerve. You are the most influential person I have ever encountered. And I am the one person who can ensure your continued health.

Vanity is not only a sin, Doctor Pasqua, he said. It can also prove deadly.

I bowed my head, fully committed to my reckless course now. Death is ubiquitous in these times, I said. The elixir of health is far rarer.

Perhaps so, but there is more than one route to securing cooperation, the Archbishop said. For instance, if you are so concerned over the safety of the Jewish doctor's family, perhaps it is best if I keep them here at the palace under my personal protection?

There was no mistaking the threat in his tone. That will not be necessary, I assured him. If you will allow me take my leave, I will go prepare the medicine for you straightaway.

Yes, yes, of course, Doctor Pasqua, he said. But double the portion.

For what purpose, Your Grace?

We are going to observe how well your remedy works on one of the already afflicted. And if it fails, Doctor Pasqua, I doubt anyone will be able to appease the flagellants.

As I hurried home from the palace, I cursed myself for my lies. I had placed Gabriella and her family at greater risk than ever. How could I produce a cure that existed only in my imagination?

I arrived back at my house to find Gabriella waiting for me. I ushered her inside and summarized my meeting with the Archbishop, but withheld mention of his threat to unleash the flagellants upon the Jews if my curative were to fail.

What will you do, Rafael? Gabriella asked as she took my hand in hers.

I am going to concoct a medicine for the Archbishop.

With what?

Most of what I described to him, although I will not burden any goats, I said. And to the medicine I will add the blood of the San Giovanni rats along with a large tincture of prayer.

I will add my own prayers, she said with a heartwarming smile.

We need to move your family to the monastery, I said. It is too dangerous to leave them where they are.

They will never go, Rafael. Not to live in a church among monks.

And you?

With Father, Ester, and Isaac departed, there is nothing left for me in our community.

You will go to the monastery? I asked in joyous relief.

She kissed my lips. From now on, I will stay with you, Rafael.

Fifty-Two

Alana answers the door to her hotel room in her bathrobe. Justine is standing on the other side with a tablet computer tucked under her arm. "Morning, sunshine!"

Alana glances at her watch, which reads 6:50 a.m. "Were we supposed to meet now?"

Justine grins. "By this time back home on the farm, we would've milked the cows, fed the chickens, and hosed the sheds."

"Not a lot of livestock around here," Alana says. "Come in."

As Justine steps inside, she makes a show of scanning the room. "Not even one stray guy lying about?" she says in mock dismay. "Was sure I'd at least find the boss here."

Alana ignores her, but, in truth, Byron left her out front of the hotel only five hours before. She has little doubt they would've ended up in her bed had both of their phones not exploded with texts and calls after the surveillance photos Sergio sent.

"So who is he?" Justine asks.

For a moment Alana thinks she's still teasing about her dating life, before realizing that Justine means the man from the surveillance photo. She shakes her head. "Haven't identified him yet."

"But you think he's the one that carried the rats to Naples?" Justine asks.

"Too soon to say."

"Kind of hope he is. Wouldn't mind having a word or two with him about cruelty to rats."

"Not to mention people."

"Them, too." Justine raises the tablet computer from under her arm. "I need to show you something."

They sit down beside each other on the unmade bed. Justine taps the screen of her tablet and the image of a dead rat appears. The animal is curled up on its side and blood is caked around its nose and mouth. "The plague, I assume," Alana says.

"Hard to slip anything past you NATO folks," Justine groans. "This ain't one of those medieval rats, neither. This is your typical run-of-the-mill local black rat."

Alana leans in closer to get a better look. "In Naples?"

"Yup." Justine flips through some more photos. In one shot, there are two dead rats lying side by side. "They've found at least six more carcasses so far."

Alana's unease deepens. "There must be a huge rat population in that Scampìa neighborhood."

"Kind of like Club Med for rats. Means the plague has found a home among the local rat population. Aside from one dead rat in the park, we haven't even seen that in Genoa yet."

"Because the sources—the construction pit and the park—were relatively isolated."

"Maybe. Either way, once the plague finds a foothold in a rat population like that . . ." Justine spreads her hands and fingers apart, mimicking an explosion.

"So what's next? Extermination?"

"Nuclear-style! I've already spoken to my colleagues. They're going in en masse. But . . ."

"It might be too late?"

Justine nods, her expression uncharacteristically somber. "This is a problem."

"It's not a problem, it's a fucking crisis. But the even bigger issue is that it didn't reach Naples on its own. We're going to face the same risk of the plague securing a rat reservoir in every city it hits. Just like what happened in the Middle Ages. We have to cut off the source."

"Agreed. Just remind me again how we're going to do that when we still don't know how or why it's spreading?"

Alana doesn't have an answer.

Justine hops up from the bed. "Speaking of cows, Byron and I have another meeting with that minister of health soon. Want to join?"

"No. I have to see someone else first."

Justine raises an eyebrow as if about to make another dating reference but seems to change her mind. "We are making some progress, Alana," she reassures her.

"I know." Alana musters a smile. "Just not sure it's enough."

As soon as Justine leaves, Alana throws on an outfit, runs a brush through her resistant hair, and heads downstairs.

Fifteen minutes later, a taxi driver drops her off at the entrance to the Seminario Arcivescovile. Don Arturo isn't in the seminary's library or the dining room. As Alana heads for the staircase, she hears someone calling to her. She turns to see Brother Samuel, the tall cleric with the widow's peak, approaching. "You have come to see Don Arturo again, Dr. Vaughn?"

"Yes."

Brother Samuel bows his head apologetically. "Father Abbot does not come down for breakfast until after eight o'clock."

Alana folds her arms across her chest. "It's urgent."

Samuel doesn't budge. "It has not been easy for him, you understand?"

"What hasn't?"

"Losing San Giovanni. The move." Samuel clasps his hands together. "He is older than he appears. And less healthy. Though you would never know either. There are few men with stronger spirits."

"Did you live at San Giovanni, too, Brother Samuel?"

"I did."

"Do you know about its history? The rats below the monastery?"

Samuel wrinkles his nose. "Rats? We did not have a problem with rats."

"What about the chute—the *scivolo*?"

"What does the *scivolo* have to do with rats?" he asks in genuine confusion.

"I really need to speak to Don Arturo."

Samuel eyes her for a moment and then nods. "I will take you."

He leads her up to the second floor. Arturo answers the door dressed in the same black tunic as before, with his gray hair as meticulously combed. Samuel speaks to Arturo for a few moments, before the abbot cuts him off with a raised hand. "It is fine. Please, Dr. Vaughn, come in."

"I am sorry to call so early," Alana says as she follows Arturo into his small but tastefully furnished living room. The smell of espresso wafts as strongly as inside a café. Numerous books line the shelves, but the room's tidiness stands in stark contrast to Brother Silvio's overrun apartment. He insists on brewing her a fresh cup and disappears into the kitchen.

Minutes later, Arturo reemerges, holding a cup and saucer. She bites back a grin when she sees the two biscotti on either side of the cup, resembling something her grandmother might have served. He sits down across from her. "How can I be of assistance?"

"You're aware of the legend of the San Giovanni rats, right?" Alana asks. "And the crypt that housed them below the church?"

"Yes." His brow furrows. "Mainly from Brother Silvio, of course. He was our unofficial historian. The legend, it dates back to the Middle Ages."

She sips the espresso, enjoying the rich, bitter bite. "Brother Silvio gave me a copy of that medieval doctor's diary."

"Ah, yes, the diary. I read it, too. With all the nonsense about the *Custodi di ratti* and rat worship."

"You didn't believe it?"

"No." He smiles. "None of us did. It's merely superstition. Typical for the time."

"And yet the brothers have been feeding those rats down the *scivolo* ever since."

"Feeding them?" He laughs. "No. No. It was how we cleared our table scraps. The ancient ritual was a practical one, too."

She lowers her cup. "We found a rat that was carrying the plague, Don Arturo."

He shrugs. "It only makes sense."

"It wasn't just any rat. We suspect the animal is a direct descendant of the medieval rats Pasqua describes in his diary. The ones from the crypt."

He frowns. "They couldn't have survived. Not all this time."

"We have reason to believe they did."

"Incredible," he mutters. "And you are suggesting this has led to our city's epidemic? Because the builders freed the rats from captivity?"

She nods. "Except we're not entirely sure who freed the rats."

The creases around his eyes tighten. "I do not follow, Dr. Vaughn."

"The plague has spread to other cities, too. We know it was brought to Rome by a man with a chest infection. But Naples is a different story. It couldn't have spread there by human contact. And no rat alive can wander four hundred miles in just a few days."

Arturo gapes at her. "You are telling me that someone deliberately transported an infected rat from Genoa to Naples?"

"We believe so, yes. So we need to figure out who else knew about the crypt and what exactly it housed."

He looks down in silence, digesting the news. "Most of the brothers would have heard the stories. A few would have read the diary. But if you are suggesting . . ."

"We have to consider it, Don Arturo," she says with genuine

sympathy. "Were any of the monks particularly interested in the legend of the crypt?"

He pauses for a moment. "No. None that I can think of."

Alana leans forward. "Some of the brothers must have been upset when they heard the monastery was going to be torn down."

"Yes, of course. We all were. I was, too. It was our home."

"Can you think of anyone who was particularly upset or . . . behaving strangely around the time the monastery closed?"

"Aside from Brother Silvio and his vigil at the construction site?" He rubs his eyes. "No. No one else comes to mind."

Alana clears her throat. "Don Arturo, have you left Genoa in the past week or so?"

If the abbot is insulted by the insinuation, he doesn't show it. "No, Dr. Vaughn. I have not left in years. Too long, in fact."

"And there's no other direction you can point me? Anyone who might be remotely connected?"

"It hurts me to even consider that this plague might have originated from inside San Giovanni. But if it did, then it must have happened by accident." Arturo rises to his feet. "I wish I could be of more help, Dr. Vaughn."

Deflated, she rises to join him. As an afterthought, she reaches for her phone and clicks on the photo that Sergio had forwarded to her. She turns it around to show him. "Do you know this man?"

Recognition flashes across his face.

Her mouth goes dry. "You do know him!"

"Yes. He is—he was—a brother at the monastery."

Adrenaline washes over her. "Who is he?"

"Brother Stefano," Arturo says, grimacing as he conjures a surname. "Stefano Russo."

"How long has Brother Stefano been at San Giovanni?" she demands.

"Six or seven years, perhaps. Stefano came to us as a young novice."

"Describe him," she says, struggling to contain her urgency.

"Stefano? He is most shy. Quiet as a mouse. Very hardworking, very studious. A good boy."

"Nothing else about him?" she presses.

"He's a simple and dedicated monk. A timid young man." Arturo shakes his head. "Where does this photo come from?"

"A colleague sent it to me."

He folds his hands on his chest. "I simply cannot imagine Stefano being involved in any of this."

Alana resists the urge to grab Arturo and shake him by the shoulders. "Where can I find Brother Stefano?" she asks as calmly as she can.

Fifty-Three

The freighter cast off two days earlier at exactly six p.m. Before this voyage, Stefano had never been aboard a vessel larger than a ferry, and he has never been on the open sea before. He wondered if seasickness would be an issue, but so far he has experienced only slight queasiness.

It was more difficult to land a berth on the cargo ship than he had assumed. The first four shipping companies turned him down out of hand. Others viewed him with bewilderment. Apparently almost all the unskilled laborers working on freighters came from developing countries. The man at the head office of Napoli Marittima told him the only reason he had offered Stefano the job aboard the *Cielo di Asia* was because one of the workers had broken his leg in a forklift accident that very morning.

In the end, Stefano couldn't have planned it better. The *Cielo di Asia* is on its way to Singapore and, after, will sail to Hong Kong to unload the rest of its cargo. Each port will make a perfect destination for his special cargo.

After his initial trepidation, Stefano has begun to enjoy the work aboard. The monastic life prepared him well. He even finds a renewed sense of purpose in the hard labor, as he prepares for his final mission.

The Lord speaks to him infrequently now but never fails to remind him of his purpose. "Man has turned from me, and to me belongeth vengeance and recompense," the voice tells him. "You will release my creatures in the East. They must learn what they have reaped upon themselves."

The only complication Stefano did not anticipate was the accommodations. He didn't realize he would have to share a room. He is fortunate to have only one roommate, as some of the crew have to share their quarters with three others. Stefano is luckier still that Nino, his Filipino roommate, is devoutly religious. He reads the Bible morning and night. And Nino is respectful, even deferential, to Stefano because of his previous work at the monastery.

Stefano had no choice but to tell Nino that he had smuggled animals aboard. But he told his roommate that, instead of six rats, he was hiding two hamsters and a gerbil that were terrified of strangers. At first Nino was doubtful, but Stefano dispelled his roommate's suspicion with one simple truth: the animals had once been considered sacred within the walls of the San Giovanni Monastery.

Fifty-Four

Alana calls Monique Olin before she has even left the grounds of the seminary.

"Stefano Russo!" she says as soon as her boss answers.

Olin doesn't need more explanation than that. "He is the one from the photograph?"

"Yes." Alana summarizes what she knows of the monk, and how he was sighted in the same Neapolitan neighborhood where the outbreak had spread.

"That is a substantial coincidence," Olin says.

"It's way beyond coincidence, Monique!" Alana has to struggle to keep her voice down. "Christ, it's basically a DNA match."

"Remember what happened the last time?" Olin points out. "With Yasin Ahmed?"

Alana remembers all too well. But beyond the strength of evidence against Stefano Russo, her gut tells her that he has to be the link. "It's him," she says.

"All right. And his last known sighting was in Naples?"

"Yes."

"Unfortunately, he has a common first and last name."

"The 'John Smith' of Italy?"

"Not far off. Send me everything you have on him. Birth date, passport number, whatever else you can find."

"I'll see what we can dig up through AISI or the Church."

"Alana?"

"Yes?"

"Good work." Compliments from Olin are rare. "But be careful moving forward. Do not let your enthusiasm get the better of your judgment."

As soon as the cab picks her up, Alana calls Byron to update him. And then she dials Sergio, who asks her to meet in thirty minutes at AISI regional headquarters in Genoa.

Alana smiles to herself when she steps out of the elevator at the unmarked offices on the fourth floor of a nondescript building on Via Cairolli. *Typical spy stuff*, she thinks as she clears a security checkpoint outside the door to the domestic intelligence service's office.

A baby-faced agent leads Alana to an inner office. Sergio sits behind a desk with the phone to his ear, but he waves her inside. As she sits down across from him, he shoves a photocopy of Stefano Russo's passport across to her.

"You work fast," she says as soon as he hangs up.

He nods. "Especially considering how many Stefano Russos there are in this city."

She notices his birth date. "He's only twenty-five."

"Old enough."

"Have you tracked him down?" she asks hopefully.

"No. We've alerted the police and other intelligence agencies across the country. And we just released his photo to the media."

Alana thinks of the possible consequences, but her resolve doesn't waver. "Good."

"Brother Stefano has no cell phones registered to his name. He doesn't appear to use any bank or credit cards. We haven't even found any social media or email accounts for him." Sergio lifts another page off his desk and passes it to her. "We do have this."

Despite the Italian wording, Alana recognizes the printed form as a typical electronic medical record that many regions use to track patients' pharmaceutical histories. She studies the names of the medications on the list, most of which are the same or very similar in English. She taps two of the items near the top of the list. "These antibiotics—ciprofloxacin and doxycycline—are both first-line treatments for *Yersinia*."

Sergio frowns. "Do you think he has been infected by the plague himself?"

"Look at the dates. They were prescribed over a month ago." She takes a closer look. "And check out the quantities! He was given a three-month supply of each."

"Is that a lot?"

"Yeah. Normal treatment would be for a maximum of two weeks, but . . ." She snaps her fingers. "Prophylaxis!"

"I don't understand."

"Stefano has enough antibiotics to protect himself for months from getting the plague. Because he knew he was going to be exposed to it for a prolonged period!"

Sergio studies the page for a long moment and then finally nods. "Yes, I think so, too. To protect himself while he was carrying infected rats."

She taps the page again. "We need to talk to the prescribing doctor. Dr. Giannini. He or she might know something."

Sergio nods and reaches for the sheet, but she pins it to the desk with her hand. She runs her finger down to the medications listed below the antibiotics. "Look at these other drugs: lithium, olanzapine, and sertraline."

"What are those?"

"Psychiatric medications."

"For what?"

"Has to be some kind of psychotic disorder. They were prescribed by a different doctor. Dr. Lonzo. Probably Stefano's psychiatrist. We need to speak to him, as well."

Sergio makes a phone call and, a minute or two later, gets one in return. He stands up from the desk and adjusts his dark tie as he closes the top button of his navy suit. "We have the doctors' addresses," he announces.

They head down to the garage and his car. Sergio drives them eastward to the same neighborhood as the Ospedale San Martino. He parks over the sidewalk in front of a medical building that has an outpatient clinic on one side and a pharmacy on the other. They rush through the clinic's crowded waiting room and up to the desk of a harried-looking older receptionist. Sergio and the woman argue for a few minutes before she throws up her hands in defeat and stomps away. Moments later, a young doctor with a messy mop of dark hair and a short white coat, who appears as stressed as his secretary, follows her into the reception area. Dr. Giannini guides them down a narrow hallway and into a small office that is equipped with an old-fashioned examining table and a blood pressure cuff mounted on the wall.

Giannini speaks no English. Sergio shows him a photo of Stefano, and Giannini's eyes widen as he listens. The young doctor shakes his head frantically as he sputters his reply.

"He swears he has only seen Stefano a few times," Sergio translates. "Apparently the monk told him he had a chronic chest condition that required long-term antibiotics."

"And he just took his word for that?" Alana asks.

Sergio speaks to the doctor, whose waving grows even more frantic.

Sergio turns back to Alana. "Dr. Giannini says he sometimes has to see more than fifty patients a day. I believe him. Our medical system . . ." He grunts in disdain. "He also says he trusted Stefano because he was a monk. He keeps asking, 'Why would the brother lie?'"

To wipe out the planet. Alana doesn't verbalize the thought.

Sergio questions Giannini further, but even without the benefit of translation Alana can tell the skittish physician has nothing else useful to offer.

Sergio and Alana return to his car, and he drives westward toward the center of the city. He pulls up in front of a more modern building, perched up a hill. They ride the elevator to an office on the fifth floor, where the receptionist is politer than the previous one but equally as reluctant to disturb her doctor. Eventually she makes a call, and moments later, a short balding man in a bow tie joins them at the desk. He introduces himself as Dr. Lonzo, and then escorts them down a hallway and into his private office. With its light color tones and soothing décor, the room epitomizes psychotherapy to Alana.

Once they're all seated, Lonzo asks in English, "How can I help you?"

"We wanted to discuss a patient of yours," Alana says. "A monk by the name of Stefano Russo."

Lonzo strokes his chin with a finger and thumb. "Dr. Vaughn, you must appreciate the sanctity of doctor-patient privilege. I am not at liberty to discuss my clients."

"We already know you prescribed him several psychotropic medications," Alana persists. "I am assuming he suffers from schizophrenia or, perhaps, bipolar disorder."

"I really cannot comment."

"Dr. Lonzo, this is a matter of national security," Sergio says.

"Maybe so," the psychiatrist replies. "But unless you have a legal order, I am ethically and professionally bound not to discuss my patients."

"Your patient is deliberately spreading the plague across Italy," Alana says quietly.

Lonzo shakes his head as if he misheard. "No, no, no . . . How could this be? This is not possible."

"It could be and it is," Alana says. "Stefano disappeared right before the outbreak here in Genoa. We have photos of him in Naples days before it hit there, and a witness who saw him acting suspiciously. And we know he was carrying a supply of several months' worth of antibiotics."

"Antibiotics?"

"To protect himself from becoming infected by his own rats."

Lonzo slumps back in his seat, shaken. "Schizoaffective disorder," he finally says.

"What is that?" Sergio asks.

"A condition somewhere between schizophrenia and bipolar disorder," the psychiatrist explains. "With elements of both illnesses. In Stefano's case, he has delusions—or unfounded beliefs—and he hears auditory hallucinations."

"Voices?" Sergio asks.

"Yes." Lonzo sighs. "Stefano is particularly susceptible to bouts of depression. And with those episodes, he experiences persecutory hallucinations that are mood-congruent. In other words, he hears voices in his head that are very critical of him."

"Whose voices?" Alana asks.

Lonzo thinks for a moment. "Different ones. Authority figures. Priests and abbots from his past. And of course, being as religious as he is, he also believes he can hear the voice of God."

"God?" Alana echoes. "And the Church let him continue to work as a monk in spite of all these auditory hallucinations?"

"The Church is very protective of their own, regardless of . . . health issues. Besides, his mood and symptoms stabilized on the medication. Stefano was functioning quite well. Even the abbot seemed to think so."

"Don Arturo?" Alana asks in surprise. "He knew about Stefano's condition?"

"And his treatment, yes, of course."

"When was the last time you saw Stefano?" Sergio asks.

"Perhaps two months ago. I can ask Lia to look up the precise date."

"Two months ago?" Alana repeats. "That would've been right around the time the monks were being evicted from the monastery?"

"Yes. In fact, he was supposed to move out the week after our last appointment."

"To where, Dr. Lonzo?" she asks.

"I believe he was being sent to another monastery. He told me he might not be able to see me for a while because of his move. And he asked for extra refills to his prescriptions."

"What was he like that last visit?" she asks.

"To be honest, I was concerned."

"Why was that?" Sergio asks.

"He was becoming somewhat paranoid. His delusions and hallucinations had shifted away from the usual self-persecutory themes."

"What do you mean, shifted?"

"He told me that God was very angry."

"About what?"

"The state of the world. The excess of sin and godlessness. These are common religious themes in the delusional, of course." Lonzo pinches his chin again. "Stefano is a mild-mannered young man, you understand. I assumed he was merely projecting his own hurt and anxiety."

"Over the destruction of the San Giovanni Monastery?" Alana asks.

"Perhaps." Lonzo's forehead creases. "Regardless, the last time I spoke to him, Stefano was quite convinced that God was out for vengeance."

Fifty-Five

Today is the fourth day of March. My heart is fuller than it has been since the day the pestilence claimed my Camilla. While I remain ashamed of recent deceptions, I believe she would have seen the necessity in them. I pray, too, that she would understand the affection which has grown in my heart for Gabriella.

How God will judge me remains to be seen. For last night I lay with Gabriella. I had insisted she sleep in my bed while I made a mattress of straw on the floor. However, she woke me in the night and guided me by the hand to join her. While there is no excuse for our sin, I do not regret the behavior. For I have fallen in love with this enigmatic yet enchanting woman.

Gabriella understands as well as I do that our fates are now intertwined. Even in the time before the pestilence, the coupling of a Christian and a Jew would have been an unforgivable sin for people of both faiths. Now, in such apocalyptical times, I cannot imagine how they might respond. Even without me by her side, the danger will only grow for Gabriella the longer she remains in Genova. And if I fail to provide the Archbishop with an effective curative, her fortunes will turn truly dire.

I raised these concerns with Gabriella as she prepared breakfast.

Surely the doge and the councilmen will not allow the flagellants to assail your neighborhood as they did mine, she said.

It is not the councilmen I fear.

Is it the Archbishop?

I wrapped my arms around Gabriella from behind. Darling, the Archbishop holds sway over all of them, I said. He could release the flagellants with a swipe of his quill.

Is that really so?

Yes, despite his empty words to the contrary. And if they come for you, they will have to kill me first.

She put down her knife and turned to face me. Tears ran down her cheeks. I cannot lose anyone else dear to me, she said as she buried her face in my neck.

Then come away with me.

Where could we go without our troubles following? she asked as she dried her eyes on her sleeve.

Anywhere. Best if we go north, to the lands well beyond the Alps where the plague has not yet ventured. For the time being, we can take shelter at San Giovanni.

How can we live in a monastery?

Only temporarily, I said. We will be safe among the brothers. The plague has already consumed what it can there. When the time is right, we can determine where to go next.

Gabriella gazed deeply into my eyes. Would we go there as husband and wife? she asked.

Yes, I said without hesitation.

Good, I will gather my belongings, then, she said, as though we had just agreed on a choice of taverns rather than having committed to marriage.

On our way to the monastery, we visited the Jewish quarter. None of the Jews were outside their homes, despite the midday hour. We spoke with Gabriella's siblings inside her brother's house. I implored the family to join us at the monastery, but, as Gabriella had predicted, they were unwilling to live under the roof of the Church. I urged them to at least find sanctuary outside of the city, and her brother agreed to take my suggestion under advisement.

Gabriella and I carried our belongings in sacks on our backs for the climb to the monastery. Rather than complain over the exertion, she was exhilarated. She stopped often to marvel at the view of the city and the harbor from our perch.

When we reached the monastery, I was relieved to see that work on enclosing the crypt for the rats had not yet been completed. I could still see a narrow dirt passageway that led to the channels below. I wondered warily if my life might rely on that slim opening.

Several of the brothers viewed Gabriella with consternation, embarrassment, or even shock. However, Don Marco greeted both of us with his usual congeniality. He shook my hand warmly and bowed to Gabriella.

It is a pleasure to make your acquaintance, good lady, Don Marco said.

It is an honor to make yours, good sir, Gabriella replied.

Come, let me show you to your quarters, he said, accepting us as lodgers without further inquiry.

Don Marco led us to a building beyond the dormitory where I had never before ventured. He opened the door to a small room that bore only a bed and a chamber pot, but the floors were swept and the wall was free of cobwebs.

I apologize, dear lady, but we are a simple abbey and this is the best accommodation I have to offer you, he said.

It exceeds my wants or expectations, she said. Your hospitality is most generous, Don Marco. Thank you.

Any friend of Doctor Pasqua's is welcome at San Giovanni. Now let me show you to your quarters, Don Marco said to me with an expression that made it clear I would not be dwelling in the same vicinity as Gabriella.

Don Marco led me back to the dormitory. He showed me to an open room where there were several unoccupied beds.

I wish it were not so, but, in the wake of the affliction, we have an abundance of empty beds, he said.

Thank you, Don Marco, you are an honorable man and a noble abbot.

I am nothing of the sort, he said with a laugh. I am a humble monk, nothing more.

We will have to disagree on that score. But, Don Marco, I do need to impose upon you for yet another favor.

I cannot allow you to lodge any nearer to your charming lady friend, he said with palms held open. The brothers would be apoplectic. It is most unorthodox to have a woman staying among us. Many of the brothers will be distressed over her mere presence.

I would never dream of asking. No, I am requesting a few more of the rats before the crypt is sealed.

Doctor Pasqua, we have discussed this. I cannot abide such experimentation. We consider these animals to be blessed, and our sacred mission is to protect them.

I understand. However, Don Marco, I fear that both Gabriella's and my life might depend on those rats.

Why? he asked with concern. Is one of you afflicted?

I told Don Marco the truth of how I had misled the Archbishop and what I had promised to provide him.

When will you ever learn? Don Marco said as he clasped his hands in front of him. The Archbishop is not a man to trifle with.

I could only hang my head in shame.

In the end, the abbot granted me my request. He introduced me to Brother Piero, who was the current keeper of the rats. Unlike other monks at San Giovanni who wore simple black robes and sandals, Piero was covered from head to toe, including a veil over his mouth and nose to protect him from the pestilence. He led me to a room full of cages where the brothers were housing the rats until the crypt was completed. I was astounded by the sheer quantity of the creatures. The cages were teeming with them. In one, they were packed so tightly that when they crawled over one another it created the effect of a blanket moving of its own accord.

When Piero realized I intended to use my bare hands to collect the animals, he interceded. I had to reassure him that, because I was a survivor of the plague, the creatures posed no further threat to me. I opened one of the cages and selected two of the biggest male rats. I tried to grab each nimbly by the tail, but the second one was too fast and managed to bite my finger deeply, drawing blood.

I carried the animals in my sack to a patch of grass several paces behind the monastery. I did not bother to assemble all the ingredients I had invented for the benefit of the Archbishop. Instead, I gathered some dirt and grass and ground them into a coarse paste. I sliced the necks of the two rats and stirred their warm blood into the mixture until it resembled wet mud. I packed the slop into a clay pot.

On my way back, I visited Gabriella. She sat on the bed, staring at the floor.

What is wrong, darling? I asked.

I fear for my brother and sister and their families.

Do you think they will heed my advice and leave Genova?

I am not convinced. My brother is as stubborn as my father was.

If I can appease the Archbishop with this, I said as I raised the pot, then life will be safer for your family.

Gabriella noticed the blood on my finger. What happened?

One of the rats bit me.

She got up and rushed over to me, taking my finger in her hand and bringing it to her lips. She sucked on it as though trying to withdraw the poison of a snake.

It is only a tiny flesh wound, I said with a laugh.

That is how it began with my Ester after the dog bit her, she said fearfully.

The same will not become of me. I have had many such bites of late.

She released my finger, but then she hugged me tightly.

I have to leave for the Archbishop's palace soon, I said. So that I may return before nightfall.

Why must you go today?

I promised the Archbishop. He might send his soldiers to look for me if I do not arrive. Besides, if this mixture is to have any effect, the blood must be fresh.

What if it is not effective for the ones already afflicted in his palace?

I have considered this. I will tell the Archbishop that the pestilence was too advanced, and that the remedy works better as preventative than as cure.

What if the Archbishop falls ill despite your medicine?

If he is like most of the afflicted, he will be too ill or too consumed to seek out his vengeance.

Gabriella took my hand in hers. Can you really trust him, darling? she asked.

Yes. I uttered yet another lie. By tonight my dealings with the Archbishop will be done, I said. You will see.

I hope so, she said with a stoic expression that could not conceal the deep sadness in her eyes.

I love you, my darling.

And I, you.

We held each other for several silent minutes, before I finally kissed her goodbye.

I went to my room to fetch my cloak. I had intended to leave directly for the Archbishop's palace, but I felt compelled to stop and record the many happenings of today before I departed.

As I reflect upon the past few terrible months since I began to write about my experience, I realize that while the world has seen the very worst of times, I truly have been blessed. Gabriella and I have found each other, and together we have found sanctuary here at San Giovanni.

I depart now for the Archbishop's palace with renewed hope for tomorrow.

Fifty-Six

Ignoring Brother Samuel's protests, Alana and Sergio march past him and up the stairs to Don Arturo's room.

The abbot's face creases in surprise when he opens the door to them. But his confusion quickly gives way to an amiable smile. "Dr. Vaughn, you have become my most frequent visitor."

Samuel is breathing heavily as he catches up to them. Before he can say anything, Arturo dispatches him with a small flick of his wrist. Brooding, Samuel turns and trudges away.

After Alana introduces Sergio to the abbot by his full title, they follow Arturo back into the living room where Alana had been only hours before. But this time she refuses his offer of coffee, as does Sergio. Neither of them sits down. "We need to discuss Brother Stefano," Alana says.

Arturo only nods.

"You told me this morning that he was a simple and dedicated monk," she says.

"He is," Arturo says.

"You didn't mention anything about his mental health issues."

"Of course I did not," Arturo says, as though it should be self-evident. "That is extremely private information. How did you even learn of it?"

"We spoke to Dr. Lonzo," Sergio says.

Arturo grimaces. "And the doctor shared such confidential information with you?"

"He did," Sergio says. "As a matter of national security."

"National security? Brother Stefano?" Don Arturo's voice rises in surprise.

"The photo I showed you this morning—" Alana starts to say.

"You never told me where it came from or how it related to your inquiry."

"It was taken in Naples," she says. "It confirms Brother Stefano is the link to the deliberate spread of the plague."

"Stefano? The plague?" Arturo drops into the chair behind him. "How can this be?"

"Stefano got his hands on the infected rats that had been living under the monastery since the Middle Ages. He has been releasing them in public places to spread the plague."

"Such a suggestion is very . . . distressing." Arturo shakes his head. "I cannot believe such a thing."

Sergio folds his arms across his chest. "What do you know about his illness? His delusions?"

"He hears voices sometimes, yes. But his condition is controlled when he is on the right medicine. Stefano always fulfilled his monastic duties. He never caused me concern."

Alana locks her eyes on his. "Don Arturo, you also told me none of the brothers were acting strangely at the time the monastery was closed."

"It is true. Stefano was acting as he always did. He has suffered this same condition since his first day at the monastery."

"Dr. Lonzo told us he'd become more paranoid of late," Alana says. "That he believed God was seeking some kind of vengeance."

Arturo holds her gaze. "Stefano did not speak of this to me. Nor did Dr. Lonzo."

"And you have no idea where Stefano might be?" Alana asks.

"I thought he was at the new monastery. No one has told me otherwise."

"He's not there," Sergio says.

"We know Stefano is behind the spread, Don Arturo," Alana says. "What we *don't* know is whether he is acting alone."

"You think others at San Giovanni could have helped him?"

"How does a twenty-five-year-old schizophrenic monk learn the secrets of San Giovanni and then retrieve the rats from an enclosure that has been untouched in more than six hundred years?"

Sergio nods. "And how is he able to move, undetected, from city to city without a phone or a credit card to his name?"

"Who would help him?" Arturo asks. "Besides, Brother Stefano is a very private man, even by monastic standards." His brow furrows. "Well, he did spend much of his spare time with Brother Silvio in the library . . ."

"Stefano was close with Silvio?" Alana asks.

"As close as with any of the brothers, I suppose. And, of course, if anyone was acting strangely after the closure of our monastery, it was Silvio. With his vigil at the construction site."

Alana and Sergio fire other questions at Arturo but learn nothing more of use before they leave.

As Sergio drives them back across town, Alana asks, "Do you believe him?"

He shrugs. "I never fully trust anyone. Not without researching first."

"How will you do that?"

"I have already requested Arturo's phone and online records. Those of Silvio and Stefano, as well. My team is scanning them as we speak."

Sergio pulls the car up in front of Brother Silvio's building. Inside, at the door to the monk's apartment, Sergio knocks three separate times, banging so hard that eventually an elderly woman pokes her head out of a neighboring unit across the hallway.

The woman speaks to Sergio for a few seconds and then disappears back behind her door.

"What did she tell you?" Alana asks.

"Silvio left yesterday."

"Left? For where?"

"The old woman didn't know. Apparently he was carrying a suitcase. And she said he looked as if he were in a big hurry."

Fifty-Seven

The captain announces that in less than forty-eight hours the *Cielo di Asia* will reach the Egyptian city of Port Said, where they will stop to replenish supplies. Stefano has never heard of the city before, but he is told that it's the gateway to the Suez Canal. What excites Stefano far more is how close Port Said lies to the Holy Land. From there, he will even be able to see the Sinai Peninsula. He knows in his heart that he will never get closer, but for him, it will be close enough.

The Lord has spoken to him more in the past few days than ever before, but Stefano is still not accustomed to His voice. When the Almighty first started communing with him, Stefano was confused, even doubtful. He suspected it was just one of the auditory hallucinations that Dr. Lonzo had told him were so common to his illness. He even asked Brother Silvio, the wisest monk he knew, what God sounded like. Brother Silvio replied that if anyone could hear His voice, it would sound as pure as the love of a mother or a father.

But love is not what Stefano has been hearing inside his head. The voice has been more unforgiving than ever. And last night, the Lord could not have been clearer. "Even the Promised Land will not be spared my wrath. You will release one of my creatures to Canaan."

It wasn't until morning that Stefano figured out how he would fulfill God's latest command. As soon as the resupply crew boarded the ship, he would a find a way to hide one of the rats in one of the empty containers that they would take back with them.

As Stefano lies on his upper bunk, his thoughts turn again to the containers. The massive freighter has countless matching modular boxes stacked aboard. They are sealed, but if he can somehow find an opening into one or two of them, he can conceal the rats inside. All the animals will need is a little food. If they have been able to survive for almost seven hundred years in the crypt below San Giovanni, surely they can survive a few days or weeks as stowaways? Then the containers can do the work of spreading God's wrath.

He is pulled from the thoughts by his roommate, who lies on the bunk below him. "Stefano?"

"Yes, Nino?"

"I am not feeling so good," his roommate says.

Stefano hears the sheets rustle below him. "What is it, my brother?"

"I was very cold. Now I think I have a fever."

Stefano sits up in the bed.

"And my underarm hurts. I can feel a lump under there."

"Oh, it's probably the flu," Stefano says, trying to sound calm despite the panic welling inside.

"I will see the doctor in the morning."

"No, no," Stefano says, desperate to find some way to talk him out of it. "The old Ukrainian doctor, he's not very good. I . . . I would not trust him."

"What shall I do, brother?"

"I have medicine," Stefano blurts. "Antibiotics. They will take care of your flu. They will make you well again."

"All right," Nino says acceptingly. "God bless you, Stefano."

"I will pray for you, Nino."

Fifty-Eight

The exhaustion begins to catch up with Alana in the back-seat of the cab. All the adrenaline-fueled excitement and anticipation from earlier in the morning has given way to the frustration of mounting dead ends. The media has splashed photos of Stefano and Silvio over the screens of TVs, computers, and mobile devices across Italy. But so far, nothing, except a bunch of false alarms.

The driver drops Alana off at the familiar entrance of the Ospedale San Martino. There are only a few reporters and cameramen left outside to circumvent. She suspects the others must already be staking out the hospitals in Naples where the crisis has deepened.

As soon Alana enters, she spots Nico and Byron talking heatedly just beside the exit to the decontamination station. Nico is angrily gesturing, while Byron's arms are folded and his expression is fixed in one of his defensive smiles.

For an embarrassed moment, Alana wonders if they might be arguing over her.

"He's just going to let my patient die!" Nico cries as she nears. "Talk some sense into him!"

"About what, Nico?" Alana asks, relieved their disagreement doesn't involve her.

"I have a forty-year-old woman in the ICU dying of antibiotic-resistant *Yersinia*. And this one"—Nico thumbs dismissively at Byron—"refuses to release the only medicine that could save her life."

Byron's smile softens briefly as he glances over to Alana, but his posture is unwavering. "I told you, Nico. We've only got the one dose of the antiserum ready to use. Could be days before we have another. And there are at least two other patients who need it just as urgently as yours."

"How can you say this with certainty?" Nico demands. "What is certain is that my patient—a mother of three—will not survive the night without the antiserum."

"Dr. Montaldo says the exact same thing of a six-year-old boy at the children's hospital," Byron counters. "And there's another woman in the ICU here who is almost as sick. They can't all split a single dose."

Alana empathizes with both of them. Such life-and-death rationing reminds her of missions with the WHO where she was also forced to play God due to limited resources. "Why not share it, Byron?" she suggests. "At least between Nico's patient and the little boy?"

"Yes!" Nico nods rapidly. "Maybe even two-thirds for the woman and one-third for the boy."

"And what if they both die, having been underdosed?" Byron asks.

"Then at least you will have given both of them a chance!" Nico cries.

Byron uncrosses his arms. "All right," he finally agrees.

"Thank you," Nico says, and then turns to Alana. "Come to the ICU, Alana. You can meet the patient."

She shakes her head. "I don't have time."

"Ah," he says, looking warily from Byron back to her. "You've come to see him?"

"Yes. We're going to see Sergio Fassino."

"I better get back to my patients, then," Nico says as he begins to turn away.

"Do you have a moment, Nico?" she asks.

Byron tilts his head but doesn't comment. He pulls his phone from his jacket. "I'll meet you outside, Alana. I have to sort out the distribution of the antiserum to both hospitals."

Alana pulls Nico over to a quiet corner of the lobby by the elbow. "I'm leaving Genoa tonight."

"For where?"

"Naples."

"I see," he says quietly.

"The outbreak is stabilizing here, Nico."

"Stabilizing?" he groans. "My patient is on the brink of death."

"No doubt. But there are fewer cases today than yesterday. Two days in a row with a drop. In epidemiological terms, we're winning in Genoa. Not so in Naples. Besides, Stefano was last seen there."

"And Byron will go with you?" Nico asks.

"I think so."

A momentary silence falls between them. Then Nico breaks into one of those open-mouth smiles that used to make the English nurse swoon on their Angola mission. "It was good to see you, Alana. To work together again."

"And you, Nico." She reciprocates the grin. "We can't let it go so long next time."

"Yes, but we do need to give it a little time. At least I do." Nico takes her by the shoulders and kisses her on both cheeks. "Time for me focus on the family again."

A pang of melancholy hits her as they step apart. "I hope you can sort things out with Isabella. I really do."

Outside, Byron doesn't ask Alana about her conversation, but once they're clear of the entrance, he takes her hand in his and gives it a quick squeeze.

They climb into his rental car, and he drives them to the building on Via Cairoli that houses the AISI headquarters. Sergio greets them personally outside the fourth-floor elevators and guides them past the security checkpoint and down the corridor into his office.

"Your timing is good," he says.

"How so?" Alana asks. "Have you found Stefano?"

"No. But we did locate Brother Silvio."

Alana's pulse picks up. "Where is he?"

Sergio motions down the hallway. "Here."

"Where was he?" Byron asks.

"At San Fruttuoso di Camogli," Sergio says. "A famous monastery up the coast from Portofino. There are no roads in—the only access is by foot or by sea. One of the other brothers saw the alert online, which we added Brother Silvio to, and he tipped us off. We picked him up a few hours ago."

"What is Silvio saying?" Alana asks.

"Not much, so far. He speaks highly of you, though. Why don't we question him together?"

Sergio leads them inside an interview room with a table and a few chairs. A plainclothes guard stands at the door and closes it behind them. Silvio sits across a table in his usual black robe. As they enter, the monk smiles in recognition, but his face is haggard and he seems years older. "Ah, Dr. Vaughn, have you had time to finish the diary yet?"

"Not yet, Brother Silvio."

"But you will?" he asks hopefully, as if it were the reason for their meeting now.

"I will." She sits down between Byron and Sergio across from the monk. "Right now we have to find Brother Stefano. Urgently."

There's a knock at the door. The guard answers it and, after a brief verbal exchange, accepts a few sheets of paper. He closes the door and then passes the pages over to Sergio.

"That poor boy." Silvio shakes his head. "Stefano, he suffers so with his illness."

"You mean the voices?" Byron asks.

"*Prego*." Silvio blows out his lips. "Most times, Stefano, he knows they are not real, but sometimes . . ."

"Especially around the time the monastery was demolished, right?" Byron presses. "His symptoms had gotten worse around then?"

"I would not say so," Silvio says. "To me, Stefano was improving. He did not mention voices. He was too fascinated with the history of our old monastery."

Alana reaches across the table and takes Silvio's bony hand in hers. It's dry and callused in her palm. "Brother Silvio, did you help Stefano free the rats from the crypt?"

Silvio stares at her for a moment and then breaks into a small laugh. "I never believed the rats were still there. I still find it impossible to believe. If Stefano had asked, I would have told him so." He pats the back of her hand. "Stefano, he did not ask. He never spoke to me of rats at all."

"Then why did you run away yesterday?" Byron asks.

"Run?" Silvio laughs again. "I am far too ancient to run. No, Don Arturo, he arranged it. He requested I spend time at San Fruttuoso di Camogli. To see their library. And to see what they could absorb of the San Giovanni collection."

"When did Don Arturo arrange this?" Byron asks.

"He called me yesterday. He told me they were ready for me right away. He booked my train and arranged the boat."

Sergio looks up from the pages, his expression neutral but his eyes afire. "Excuse us for a moment, brother," he says as he rises to his feet.

Alana and Byron follow him out of the room and down the corridor to his office. He closes the door behind them and then passes the sheets over to Alana. The words are all in Italian, but the pages clearly are a printout of an email exchange. There are only eight or nine entries, most of them two sentences or shorter. "Is this from Stefano?" she asks.

"Yes," Sergio says.

"How did you get it?" Byron asks.

"We tracked down the IP addresses for the homes of both Brother Silvio and Don Arturo. The team just intercepted these."

Her breath catches in her throat. "Which one of them has been communicating with Stefano?"

Sergio flashes her a grim smile.

Fifty-Nine

Stefano lies on the top bunk, staring at the ceiling. The room smells of sweat and disease. Nino isn't speaking anymore, not even in the delirious rambling he lapsed into over the last few hours. Stefano isn't certain if his roommate is even still breathing, but he's not willing to get close enough to find out.

O Lord, I have never needed Your guidance as I do now. But even God has gone silent.

Stefano feels the doubt worming its way back into his head. He thinks about when the scheme was first hatched. He was skeptical then, too, but Don Arturo had been so convincing. Stefano thinks of their many conversations, which began as philosophical musings but somehow evolved into planning sessions without him ever noticing.

"There must be a reason for this blessing, Stefano," Don Arturo had told him one evening, a few weeks before they were evicted from their home.

"Which blessing, Don Arturo?"

"Your ability to commune directly with the Lord."

"Dr. Lonzo tells me that none of it is real, only a symptom of my disease."

"Doctors!" Don Arturo scoffed. "Such arrogance. They are as flawed as every other man. They simply do not recognize it. And those poisons he feeds you . . ."

"Dr. Lonzo says the medicines stabilize my mood."

"Nonsense, Stefano!" Don Arturo shook his head gravely. "They dull your mind and cloud your soul. They separate you from God." His brow creased as if he were in pain. "Is that what you want?"

"No."

"You have stopped taking the medicine, as we agreed?"

Stefano nodded.

"Good boy." Don Arturo gripped his arm.

Stefano hesitated. "But, Don Arturo . . . what if Dr. Lonzo is right?"

"He is not!" The abbot squeezed his arm until it ached. "God speaks to you! I have never been more certain of anything in my life!"

"But what He is asking—"

"Is to make His Kingdom whole again."

"By bringing back the Black Death?"

"Even the most merciful reach a breaking point. Remember the Old Testament? Noah and the flood?"

"Yes."

"There are times when God must cleanse the world of evil, regardless of the cost."

"Yes, but—"

"Think of it, Stefano! They will soon tear down San Giovanni. Our home. A house of God!" The abbot's voice quavered with passion. "It is no coincidence. This is precisely why Don Marco and the medieval monks buried those creatures there all those years before. So that if the faithful were to ever come under attack, we would have a way to strike back. To unleash all God's fury."

"Do you really think so?"

"I know so." Don Arturo smiled encouragingly. "Besides, if not us, then those bulldozers, diggers, and other infernal machines would free the creatures anyway. We are simply expediting the inevitable."

Even months later, the memory of Don Arturo's conviction is reassuring to Stefano. But the guilt is near-crippling. So is the fear.

Stefano gave Nino the antibiotics as promised. But he was so afraid his roommate might still try to go see the ship's doctor that he also crushed ten pills of the sedative trazadone, which Dr. Lonzo had prescribed him, and slipped the powder into Nino's orange juice. Stefano can't tell whether Nino has succumbed to an overdose or the plague.

Stefano checks his watch again. By his calculation, the freighter will reach Port Said in less than eighteen hours. The moorage will only complicate matters. It is one thing to smuggle a live rat out with the restocking crew, but the same strategy will not work for a dead sailor. Stefano wonders if he could toss his roommate's body overboard before they dock. Nino is slight, but even if he could possibly lug him all the way above deck, how would he throw him into the Mediterranean without being spotted?

He thinks again of Don Arturo. Stefano's mother was only sixteen years old when he was born, and he never met his own father; the wise abbot is the closest anyone has ever come to filling the role. Surely Don Arturo will know what to do about Nino. They were not supposed to have further contact during the mission, but Stefano sees this crisis as reason enough to break the silence and consult his mentor.

He leaves his room and locks the door behind him. He slinks down the narrow corridor of the belowdecks hallway, takes the stairs down to the computer room on the lower deck, and is relieved to find it empty.

He sits down at the far terminal of the two computers but has to wait a minute or so for the slow satellite Internet connection to engage before he can log on to his account. As he waits, a minimized photo on the side of the browser's home page catches his eye. He clicks on the icon and watches, with horror, as his own image fills almost half of the screen. Beside his own passport photo is a picture of Brother Silvio. The text underneath screams: "*Source of plague?*"

Sixty

Sergio has no flashing light or siren, but he drives as if he does, leaning heavily on the horn as he weaves along the crowded curving streets. The black sedan jerks so hard at times that Alana has to grip the armrest in the backseat to steady herself.

"What exactly did the emails between them say?" Byron asks from the passenger seat.

The car slows to a halt behind a line of traffic, and Sergio uses the opportunity to grab the pages off the console between them. "Stefano sent the first email four weeks ago. It says: 'All is well, but the males fight over the food. Can this really be what God intends?' And Don Arturo replies: 'He speaks to you alone. His blessing is righteous, my brother. Do not ever doubt His word.'" Sergio flips a page. "And then three weeks ago Stefano wrote: 'I freed Asiago at the construction site, just as you advised. Should I still release Robiola in a park now?' And Arturo responded: 'Yes, the Parco Serra Gropallo will be perfect. He will easily find a home there. Just as the Lord intends it.'"

Alana can barely bite back her anger. "The son of a bitch was feeding into Stefano's psychosis! Goading him on."

The cars ahead of them begin to move and Sergio drops the pages back onto the console. "The last few emails were sent seven days ago," he says. "Arturo told Stefano that God wanted him to spread the plague in Asia. He even suggested that Stefano hire on as a crew member on a freighter."

"Asia!" Alana slaps the armrest with an open palm. "What if he's already left?"

Sergio shrugs. "No freighter can reach the Far East in under a week. We will search the manifests and crew lists of every ship that has recently departed Naples, or will soon. We will find him."

"What if he's not traveling under his own name?" Byron asks.

Sergio motions to the pages. "Arturo specifically asks Stefano if his passport is in order. And he confirmed it."

Alana exhales heavily. "If Stefano releases those rats in Asia . . ."

"Can you imagine trying to contain this plague in cities like Jakarta or Shanghai?" Byron says.

"Jesus! It's like the plague ships of the Middle Ages all over again. Only this time in reverse. They'll be carrying the Black Death back to Asia."

Sergio veers off into the driveway of the Seminario Arcivescovile and abandons the car in front of the main doors. The three of them race through the common area and up the stairs to Don Arturo's apartment.

Sergio slips the gun from his holster as he pounds on the door with his other fist. No one answers. Just as he lowers his shoulder to ram the door, it opens a crack. Alana recognizes the widow's peak through the gap. "*Vattene, per favore!*" Brother Samuel says.

Without replying, Sergio thrusts his shoulder against the door. It flies open. Samuel stumbles back. He regains his balance and tries to block their entry with his body, his arms spread wide. "Leave Father Abbot be!" he cries.

Sergio levels the gun at his chest.

"*Basta!*" Arturo cries, as he steps out from behind Samuel. "It is enough."

Samuel hesitates and then steps aside, his chin hung in defeat.

The abbot doesn't appear the least surprised. "You know, then?"

Sergio addresses Arturo in Italian. The abbot only juts his lower lip and nods, showing not an iota of contrition.

Head held high, Arturo accompanies them back down to the car. He sits next to Alana in the backseat, his mood seemingly tranquil.

She knows Sergio intends to formally question the abbot in the controlled setting of an interview room, but she's too enraged to hold her tongue. "Why?" she growls.

"Why what, Dr. Vaughn?" Don Arturo smiles as if they were still making small talk over coffee.

"Why the hell would you encourage someone as ill and deluded as Brother Stefano?"

Arturo frowns. "How do you know Stefano is ill?"

"He was diagnosed by a qualified psychiatrist," she says in disbelief.

"Yes, with delusions and hallucinations. How does Dr. Lonzo know those are manifestations of his imagination? What if the voices are real?"

"You honestly believe Stefano speaks directly to God?"

"He would not be the first," Arturo says. "The English thought Joan of Arc was crazy, too."

"What is wrong with you?" she snaps. "The man is a schizophrenic. And you were enabling his lethal delusions."

Arturo folds his arms over his chest. "I believe Stefano is an agent of God."

"So God intends for the Black Death to reign again?" Alana resists the urge to grab the abbot by the neck. "To wipe out half the world like the last time?"

Arturo smiles and then slowly shakes his head. "God must be so fed up with the world as it is. All the greed. All the sin. And so little faith or repentance. This world is not worth saving."

"You're as delusional as Stefano!"

But Arturo doesn't seem to hear her. "To rend asunder such a holy place? A monastery of almost eight hundred years? And for what? To build more extravagant condominiums for the rich and godless to dwell in, instead of us true believers?"

Alana's jaw drops. "That's it, isn't it?"

Arturo locks his eyes on hers. When he speaks again, his tone is harsh and the façade of the grandfatherly cleric melts away. "What would you know of any of this? You brash American. You understand nothing of faith, devotion, or sacrifice!"

"This has nothing to with God!" Alana leans in closer. "You've done this out of some warped sense of vengeance. To settle a personal score. Nothing more!"

"I was sent by the archbishop of Genoa and the Benedictine primate in Rome to make San Giovanni whole again. I did everything they asked of me. I breathed new life into the monastery. And how did the Church reward that? They sold it to the devil!" His voice rises as his nostrils flare. "And then they stripped me of my abbotship and, with it, my dignity. They cast me aside."

"Oh, my God." Alana clenches her fist. She has never wanted to hit someone more in her life. "You'd destroy the world because they took your *job*?"

"It's too late to stop Stefano, Dr. Vaughn. What's done is done." Arturo relaxes back in his seat. A self-satisfied smile crosses his lips. "And the legacy of San Giovanni will not be soon forgotten."

Sixty-One

The night passed in a sandstorm of activity. Alana spent much of it at AISI headquarters, helping to scour the ship manifests with the other agents. She only returned to her hotel after four a.m. to have a quick shower.

She doesn't realize she has dozed off in the chair until she's startled awake by the ringing phone in her hand. She jumps to her feet when she sees Sergio's name on the screen. "You found him!"

"Yes," Sergio says.

"Where?"

"On a cargo ship off the north coast of Egypt."

He hasn't reached Asia yet, thank God! "Heading for the Suez Canal?" she asks.

"I will fill you in when I see you. How soon can you be ready?"

"Five minutes. Less, if need be."

"I will pick you up."

"What about Byron?

"Military personnel only." Sergio disconnects without another word.

Alana throws on clothes and hurries down to the lobby. A black SUV screeches up to the entrance just as she reaches the sliding doors. She climbs into the backseat next to Sergio. She recognizes the two dark-suited AISI agents in the front seats from the previous raid on the bomb makers' lair.

"What do you know, Sergio?" she demands as the car pulls away from the curb.

"Stefano was hired on to the *Cielo di Asia*—a transpacific freighter out of Naples—on the same day it sailed. We came close to missing him. The shipping company, Napoli Marittima, had misspelled Russo with one *s* instead of two."

"Are you sure it's him?"

He nods. "I saw the copy of his passport."

"Where is the ship now?"

"Moored outside of Port Said."

"Already? How long have they been there?"

"Since early this morning."

She grabs his arm. "Has anyone left the ship?"

"No. We're in contact with the captain. He understands no one is to get on or off until we arrive."

"Does he know about Stefano?" she asks, releasing her grip.

Sergio shakes his head. "We didn't want to alarm him or put the rest of the crew at risk. We don't even know if Stefano is armed."

"So how do we get there?"

"Our navy has an amphibious landing ship, the *San Giorgio*, in the region. It should reach Port Said in less than three hours."

Alana was army, not navy. She can't remember exactly which class of vessel qualifies as an amphibious landing ship, but she recalls it's large enough for both fixed-wing and rotary-wing aircraft to land on. She assumes the plan must be to launch a raid on the freighter by air. "Are we heading to the *San Giorgio* now?"

"Yes." Sergio shows a hint of a smile. "It is not quite . . . direct."

After their driver drops them off at a helipad outside of Naples, a small noisy chopper carries them to an Italian military base outside of Rome. From there, they board an air force jet that flies them to a base in Egypt, outside of Alexandria. Alana spends most of the flight on the phone, updating Monique Olin and then Byron. She's disheartened to hear that all the gains in Genoa have been more than offset by the outbreak in Naples, where the plague continues to spiral out of control and the hospitals have been flooded with suspect cases.

On the tarmac in Alexandria, a sleek gunmetal-gray helicopter is waiting for them with its rotor already turning. As they lift off, the talkative pilot explains with great pride, in broken English, how his AB 212 chopper has a range of several hundred miles and flies as smoothly as a seagull. Alana's slight airsickness tells her otherwise.

Forty minutes later—and four hours after they left Italy—a naval ship appears out of the mist below them.

"Is that her?" Alana asks Sergio over the headphones.

"The *San Giorgio*, yes. A COMSUBIN team is already waiting for us onboard."

"What's that? Special ops?"

"Yes. Italian special operations maritime assault force. Similar to your Navy SEALs." Then he adds, with obvious pride, "Only COMSUBIN has a much longer history."

The pilot eases the helicopter down on the ship's deck. There are two other choppers, larger than theirs, lined up on the deck beside them. Mechanics are attending to both aircraft while sailors load equipment and boxes inside each of them.

An officer in forest-green fatigues appears outside the door of the helicopter. He reeks of special forces, from his thick neck and chest to his crew cut and rigid posture. He salutes crisply and then shakes hands with Sergio. They speak in Italian for a few moments. Sergio turns to Alana. "This is Capitano Monti. He will lead the assault team onto the *Cielo di Asia*."

Alana shakes Monti's strong hand and, assuming he doesn't speak English, glances over to Sergio. "How soon do we leave?"

Monti answers for him. "Forty-five minutes, Doctor," he says with minimal accent. "After the briefing. Come now, please."

Monti leads Alana and Sergio inside the ship and into a long narrow conference room where several men are seated in rows of chairs, all wearing the same dark green fatigues. The room goes silent. Monti stands with arms folded below a screen that fills the wall above him. Alana counts eleven other men. Each one of them is stone-faced and sits bolt upright. There are a few impassive nods for the guests after Monti introduces them.

Alana and Sergio claim two empty chairs near the front. Sergio leans closer and says in a low voice, "The capitano described you as a soldier with the NATO counter-bioterrorism force."

"Does that mean he will let me join the raid?" she whispers back.

"I believe so, yes."

Monti clicks a button in his hand, and an image of a modern freighter fills the screen. The sheer size of the *Cielo di Asia* is daunting. And the vessel appears even bigger when the image flips to a cross-sectional blueprint. Modular containers are stacked six stories high and there are three levels belowdecks.

Monti speaks rapidly. Sergio can only translate in snippets. Alana gleans enough to understand that if Stefano is not immediately found, the soldiers will scour the ship in pairs from top to bottom.

Monti clicks the button again, and the screen fills with a photo of a smiling Stefano that Alana hasn't seen before. There's something lonely in his self-conscious grin. Monti advances through a few more photos of the monk. Then he extracts a printed photo from his front pocket and waves it around, indicating that everyone should be a carrying the same picture.

Monti advances the slide and an image of a self-contained breathing apparatus appears on the screen. He switches to English. "Dr. Vaughn will discuss the safety requirements now."

Surprised, Alana rises to her feet. She pulls Sergio up by his arm. "Will you translate for me?" she asks, and he nods.

She walks the soldiers through the steps involved in securing their biohazard suits and then describes contact precautions, stressing the importance of washing their hands during decontamination, especially their thumbs, which she knows people, even doctors, sometimes forget. She reminds the soldiers to avoid any direct contact with potentially infected people or with rats, and emphasizes the importance of sealing any trapped or dead animals inside biohazard bags.

"We believe Stefano is carrying several infected rats," she says, and waits for Sergio to translate. "Ideally, we would capture the rats alive. But do *not* take chances with them. A bite through the glove could lead to infection. If you're in doubt, kill the animal."

Monti says something in Italian and a grim laugh ripples through the room. "The capitano says that the same applies to Stefano," Sergio translates.

The meeting breaks up. Sergio and Alana follow the soldiers to a room full of biohazard equipment. They suit up in complete silence. Alana's mouth goes dry when Sergio passes her the same Beretta handgun he gave to her during the raid on the bomb makers' hideout. It feels heavier in her hand.

The team assembles on deck and then breaks off into two groups. Six men head for one of the awaiting assault helicopters whose rotors are spinning slowly. Monti beckons Alana and Sergio over to join him in the second helicopter.

As soon as the doors close, their chopper takes off with a jerk. The staccato of the beating blade fills the otherwise tense silence in the cabin. This time the butterflies filling Alana's stomach are not from motion sickness.

Fifteen minutes later, the coastline of northern Egypt comes into focus. A city emerges ahead of them. As the choppers fly lower, she can see that the harbor below is crowded with cargo ships. They descend steadily, until a freighter that matches the one shown in the briefing comes into view. Alana's breathing picks up when she sees the Italian flag. She squints to read the markings on the side: *Cielo di Asia*.

The pilot slows the aircraft down to a near-standstill. Alana cranes her neck to watch the other chopper drop down and hover twenty feet or so above the ship's deck. Its door opens and a rope drops to the deck. Moments later, the first soldier, with his rifle strapped to his back, rappels down the line and lands on the deck in a defensive crouch.

As the others follow, the soldiers on her aircraft stand and shuffle toward the door. Alana tucks her gun into the back of her waistband and rises to join them, her heart in her throat.

Sixty-Two

Stefano hears more thumping overhead, and he wills the trembling out of his fingers. Everything is wrong, and has been since the moment he saw his own image on that website and bolted from the computer room without bothering to email Don Arturo. They had stripped Stefano of his one gift: his anonymity.

He is surprised he hasn't already been caught. Yesterday, the ship's security officer checked his room looking for his missing roommate. Stefano hardly breathed during the brief inspection. But the officer never thought to move the stack of clothes, blankets, and pillows in the closet, behind which Stefano had stuffed his diminutive roommate along with the knapsack full of rats.

The thuds grow louder. They are coming for him. He has been certain of it even before they reached Port Said, even before the captain announced on the speakers that all shore leaves were canceled until further notice.

God is also refusing him leniency. "Carry my creatures ashore!" The voice of the Almighty commanded just after they laid anchor.

But how, O Lord?

"Hide them!"

I cannot access the containers. I have tried. They are too securely locked and bolted.

"Find others!"

Which others?

He waited, but the Lord shared no further guidance.

It is only now, as Stefano skulks past the galley in search of a place to hide himself, that he recognizes his salvation.

The galley is far more spacious than San Giovanni's kitchen was. And the pantry is larger still. No one else is around, as the captain has called the entire crew, including Cook and his assistants, to the assembly deck.

The dried food bins stacked at the side of the pantry might prove to be his salvation. He pops the lids off the containers full of flour, rice, and even corn chips. When he finds the three bins piled with dried cereal, he recognizes them as the ideal temporary home for the rats.

Stefano was going to bring all six rats, but he decided not to, opting instead to leave three of them in the bag in his room. After all, when they do find him, how will they know how many animals he has brought on board?

The knapsack is squirming as he lowers it to the floor. The rats sense the danger even more acutely than Stefano does. He slips his glove on and extracts the first of the animals by the tail, recognizing him as Puzzone by the ear that was gnawed in a previous fight. As soon as Puzzone falls onto the bed of cereal, he burrows down through the flakes until his whole body disappears. "Well done," Stefano whispers.

He drops the other rats into the two other bins of flavored cereals. Tuma tunnels through the chocolate rings as quickly as Puzzone did the flakes, but Ormea perches warily on the surface, his whiskers twitching with suspicion. Eventually Stefano has to reach into the container and scoop the flakes over Ormea until he is finally concealed.

Satisfied, Stefano snaps the lids back on the containers and piles them against the wall exactly where he found them.

The stomping is louder. They are close now. His hand trembles again as he snatches the knife up off the floor where he laid it earlier. He had overheard Cook bragging that it was sharp enough to cut through bone. Stefano wonders if he will have to find out for himself.

He hurries across the pantry to a shelving unit that is stuffed with boxes. He has already nudged the unit a few inches away from the wall, but he still has to suck in his breath just to wedge his thin frame into the narrow space he created behind it.

The footsteps are heavier. They are in the galley now. But Stefano cannot see anyone through the crack between boxes that offers only a sliver of a view. Suddenly a blur of dark green darts across his field of vision. Stefano tenses as the source pauses and comes into focus. A soldier wearing a full body suit and helmet stands a few feet in front of him, pointing a rifle directly at him.

Stefano's breath catches in his throat. He's overcome by a mix of terror and relief. *Is it finally over, O Lord?*

But the soldier doesn't seem to notice him. He swivels his head from one side to the other, scanning the room, and then moves off to the right. Stefano cannot see the soldier anymore, but he hears cupboards opening and boxes moving. He grips the knife so tightly that his palm throbs.

What am I doing? I am a simple monk. A man of peace.

"You serve me!" The voice in his head is so loud that Stefano is convinced it will give away his hiding spot. "Do not waver! Kill in my name! Vengeance will be mine!"

Chapter

Sixty-Three

Alana stands impatiently beside Sergio on the raised bridge deck of the *Cielo di Asia*. The air is electrified. They've been aboard the cargo ship for twelve minutes. COMSUBIN soldiers are scouring the vessel but have yet to find any sign of Stefano, and a canine search team is already en route for backup.

The freighter's commander, Captain Murdoch, a bearded Englishman with a lazy left eye, is implacable. "If you had only notified us, we could have apprehended this man!" he mutters, as he paces around the high-tech navigational equipment. "He could be anywhere now."

"We didn't want to place your crew at risk," Sergio repeats for the third time.

"Well, you bloody well did that, didn't you?" Murdoch growls.

"No, Stefano Russo did that. So did your company when they hired him without screening."

"A hundred fifty thousand metric tons on board a ship that is as long as a football pitch!" Murdoch rails on. "There's no end of places for your man to hide!"

"What's done is done!" Alana snaps.

Murdoch shoots her an icy glare, but says nothing.

Sergio brings his hand to the Bluetooth receiver in his ear, and says a few words. He turns to the captain. "There's something in Stefano's room. Take us there, please."

Murdoch leads them down three flights of stairs to the lowest deck. As they turn a corner, Alana sees a soldier standing outside a doorway down the hallway. They head for him. Murdoch begins to follow, but Alana stops him with an open palm. "Stay here."

"This is my ship!" he protests angrily.

"Maybe so, but you're not wearing protective gear. Or would you prefer to expose yourself to the plague?"

Murdoch pivots and marches back the way he came.

Before Alana reaches the room, she spots a hand and part of an arm extending out the doorway. She bolts ahead until she reaches the open door. Inside, a body is sprawled across the floor. The dead man is Asian.

Capitano Monti is already in the room, but he's not focusing on the corpse. Instead, he leans over the lower bunk and sweeps a flashlight over an unzipped black canvas bag.

"Capitano, who is this man?" Alana asks.

Monti looks over his shoulder. "The roommate. We found him in the closet." He beckons her over with a flick of his wrist. "Come, *Dottore*. You must see this."

Alana steps over the body to reach Monti. She peers over his shoulder into the canvas bag. The inside resembles the old mouse cage she remembers from her grade school, with a feeder and fleece-like material lining the bottom. There are three rats inside, dividers separating each of them. Two of the gray-black animals freeze in the light, while the third stands on its hind legs and sniffs the air.

Alana recognizes their distinct markings as similar to those of the rat from the necropsy Justine performed. She goes cold at being so close to the source of the Black Death. "How do we know if these are all the rats he brought on board?"

"We don't." Monti nods toward the sack. "There are six slots here."

Alana turns her attention back to the dead man. She kneels closer to him. His open eyes are bloodshot and his lips are chapped and cracked at the corners. She palpates with her gloved hand along his neck, but feels nothing. Then she slides her hand under his arm. As soon as her fingers reach his armpit, she feels the golf ball–sized lump. "Plague!"

"You are certain?" Sergio asks.

"Absolutely."

Monti barks something into the receiver of his headphones and spins away from the bed. He spouts something else as he races out the door.

"There is movement in one of the cargo bays. It could be Stefano," Sergio translates as he starts after Monti. "Stay here, Alana, and secure the room. Contain the infection."

Alana is tempted to follow, but she knows Sergio is right. She walks back over to the canvas bag that serves as a portable rat cage. She stares down at the nervous animals inside. "How many more of you are aboard?"

She knows Stefano could have freed other rats almost anywhere on the massive freighter. There are thousands of containers where he could conceal them. All they would need is a food source.

Food! The word hits her like a blow to the chest.

She turns and rushes for the door. "Where is the galley? The kitchen?" she asks of the lone soldier who stands guard outside.

He shakes his head, clearly not understanding what she is asking.

She struggles to think of the word. "*Cucina!*" she says.

The soldier frowns. "*Il terzo piano.*" He motions to the ceiling and then holds ups three fingers.

Alana bolts down the narrow corridor and flics up the stairs to the third deck. She runs past the mess hall and through a set of swinging doors into the galley. Inside, all the closet and cupboard doors are wide open. She assumes the soldiers must have already searched the area, but she has a quick look around. Nothing. She hurries through the open door into the large pantry.

Alana groans as she scans the scope of the storage area. A whole shelving unit is filled with boxes. It will take her forever to go through them. Then her eyes are drawn to a group of plastic bins, the size of large laundry baskets, stacked together in twos on the far wall. She steps over and lifts one off the top of the stacks. It's heavier than she anticipated, and she struggles to lower it to the floor. She pries open the lid and sees that it is loaded with white flour.

Alana reaches for the next bin, which is almost as weighty as the first. She opens it to find it full of rice. She lifts another container that is much lighter. It's filled with corn chips. She darts back into the kitchen and grabs one of the large serving spoons. She sifts through the bin with the spoon, but feels nothing except more chips. Discouraged, she reaches for another, lighter bin, to discover that it's packed with plain cereal. She digs the spoon through it, as well, but finds only cereal.

She opens the next container, which turns out to be packed with corn-flakes. As she's about to lower the lid back into place, a few of the golden flakes on one side begin to vibrate. She jams the spoon into the spot and starts sweeping flakes away to one side. After the fourth or fifth scoopful, she spots a trace of gray.

She leans forward and gently touches the spot with the back of the spoon. Suddenly a rat shakes, spraying flakes everywhere and exposing its furry body among the grains. Alana yanks her arm back in surprise and immediately feels the heavy pop of her shoulder dislocating. She gasps in pain.

She clasps her wrist with her other hand and jerks it outward. Just as she feels the relief of the bone slipping back into place, something sharp pokes between her shoulder blades.

A chill rips through her. "Stefano?" she asks, without moving.

There's an agonizing silence. "*Sì*," he finally says.

Alana flinches as the blade's pressure increases. She's afraid to even inhale with the knife so close to her spine. "Do you speak English?" she asks.

"Yes."

"Stefano, I am a doctor," Alana says slowly. "You understand?"

"You look like the others. The soldiers." His voice is soft, but there's menace in his tone.

"I'm not a soldier. I didn't come here to harm you. Only to make sure no one else gets sick from the plague."

"That is not the will of God."

The knife presses even harder. She feels something cool against her back and realizes her biohazard suit is cut. She wonders if the blade has already penetrated her flesh. But she forces herself to focus. She remembers Dr. Lonzo's description of Stefano's fluctuating level of belief in his delusions. "It is not God, Stefano."

"What did you say?" His voice cracks.

"I spoke with Dr. Lonzo," she says, as she tightens the grip on the spoon, realizing she won't have time to reach for the gun tucked behind her back. "He is a good man. A smart man."

"Dr. Lonzo is wrong!"

"In your heart, you know he is right." She can feel his thigh against the back of her leg. Her mind darts back to her hand-to-hand combat training. One blow to the groin might be enough to immobilize him. She squeezes the spoon tighter and edges sideways, trying to create access. "God is not speaking to you, Stefano. Those voices are inside your own head. They're part of your illness."

"No!" he cries.

Alana freezes, expecting the blade to plunge into her back, but the sharp pressure holds steady. "Think about it, Stefano. What kind of merciful God would spread a disease like this?"

"The world is disease now. And He has done so before. Noah and his ark. The ten plagues of Egypt!"

"I've seen children dying of this plague, Stefano."

"*Bambini?*"

"Yes. A little three-year-old." She inches over again, testing him. "She was so beautiful—with little blue and pink ribbons in her hair. She would break your heart. She died in her mother's arms. God is not so cruel. He would never do such a thing."

"You saw this?" His voice cracks

"Yes, I did. But it wasn't your fault, Stefano. Don Arturo is responsible!"

"Don Arturo?" he echoes in confusion.

"Yes." She edges farther away. "We know he was encouraging you. Making you stop your medication. Convincing you to scatter the infected rats. He was only taking advantage of your illness."

"Don Arturo is a good man," he says, but she can tell doubt has crept into his tone.

"No, Stefano. He is a bad man. A bitter, angry man. He was filled with fury that they took his monastery away. This has nothing to do with God. Don Arturo only wants revenge. For others to share in his misery."

Stefano is silent for a moment, but the blade doesn't budge.

"No, no, no!" he groans. "*Lasciami solo!*"

For a moment Alana wonders if someone else has entered the room. Then she realizes that he must be arguing with his own hallucinations. "Listen to me, Stefano!" she commands, as she tenses her wrist, preparing to strike. "The voices are not real. Dr. Lonzo has been right all along!"

"And Don Arturo knows this?"

"Yes! He was just using you to settle a score with the Church."

There's another combustible silence, then the pressure of the knife's tip lightens. "What did I do . . ." Stefano murmurs.

"It's going to be okay, Stefano."

"The children . . ."

The blade leaves her back. When she's certain it's gone, she whirls around to face him, raising the spoon as she does so.

Stefano stands a few feet away from her. Tears stream down his cheeks as he holds the blade leveled against his own throat. "O Lord, take my life instead," he says.

"No, Stefano!"

She lunges forward, but it's too late. He has jerked the blade across his neck, splattering her mask in a shower of crimson.

Sixty-Four

*Today is the fourth day of June. However, I, Gabriella, daugh-*ter of Jacob ben Moses, inscribe this journal entry in the place of Doctor Rafael Pasqua.

For weeks I have fought the urge to add my words to those of my beloved Rafael. Today, I could resist no longer. My Rafael was so dedicated to documenting his experience with the pestilence that, in my heart, I know he would have wanted his story completed for the sake of posterity. And I consider it my duty, and my debt, to him to do so.

I have heard that more than half of the city's inhabitants have succumbed to the plague. I cannot recall the names of all those I have lost over these cursed months. It pains me too much to remember any one of them, let alone to think of them all. However, the pestilence has finally blown through Genova like the worst of storms passing. People are returning to the streets and markets. Life will never be as it was, but the city has endured, which is more than most expected.

Three months have passed since Rafael left San Giovanni to deliver his hastily improvised remedy, if it can be even considered as such, to the Archbishop. When he did not return home as promised that evening, I stayed up all night praying for his safe return. My prayers, as they often do, went unanswered. The next day, I implored Don Marco to inquire after my Rafael. The kindly abbot assured me that God would watch over him and he would come back soon. When two more days passed without any sign of Rafael, Don Marco set off to visit the palace of the Archbishop.

Don Marco would not return to San Giovanni for three more days. When he finally did, he was alone. He limped heavily, and his right eye was swollen shut. Before he would recount the events that unfolded at the Archbishop's palace, he invited me to sit with him in the Warming House and insisted we share a skin of wine together, an occasion that would have been unthinkable under almost any other circumstance.

Once we had finished our drink, Don Marco asked me how much of Rafael's ordeal I wished to hear. I begged him to share every last detail, regardless of how painful or indelicate. However, I have come to regret such vehemence, as my tears have hardly abated since.

Upon reaching the palace, Don Marco learned the Archbishop was gravely ill. Inside his chambers, the Archbishop was too weak even to rise. His breathing was ragged with pestilence. So incensed was the man that Don Marco could not discern whether he shook with fever or rage. Not only did the Archbishop falsely charge my kindhearted Rafael of being a heretic and a sorcerer, he further accused Don Marco of colluding with him. When Don Marco mustered the courage to ask what had become of Rafael, the Archbishop only said he would learn soon enough and then called for his guards.

They dragged Don Marco to the dungeon. It was there that Don Marco found my Rafael, curled up on the cold stone floor. His face was so swollen that Don Marco struggled to recognize him. At first he believed Rafael to be already dead. It was not until my beloved spoke that the abbot realized otherwise.

Rafael's voice was no stronger than a whisper, but his wits were still about him enough to describe his experience to Don Marco.

The Archbishop had manifested the first signs of the plague only hours before Rafael arrived. He hungrily consumed Rafael's remedy and commanded him to remain at the palace as his personal physician. Over the next day, Rafael drained his sores and fed him more of the medicine. However, the Archbishop's fever did not break. And how he blamed my Rafael! In his outrage and delirium, the Archbishop even accused him of instigating the infliction through sorcery. He ordered the guards to torture Rafael.

My poor Rafael had been beaten mercilessly and flogged for two days before Don Marco encountered him. The abbot himself would have most probably died there as well, had the Archbishop not succumbed to the plague, thus permitting one of the other priests to free him.

My tears stain the parchment as I record these last moments of Rafael's life. He understood that death was hovering over him as he lay on the floor of that dungeon. Still, Don Marco assures me that Rafael died as he had lived, with such bravery and generosity of spirit. He used his final words to implore the abbot to relay the depth of his love for me, and he made Don Marco promise to protect me. Only after the abbot had sworn his word did Rafael close his eyes and inhale his final breath. How the thought of that moment breaks my heart anew.

The Archbishop's misguided vengeance was not confined to my Rafael. He also ordered his soldiers to raze the Jewish quarter. I have heard from one of the other monks that there is nothing left of our village but ash. I only thank God that Rafael had succeeded in convincing my brother and sister to flee eastward with their families prior to the Archbishop's fit of rage.

In the past three months, Don Marco has been true to his word. I have remained under the protection of the monks here at San Giovanni. I had considered going off in search of what remains of my family. However, two months ago, when the bleeding stopped and the morning sickness descended, I found a new purpose in my existence. For I now carry the child of Rafael Pasqua.

It is fulfillment enough of my life to know that the legacy of this great doctor, a man who showed such courage and kindness in the darkest of times, will live on not only through this written record but also through our son or daughter and, God willing, the many offspring that are to follow.

Sixty-Five

Concrete forms still crisscross the pit. Mounds of dirt and rubble are piled higher than ever. But everything else is different. The ground no longer vibrates. The buzz and whir of heavy machinery has been silenced. And the diggers, trucks, and bulldozers are nowhere to be seen. Even the smell of diesel on the breeze has been replaced by an earthy petrichor after the recent rainfall. The construction workers are all gone, too. Only a few white-clad WHO technicians wander the site scouring for last vestiges of the plague and the rodents that carried it.

Alana stands between Justine and Byron at the top of the pit, watching the technicians work below them. "I kind of wish I had seen it," she says.

"What?" Byron's brow creases. "The old monastery?"

"Yeah. While it was still standing."

"What's wrong with you?" Justine grimaces. "That creepy old church was harboring the next Armageddon under its floors."

"Maybe so," Alana says, thinking of the translation of Pasqua's diary that she just finished reading. "But also a ton of history."

"Thank God it's just history now," Justine says. "Zanetti, too."

Byron nods. "Sergio told me they've arrested Zanetti and his man Paolo. For obstructing justice and tampering with evidence."

"Good riddance," Justine says.

"They didn't plan any of this, Justine, they just panicked," Alana says. "Marcello is a broken man. I feel kind of badly for him. Nico, too. After all, Marcello is his wife's uncle."

Byron glances over to her. "How's Nico doing?"

She's glad to realize there's no jealousy in his tone. "He's got a lot to sort out. But Nico will land on his feet."

No one speaks for a moment or two, and Alana watches as a technician crouches down to examine something in the dirt below him. She shakes her head. "For Arturo and Stefano to even believe the rat colony might still exist at the bottom of that chute after all those centuries . . ."

"And then to trap them and deliberately infest the rats with fleas," Byron says, "without knowing if they even still carried the plague."

"Oh, my God," Justine groans. "After all this, I would've thought you two would have developed a bit more respect for rodent ingenuity."

"Trust me, Justine, I'll never underestimate that again," Alana says.

Byron shakes his head. "I'll give Arturo and Stefano this, they were committed."

"They sure as hell ought to have been," Justine snorts.

"Poor Stefano. What he needed was help. Instead, the man he trusted most in the world preyed on his mental illness." Alana exhales. "I keep thinking about him in those final moments. What an awful way to go."

Byron shakes his head. "I hope Don Arturo realizes the hell he put that kid through."

"And I hope he rots in jail chewing on it," Justine says.

Alana glances around the empty site again. "At least we've got Arturo's handiwork under control now."

"We're not out of the woods yet, though," Byron says. "Not even close. The plague is still raging in Naples."

"There were fewer new cases reported today than yesterday," Alana points out. "And none here in Genoa."

He nods. "Let's celebrate after a week goes by without a new case *anywhere*. Until then, it still could only take one stray rat—or person—to launch this globally."

Alana holds his gaze for a moment. "It's not the same as when Stefano was rogue. We've cut off the source now. Also, they'll be mass-producing antiserum soon. The outbreak control measures you put into place are working. It's going to settle."

"Never a good idea to be overconfident," he says, but his tone suggests that he agrees.

"Well, much as I'd like to listen to more of this awkward self-congratulation that passes for flirtation"—Justine points to the technicians in the pit—"I better go check on the boys' progress."

Alana laughs. "I can't believe I'm saying this, but I'm actually going to miss you, Justine."

"They always do," Justine says as she turns away.

Alana watches her descend the wooden steps into the pit and disappear behind one of the concrete forms. "I just finished reading the translation of Rafael Pasqua's diary, Byron."

"And?"

"It was sadder than I expected."

"You're surprised a diary about the Black Death turned out to be sad?"

"I just didn't expect it to be a love story."

"The doctor and the Jewish woman you mentioned before?"

Alana nods.

Byron reaches over and gives the back of her neck a quick squeeze. "Who knew the Black Death could be so damn romantic?"

"Funny." She elbows him in the side. "We're not so different from them, you know?"

"How so?"

"Once fear took hold, their society crumbled. People just turned on each other."

"People were scared this time, sure, but I wouldn't say we turned on each other."

"It's just been a week or two, Byron. Imagine if it had gotten anywhere near as bad as it did in the fourteenth century. Who knows where it would've ended? Back then, they scapegoated the Jews. This time, it could've been the Muslims."

"I suppose." He chews his lower lip. "By the way, that was when I realized you were kind of worth it."

"What are you talking about?"

"After I decided to release Yasin Ahmed's photo to the media—"

"Oh, yeah." She stretches the words. "That I do remember."

"You could've thrown me under the bus, but instead you blamed yourself for those hate crimes." He lays his arm across her shoulders. "That's when I realized you're quite something."

Alana rests her head against the crook of his neck. "Rafael Pasqua . . . now, he really was something. A hero."

"Don't sell yourself short, Alana. The way you stared down Stefano when he was wielding that knife—"

"Stared him down? He was behind me. I couldn't even see his face."

"You were also the one who figured out where he hid the rest of the rats."

"The dogs sniffed out the last two rats in the galley."

"But if it weren't for you . . ."

"Yeah, I guess." She feels her cheeks warm. "We did okay, huh?"

"Yes, we did." There's genuine pride behind his small grin.

"Listen, Byron, I have to leave for Brussels in a couple hours."

"I've got to stay here. There's still a ton left for us to do."

"I wasn't inviting you."

He looks down with obvious embarrassment. "Oh, I . . . I see. I was just—"

She leans forward and skitters kisses across his cheek and onto his mouth. "I'm teasing. Come visit me once you're done. I'll give you the whole Belgian experience."

"Which is?"

"No idea. Waffles in bed?"

Laughing, he wraps her in a tight hug.

Alana squeezes back. She feels comfortable in his arms. She thinks of Pasqua's final entry in his diary. She, too, feels renewed hope for tomorrow. She also hopes it isn't misplaced.

Acknowledgments

While my story is fictional, the science and the history behind it are anything but. And I needed help to accurately envision a world where the Black Death—the most deadly natural disaster ever to devastate humankind—recurs in contemporary times. Two esteemed colleagues, Drs. Victor Leung and Marc Romney, provided me with fascinating insights into the microbiology behind this enigmatic and, at times, terrifying plague. And I learned much more from several excellent books, including *The Great Mortality* by John Kelly, *The Black Death* by Philip Ziegler, *In the Wake of the Plague* by Norman F. Cantor, and *The Decameron* by fourteenth-century author Giovanni Boccaccio.

I'm also blessed—in the fortunate, not religious, sense—to have the support of friends and family members who read my books, often in the form of the unpolished first draft, and provide useful feedback, along with tons of encouragement. I would list each one individually, but I worry I might leave out a significant name, so I'm going to play it safe and thank them as one. But you know who you are!

There are a few people I do have to single out for their unique contributions. I am deeply indebted to the wonderful Kit Schindell, a freelance editor and friend, whose detailed feedback always helps to improve my stories. Glen Clark has been a champion for my writing. My mom, Judy, is a stalwart of support and a constant inspiration on living to the fullest. And, as always, I rely heavily on the wisdom of my agent, Henry Morrison.

I am excited to launch into a publishing relationship with my new friends at Simon & Schuster. The support and feedback from Nita Pronovost, Anne Perry, Adria Iwasutiak, and, especially, Kevin Hanson, have proved invaluable. And, finally, I owe a huge thank-you to my wonderfully talented editor, Laurie Grassi, who has helped to transform this novel from rough first draft to final product, improving it vastly with each dedicated editorial pass.

Finally, I'm grateful to the readers who share this journey with me. In this novel, I return to my global thriller roots, but I also get to capitalize on my recent experience in writing historical fiction to flavor the contemporary story line with one from the past. For me, it is the perfect symmetry. And I want to thank you for your loyalty and interest.

About the Author

DANIEL KALLA is the international bestselling author of *Pandemic*, *Resistance*, *Rage Therapy*, *Blood Lies*, *Cold Plague*, and *Of Flesh and Blood*. His books have been translated into eleven languages, and two novels have been optioned for film. Kalla practices emergency medicine in Vancouver, British Columbia. Visit him at **danielkalla.com** or follow him on Twitter at **@DanielKalla**.